About the author

Claire Miller is a senior journalist with *The Age* newspaper in Melbourne. She was born in 1964 in Alexandra in Victoria on the edge of the high country, but grew up in the city.

In 1983 she began work as a cadet journalist in suburban newspapers and moved to *The Age* as a general reporter in 1985. Since then, she has covered state and federal politics, rural and regional affairs and transport, and reported on international news and events from the United States, Germany, Nauru, the United Kingdom, Japan and Chile.

From 1993 to 1995, Claire was news editor at *The Age*, and from 1998–2002 was *The Age* environment reporter. She has won numerous awards including a World Press Institute fellowship to the United States in 1996 and the 2000 JD Pringle Journalism Award from the British Embassy and the National Press Club.

Claire lives in Melbourne with her husband Chris Agar, and children Imogen and Tom.

SNOWY RIVER STORY

THE GRASSROOTS CAMPAIGN TO SAVE A NATIONAL ICON

CLAIRE MILLER

ABC
Books

Published by ABC Books for the
AUSTRALIAN BROADCASTING CORPORATION
GPO Box 9994 Sydney NSW 2001

Copyright © Claire Miller 2005

First Published April 2005

National Library of Australia
Cataloguing-in-publication entry:
Miller, Claire
  The Snowy River Story
  Bibliography

  ISBN 0 7333 1533 X

  1. Snowy Mountains Hydro-Electric Scheme — Environmental aspects
  2. Political Activists — New South Wales — Snowy Mountains Region
  3. Snowy Mountains Region (N.S.W.) — History 4. Snowy River (N.S.W. and Vic.) —
  Environmental conditions. I Australian Broadcasting Corporation. II Title.

333.9162099447

Cover design by Christabella Designs
Cover photography by courtesy of Snowy River Alliance
Typeset by Kirby Jones
Printed and bound by Griffin Press, South Australia

5 4 3 2 1

For my daughter Imogen and my son Tom,
who joined me on my travels through the Snowy River country,
and always knew I could do it.

Contents

Foreword

No river has captured the Australian imagination like the Snowy. For centuries it roared through the high country to the coast and became, over time, equally famous for its rugged beauty and the legends it inspired.

But by the 1940s the powerful Snowy flows were considered a wasted resource — and all but 1 per cent was diverted for use in the Snowy Mountains Hydro-Electric Scheme. There is no doubt the scheme was one of the greatest feats of modern engineering. But it came at a huge environmental cost, with the river reduced in parts to little more than a muddy, weed-choked stream.

For decades dedicated environmentalists and Snowy users warned the river was dying — and by 2002 their voices had been heard. Our governments worked with them to reverse the decline of this great river in a way that also recognised the needs of the Snowy hydro scheme and farmers. And on August 28, 2002, we were both privileged to release the first waters back into the Snowy. This historic act — the first step in a $300 million, decade-long plan to return 21 per cent of the river's original flows — has already lead to new signs of life. More importantly, it symbolises what can be achieved when governments act across state borders and political lines to undo the mistakes of the past.

The Snowy rescue plan is a testament to the men and women who fought for the river they loved, and their stories of strength, resilience and character have been lastingly captured in this book. It is their stories that we listened to. And it is their stories that will help all Australians face the challenge of protecting our country's precious water resources well into the future.

Steve Bracks
Premier of Victoria

Bob Carr
Premier of New South Wales

Foreword

The Snowy Mountains Scheme was an engineering triumph and a key pillar of Australia's post-war development. So, when the Jindabyne Dam was commissioned in 1967, only a few dared to question the legitimacy of taking 99 per cent of the Snowy River's flow, leaving but a dribble to flow past Dalgety and removing the annual snowmelt high flow past Orbost. At the time, this was accepted as the price of national development.

With time, concerned citizens of the Monaro and Orbost sought a better deal for the Snowy, but were ignored. However, the persistent and dedicated few steadily gained strength in numbers and effectiveness, forming committees, calling meetings, lobbying politicians and questioning managers. With the announcement that the Snowy Mountain Scheme was going to be corporatised, the opportunity arose to seek a reviving flow from the Jindabyne Dam. An expert panel recommended restoring a flow of 28 per cent and this flow became the target of an immense, drawn-out campaign.

Claire Miller has produced a detailed yet gripping account of the meetings, demonstrations and political lobbying of these dedicated voluntary campaigners. She recounts the debates, fierce exchanges, complex deals, intricate negotiations, ultimatums and pronouncements that finally led to the state governments' agreement on environmental flow. The struggle for the environmental flow involved many players — from grassroots voluntary organisations up to senior levels of political and governmental bureaucracy. It was an incredibly complex exercise and one must admire the author's perspicacious and dedicated research, which has enabled her to unravel this complexity and produce such a lucid and moving story.

What I think is inspiring about this whole struggle is how concerned citizens who were acting on behalf of the river set out to correct a wrong and banded together to take on the powers of management authorities, government bureaucracies and politicians and achieve a just result. Mind you, it is a result that still has to eventuate and may yet be compromised.

Snowy River Story highlights the immense difficulties that have to be faced to obtain just one worthwhile environmental flow for just one river. Development is still rapid, even in these days of EIS's, while restoring the excesses of development is a slow and tortuous business. The difficulty involved in achieving worthwhile environmental flows for the Murray further illustrates this disparity.

In the David and Goliath-like struggle for the Snowy, the citizen campaigners had one asset — the Snowy itself. A national icon with a high public relations profile, this area is instantly recognisable as an area of wild beauty. But the campaign was also also pitted against other icons — the Snowy Mountains Scheme and the inland irrigation industry Sadly, there are many other degraded rivers that need ecologically worthwhile environmental flows that are not national icons — let's hope that their flows might be restored without such a long and painful struggle.

As concern for the environment in Australia rapidly increases, one can take heart from the struggle for the Snowy River, which is related so well in this book. This story dramatically illustrates what dedicated citizens may achieve. Let's hope that we're not in for an age of environmental battles, but that governments at all levels may adapt to meet environmental concerns effectively and that resolving environmental problems is viewed as being as important as dealing with economic difficulties.

Professor Sam Lake,
Professor in Ecology,
School of Biological Sciences, Monash University

Author's Note

I was one of those horse-mad girls, and so the romance and excitement of *The Man from Snowy River* resonated in my imagination. I was in my twenties, however, before I realised there was in fact a real Snowy River, and in my mid-thirties when I first laid eyes on the legendary waterway. What an anti-climax. It was March 1999, and Max White from Orbost had phoned me at *The Age* where I was the environment reporter. He asked if I was interested in writing an article about the community's campaign to get more water released into the river from the Snowy Mountains Hydro-Electric Scheme. Like most Australians, I had no idea the scheme had trapped more than 99 per cent of the Snowy River's headwaters, and I was shocked to see the effects downstream: the slime, the shallow rivulets over sand, the weeds and willows taking over where a rambunctious larrikin of a river once flowed. It seemed all wrong, and there was a quixotic poignancy in the community's belief that history might be undone and the river restored to something like its former glory.

The Snowy River story became a professional and personal favourite, and I covered the campaign closely for *The Age*, right up to the unexpected fall of Jeff Kennett's coalition government in October 1999 and the subsequent deal struck between the Victorian and New South Wales Labor governments to restore at least 21 per cent of the Snowy River's original flow at Jindabyne. By October 2000, when the Victorian and New South Wales Premiers Steve Bracks and Bob Carr announced the ten-year restoration plan, I knew enough about the inside story to think it had all the elements required for a good book: strong characters, fateful twists, accidents of history, political intrigue, drama, humour, failure and triumph. It was a great yarn crying out to be told.

Still, it took me another two and a half years, and a serendipitous meeting with Graeme Enders, the New South Wales Snowy River recovery program coordinator after the catastrophic 2003 bushfires, before I got my act together and put a submission to ABC Books. I then spent a marvellous year researching, writing and travelling around the spectacular Snowy River country the better to understand the raw, natural stuff from which the community campaigners were made. Tough stuff, I can tell you that.

The book is based on information and documents gleaned from many sources, too many to be listed individually. More than 150 people were interviewed, most between September 2003 and August 2004. I talked to everyone from the Premiers of New South Wales and Victoria right down to the bloke who cleaned graffiti off Craig Ingram's electorate office window after Ingram controversially announced he would support Labor to form government in Victoria in 1999. Only three major players declined repeated requests for interviews: the New South Wales Treasurer, Michael Egan; the former federal Environment Minister, Senator Robert Hill; and the former Liberal Premier of Victoria, Jeff Kennett. However, I interviewed people who worked closely with them or witnessed events in which they were involved. In Kennett's case, I forwarded contentious passages to give him the chance to give his side of the story, but he did not reply.

Many interviewees gave access to personal files containing minutes of meetings, letters, briefing notes, photos and archival footage of the Snowy River. Government documents were obtained through Freedom of Information and various sources. Documents included letters, briefings and official reports. The Total Environment Centre in Sydney opened its comprehensive files for my research, providing minutes of phone hook-ups, letters, press releases, ministerial briefing notes and emails among other useful documents. Most of my primary source material is, or will be, available in state and national archives.

I also drew on media reports published or broadcast from the following outlets: *Snowy River Mail; Cooma–Monaro Express; The Age; Herald Sun; Sydney Morning Herald; Daily Telegraph; Weekly Times; The Summit Sun; Bairnsdale Advertiser; East Gippsland News; The Adelaide Advertiser; The Australian Financial Review; Shepparton News; Country News;* ABC Radio National; ABC Radio, Bega; ABC TV's *7.30 Report;* ABC TV news; Radio 2XL in Cooma; *Today Show* on Channel Nine; Nine Network News; Channel Ten News; Channel Seven News.

I have been interested to discover along the way that so many people confuse the Snowy River with the Snowy Mountains Hydro-Electric Scheme. They would ask me if my book was going to include stories about all the migrants coming out to build the dams, the deaths during construction and so forth. Many books have already been written about the scheme and readers will be disappointed if they think mine is yet another one lauding the great engineering feat. This is a book about the Snowy River alone, which never got the chance to tell its side of the story.

I think the river is like everything else — it was taken for granted, and we did not think enough of it until we lost it.

SHEILA ROBERSON, AVALON, DALGETY, NOVEMBER 2003

⌣

Our battle will form part of the written history of the Snowy River Country, and a display of indifference by public figures in that setting will look very stupid and will be permanently recorded.

JOHN HARROWELL, ROCKWELL, DALGETY, JULY 1993

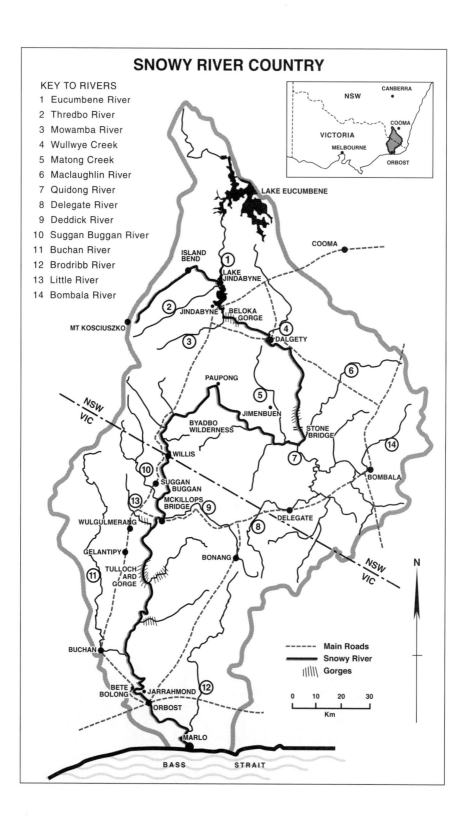

SNOWY RIVER COUNTRY

KEY TO RIVERS

1 Eucumbene River
2 Thredbo River
3 Mowamba River
4 Wullwye Creek
5 Matong Creek
6 Maclaughlin River
7 Quidong River
8 Delegate River
9 Deddick River
10 Suggan Buggan River
11 Buchan River
12 Brodribb River
13 Little River
14 Bombala River

NSW
CANBERRA
COOMA
VICTORIA
MELBOURNE
ORBOST

LAKE EUCUMBENE

COOMA

ISLAND BEND
LAKE JINDABYNE
JINDABYNE
BELOKA GORGE
MT KOSCIUSZKO
DALGETY

PAUPONG

JIMENBUEN

NSW
VIC

BYADBO WILDERNESS
STONE BRIDGE

WILLIS

SUGGAN BUGGAN
MCKILLOPS BRIDGE
BOMBALA

WULGULMERANG
DELEGATE

GELANTIPY
BONANG

NSW
VIC

TULLOCH ARD GORGE

N

BUCHAN

BETE BOLONG
JARRAHMOND
ORBOST

MARLO

- - - - Main Roads
▬▬▬ Snowy River
|||\ Gorges

0   10   20   30
Km

BASS   STRAIT

The Drought Breaker

They dammed the Snowy River and they damn well stuffed it up
They've ignored the cries of nature to fill their golden cup
And the wild old Snowy wonders why it has been cursed
And why they have condemned it to a slow cold death of thirst

— 'Rhubard', aka Reg Silvester, Snowy River, 1997

Chris Todhunter lay in bed, wide awake. Her children were rustling in their dreams; her husband, Greg, breathed peacefully in the deep of the night at her side. But it wasn't those familiar sounds she was listening for; it was the Snowy River gurgling over the Dalgety weir a few hundred metres away. Tonight it was too quiet. She sprang up and threw open the door of the caravan annexe. Water was swirling past the step where there should be dry land. For the first time in more than twenty years, the Snowy was in flood.

Chris raced back and shook Greg hard. 'Get up!' she cried. 'The river's rising — it's here, right here. Hurry, get up!'

Greg was groggy and confused. 'What? Where's the river?' He stumbled to the open door where freezing water was now lapping over the sill. He stood there with his wet toes turning blue and thought he must be dreaming.

The river had been a sad shadow of its legendary wild self ever since 1967, when the Jindabyne dam was completed. The dam was the last of three on the Snowy River, built as part of the iconic Snowy Mountains Hydro-Electric Scheme. Together the three dams trapped more than 99 per cent of the Snowy's headwaters. The water was diverted west through tunnels under the mountains to generate electricity and help green the inland desert. Dalgety's inhabitants, living thirty kilometres downstream from the Jindabyne dam in New South Wales, were left with a dying river, a dying town, and the sour feeling that somehow they had been robbed.

By 1991, the Snowy River was little more than a greasy trickle in a huge channel choked with willows, weeds, sand and slime. The last thing anyone expected was a flood, but it was an exceptionally wet winter that year. When the heavens opened yet again one night in late June, the ground was waterlogged and the rain had nowhere to go but into the Snowy River.

The council-owned Dalgety caravan park on the Snowy's overgrown banks bore the brunt. As morning dawned, a small crowd gathered on the Dalgety Bridge to watch Greg Todhunter, the park's caretaker, bobbing about in a boat, reaching into caravan windows and trying to salvage bedding, furniture and appliances. It was still raining intermittently, but the drizzle did not deter the onlookers, including a Snowy River Shire officer taking notes.

No one thought much of it at the time, since the shire generally took little interest in this municipal backwater. Then five months later, early one sunny morning in mid-December 1991, the shire paid another rare visit. At least, Todhunter assumed so when he got up to find notices pasted on the regular campers' permanent vans.

> Dear owner, the Snowy River Shire wishes to notify that the caravan park will be closed down on 31 December 1991. All permanent vans must be removed by 1 January 1992. Any vans remaining in the park after this time will be auctioned.

After years of neglect, the caravan park was overdue for a major upgrade under new state regulations and now it needed additional work after the flood. The combined works would cost about $20,000[1] when camping fees barely paid for the caretakers. The easiest and cheapest thing to do was shut the place down.

Dalgety's residents were alarmed. The post office had closed just after the flood. The general store, the pub and the servo relied on campers to survive. The caravan park was not exactly thriving, but if it went, those other businesses could well be next. If the store and the pub closed, it would be only a matter of time before the school went too, and after that, the town. It would be the classic country town's slide into oblivion: slow death by a thousand cuts. Dalgety did not want to be another statistic.

The Snowy River Shire Council told the residents the caravan park's future was not yet decided, and council would consider the matter at its next meeting in a few days. Dalgety was not reassured. When the councillors took their seats on 17 December 1991, they were startled to find the small room jam-packed and overflowing into the foyer with residents and anxious caravan owners.

The overwhelming public display impressed the councillors. 'I didn't think there *were* sixty people in Dalgety,' said the mayor, Keven Burke, looking over the throng. He said the council was as surprised as Dalgety to learn about the closure notices. It postponed its decision pending further investigation, and ultimately dropped the proposed closure, but Dalgety remained restless.

About seventy people attended a public meeting in the Dalgety Memorial Hall on 23 January 1992 to talk about what was going wrong. Everyone was bewildered as to why the shire would want to do such a thing to Dalgety; why, indeed, the town was dying. Everyone except retired accountant John Harrowell. 'The town is dying because the river is dying,' the seventy-three year old told the meeting. 'If we want to save Dalgety and the caravan park, we have to get more water back into the Snowy River.'

It was a heretical thought. The Snowy River's sorry state was a hot topic of conversation in the pub, but it had never occurred to anyone that history could be undone. The Snowy Mountains Hydro-Electric Scheme enjoyed mythical status as an absolute and unquestionable good; the Snowy Mountains Hydro-Electric Authority managed the water, and it was like God: unreachable, impenetrable, unaccountable. 'It seemed as if whatever Snowy Hydro said was gospel, and no one questioned it,' said Moina Hedger, from Cave Creek station. 'No one knew we could.'

The challenge could not be underestimated. John Harrowell was suggesting that little Dalgety — population about 100, with maybe another 200 on surrounding farms — take on a monolithic federal authority and the powerful irrigation lobby, both very used to getting their own way. It would involve trying to shift a mountain of political indifference and going against regional sentiment, which favoured the hydro scheme for bringing jobs, people and development to the Monaro high plains.

Dalgety decided it was up for a fight. Its inhabitants found kindred spirits in Orbost, the only other town on the Snowy River, down in Victoria. Like modern-day Oliver Twists, the men and women from the Snowy River went to the powers-that-be and asked for more.

ONE

The Throwaway River

*I took my son to Australia's Wonderland in 1997, and we found a
wild water ride called the Snowy River Rampage. It had white water
everywhere and I reckon it had a stronger flow than the river. The
tragedy is that a whole generation of Australians have grown up to
believe that the Snowy is still mighty when it is not.*

PAUL LEETE, DALGETY, 1998

The dog finally demonstrated what the others had tried to explain for the
last two hours. I was standing on a sandbank on the Snowy River in the
late summer of 1999 with four men from the Snowy River Alliance: Max
White, Gil Richardson, Ian Moon and Chris Allen. I had come to Orbost to
write a newspaper article about the community's campaign to get more
water released from Jindabyne dam into the Snowy River. In town, where
we met and talked initially, the Snowy rises and falls with the tide; it looked
deceptively as if it had plenty of water.

The same, however, could not be said here, 10 kilometres upstream,
opposite Richardson's farm at Bete Bolong.

'Does it get any deeper?' I asked Richardson, as we watched one of his
farm dogs gambolling ankle-deep across the shallow rivulets running over
the sand. We were standing at the spot where his children used to swim in
holes five metres deep in the 1960s, with a warning to keep out of the main
channel or risk being swept away.

'Oh, yes,' replied Richardson, a fourth-generation farmer on the Orbost
flats. 'There is a bit of a channel left over by the other bank. The dog still has
to swim.'

We watched in silence as the dog waded through the channel and
scrambled dripping up the far bank. It barely got its elbows wet. 'For a kid
who grew up in that and played in boats and canoed upstream and
downstream, it is terribly disappointing,' said Richardson.

If Percy Charles 'Toby' Nixon were still alive, he would be saying with
grim relish, 'I told you so.' The Snowy Mountains Hydro-Electric Scheme
was still in its planning stages in the late 1940s when Nixon first predicted

Gil Richardson's mother Penuel enjoys a dip at Bete Bolong near Orbost, with her grandchildren Marion, John and Susan, in 1966. *Source: Gil Richardson.*

dire consequences for the river's lower reaches. But few took him seriously, even his fellow townspeople in Orbost. 'People here did not oppose the hydro scheme,' said his son, former federal Country Party minister Peter Nixon. 'We were told its value for the national economy and irrigation. We were told it would cure the floods, so we were naturally delighted and we supported it.'

The Snowy Mountains Hydro-Electric Scheme takes in the top 14 per cent of the Snowy River's vast 15,540-square kilometre catchment. The snowmelt from this area contributes about half the average annual flow past Orbost, more than 350 kilometres away. That sounds okay, if a river's health is judged only by how much water runs out to sea. But ecology is more complex than that. The Snowy was a highly dynamic river; its level rose and fell constantly. For three-quarters of the year, it was a torrent. In summer, the flow was lazy and low, with drought levels experienced maybe one in twenty years.

After the hydro scheme was built, the river at Orbost began to flow at drought levels virtually all year around, apart from occasional floods caused by storms in its middle catchment. Without its headwaters and the spring snowmelt flush, the Snowy could not keep its channel clear of weeds, reeds, willows, silt and slime. Down on the flood plain, the bed rose several metres and smoothed out to create a 'table-top' river; the flow was no longer strong enough to push the sand aside and re-establish a deep channel with deep

Gil Richardson with his grandchildren Penny, Kelly and Sam, standing in the family's swimming hole in 1998. *Source: Gil Richardson.*

pools. A sand plug 14 kilometres long developed, making it difficult for native fish to travel up and down the river past the Richardsons' farm to spawn in the estuary. As the years passed, the rate of degradation accelerated until, by the late 1980s, the river was in ecological crisis.

Yet its plight was not obvious. The Snowy flows through sparsely populated country far off the beaten track. It is not readily visible or accessible for most of its course. Dalgety and Orbost are the only two towns, and there are only three bridges along its entire length. Most people nowadays only see the Snowy when they drive into Jindabyne, or rather, until recently, they saw a small sign on the dam wall saying 'Snowy River'.

On one side of the road was the picturesque expanse of Lake Jindabyne. On the other side there was nothing but the rocky Beloka Gorge. There was no river, not even if you parked and walked back to look over the side. There were water lilies floating in a serene green puddle, a bit of a pool among the reeds further down, and a line in the lichen on the rocks on the sides — a ghostly marker of the Snowy's old water level. 'In the minds of the rest of Australia, the Snowy scheme stops at Jindabyne dam wall,' said Dalgety resident John Harrowell in 1992. 'No one, except the people of Dalgety and Orbost, is aware of the destruction east of that wall.'

∽

You have to admire the tenacity and ingenuity of it on one level, but then on another level, you wonder, 'How could they have thought it was okay to do this?'

CANDY BROAD, VICTORIAN RESOURCES AND ENERGY MINISTER, 1999–2002.

The Snowy River was doomed almost from the moment white people set eyes on it. Long before 1890, when A. B. 'Banjo' Paterson made the river shorthand for all things Australian, the Snowy was singled out for a special role in Australia's national development. Another quintessentially Australian phenomenon — drought — sealed its fate. Settlers fanned out into far western New South Wales in good seasons during the nineteenth century, convinced the inland climate was fair conditions punctuated by occasional drought. When they discovered, to their everlasting despair, it was the other way around, they turned longing eyes towards the Snowy Mountains.

The snowmelt sustained the Murray and Murrumbidgee rivers, but sometimes it was just not enough to keep the rivers going on their long 2500-kilometre journey across the semi-arid plains to the Southern Ocean. In severe droughts, they dried up to little more than strings of salty, muddy pools. The Snowy River, on the other hand, never failed. It got the lion's share of the snowmelt, but raced it south to the Tasman Sea through a poor and sparsely populated wilderness.

'It was the thought of this continuous waste of this river, while inland areas could not be adequately developed for lack of water, that led to various proposals for diverting the Snowy inland,' observed the Commonwealth and States Snowy River Committee in 1946.[1]

The first serious proposal was made in 1884, when the NSW Government initiated a Royal Commission on water conservation at the end of yet another long drought. The state's Surveyor-General, Mr P. F. Adams, told the NSW commission chair, William Lyne, that the snow never failed in the alps, giving one or two rivers an apparently inexhaustible source. 'The Murrumbidgee has been almost dry when [the Snowy River] was pouring out an unlimited supply,' he said. Adams suggested the Snowy River could be diverted via a canal into the Murrumbidgee, but then the rain fell again and dissolved the urgency of the matter.[2]

The Snowy River next came to political attention in 1901, when Dalgety was selected as the site for the new national capital following Federation. The NSW Royal Commissioner, Alexander Oliver, whose team assessed potential sites, recognised the Snowy River's 'incalculable' potential for generating hydro-electricity. 'The applicability of that power, procurable as it is from various points in the course of the river … marks southern Monaro as the most richly endowed district, in respect of natural power, of any state of the Australian union,' Oliver wrote.[3]

The new federal government agreed with Oliver's choice. It duly passed legislation to that effect in 1904, with New South Wales granting the Commonwealth 'the right to use the waters of the Snowy River or such other rivers as may be agreed upon … for the generation of electricity for the [Australian Capital] territory, and to construct the works necessary for that purpose'.[4] In 1909, the national capital site was moved from Dalgety to Canberra, but, significantly, the law giving the Commonwealth rights to the Snowy River for power generation was never rescinded.

Various state plans were put forward over the next three decades to divert the Snowy for irrigation or harness it for hydro-electricity generation. In 1913, a Mr J. S. Gregory from Swan Hill presciently told a conference of engineers that the Snowy River should be diverted west into the Murray by means of tunnels. In 1920, the chief engineer in the NSW Department of Public Works, William Corin, suggested the river be diverted south across its loop through a series of tunnels and two power stations, to rejoin its course where it turns down towards Victoria.

The ideas began to get some serious traction in 1936, when community leaders on the Monaro plains formed the Snowy River Hydro-Electric Development League to promote Corin's scheme. The league believed the power stations would provide much-needed jobs during the Depression, and transform the Monaro and East Gippsland from sleepy agrarian backwaters into an industrial engine room. They envisaged Cooma as a thriving city, Eden as a bustling port, and smoking factory chimneys over Bombala.

Councillor Leo Barry was prominent in the league. His son, Tom, remembers his father describing the Snowy in flood. 'Dad said the horses began to take fright because the ground was shaking with the power of the river in this gorge below them.' From Leo Barry's perspective, most of the Snowy ran through unpopulated country useless for anything but light grazing. 'Now, in an enlightened age, we can see there were mistakes made, but people like my father saw the incredible power and energy of the Snowy and thought there must be some way to harness what they saw as its surplus energy for the good of mankind,' said Tom Barry. 'They knew the river, they saw it on horseback. They were not people who come in from outside for six-minute grabs in a helicopter. To them, the Snowy was just going to waste. They couldn't see any need for the water in the Snowy, except as a natural stock boundary.'

In the late 1930s, when Leo Barry was promoting the plan in Sydney and Melbourne, drought again gripped the newly established irrigation communities along the Murrumbidgee and Murray rivers. The Murrumbidgee Irrigation Area had expanded during good seasons early in the decade, but by 1938 there was not enough water to meet demands. The irrigators formed the Murrumbidgee Valley Water Users Conservation Committee and revived the 1884 proposal to divert the Snowy River into the Murrumbidgee via a canal.

The NSW Agriculture Minister, A. D. Reid, told the irrigators in June 1939 that the Snowy was to be used to generate power for Sydney in a variation of Leo Barry's proposal. But then the government changed its mind when state engineer, F. H. Brewster, suggested internally that a dam be built near Jindabyne, and the Snowy's water diverted into the Murrumbidgee through tunnels with turbines inside. It was the first combined irrigation/power plan put forward.

In 1941, at the height of World War II, Leo Barry suggested a compromise in which the Eucumbene River, a major Snowy tributary, might be diverted to the Murrumbidgee, while the rest of the Snowy River was still used to generate power for the Monaro/East Gippsland region. The irrigators refused to countenance sending Snowy water anywhere but their way. The NSW Water Conservation and Irrigation Commission championed the irrigators' cause inside government. The Snowy River country had been settled long before the irrigation districts, but its sparse population did not stand a chance of being heard above the inland clamour.

The NSW Government considered the various proposals carefully, and in 1944, a NSW technical committee finally recommended that the Snowy River be diverted to the Murrumbidgee via a series of reservoirs, tunnels and power stations. But the Commonwealth refused to relinquish its legal rights to use the Snowy River to supply power to Canberra. Federal engineers instead suggested a dual scheme with power stations diverting water into both the Murray and the Murrumbidgee. The Commonwealth supported this proposal as a post-war reconstruction project, although it was on shaky constitutional ground.

Section 100 of the Constitution stipulates that 'the Commonwealth shall not, by any law or regulation of trade or commerce, abridge the right of a State or of the residents therein to reasonable use of the waters of rivers for conservation or irrigation'. The Commonwealth got around this by invoking its defence powers, arguing that its scheme was necessary to secure power supplies in the event Australia was attacked and lost its big coal power stations near the coast.

Victoria also staked a claim. Two-fifths of the Snowy River is in Victoria. The Victorian Government had surveyed the lower gorges in 1928, confirming the potential for big hydro-electric dams to service East Gippsland. Diversions in New South Wales would diminish the capacity of these dams. Further, if the Snowy's water had to go anywhere, then Victoria wanted all of it diverted into the Murray to improve navigation and benefit irrigators in both states.

The Commonwealth, New South Wales and Victoria agreed to work together in 1946. A joint technical committee of engineers was appointed to investigate all options. In November 1948, the committee submitted an ambitious plan for a dual-purpose scheme diverting water through separate power stations into the Murray and the Murrumbidgee rivers. The proposed design had a potential power capacity almost ten times higher than earlier designs. It also satisfied the claims of both states to the Snowy River's water. The states and federal government formally approved the plan at a meeting on 13 July 1949.

The Commonwealth's *Snowy Mountains Hydro-Electric Power Act* had already come into effect a week earlier, on 7 July 1949. It established the Snowy Mountains Hydro-Electric Authority to construct the scheme and operate its power stations. Work officially began on 17 October 1949, with a small ceremonial dynamite blast near the old township of Adaminaby on the Eucumbene River.

Yet the states still did not wholeheartedly support the scheme; New South Wales, for one, persisted in wanting all the Snowy River's water diverted into the Murrumbidgee alone, for irrigation purposes only, and it had the Constitution on its side. The Commonwealth hoped that by getting work underway quickly, the states would have little choice but to fall into line. After nearly a decade during which the scheme's legal status remained uncertain, New South Wales and Victoria finally passed complementary legislation in 1958 confirming the 1949 pact on sharing the water and power.

'This outlaw of a river, whom nobody has yet been able to tame, is to become a broken lady's hack,' observed one journalist as construction began. 'This rip-roaring terror, whom engineers have been unable to hold, is to become the driver of electric irons and sewing machine motors that turn out shirts for little Willie. Well, they may tame the outlaw eventually, but it will be a job ... I suppose they know what they are up against.'[5]

The engineers did, and they triumphed. The design brief aimed to catch as much water as possible to maximise the economic value of hydro-electricity generation and maximise the amount of water available to irrigators. By the time construction ended in 1972, the scheme had diverted twelve major rivers and seventy-one creeks. It had sixteen dams, eighteen aqueducts, nineteen trans-mountain tunnels, seven power stations and two pumping stations. The Snowy River accounts for just under half the average 2410 gigalitres that the scheme traps each year. The other half comes from montane rivers that would eventually flow inland anyway, including the Murrumbidgee and tributaries to the Murray River. The scheme's total storage capacity is 7000 gigalitres. Irrigators are entitled to 2100 gigalitres a year; another 1000 is held in reserve and can be used to generate power at the discretion of the Snowy Hydro Authority. The reserve can also be used to top up irrigators in severe droughts.

The scheme's thirty-one turbines have a total generating capacity of 3756 megawatts, but only holds enough water to run the turbines at about a quarter of their capacity. The turbines feed an average 4500 gigawatt/hours of energy into the national grid every year. This is 3–4 per cent of the total electricity consumed in eastern Australia.

As an engineering feat, the Snowy Mountains Hydro-Electric Scheme is truly remarkable. It is almost as impressive a social engineering feat. More than 100,000 men and women worked on the scheme, two-thirds of them migrants from thirty countries in war-torn Europe. The scheme enabled irrigation to expand along the Murray and Murrumbidgee rivers; the New South Wales areas receiving water from the scheme grow produce worth $750 million a year. The irrigation lobbyists did not quite get the 'million healthy happy people' they imagined living in golden cities in the desert, but close to 24,000 people live in prosperity in Griffith, with another 40,000 in surrounding districts.

By and large, the hydro scheme had overwhelming public support. How could it not? The Snowy Mountains Hydro-Electric Authority not only presided over a massive development project, but also designed an impressive public relations machine. The propaganda was in part pragmatic: the authority's first commissioner, Sir William Hudson, was well aware of the need to get and keep the public on side given the scheme's uncertain legal status in its first decade. But the evangelical tone also reflected the faith of a true believer.

Hudson, knighted in 1955, was a renowned engineer with expertise in hydro-electricity projects in France, Scotland and New Zealand. He believed unequivocally in the Snowy Mountains scheme's capacity to do good for Australia, and he shared his vision through a communications department that produced dozens of celebratory books, films and songs. All that ordinary Australians understood about the scheme, they understood from information provided by mythmakers of the first order. 'The Nation's regard for the Scheme may be high because nowhere in its history is reference made to the loss and damage suffered by a large area of country which once had the full use of a famous river,' complained John Harrowell in 1992, in a letter to Democrats Senator John Coulter.

Even today, the scheme's pamphlets, books and videos barely mention the Snowy River, much less admit the damage done to one great Australian icon in the process of creating another. The scheme turned off the Snowy River in three stages. The first third of the Snowy's headwaters was trapped in 1958 when Eucumbene dam was completed. The second third went west with the completion of Island Bend dam in 1965. The Jindabyne dam cut off the last third in 1967. Less than 1 per cent of the Snowy River's original flow was left gushing through a small concrete drainpipe at the bottom of the Jindabyne dam spillway.

Very occasionally, in extremely wet weather, the Snowy River gets a little more water if the weir overflows on the Mowamba River, one of its tributaries. The drainpipe on the dam and spills from the weir provide virtually the only water the Snowy River now gets for 60 kilometres, before the Quidong River enters near the Victoria border. Most Australians understood vaguely that the Snowy Mountains Hydro-Electric Scheme dammed and diverted the Snowy River inland, but somehow they also sustained a mental picture of the legendary torrent still thrashing through the wilderness. The people living along the Snowy River thought the same thing too — at first.

⌒

The residents failed to fight for their river thirty years [ago] not through indifference but through bewilderment. At that time the air was filled with the sounds of 'cusecs',[6] 'a vast engineering project' and the 'dead heart of Australia' and many other catch phrases. What was never said at that time in clear English was, 'You are about to lose 99 per cent of your river'.

JOHN HARROWELL, ROCKWELL, DALGETY, 1992

Cec Bottom grew up on a farm near old Jindabyne town. The Snowy Mountains Authority compulsorily acquired the property, which is now under Lake Jindabyne. As a teenager during the hydro scheme's construction, Bottom bought another property backing onto the rugged Beloka Gorge, below Jindabyne. 'In old Jindabyne, people did not know much about the scheme and what it would do,' Bottom remembered. 'I don't know whether they found out in letters or by word of mouth, but people were certainly under the impression the dam would be catching only the snowmelt, and the river would still have its normal, average flow. The dams would just catch the surplus.'

Local people understood 'catching the snowmelt' to mean skimming off the extra water running in spring over and above the Snowy's flow the rest of the year. The reality dawned after Jindabyne dam was completed. 'It was not until 1968, after Jindabyne dam went in, that people thought, wait, the river has dried up,' said Bottom.

'It was in a drought, and the hydro thought the dam would take three years to fill, but it filled almost immediately because it was a big snow season. I wondered what effect the dam would have on the river below my place and went down, and sure enough it was shocking. We thought the scheme was special because it was developing the area, but we never thought about the repercussions of water not being there in the river. People grieve for the river now that they know the repercussions.'

The Snowy was so big, so irrepressible, such a powerful presence, it was hard to believe it could disappear, virtually overnight. Bernie Power, whose family property fronted the Snowy River a few kilometres upstream from Dalgety, said no one really understood the figures being bandied about. 'The engineers would come and say there will be so much running down after the dam is built, like so many cusecs, and people could not envisage what it meant in terms of the flow.'

Landholders received letters explaining that the Snowy Mountains Authority would help pay for fencing because the river would be too low to keep stock contained, but 'I don't think even then people realised how low it would be,' said Power. 'I think they thought it would be sheep-proof, if not cattle-proof. And then the sheep spread out after the dam went in.'

Kevin McMahon grew up in Dalgety and ran the local service station for more than twenty years. As a child in the Depression, the spring snowmelt meant money for jam. He and other little boys would wade into the torrent as far as they dared, and grab the rabbits washed out of their burrows and swimming for their lives. The meat went in the pot for dinner and the skins were worth a few bob. In summer, the river ran low, but so clear over its gravel bed that a shilling could be dropped into the 7-metre 'Blue Hole' under the bridge and still be seen bright as day. So could the false teeth someone once lost peering over the railings.

McMahon said the town was promised the river would still have 98 per cent of its average summer flow after the scheme was built. 'It was common knowledge we would get 98 per cent, but then some other fellows came along and said Dalgety could do without that much water and they gave us only 2 per cent,' Kevin said. 'They just went ahead and did it and said it would be a good thing.'

Max and Glenice White, who moved to Orbost in the early 1960s and were to become key players in the fight to restore the Snowy, were also under the impression the scheme was originally designed to take only one-third or two-thirds of the river. They understood the plan changed in the late 1950s, when American engineering companies got involved. 'It was the Yanks,' said Glenice. 'When they took the scheme over, they said, "Why pussyfoot around — y'all might as well take it all!" They didn't tell anyone, they just did it.'

John Kelly, an engineer, who helped design the scheme, is mystified as to where such ideas come from. For a start, the Snowy Mountains Authority told its contractors, American or otherwise, what to do, not the other way around. Secondly, it was always the intention to take all water in the Snowy River coming from the mountains, including the Mowamba River which enters the Snowy 2 kilometres below Jindabyne dam wall but is diverted into Lake Jindabyne via a weir and pipe higher up in the catchment.

The intention was clear in November 1948, when the Commonwealth/state joint technical committee of engineers submitted the scheme's broad design to the Commonwealth, Victorian and NSW governments. The governments approved the design in July 1949. It included a pipeline to divert the Mowamba River. It also stated that two-thirds of the Snowy River's water would be diverted into the Murrumbidgee and one-third into the Murray.

As a young engineer with the scheme, John Kelly's responsibilities included public relations. He showed politicians and journalists around the scheme and explained how it worked. Kelly cannot remember public information meetings being held, but said that if there were, there was 'no way that anybody from the Authority would have said what these people claim. It would just not have been true, and besides which, you would have been as good as shot if you had said anything to the contrary.'

Kelly said Sir William Hudson expressly forbade distortion or exaggeration. In the foreword of Kelly's 1965 conducting officers' manual, Sir William said, 'Information given by Public Relations Officers, whether in talks on the Scheme and during tours of inspection, should be factual. Exaggeration must be avoided, so must anything in the nature of propaganda'. The manual has a detailed index with more than 100 topics, but none dealing with releases from Jindabyne dam into the Snowy. 'As far as the Authority was concerned, it was just not an issue. Otherwise, there would have been something to say about the subject in the manual,' Kelly said.

John Brown, a fellow engineer who worked for the Snowy Mountains Authority from 1953 to 1971, concurred. He was involved in estimating how much the snowmelt contributed to the overall runoff. If flow regimes below the dam were raised as an issue, he would have been aware of it. But no one asked, so he did not tell. 'I am sure that nobody in authority would have ever told riparian residents that the scheme would only divert snowmelt runoff,' he said. 'They would have been told that arrangements would be made to release a very small amount of water to supply existing licensed pumps, and another very small amount to meet other riparian requirements such as fish.'

Just how small an amount was decided in 1961. The Snowy Mountains Authority wrote to the NSW Water Conservation and Irrigation Commission, asking how much water they should release into the Snowy River from Jindabyne dam. The commission calculated existing licences for stock, crops and domestic consumption. It allowed a margin for future increases in licences, and losses in evaporation and seepage. The commission then advised the Snowy Mountains Authority to allow for 50 megalitres a day at most, to be released from Jindabyne dam; that is, about 1.5 per cent of the river's original flow at this point.[7]

The commission also advised that on a daily basis the authority only had to maintain a visible flow below the dam wall, and a mean flow of 25 megalitres under the Dalgety bridge. This amounted to 0.78 per cent of Dalgety's daily average of 3200 megalitres, including inflows from several tiny creeks below the dam wall. It was worse than the worst droughts experienced on the Monaro plains. The flow at Dalgety had dropped temporarily below 50 megalitres a day only five times between 1902 and 1956; now the river would permanently have less than half that amount.

'The releases from Jindabyne dam were set by New South Wales,' said engineer John Kelly. 'In all probability, had the commission asked for three or four times as much, they would have got it because the Authority had to keep the states on side, and this would have been a small portion of water compared to the whole thing. But New South Wales said this much, and so the Authority said yes.'

In the meantime, the 'only the snowmelt' impression persisted in the community, possibly due to the scheme's promotional movies made in the 1950s and '60s. Ross Walters, who has a property south of Dalgety, watched these films as a child at school in the 1970s. He remembers them emphasising the scheme would take only the snowmelt.

The films actually weren't that explicit. They make passing reference to diverting the Snowy River's snowmelt and 'excess' water into Lake

Eucumbene for storage, but say nothing about the rest of the river being trapped behind Jindabyne dam.

'Roll, roll, roll on your way/Roll on your way until judgment day/Snowy River, roll' went the chorus in the song opening some promotional films, as if somehow the Snowy would remain forever despite what the engineers planned. The community was not alone in thinking the scheme would take only the river's floods or snowmelt. As late as January 1994, the new Snowy Mountains Authority commissioner, Murray Jackson, told the *Canberra Times* 'the scheme was designed to harness the floodwaters of the Snowy and turn those into irrigation supplies'.[8]

The community's initial confusion is not surprising. The scheme was conceived and built in an era when few people questioned the authority of governments and engineers, much less expected the community ought to be consulted about such projects. The design process and official deliberations were secretive, but the Snowy Mountains Authority, the politicians and bureaucrats saw little need to keep the public informed; to a large extent they believed the technical details were beyond ordinary people's comprehension. And most people did not need the Authority to persuade them it was a wicked waste to let the Snowy River run to the ocean: it was common wisdom at the time.

Community confusion also arose because so many different design variations were bandied about. In mid-1949, the United Country Party member for Gippsland, Colonel George Bowden, complained to Nelson Lemmon, the Minister for Works overseeing the scheme's construction, that the plethora of combined and recombined options under consideration was causing a 'good deal of confusion' in his electorate about 'what exactly is meant' by the proposal to divert one-third of the Snowy River into the Murrumbidgee River and the other two-thirds into the Murray River.

Lemmon spelt out what was meant: all water in the Snowy River above Jindabyne was to be diverted, including the Mowamba River. Tributaries below Jindabyne dam would be the only source of water in a truncated Snowy River. Although it meant virtually no water in the Snowy for its first 60 kilometres, Lemmon said the river would have 53 per cent of its annual average flow[9] by the time it reached Orbost.

So the right information was out there from the start, although apparently not widely known. People in Dalgety sixteen years later were shocked to discover they were losing the Mowamba River as well as the Snowy's headwaters.

Colonel Bowden took the matter to Nelson Lemmon in 1949 because alarm bells were ringing in Orbost. Farmer Toby Nixon initially accepted the hydro-electric scheme when he thought it only involved diverting about a third of the Snowy's headwaters inland. When he heard there might be not one but three dams diverting all the river's headwaters, he became among the most vocal in a group of farmers who feared the Snowy would silt up on the flood plain.

The farmers took the matter to the Orbost Shire Council in early February 1949. Spokesman Jim Luckins warned the lower flats could be flooded and permanently salted by brackish water if the mouth closed. He said the national benefits precluded an attempt to stop the hydro scheme being built, but the district had rights under the Constitution, and immediate action was necessary to protect those rights. Luckins said the states had a responsibility to indemnify the Snowy River's lower reaches against negative impacts.[10]

The council decided to hold a public meeting to test the depth of public opinion, and to ask Colonel Bowden to take up the cause in Canberra. Bowden was requested to protest against the summer flow being reduced 'below a certain amount', lobby for an indemnity fund to cover proven damages, and ask for a breakwater at Marlo to keep the mouth open all year.

Any rumbling about the scheme's Constitutional validity was bound to attract the politicians' attention. A Commonwealth/state ministerial conference on 14 February 1949 agreed that further investigation into the implications for the lower Snowy was warranted.[11] The Victorian Deputy Premier, Colonel Kent-Hughes, represented the Orbost farmers' interests at the ministerial conference, then went to East Gippsland for the shire's public meeting on 25 February 1949. Captain Green, an officer from the State Water Commission, accompanied Colonel Kent-Hughes. They faced a hostile audience.

Orbost's Councillor R. R. Johnston opened the meeting by saying he believed the Orbost flats would develop into a barren desert if the hydro scheme went through as planned. Farmer Jim Luckins said the authorities had not considered Orbost in their deliberations. In his opinion, 'Ned Kelly would not have done more. [The authorities'] opinion was "We want the water, we take it".'

Colonel Bowden said news of the scheme came like a bolt from the blue and he, like others, knew little about it. He felt it was 'beyond the conception of normal thinking', and the authorities would have to fight to get the scheme through.[12]

In a blunt realpolitik assessment, Colonel Kent-Hughes told the meeting Orbost had the least political pull among all the districts laying claim to the Snowy River's waters, and the sooner a local committee formed to defend the district's interests, the better. He said experts considered the scheme would not have any effect on the flats (although none of these experts had visited Orbost). He also assured the community that the current design of the scheme would take only 35 per cent of the Snowy's flow, and 50 per cent later, subject to a technical committee investigation. He clearly meant 50 per cent of the flow at Orbost, but the newspaper report of the meeting did not spell this out — no doubt contributing to the misconception up and down the river that the scheme would take only a third to half of the *headwaters*. Several months later, when it was too late, Nelson Lemmon spelt out the real situation to Colonel Bowden.

In the meantime, Colonel Kent-Hughes said the technical committee would investigate the farmers' concerns before June 1949. He finished with some soothing noises about the Victorian government's desire, in tandem with New South Wales to explore the economic possibilities for developing the 'neglected' South Coast and East Gippsland. He assured the meeting that the area's interests would be safeguarded. 'No water should be taken if needed in this area,' he said.

A week later, the farmers formed a protest group called the Snowy River Protection League and appealed for donations to fund a campaign.[13] The league wrote to the Prime Minister, Ben Chifley. They asked what protection would be afforded the Orbost flats, and flagged their intention to seek advice on the scheme's legality and Orbost's rights.

In the meantime, the scheme's technical committee prepared to visit Orbost. It did not take the task seriously and didn't think the issues so important as to warrant all members going to Orbost. 'If four of us went down, that would be ample,' Ronald East, chairman of Victoria's State Rivers and Water Supply Commission, told the others in a meeting in April 1949. 'It is really just for the purpose of "showing the flag", rather than making any real investigation.'[14]

The committee visited Orbost on Friday 29 April 1949. In the morning, Toby Nixon took the committee upstream, to Bete Bolong. After lunch, the committee looked at the section around Orbost, before Jim Luckins took them to see around the mouth at Marlo. At dinner that night, the Snowy River Protection League told the committee its concerns. The farmers said the proposed flows would cause the Snowy to silt up; lower the ground water table under the flats in summer; allow salty water further upstream, affecting livestock and household wells; and cause the mouth to close, flooding low areas. The farmers emphasised they were all for the hydro scheme in the national interest but they wanted assurances Orbost would be protected.

Ronald East assured the farmers the committee would recommend compensation for known and unknown damages. Dr Louis Loder, the committee chairman, also assured the farmers their case would be fully investigated before any final decisions, although he warned the committee was only acting in an advisory capacity to the three governments.[15]

That was about as much thought as the technical committee gave the matter. Its members met again in on 23 May 1949 to finalise their comprehensive report to the Commonwealth, Victoria and New South Wales, detailing the options for a grand hydro-electric scheme diverting all the Snowy's headwaters inland. They discussed their Orbost excursion. East doubted local opinion that the Snowy would become too brackish for stock to drink, 'as even now, there were times the water was not drinkable by stock'. The potential for the river to silt up and the mouth to close was more serious, but the committee decided not to mention the prospect of damage in the final report. Instead, they suggested remedial works if and when a problem arose.[16]

'After inspection of the area and consideration of the problem, it was decided there was little justification for the fears mentioned,' said the committee in its report, which it submitted in late June 1949. It said any problems in the lower reaches of the Snowy could be overcome with minor works such as a small dam on a tributary in Victoria, to supplement the flow if it fell to dangerous levels. Moreover, since 'any such minor work would be wholly in the state of Victoria ... it was decided that Victoria should accept full responsibility for dealing with any deleterious effects on the lower reaches of the river caused by the diversion'. The committee recommended, that in return, Victoria would be guaranteed a quarter of the diverted water for use by its irrigators along the Murray and a share of the power generated.[17]

The technical report was considered at another conference of Commonwealth and state ministers on 13 July. Victoria readily agreed to the engineers' recommended trade-off. It further agreed that the state would 'not require at any time that any water be released from Jindabyne to the lower Snowy and so become unavailable for power and irrigation'. It also agreed that the Snowy Mountains Authority be indemnified against all claims arising out of the loss of water or stream flow due to the scheme's diversion.[18]

Orbost was sold out, and most residents did not even know it. A month earlier, the *Snowy River Mail* carried reports of the Commonwealth legislation for building the scheme. The federal Minister for Works, Nelson Lemmon, emphasised in his second reading speech that 'the Government was ever mindful of the fears that had quite naturally been expressed by residents of the lower Snowy valley as to the effects on rural lands of the diversion of the Snowy waters'. For that reason, 'power had been given to the [Snowy Mountains] authority to carry out works, even outside the prescribed area, which may be necessary to prevent or mitigate any such danger. It may be necessary to provide some small storage to the lower Snowy valley to augment the summer flow in that area'.[19]

The public record was not corrected when, a few weeks later, the politicians decided instead to absolve the Commonwealth and the Snowy Mountains Authority of all responsibility for what happened to the Snowy River in Victoria.

The Orbost community remained under the misapprehension that the Commonwealth Government remained liable for compensation if damages arose. Toby Nixon was never satisfied with official assurances that all would be well, and kept up his letter-writing campaign. In the late 1950s, he urged the Victorian Premier, Henry Bolte, not to pass complementary legislation rubberstamping the 1949 agreement to divert all of the Snowy's headwaters. Nixon argued that Jindabyne dam should not be built, so that one-third of the river's headwaters could still flow down to the sea. Bolte told Nixon the condition of the lower Snowy was a state matter. 'Dad wasn't happy about the Victorian agreement taking responsibility, but people thought it meant something,' Toby's son, Peter Nixon, recalled. The Premier gave more money to the Snowy River Improvement Trust, a community-based statutory agency set up in 1952, to undertake remedial river works as required 'and washed his hands of it all', said Peter Nixon.

Toby Nixon joined the Trust but continued to agitate against the river being totally blocked off at Jindabyne. His son remembers his father writing endless letters to Prime Ministers — Toby Nixon and Bob Menzies were Wesley College old boys — state Premiers, ministers, Country Party powerbrokers, the Liberal and Labor Parties. He spoke at Country Party conferences, complaining that the state and federal governments were taking away East Gippsland's water. 'What, without an anaesthetic?' a bored Deputy Prime Minister, Artie Fadden, heckled on one occasion.

In 1961, Peter Nixon was elected to Federal Parliament for Gippsland: he held the seat for twenty-three years. On arriving in Canberra, he began getting out the files on the scheme and asking questions about its implications for the lower Snowy. He discovered how effective his father had been in raising the issue when he talked to the Minister for National Development, Senator Sir William Spooner. 'Are you Toby Nixon's son?' the minister asked the young backbencher. 'God help us!'

Toby Nixon's relentless campaigning eventually prompted the Snowy Mountains Hydro-Electric Authority to send engineer John Kelly to Orbost to tell the landholders nicely, but firmly, where they stood once and for all. Kelly explained to a meeting of about ninety landholders that Victoria had accepted all responsibility for 'any consequences whatsoever of the diversion of the upper Snowy River by the Snowy Mountains Authority'. He said that ultimately the scheme would take the equivalent of 55 per cent of the Snowy's average flow at Orbost; in droughts, the scheme would take virtually all of it. Spills from the dam would occur rarely, if ever, which meant floods from rain and snow in the montane catchment would be greatly reduced. He finished by saying that no one could really predict how the diversion would affect the river in the lower reaches.[20]

Toby Nixon had a fair idea. 'Dad said the Jindabyne dam would ruin the river because the melting snow and the summer storms that brought the medium floods every year kept the river in its prime condition,' said Peter Nixon. 'He said Jindabyne would lop these off and ruin the Snowy. But he was a one-man band and people thought he was obsessed by it. I suppose he was, but he never stopped. People in this district thought he was exaggerating, that it would not be as bad as he thought.'

Years later, during a drought, Peter Nixon appealed for an emergency release of more water from Jindabyne to help Orbost farmers irrigate their crops. He learned then that it was a physical impossibility given the small size of the outlet pipe. 'And then we knew there was no way we would ever get water into the river,' he said.

Several months after John Kelly's visit to Orbost in 1964, Dalgety learned that the Snowy Mountains Authority intended to divert the Mowamba River into Jindabyne dam, which left the Snowy River with no significant inflows until the Quidong River 60 kilometres downstream. Keeping the Mowamba meant the Snowy would still have about 6 per cent of its original flow.

Councillor Leo Barry, who had fought so hard in the 1940s for a hydro-electric scheme to power industrial development on the Monaro plains, complained. He told the then Dalgety council the Snowy River 'would be reduced to no more than a string of muddy waterholes unless something was done to dam water for the township next summer'. The council agreed to hold a public meeting in Dalgety in May 1965 to discuss what might be done. The options included leaving the Mowamba to run free; a series of five or six small dams for fish, irrigation and watering stock; or a weir near Dalgety to raise the water level and secure the town's water supply.[21]

Dalgety was in uproar when only a couple of weeks later the Snowy Mountains Authority put out the tender to begin building the Mowamba

The drainpipe built into the Jindabyne dam to release a maximum of 50 megalitres a day or about 1.5 per cent of the Snowy River's original flow at this point. *Photo: Claire Miller.*

diversion. The president of the Dalgety Progress Association, Mr John Melham, said the proposal was 'disgraceful'. He accused the authority of going ahead 'without a thought about what effect its diversion scheme would have on Dalgety residents and graziers'. '[This water] is used in the homes, shops, hotel, cricket, football, hockey ovals, etc,' Melham said. 'It is essential to the whole district. And if it is taken from us, particularly in drought periods such as this year, the situation would become intolerable.'

The local newspaper said every Dalgety person it contacted opposed diverting the Mowamba, and believed it would ruin Dalgety and surrounds. 'Dalgety has been made the sacrificial scapegoat without a moment's consideration,' declared the hotelkeeper, George Moore, appealing to everyone in the district to oppose the diversion to 'the bitter end'.[22]

They didn't. Councillors Barry and A. M. Kingston sought and were granted an urgent deputation with Sir William Hudson, the Snowy Mountains Authority commissioner. No doubt he pointed out that diverting the Mowamba was long part of the plan, and there was nothing they could do about it. The authority did agree to pay for a weir near the Dalgety bridge for cosmetic appearances and to keep the water level high enough to pump into the town treatment plant. People whose squatter ancestors had defied government strictures grumbled but accepted the loss of their river as inevitable — an act of government, if not God.

⌁

Peter Nixon said his father Toby claimed the Snowy River was getting worse every year until he died in 1976. And, eventually, 'we could all see it was slowly being ruined'. The community woke up to the truth after the biggest flood on record swept across the flats in February 1971. Peter Nixon's house was left hanging out over the river as the flood tore away the banks. Huge mahogany trees crashed past, tossed end on end like matchsticks in the current. The railway line crumpled as the logs banked up and the causeway gave way. Stock and crops were lost. The fertile soil was smothered in metres of sand. Robert Greenwood from Marlo drowned when he rowed into the current to intercept his motor cruiser, which had broken its moorings; his dinghy was swept out to sea and capsized in the waves. 'My husband saw that, and came back in a terrible state,' said Margaret Adams, from Marlo. 'He said the waves at the entrance were rolling backwards, and the boat went around and around and disappeared from sight.' A few days later, a fisherman found Greenwood's cruiser bobbing undamaged in the sea near Lakes Entrance, and towed it into port.

Orbost learned in 1971 that while the scheme trapped the vital snowmelt flush and 'freshes' from storms in the Snowy Mountains, it did nothing to stop the damaging floods that swept all before them. Those monsters originated in the middle catchment, well below the dams. The 1971 flood receded after five days and the clean-up began, but people living alongside the river say the Snowy itself never recovered.

Peter Nixon noticed the river deteriorating early because he lived beside it and had his father constantly in his ear. 'But it was not till the 1971 flood, I suppose, that the whole district woke up that the river was gone for good,' he said. 'It showed that the river could no longer carry a decent flood, and it changed the Snowy. It was the real awakener for people who had taken no interest before. After the floodwater went down, the river had moved course, washed away islands and dumped big sand banks, so there was a realisation that everything my old man had said had come true.

'Dad always said we would rue the day it was dammed, and we do.'

TWO

The Snowy River Alliance

Welcome to the Hotel Snowy River — you can check out, but you can never leave.

BRETT MINERS

Glenice White's pantry is a sight to behold. Shelves rise from floor to ceiling, packed with bags of flour, jars of jam and pickle, packets of dried fruit and tins of vegetables. The smell is piquant, slightly ticklish; it must be all those spices on the shelf at eye level. Glenice spends a lot of time looking at them — the cumin, paprika, whole cloves and cinnamon — but sadly not because she gets to cook as much as she would like. The pantry is also home to the telephone.

Glenice White and her husband, Max, are often on the phone, talking about the Snowy River. Both grew up in the irrigation districts that took its water, but moved to Orbost as young adults, where they met and married. Glenice was drawn there in part for the river. 'I had wanted to see the Snowy ever since I was kid,' she said. 'When I came to Orbost and found it was running right through the place, I was delighted. I did not realise it would be so close to hand.'

The Whites' lives moved closer to the river in 1974, when Max became the secretary of the Snowy River Improvement Trust and the Flood Warning Officer for the better part of twenty-five years. His work was always in an informal partnership with his wife: Max was the mathematics wizard and Glenice could spell. She usually updated the flood bulletins on the recorded message service, disconcerting the farmers. They would hang up on hearing a female voice and call the Whites' private line to talk to Max. 'How's the river going?' they would say. 'The message has been updated — have you rung the recorder?' Max would reply. 'Yes, but I don't take much notice of that. I thought I would ring you to find out what it's *really* doing!' Glenice forgave them; in those days, it was expected that good women let their husbands do the talking.

The men of the Snowy River Improvement Trust were talking at that time about the river dying. The Trust was set up in 1952 to maintain the banks and the channel. After the devastating 1971 flood, it became a losing battle. Despite the Trust's best efforts, the channel silted up, riparian vegetation died through saltwater pushing upstream from the estuary, the banks eroded and weeds took over. The Trust pointed the finger at low flows. Before the Snowy Mountains Hydro-Electric Scheme, the annual snowmelt flush swept out the channel and gouged deep holes 'up to a kilometre long and 10 metres deep', said Max White.

After the dams went in, the Snowy slowed to a near-permanent drought flow; in summer, it barely ran at all. The current was too weak to sweep sand and silt to the sides, and the holes filled in. Saltwater invaded the flats from the mouth, tainting rich farmland and killing trees holding the banks together. 'It takes a long time for the holes in the river to fill up, and then, all of a sudden, be buggered, there's not many fish here,' White explained.

His wife is the first to admit the state of the river became an obsession. 'What we could never get away from was they just cut off this great river and cut off everything past the wall and they did not care,' Glenice said. 'They just thought they had every right to do it — destroy that magnificent natural resource. It was just total ecological vandalism, quite apart from the fact we had always loved the Snowy. I don't understand why they were so greedy.'

The Trust asked the Victorian Water Conservation and Supply Commission to investigate. Max White and farmer Gil Richardson wrote

The sand plug choking the Snowy and creating a "table-top" river in its lower reaches and across the Orbost floodplain. *Photo: Gil Richardson, February 1998.*

letters, made phone calls, sat through endless meetings and generally bashed their heads against a brick wall. Richardson said half the letters were not even answered. The Trust was up against an official mindset that saw rivers as little more than supply and drainage lines. 'We think the Snowy needs more water,' the men from Orbost would say. 'No, it doesn't,' the public servants from head office would reply. 'Yes, it does!' 'No, it doesn't!' — and so on, and on. One such exchange during an inspection down by the Orbost bridge ended with a frustrated Trust member chasing a hapless bureaucrat up the road, threatening to knock his stupid bloody head off. 'They were on a different planet,' said Max. 'They thought we were idiots, a bunch of hicks.'

The Trust was before its time. Luckily, times change. The battle to stop the Tasmanian Hydro-Electric Commission damming the Franklin River in 1982–83 captured the public imagination. It catapulted environmental issues into mainstream thinking, and a new generation of public servants emerged, speaking a new language with terms like 'environmental flow'. In these more enlightened times, two public servants — one from New South Wales, one from Victoria — visited East Gippsland in 1989. Campbell Fitzpatrick, a researcher in Victoria's then Department of Conservation and Environment, flew the length of the Snowy with Gil Richardson; from the air, the degradation was obvious in its scale and severity.

The inspection led to Victoria and New South Wales setting up the Snowy River Interstate Catchment Coordination Committee. The committee, made up of community representatives and public servants, developed a LandCare strategy to deal with erosion and weeds in the middle catchment where the first decent tributaries kick into the Snowy River. The committee hired Brett Miners, a young natural resource management graduate fresh out of university, as coordinator. The tall, angular public servant was to tread a fine line in coming years between public service and community advocacy.

The sweetly relentless Glenice White joined the committee, to ensure low flows did not fall off the agenda, even though the committee had no power to deal with that problem. Max White and Gil Richardson continued to press the case inside the bureaucracy. The wheels of government turn slowly. It was a major breakthrough when the Department of Conservation and Environment officially, in the draft Gippsland Water Strategy, released in April 1992, accepted low flows in the Snowy were indeed a legitimate issue. The interstate committee then prepared a report identifying the river's problems. It concluded that the only permanent solution involved renegotiating the releases from Jindabyne dam.[1] However, the public servants maintained nothing could be done because Victoria had signed away its rights to more water in 1949.

The issue was still sitting there in the bureaucratic too-hard basket when Glenice White picked up the ringing phone in her fragrant pantry. Jo Garland was on the other end, from the Dalgety and District Community Association. Glenice had never heard of them before.

'I hear you are one of the movers and shakers on the interstate committee,' Garland said.

'Oh, I don't know about that — I'm just a member,' White replied.

'Well, can you tell me why Dalgety isn't on it?'

'I don't have a clue.' White and Gil Richardson had simply received an invitation in the mail. She promised Garland to follow it up.

'Why isn't Dalgety represented on the committee?' she asked at the next meeting. Everyone shrugged. The committee was focused on erosion and other problems in the middle catchment. The river section upstream was not on its radar.

'Is it worth having Dalgety on the committee?' someone asked.

'Who are we to judge that?' White said. 'They live right on the Snowy River. I'd say that makes them important.'

⌐

When you've had a river thundering by at 3200 megalitres a day and that's turned off to almost nothing, to want it back is not being a greenie. We are political, but we are not about getting the hairy-chested quoll protected, or something like that. We are after a simple thing: we want our water back.

JOHN HARROWELL, CANBERRA TIMES, 9 JANUARY 1994

Peter Cochran, the former National Party member for the state seat of Monaro, said he could see trouble on its way when Carl Drury and Jo Garland moved to the Monaro plains in the late 1980s. Cochran knew their type. Greenies. Outsiders, who infiltrated and sowed the seeds of discontent. Knew it, he thought, when Dalgety started complaining about the Snowy River in 1992.

'It was all driven by Carl and Jo, claiming to be locals,' Cochran said. 'They were blow-ins, but they ran the campaign targeting locals and claiming they had been deprived of their river. The locals had lived with the river since the dam was finished in the 1960s, and most did not have real concerns about it, but the huge publicity began to persuade them water should be restored.'

It is true 'blow-ins' spearheaded Dalgety's campaign. 'We would get cranky about our river, but we felt there was nothing we could do,' said Kevin McMahon, seventy-five and one of the 'local locals'. The likes of Jo Garland, on the other hand, 'have the gift for the gab, do not take no for an answer, and they know who to torment'. Cochran, however, was convinced that the environment movement planted Drury and Garland, even though neither knew the other, and neither had much respect for what Drury calls the 'corporate' green groups.

Carl Drury moved from Darwin to Jindabyne in 1988, 'after I felt a cool breeze blow through and called a friend at Thredbo who said, "Mate, we are in a full powder blizzard!"' After a fifteen-year hiatus, Drury became a born-again skier, and then picked up canoeing and rafting. He got to know the Snowy during the wet years of 1990–92. 'You picked up subtle signs, like the driftwood left 4 metres up in trees from floods, and knew she was a shell of her former self. Then the [canoeing] seasons began to end earlier and earlier until there was just a flush of water in November-December. And then it was too dry to float the canoes, and the business died.'

Drury drifted into Dalgety and the campaign in 1996, after hearing the Snowy River Alliance chairman, Paul Leete, on radio.

In Jo Garland's case, she just likes trees. After moving from semi-tropical Grafton, Garland said the lack of green on Dalgety's spare brown plains

Canoeing in the Snowy River at Bete Bolong, near Orbost, before the dams were built. *Source: Gil Richardson.*

More rocks than water confront canoeists tackling the Snowy River after the dams were built.
Photo: Craig Ingram.

'hurt my eyes'. So she sought funding to plant a few trees around town, which was enough for the postman to begin introducing her as 'our local greenie'. 'But you wouldn't have a hope around here if you really were a greenie,' Garland said. 'I try not to be one, but I suppose I do have a green tinge. I am accepted here though, because I do stuff and I don't whinge. Here they think of greenies as people who whinge but don't do anything, and don't have to make a practical living like farming.'

Anyway, the Dalgety and District Community Association did not need greenies to stir things up. It had John Harrowell. He was also a blow-in by local standards, having retired with his wife Janet a few years earlier to Rockwell station, just out of Dalgety, but he commanded great respect. The seventy-three year old was a prominent accountant in Sydney. He served on the Taxation Board of Review and as president of the Institute of Chartered Accountants. He was on the NRMA board and treasurer for the Royal Alexandra Hospital for Children. After retiring to Dalgety, he was a Snowy River Shire councillor. Harrowell was patrician, conservative and a natural leader. When the townspeople formed the Dalgety and District Community Association in mid-1992, with the express purpose of saving the caravan park and getting more water in the Snowy River, there was no question that Harrowell was the right man for the job as president and press secretary.

The caravan park proved easy: while the association was still getting itself organised, the Snowy River Shire Council decided to lease the park to private operators. That just left fixing the Snowy River. Early in the campaign, Harrowell entertained Charles Halton, the Snowy Mountains authority commissioner, at his house. His wife, Janet Harrowell, remembers Halton sitting over coffee, explaining there was nothing the Authority could do even if it wanted to — it was a decision for the federal, NSW and Victorian governments. 'He said to John, "If you have the determination to go on, and go on, and go on, and don't flag, and just keep working at it, then you will get somewhere — but it will take 10 years, at least".'

There were plenty of doubters and sceptics in and around Dalgety too. Liz McMahon, the Dalgety Association's secretary since its inception, said many locals accepted the river was gone and did not think it was a high priority. Others believed there was nothing wrong with the Snowy River that drought-breaking rain would not fix. Even Moina Hedger, who was active on the executive committee for years, said she did not believe at first they could get more water. 'I thought there were too many obstacles ahead of us. Other people said it was impossible, that it could not be done.'

David Glasson and his wife, Jane, encountered hostility from within family ranks when they joined the Dalgety Association. Glasson's father, Mark, thought the campaign ridiculous. Now in his eighties, Mark Glasson, like his son, grew up at Jimenbuen station with the Snowy River as the backdrop to his childhood, but he could not see what everyone was complaining about. Yes, the river was much smaller, 'but it had to be, they took a lot of water out of it, but what was wrong with that?' As for the Snowy's heritage appeal, Mark Glasson snorted, 'What a load of rubbish!'

'I was always of the opinion that Australia is a very dry country and the more we store and use a precious commodity like water, the better,' he said. 'Harrowell was the first who said we must have more water in the Snowy River, which I just totally disagree with because it is such a scarce resource. I think we have to use every drop as best we can, going through the turbines, and irrigation is a very important part of our rural economy. We have a duty to try to produce food in this world, and putting water in the Snowy is letting it go to waste.'

Another disapproving relative called David Glasson soon after he joined the Dalgety Association's campaign working group. 'Really, David,' the relative said, 'you're getting yourself involved in a crackpot organisation, taking on Snowy Hydro. You're embarrassing yourself being part of something like that.'

But Glasson remembered lying in bed as a small boy, listening to the river during the spring snowmelt when it roared through the gorges to the east of Jimenbuen. It was a poignant sound to young ears. In summer, his mother, Pam, took to him to Dalgety for swimming lessons, where he watched in awe as the big boys jumped from the bridge into the 7-metre deep 'Blue Hole' underneath. After the river was dammed in his teenage years, he envied his father's generation that they had had this wonderful river while he spent his adult life watching the Snowy die. He regretted that his own children would never know the river as it was at all. 'For our kids, it was just a swamp.' Arguing with his father around the barbeque, Glasson's bottom line was simple: 'If we don't fight for the river, my children will never get to see the Snowy.'

Glasson said Harrowell gave the community a reason to believe in itself. 'Things kept being taken from Dalgety and then he stood up and said let's make a stand. He had the people skills and the knowledge. John felt we owed it to the people of Australia to do this. It was a rallying call.'

Harrowell was well aware that anything with a whiff of environmentalism or political activism could be anathema in this conservative community, no matter how good the cause. This genial, grandfatherly man, hardly a greenie by an anyone's standard, overcame the environmental taint by saying the

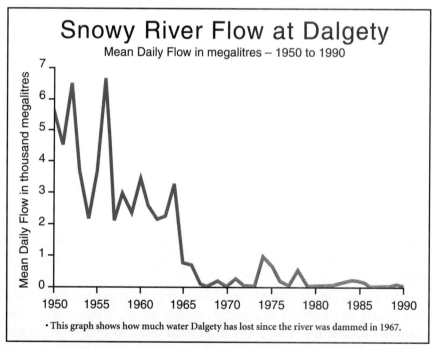

Snowy River Flow at Dalgety

Mean Daily Flow in megalitres – 1950 to 1990

• This graph shows how much water Dalgety has lost since the river was dammed in 1967.

The change in flows down the Snowy River past Dalgety before and after the Snowy Mountains Hydro-Electric Scheme was built. *Source: Dalgety and District Community Association.*

campaign was about righting a historical injustice and defending Dalgety's legal right to adequate water in its river. In his first press release in July 1992 he demanded no less than a government review of the hydro scheme's water-sharing agreement. 'A wrong decision made over forty years ago is not sacred, nor is it engraved in stone,' Harrowell wrote in the release to federal and state ministers, senior public servants, the Snowy Mountains Authority and the local media.

Of course, they all attempted to brush Harrowell off at first. The community would hear variations of the same dissembling excuses for the next seven years: the scheme was an engineering triumph, a source of environmentally friendly power, an irrigation success story; an 'environmental impact assessment' had determined flows in 1961. Garry West, the NSW Minister for Conservation, Land Management and Energy, assured Harrowell in a letter in August 1992 that 'I am concerned with the well-being of all communities and I am keen to see that the current Snowy River riparian rights are maintained and pollution is controlled.' The minister chided Harrowell when he persisted. 'We all have a responsibility to see that [the scheme's] value to New South Wales is maintained,' the minister wrote in September.[2]

The region's main newspaper, the *Cooma-Monaro Express*, ignored Harrowell's press statement, but published a response from the Snowy Mountains Authority. The authority blamed the sorry state of the Snowy River on bad land management. It lectured the community, saying it had to look after the diminished flow better by controlling storm runoff carrying sediment and pollutants. It claimed that merely increasing the flow from 25 megalitres to the maximum 50 megalitres that the outlet pipe at Jindabyne could handle would cost at least $1 million a year in irrigation and electricity losses.

'It will be quite non-productive for them to start by saying how difficult it is now to change things or what a blow it would be to the irrigation areas or the electricity authorities,' Harrowell wrote to his local federal member, Jim Snow, asking for the Prime Minister, Paul Keating, to take action. 'Before talking on any of these things, they must first look at the original concept. Was it right to decide for all time that the country east and south of Jindabyne, including Dalgety, should be deprived of their river, one of the three most famous rivers in Australia?'[3]

Harrowell complained of bias to the *Express*. Chastened, it printed his next statement in full, with Harrowell putting the Snowy Mountains Authority back in its place. He said the authority was required to run the scheme according to the law; whether or not those laws were just and should continue was a matter for government to decide, not the hydro authority.[4] He also complained to the politicians about the authority entering the political fray. 'It is not its role to tell us to be quiet and do without our water until the end of time,' Harrowell wrote to Jim Snow.[5]

When Dalgety settled on returning 800 megalitres a day — or 25 per cent of the river's original flow under the town bridge — as fair, the Snowy Mountains Authority told the Commonwealth Government it would cost $20 million in lost electricity revenue. Harrowell challenged the authority to reveal the accounting basis for its claims. Anyway, he said, of course it would cost money because the scheme was over-designed to catch too much water in the first place. 'The scheme has had the benefit of excess revenue for twenty-seven years [while] the people of south-eastern New South Wales have had at least 800 megalitres a day of water taken from them, without consultation and without one dollar's compensation. That figure, too, could be measured in so many millions of dollars per year when preparing a damages claim.'[6]

'You are being unreasonable,' the politicians and engineers told Harrowell, when all else failed. 'Was it reasonable to deny Dalgety a fair share of its own river till the end of time?' he replied.[7]

Eventually, in late August 1992, Peter Cochran came to see what his constituents were complaining about. Harrowell warned his fellow

John Harrowell at his property, Rockwell, with a line of trees marking the Snowy channel behind. 'The loss of our water is wrong and must be corrected.'
Picture: Richard Harrowell.

townspeople to keep the message simple. 'It will benefit the Association if we all say the same thing to third parties,' he said in a memo.

'For example, if we talk on tree planting, the SMA could at once offer us trees to plant in the hope we will forget about releasing more water. If we talk on making Dalgety a better place for our children, the Government may offer us a playground and hope the water issue is buried. My point is that if we get the water, then these other things will come to pass. If we each quietly and firmly say that the loss of our water was wrong and must be corrected, then the opposition will have nowhere to go.'[8]

The group manager of the Snowy Mountains Authority, Clive Perrett and the commissioner, Charles Halton, also visited Dalgety once it became obvious the issue would not go away. A truce was declared, in which the Snowy Mountains Authority agreed to cease criticising the campaign publicly, recognising the decisions and justifications for the status quo should come from the governments, not the bureaucracy. In return, Dalgety would focus its lobbying and criticism on the governments. But Perrett pointed out that even if the authority was permitted to release more water, the discharge valve's maximum capacity was only 50 megalitres per day.

In New South Wales, the land and water agencies, as in Victoria, were beginning to examine factors affecting the environmental health in rivers and calling for community input. Dalgety followed up every opportunity to make its voice heard, which was why Jo Garland came to ring Glenice White that day. It was the tentative beginning of a close working relationship between Dalgety and Orbost that would eventually put the Snowy River on the national agenda.

Progress was slow, but by January 1994 the Dalgety Association, the Snowy Interstate Catchment Committee and the Snowy River Improvement Trust had persuaded New South Wales and Victoria to undertake a joint scoping study to provide a scientific basis for higher flows. The study would examine how low flows affected the river, and the benefits of more water. It was expected the study would be completed and on the respective ministers' desks by June 1994.

The community was encouraged when the NSW Department of Water Resources advised the study would probably lead to a renegotiation of the hydro scheme's water agreement. Even better, the Victorian Natural Resources Minister, Geoff Coleman, indicated he was open to revisiting the 1958 Act. In a letter to John Harrowell, Coleman said that community attitudes had changed, and there was now 'some acceptance' in government that it needed to examine the feasibility of providing additional flows.[9] It was a long way from the outright and universal 'No!' that answered the community's pleas initially.

John Harrowell in the meantime turned seventy-six, and left town. He sold his property reluctantly but he felt he was getting too old to maintain it. He and his wife, Janet, moved to a smaller place, close to family, in Oberon in the Blue Mountains. Harrowell told the local Jindabyne paper, *The Summit Sun,* that the fight for the river would continue without him, whatever some others might think. 'It doesn't depend on one person,' he said. 'I've given it a start and there are others who are more than capable of pushing forward.'[10]

One of them was Jo Garland. Harrowell handed her the reins with the advice: 'Hasten slowly — don't make enemies. Otherwise they will put your file at the bottom of the pile.' She was positive in her first annual report in September 1994: 'The politicians are slow to move, but no one has said "no" to our campaign. Rather, they have said we must wait for the NSW Department of Water Resources review findings … We look forward to some action then.'

⌒

> *Dear Minister,*
>
> *Mr Murray Jackson, the new commissioner for the SMA, has announced in Cooma that he will be issuing information on the proposed plan to form the SMA into a corporation, presumably with outside investors … It will be wrong to seek public funding of the SMA without a full disclosure to the investing public that the present scale of operations may not be maintained in the future.*
>
> John Harrowell, letters to Michael Lee, federal Resources Minister, and George Souris, NSW Minister for Land and Water Conservation, October 1993

John Harrowell was not the only person thinking the Snowy Mountains Scheme was in need of review. The then federal Treasurer, Paul Keating, had had it in his sights since 1988. His problem was with the management structure, which was a model of inefficiency and inertia.

The Snowy Mountains Authority operated the scheme's dual functions of power generation and water supply according to instructions from the Snowy Mountains Council. This council had eight members, two each from the Commonwealth, the Snowy Mountains Authority, New South Wales and Victoria. The Commonwealth effectively had control because it nominated four representatives and chaired the council. The four state members represented their energy and water bureaucracies, whose objectives were often in conflict. What was good for power generation was not necessarily good for irrigators and vice versa.

The result at times was a council mired in a morass of competing interests, jurisdictions and priorities. The 1958 intergovernment agreement required the scheme be run on a cost-recovery basis, while the state utilities onsold the hydro-electricity at premium tariff prices. Vin Good, the scheme's finance manager from 1991 until 1998, estimates that under this arrangement the authority forewent $150 million a year in profits, with as much as $3 billion going into the pockets of Pacific Power in New South Wales, ACTEW in the ACT and the State Electricity Commission of Victoria (SECV). There was no money in the water itself: the irrigators got that for free. Instead, the states used the proceeds from power sales in part to repay the Commonwealth's $1 billion construction debt, with interest, through a sinking fund over seventy years. But almost forty years after construction, the Commonwealth was still owed some $800 million.

In 1989, Keating prevailed on the Labor Prime Minister, Bob Hawke, to initiate a review of administrative, structural and financial issues associated with the scheme. In December 1990, the review recommended corporatising the Snowy Mountains Authority. Keating, however, wanted more. After taking over as Prime Minister, Keating wrote to the states on 28 May 1992, offering to buy their power entitlements so that the Commonwealth wholly owned the scheme.

By then the states and Commonwealth had agreed to an integrated national electricity market in which state utilities would compete with each other and new private suppliers. The Snowy Mountains Scheme was an anomaly in this new world, a commercially uncompetitive government structure run on a cost-recovery basis. It had to be knocked into shape to compete in its own right in the market, and Keating reasoned would be easier if it had just one owner instead of three.

Restructuring to compete in the market began under the Snowy Mountains Authority commissioner, Charles Halton, in 1989. It accelerated when Halton retired in 1993 and was replaced by Murray Jackson. Between 1989 and 1998, the authority's workforce dropped from 920 to 400, with most jobs disappearing after Jackson, a corporate slash-and-burn man, arrived. Some executives say he went too far and the authority lost a lot of its expertise and its morale. It also lost status in local eyes as a self-proclaimed community benefactor.

Keating offered Victoria $500 million for its 29 per cent share of the electricity, but Victoria's Director for Water Resources, David Downie, suspected water was the more valuable resource. Victoria was entitled to one-quarter of the average 2400 gigalitres the scheme released for irrigation. Downie worked out Victoria's share was worth $2–3 billion if Victoria had to find the water elsewhere, such as build new dams. The state said thanks, but no thanks to Keating's offer. Liberal NSW Premier John Fahey also rejected the Commonwealth purchase. In a letter sent on 30 July 1992, Fahey proposed corporatising the authority instead, followed by privatisation.

Keating did not give up. He again asked the states to sell the scheme to the Commonwealth in December 1992. Downie said Victoria again rebuffed the offer, out of fear it could lose its water if the Commonwealth, or New South Wales or a private operator controlled the scheme. Fahey again wrote back, in March 1993, suggesting corporatisation.

Finally, in June, the Council of Australian Governments agreed in principle to corporatise the scheme. Three public servants were appointed to look into the prospects and report back. They were David Downie, by now head of Victorian Minerals and Energy where he was implementing the newly elected Kennett Government's privatisation agenda; Peter Staveley, Policy Manager for Economic Development in the NSW Cabinet Office; and Russell Higgins from the Commonwealth Department of Primary Industry and Energy.

After a few months' investigation, the three men recommended going ahead with corporatisation. The three governments announced their intention in a press release on 25 November 1993 — around the same time as the states' water agencies decided to study the effects of low flows in the Snowy River.

The corporatisation announcement hardly set the world on fire; only *The Australian Financial Review* reported it, in passing at the bottom of an article on electricity market reforms. It was not news in Dalgety; Murray Jackson had been telling the local media for months he was there to corporatise the scheme. Only John Harrowell immediately understood the implications. A corporatised scheme would be focused on profit alone, and water down the Snowy would be water that did not earn money through the turbines. The river would never get more water if the scheme were corporatised before the flows issue was sorted out.

It took another eighteen months to get the corporatisation process underway. 'The whole thing took so long because we were dealing with three governments,' Peter Staveley said later. 'It was one of those things — to get hard decisions made in relation to this was like getting the planets into alignment. Also, the more you looked at it, the larger the issues became.'

The public servants were dimly aware of the Dalgety campaign, and the irrigators inland were always agitating for more than their mandated share of water. They decided it was best to avoid opening that can of worms, and so water was set to one side to be dealt with as a separate process at another time. For the purposes of corporatisation, they would proceed on the basis that the status quo in water allocations was maintained. That way, the scheme had commercial certainty about its water assets.

New South Wales got carriage of the corporatisation process because the state had the most at stake. It would be the majority shareholder based on its 58 per cent share of the power, the fact that the scheme was in New South Wales and partially inside the National Park, and the state also got three-quarters of the water for irrigation. The process was assigned to New South Wales Treasury, which was responsible for major structural reforms. NSW would draft and pass the necessary legislation first, followed by Victoria and the Commonwealth.

The governments set up a senior implementation committee to work its way through the tangle. It had three project managers from each government: Russell Higgins, Peter Staveley and Paul Dunn, from the energy project and privatisation unit inside Victoria's Treasury. They liaised with the relevant agencies within their jurisdiction, so they could bring a whole-of-government perspective to the table. This proved difficult in New South Wales, where the agencies were bitterly divided. National Parks and the Environment Protection Authority wanted to use the opportunity to address the scheme's poor environmental legacy, Treasury wanted only to maximise revenue from electricity production, and the Department of Land and Water Conservation wanted more water for irrigators. The Snowy Mountains Authority also had a seat at the table: it wanted to retain as much of its autonomy as it could. Behind them all was a small army of consultants and lawyers. The one stakeholder without a seat at the table was the public: it was thought no significant public interest was at stake because the status quo in terms of power and water shares would be maintained.

The NSW state election in March 1995 delayed the process getting underway. The Labor Party won office, with Bob Carr, a well-known environmentalist, as Premier and Michael Egan, an economic hardliner from the Right, as Treasurer. 'It took some time to attract the new government's attention,' recalled Staveley. 'Corporatising the scheme was not seen as an essential matter, and it took some time to get down the list to it. But when we were briefing Egan and Carr, the view was that it seemed a sound thing to do and so proceed. There was no great controversy about it at the time — it was looked on as an administrative rearrangement.'

Sydney consultants DJG Projects were appointed as the consultant project managers in June 1995. Everything was finally set to go. 'This will only take six months,' DJG's head Andrew Martin confidently told David Downie, who joined the consultancy as assistant corporatisation manager to represent Victorian interests.

Downie was less optimistic. He foresaw complications. The Snowy Mountains Scheme was a major industrial complex operating on state land in the Kosciuszko National Park under Commonwealth law. Historically, the Snowy Mountains Authority was almost a law unto itself. It would be difficult to straighten out a sensible commercial landlord/tenant relationship, introduce a regulatory regime covering, planning, access and use requirements under New South Wales law, and maintain the status quo in water management and shares. Then the project had to run the gauntlet for approval through six Houses of Parliament in three jurisdictions. One Parliament alone would have been bad enough. 'The horror, the horror,' thought Downie. 'I don't know — I think it'll take eighteen months,' he said to Andrew Martin, who laughed. 'Oh, really, David, it won't take that long.'

⌐

> *Now it seems so unreal but back then we spent so much time convincing people that it was a real issue. The concept that a river needs an environmental flow was new, and we had to establish a case for what now seems so obvious. People would say, 'What is wrong with the river? It has water and it is wet and the willows look okay'. If it was buggered it had to be concrete lined or totally dry, and not just turning into a soupy wetland.*
>
> BRETT MINERS

'Has anyone seen Wayne?' asked Brett Miners, coordinator of the Snowy-Genoa Catchment Management Committee. Dr Wayne Erskine, eminent geomorphologist, was missing … again. He had wandered off, engrossed in examining rocks. There were a lot of rocks by the Snowy River — a lot of very big rocks to hide behind, and a lot of scrubby forest to swallow a person whole. Miners looked at his watch. It was hot down here in the river valley, and dusty, and time to go. 'Cooee! Wayne! We're going!' Miners shouted. Stones scrabbled down the slope across the river, the willows parted and Erskine materialised.

'Sorry to hold everyone up,' Erskine said as the two men scrambled up the track to where the others were waiting in the four-wheel drives, engines running. Miners made a mental note to assign someone the 'cattle dog' job, to round up Erskine at every stop. They had already driven off once and left him behind.

The Snowy-Genoa Catchment Management Committee, which replaced the Interstate Catchment Coordination Committee in 1994, had grown tired of waiting for the joint-government scoping study and was doing its own. More than a year after the scoping study was supposed to be completed in June 1994, there was still no sign of it. Rumours were running rife that the Snowy Mountains Authority, which partly funded the study, was blocking its release because the report supported the claim for a 25 per cent flow.

While the Snowy River Improvement Trust and the Snowy-Genoa Catchment Management Committee waited patiently for the government scoping report, the Dalgety Association ramped up its publicity campaign. It produced a pamphlet, and stickers saying, 'The Snowy River must flow again'. Sympathetic shops and resorts distributed the material to thousands of tourists passing through Jindabyne and the mountains. The stickers went everywhere. Meantime, Paul Leete, the quiet new caravan park manager, prepared a graphic colour photo essay with before and after shots, and sent copies to politicians.

The state and national media swung in behind Dalgety's campaign. *The Canberra Times* picked up the story in January 1994, followed by *The Today Show* on Channel Nine. It aired a live interview with David Glasson of the Dalgety Association and Murray Jackson, the Snowy Mountains Authority Commissioner, on 18 July 1994. Several Sydney radio programs picked up the story and interviewed Glasson the same day. The *Sydney Morning Herald* ran a front-page article in June 1995, with the headline, 'The Man from Snowy Creek'. The ABC's *The 7.30 Report* followed up with an item, and *60 Minutes* rang to pick up the story. Indeed, over the years the story was a durable media favourite, attracting even international coverage with documentaries on Japanese and European television, and mention in Australia's report card in *National Geographic.*

The vibes from the two state governments, however, were not so encouraging by mid-1995. The Natural Resources ministers used to say they would address the issue once they got the scoping study. Now they were saying the issue would be settled as part of corporatising the scheme. Corporatisation had slowly seeped into the public consciousness, and the more the Snowy River's supporters learned, the greater their anxiety.

Word leaked out of the Snowy Mountains Council that regardless of the scoping study, the council would be recommending to NSW Treasury that a token 50 megalitres a day, or 1.5 per cent, be released down the Snowy to cover its 'environmental flow'. Brett Miners sent a 'please explain'. The council wrote back on 15 September 1995, emphasising the complexities of maintaining the scheme's commercial viability. It explained that the Commonwealth, New

The Snowy River at Dalgety, c1920. *Source: Brian Seears.*

The overgrown Snowy River at Dalgety, 1992. *Source: Dalgety and District Community Association.*

South Wales and Victoria had agreed to stick with the status quo for water for the purposes of corporatisation, and the governments would look into the water agreement in the longer term. '[That] will be the most appropriate time for community organisations to press for an active role,' the council advised.[11]

The governments, however, were talking about a 125-year water licence to give the corporatised scheme certainty for obtaining finance. It was unlikely the governments would undermine the scheme's commercial position afterwards to return a substantial flow to the Snowy River. Even worse, all three governments were in the grip of privatisation fervour and had indicated they were highly likely to sell their shares in the scheme once it was corporatised. A private operator was even less likely than government to give up water, not without demanding millions of dollars in compensation to damp down the politicians' good intentions.

Trouble was, there was no hard scientific data to persuade the politicians the Snowy had indeed suffered from losing 99 per cent of its flow, or tell them how much it might require to recover its health. This alone was a radical idea: that an environmental flow was not just a token amount, but determined according to ecological need.

The Dalgety Association claimed 25 per cent for the Snowy River, based on an international rule of thumb, but every river is different; the Snowy could need more or less depending on its own peculiar ecological and geological features. The joint scoping study was supposed to provide the requisite scientific information, but a few days after the bombshell from the Snowy Mountains Council, the Snowy Mountains Authority told Jo Garland the study would not be released for an 'indeterminate' period. Without scientific backing, the community had no hope of persuading governments to work out the flows issue before corporatising the scheme. With the corporatisation deadline just eight months away in July 1996, Brett Miners felt the community could not afford to wait any longer for a study that might never be released. 'We should do our own,' he suggested in October 1995.

The Snowy-Genoa Catchment Management Committee was a statutory body set up under new New South Wales laws arising from the Council of Australian Governments Water Resources Policy. This policy, adopted in January 1994, recognised for the first time that the environment was a legitimate water user whose needs had to be met. The Snowy-Genoa Catchment Management Committee, made up of public servants and community representatives in New South Wales and Victoria, had an unusually high degree of independence. The NSW Department of Conservation and Land Management, for instance, paid Miners' wages, but he answered to the committee's community chairman, Stuart Hood. The committee identified priorities in catchment management and advised the government accordingly, but it trod a fine line between advising and advocating. Still, Miners reasoned the committee could not properly advise government on the flows issue without a sound scientific foundation, so it was justified in initiating its own study.

Studies cost money, however. The Snowy River Improvement Trust in Orbost gave the committee $10,000, but it needed more. The Department of Water Resources was reluctant, since it was already embroiled in the ill-fated joint scoping study. Culturally, it was also ambivalent about the Snowy River; the agency was set up historically to manage water for irrigation, but it was trying very hard to come to grips with the new environmental flows concept.

Miners and chairman Stuart Hood went to Sydney cap in hand to ask other agencies for money. Derek Rutherford, the New South Wales Environment Protection Authority's (EPA) representative on the Snowy-Genoa Catchment Management Committee, helped them get an audience with Pam Allan, the Environment Minister. Allan lent a sympathetic ear. The EPA was developing flow objectives for all rivers, so Allan decided the study could be justified as part of the state-wide review. She signed a cheque for $20,000.

With time not on the committee's side, Miners decided to try the then novel approach of an expert panel assessment. This approach, which brings together scientists in different but related fields, had been tried only once before in Australia, by the NSW Department of Water Resources. Although the department paid Miners' wages, it refused to cooperate and give Miners information on how it had gone about its panel process. As luck would have it, a workshop on environmental flow methodology was convened at the Snowy Hydro headquarters in Cooma, so Miners went there instead to talk to local and international experts about setting up panels. Then he worked out a methodology which he thought should work for the Snowy River and be scientifically credible.

No scientific studies had been done on the Snowy before the hydro scheme was built, so Miners asked two old-timers to provide historic information. Jim Nixon from Orbost and Charlie Roberson from Dalgety knew the Snowy and its secrets well after lifetimes spent fishing the river from top to bottom. Then Miners called six of Australia's best river experts and asked them to take a trip out of their comfort zone, at a fraction of the fees they would normally charge. 'They offered us basically beer and bed,' said Professor Sam Lake, Professor in Ecology, School of Biological Sciences, Monash University. Miners was lucky. The scientists were all of an adventurous spirit and leapt at the opportunity to try something new.

They were an illustrious lot: Dr Wayne Erskine, senior lecturer in geomorphology (the study of forces shaping landforms) at the University of New South Wales; Professor Sam Lake, a leader in his field and veteran of the battle for Lake Pedder; biologist Paul Brown from the Narrandera Fisheries Centre; Ian Pulsford, southern zone manager for the National Parks and Wildlife Service; Dr John Banks from the School of Resource and Environmental Management at the Australian National University; and Paul Pendlebury, a senior hydrologist with the NSW Department of Land and Water Conservation, formerly Water Resources. Derek Rutherford from the EPA came along for the ride, to look after the interests of the NSW Environment Minister, while Anthony Hurst from the Department of Land and Water was sent to keep an eye on this rather feral exercise in November 1995.

It was an exciting ride, a kind of ecological mystery tour looking for clues to solve the puzzle of the Snowy River's degradation. The scientists had only five days to study multiple sites along the 353-kilometre length from Jindabyne dam right down to the river's mouth in the ocean at Marlo. At each site they looked around for forty-five minutes, discussed what they observed, then jumped back into the four-wheel drives and headed to the next spot.

At each stop, the question was asked: 'What did the river look like back then?' Charlie Roberson and Jim Nixon would describe how they remembered it, and the scientists would examine the river to see if the physical signs supported those memories. The clues lay in the way water had shaped rocks over millennia, the riverside vegetation, lichen patterns on the boulders, and insect life. These hinted at long-gone rapids and deep clear pools capable of supporting fish. Then the scientists tried to answer the question: 'What would the Snowy need to recover those past characteristics?'

Sitting on a rock while the scientists bounced ideas off each other, Hurst furiously took notes and Miners listened so hard his head hurt, trying to piece together the strands of information, thoughts and clues so he could ask the right questions.

'We started off with only a shell of a process and made the rest up as we went along,' Miners admitted. 'But the people and bloody good scientists made it work. It was a love job. Scientists who charge $1000 a day were saying just pay what you can afford. It was new and novel and everyone was open to it. We would give people monstrous quantities of food to sustain them, then flog them till midnight going over again and again the questions about what made the river tick and how it looked. It was a detective game — big and little clues.'

*We realised the Snowy River could be a problem from the time
corporatisation was announced. We could see agitation in New South
Wales. We had contacts in all the bureaucracies. I began to hear
stories that there was pressure on the New South Wales politicians
and the Snowy Mountains Council, and corporatisation would not be
agreed until there was a significant flow in the Snowy River.*

DAVID DOWNIE, ASSISTANT CORPORATISATION MANAGER, DJG PROJECTS,
CONSULTANTS FOR SNOWY MOUNTAINS SCHEME CORPORATISATION PROJECT

Peter Staveley had had better weeks. This one wasn't one of them. The
wrangling on the corporatisation committee was interminable. Everything
was difficult to resolve. Take land tenure. The Snowy Mountains Authority
was paying New South Wales a small rental for the use of its land, but there
was no signed record of the original lease. There was even a possibility that
the Snowy scheme assets (dams and power stations) legally belonged to
New South Wales because, technically, they were 'fixtures' on land owned by
the NSW Government. Now the tenure had to be formalised. Treasury
wanted a level playing field with the rest of the power industry, as if the
hydro scheme was not in a National Park. 'But we had to establish a business
with a licence to operate like the ski resorts,' explained Graeme Enders, who
was involved in the negotiations as the heritage manager coordinating
science and planning functions for Kosciuszko National Park.

The National Parks and Wildlife Service was also determined the
authority would rectify its poor environmental legacy. There were dozens of
construction sites still in a mess, despite earlier consultation to remediate
them. Some were major, like where the spoil from tunnels was simply
tipped over the side into ravines.

'These used to be a federal management problem,' said Enders. 'But once
it looked as if the NPWS was going to inherit them, we said they had to get
them into a condition we were happy with before corporatisation. They did
not like that because it created more and more costs on their side of the
ledger.' (Eventually, the authority agreed to pay National Parks $32.5 million
over five years to rehabilitate the sites, without an admission of liability.)
Then there were the roads the authority built — who owned them? And
where exactly were the boundaries between areas under National Park
management and areas for which the scheme was responsible?

And then there was water. There was no avoiding it. The scheme held
1000 gigalitres in useable storage over and above the irrigators' mandated

annual 2100 gigalitres. This reserve was called 'above-target' water. This was the only water the scheme could use for generating power at its own discretion, but the irrigation lobby had got used to the idea that by applying pressure on the Snowy Mountains Council, they could get extra water from the reserve for free to top them up in dry seasons. That would not be the case in a corporatised scheme, where above-target water would enable the authority to play the electricity market and charge premium prices for meeting spikes in demand. If the irrigators wanted the water instead, it would come at a high price and the irrigators would have to pay it back from future releases. Naturally, the irrigation lobby was not happy about the likely new order of things.

The scheme had also devastated dozens of montane rivers and streams. The upper Murrumbidgee, for instance, was now a trickle. The Tumut River below the Tumut dam was a series of pipes and ponds. After passing through the turbines, it flowed into Blowering dam and, when released by state authorities for irrigation, out again as an unnaturally angry torrent, ripping away the banks. National Parks had complained for years; now it insisted the rivers inside the park were dealt with before corporatisation. The Snowy below Jindabyne was on its list, but not the highest priority. National Parks was more concerned about the Snowy River up in the mountains where its rocky bed below Guthega power station and Island Bend reservoir was often virtually dry.

NSW Treasury and the Snowy Mountains Authority reluctantly agreed to review river flows within the boundaries of the scheme. This did not include the Snowy River below Jindabyne. 'Their pain was one-dimensional — just, how much money is it going to cost?' said Graeme Enders. 'The authority did not see these other issues as real but concocted, and that we were just trying to make it hard for them, especially anything that indicated they hadn't operated at the peak of environmental performance in such a significant national park. This was something of a corporate delusion, given the drastic condition of all the mountain rivers.'

The scheme's finance manager, Vin Good, defended the Snowy Mountains Authority and Snowy Mountains Council, saying they could not legally release water for environmental flows because they were required to use all water collected in the scheme for generating electricity. 'Corporatisation was the first step in being able to change the legislation so that environmental flows could be allocated and released,' he said.

The authority, however, resisted giving water back to the rivers. It made progress difficult in other ways. Peter Staveley got the impression the authority initially embraced corporatisation because it thought it would be freed from bureaucratic interference. Then it realised it would no longer be virtually a power unto itself under federal law, but be subject to New South Wales law. It would have to be more consultative. Its activities would have to be approved under rigorous planning processes. It would pay more for the lease. Its representatives began to challenge changes, protesting, 'But we have always done it this way!'

On top of that was the difficulty of coordinating the process across three governments. Each jurisdiction had different priorities, election timetables and occasional Cabinet reshuffles. Progress ebbed and flowed as points agreed at one meeting had to be revisited again and again because people forgot what was previously agreed, or a minister somewhere wanted something else. The plight of the Snowy River below Jindabyne seemed the least of the committee's problems. 'From our corporatisation team perspective, the Snowy was not as bad as other rivers,' said David Downie. In his former life as a water bureaucrat, he was involved in Victoria's 1990 State of the Rivers report. It concluded the Snowy was in better condition than most of the state's other twenty-eight river basins.

'Apart from the 30 to 40 kilometres up near the dam, it was pretty good all the way to the sea,' claimed Downie. 'The thing is, you would have to put a fair bit into the Snowy, not just a few gigalitres a year. Otherwise it is tokenism. But if you put a fair bit in, then every megalitre means you can't generate power. Any water that went down the Snowy would be very expensive water because it would be taken from Adelaide and the irrigators, and they would be very angry because they have salinity and drinking water problems. To be honest, we thought the Snowy campaign was a joke and could not see how, even on an equal set of criteria, you could save the Snowy ahead of other rivers in Victoria given their problems with salinity, etc.' Besides, 'we are old-time believers that political pressure moved from votes and numbers, and basically there was no one there in the top 60 kilometres.'

Peter Staveley was not so dismissive. In late 1995, the concept of environmental flows was gaining acceptance. New South Wales was committed to restoring flows in all regulated rivers. The EPA was reviewing the state of the rivers, and the Department of Land and Water Conservation was assessing the environmental impacts of major water storages. Both agencies advised Staveley that the Snowy River was a priority because of impending corporatisation. Staveley realised the two hitherto separate processes — water reform and corporatisation — were converging. He also read the early signs of a political campaign on the Snowy, with a smattering of articles in the Sydney media. Perhaps it was best if this issue was dealt with now, so they could get on with corporatisation without at least one distraction.

The week that Brett Miners was shouting himself hoarse to avoid losing Wayne Erskine in the Snowy River National Park, Staveley took a proposition to the corporatisation committee. He sat at the table with John Grant, the assistant Director-General of the NSW Cabinet Office, who did not normally attend these meetings. 'The New South Wales Government wants to allocate 200 megalitres a day to go down the Snowy River as an environmental flow, and proceed with corporatisation on that basis,' Grant announced. 'We think that is reasonable.' It equated to about 6 per cent of the river's original flow. It was also relatively cheap and easy: it meant just letting go the Mowamba River, rather than diverting it into Jindabyne lake.

There were blank looks around the table. 'The problem with the offer was that the Snowy River was not well studied at the time, and we were not certain what needed to occur,' said Paul Dunn, Victoria's government representative. 'We were aware of the community agitation, but we wondered if there was any point in just putting 6 per cent down, whether it was sufficient and would achieve any environmental objectives. It was an arbitrary flow that was unlikely to satisfy the community and it had no scientific basis.'

Victoria's consultants advised Dunn that the offer represented an unacceptable loss of value for the scheme. David Downie thought New South Wales was trying it on for the sake of appearances. 'They are bluffing,' Downie told Dunn. 'If it was a serious offer, there would be a letter from the Premier. It is just so they can go back and say they tried, so tell them to get lost.'

Staveley said later it was a serious offer. It was not accepted so he let it go.

⌒

I think the greenies were looking for a war anywhere on a river, because if they could get water for environmental purposes, then it could set a precedent. The Snowy was perfect because no other river has had that size of diversion — 1100 gigalitres per annum — so it was a good model to start to push for environmental flows in all rivers.

VIN GOOD, SNOWY MOUNTAINS AUTHORITY

The expert panel report was dynamite. The scientists found fish were disappearing; the channel had shrunk dramatically with massive sedimentation; and trees and weeds had taken over. Aquatic insect numbers and diversity were way down, and the species were more typical of farm dams than a large, mountain-fed river. Algae were rampant and the salt wedge from the mouth now extended 7 kilometres upstream. The scientists also concluded that the Snowy was still declining, and would get a lot worse before it stabilised ecologically.[12]

The report recognised that low flows were only one of many factors in the degradation. Erosion and weeds played a role, as did persistent drought; 60 per cent of winters on the Monaro had been drought-declared since Jindabyne dam wall was completed. But low flows compounded and accelerated the degrading effects of these pressures. For instance, the river was no longer turbulent enough to stop rotting organic matter accumulating in the bottom of pools and turning to mud. This in turn promoted weeds and algal growth, to the detriment of water quality and fish.

'The panel was so conscious of how hard it would be to get water,' said Brett Miners. 'They identified that you could do all sorts of catchment work, but the river would still be crap without the flows. Sam Lake and the other scientists had a very strong understanding that any flow for the river would be a huge feat in itself. There were no ambit claims and a clear recognition that it is notoriously difficult to clearly define how much water a river needs to be healthy. They just said these are our best scientific guesses on what is needed to achieve the outcomes in each of their fields. Together it made a giant hypothesis that could then be tested.'

Professor Lake, from Monash University, said it was the first time a panel had given ecological meaning to the environmental flows concept. They consciously did not talk about minimum flows or figures but instead made a suite of recommendations. These incorporated returning minimum flows, some mimicking of natural seasonal variations, and the return of annual flood flows to scour out habitat holes and maintain the main channel all the way to Orbost. In total, the recommended regime added up to between 324 and 358 gigalitres a year. The scientists said any less would have benefits, but they would be limited.

The report was finished in January 1996. The community groups quickly worked out that 324 gigalitres equated to roughly 28 per cent of the average annual flow at Jindabyne. It became the rallying cry. Their confidence was boosted when Max White opened his front door one morning in the New Year and nearly tripped over a brown unmarked envelope. 'What's this, do you think?' he asked Glenice as he came back inside, tearing it open.

They were astonished to see a photocopy of the draft joint-government scoping study, due eighteen months earlier. The Dalgety Association had tried to get it through Freedom of Information laws, but was knocked back on the grounds that its public release would affect intergovernmental relations. But here it was, in Orbost, fallen off the back of a truck.

The scoping study found that a minimum 12.5 per cent was needed before the river would begin to improve, but at least an average 800 megalitres a day, or about 25 per cent, was required to achieve meaningful ecological benefits all the way to the sea. It estimated this would cost $22 million a year in lost revenue from reduced electricity generation, irrigation and reallocation of water to dilute salinity in inland rivers. On the other hand, returning just the Mowamba River's flow would cost about $3.1 million a year. The scoping study did not assess the economic benefits of returning water to the Snowy River. 'It should be noted that the costs of lost electricity generation and irrigated agricultural production are easily quantified, while the benefits to the environment of increased flows in the Snowy River are not,' it said.[13]

Miners and Stuart Hood sent the expert panel report to Pam Allan. The Environment Minister was very supportive, but said Treasury and the Energy portfolio — both under the one minister, Michael Egan — had hijacked the issue in Cabinet and it was hard to get a word in. Miners and Hood discussed how the community could best get the message across before the governments corporatised the scheme, now scheduled for June 1996, five months away. 'We did feel we had to be able to push harder politically, but the [Snowy-Genoa Catchment Management] committee had to toe the line somewhat because the government could put us out of business,' said Hood.

Until now, the Snowy River Improvement Trust, the Dalgety Association and the Snowy-Genoa Catchment Management Committee had pretty much done their own thing, only very loosely liaising with each other. They did good work, but their efforts were rather random, without a real understanding of political processes or strategy. Some members were also too inclined to play the man, not the ball, when they encountered provocative personalities in the public service, the Snowy Mountains Authority, government and each other. Miners suggested the campaign would be more effective if the different groups pooled their energy, resources and passion into one umbrella organisation whose job was to keep its eye firmly on the main game.

A meeting was called in Bombala on 20 February 1996. Harry Moss from Dalgety was there, and Paul Leete, the caravan park manager who had taken over as Dalgety Association president from Jo Garland, who stepped down in the late stages of pregnancy. Max White, Gil Richardson, dairy farmer David Adams and old Jim Nixon drove up from Orbost. They brought along Chris Allen, the new Moogji Aboriginal Council manager.

Allen started work at the council in 1995. Soon after, Max White approached him to represent indigenous interests in the Snowy campaign. Allen was reluctant at first — he had sworn 'Never again!' after spending his

twenties immersed in community development work and burning out —
but White persisted. His devotion to the cause was irresistible. 'I realised the
river really was in trouble, and if anything was worth putting time into, it
was the Snowy River,' Allen said. 'It sort of draws you in, and I really liked
the people involved because it was a real cross-section of the community
that wanted the same thing.'

Allen has fond memories of his many road trips with the four old men of
the river, attending meetings in Bombala and Cann River. 'I was the youngest
in the car at thirty-seven, and they were all third and fourth and fifth
generation. It was like going up with my granddad and uncles. I felt a sense of
camaraderie — it was like the indigenous perspective, spending time listening
to elders. I learnt a lot about the river and its history, about the boat races
from Bete Bolong to Marlo and the *Curlip* steam paddleboat, and the floods
and the fish. I was like a little kid in a lolly shop, like a big sponge.' Gunai elder
Albert Mullett was pleased to see Allen getting involved. 'Someone had to do
it,' he said. 'If we blackfellas did it, they will just say we are only blackfellas, but
with a strong group of environmental people, then we have the clout.'

A smattering of government officers also attended the first meeting in
Bombala, including Derek Rutherford from the EPA who worked closely
inside the public service with Graeme Enders from National Parks and
Miners. Ian Moon, who had cabins in Buchan, came along to represent
regional tourism interests. Eric Sjerp, the East Gippsland Shire's
environmental planner, attended with the blessing of Peter Nixon; the
former Country Party minister was the shire's chief commissioner at the
time, overseeing the controversial amalgamation of five small councils such
as Orbost into the one large regional municipality.

The meeting took place in the back room of the Mail Coach House, a
heritage red-brick landmark and bed and breakfast in Bombala's main street.
There is nothing historic about the back room — it is a modern addition
furnished with wood-laminate tables and black vinyl chairs — but the lunch
was good and the conversation productive. The meeting decided to form the
Snowy River Alliance, with Stuart Hood as chairman. The Alliance essentially
would be the Snowy-Genoa Catchment Management Committee's political
arm, coordinating publicity, lobbying and fundraising.

'We felt that if there was anything very political, we could pass it on to
the Alliance, because we were supposed to be neutral,' said Hood. 'We had
to deal with the government, so we would get the Alliance to stir the
politicians and go where we weren't prepared to go.'

The Alliance's first decision was how much water it wanted in the Snowy.
There was debate about whether to make an ambit claim, perhaps as high as

40 per cent, but the consensus was that 28 per cent had scientific credibility and could be backed up.

The expert panel report precipitated a deeper personal involvement for Brett Miners. He grew up on the Monaro plains, but near Cooma, and the Snowy River was not his river. He is a steady sort of character, thoughtful and conscientious. Until then, low flows were one among many catchment problems he had on his plate as the Snowy-Genoa Catchment Management Committee coordinator. Down in the Snowy's rocky remote wilds with the scientists, though, something happened. The river got him.

Miners understood now why two busloads of people would travel all the way from Orbost to Dalgety for the formal launch of the expert panel report. He realised they were serious. It was at the height of a misinformation campaign waged by the Snowy Mountains Authority under commissioner Murray Jackson. 'The community had been sweating on this,' Miners said. 'The range of people who turned out hammered home how important this issue was, that people would give up a day's work on the farm to travel 300 kilometres to hear the findings of a scientific study. There were people there from Bombala and Delegate, Orbost and beyond. Everyone rallied, and were so pleased about scientific backing. It was a good bit of science, a bit rough around the edges, but it was independent support for what they had been saying for years: 25 per cent; and the expert panel and even the overdue and much maligned scoping study came close.'

The Alliance and the expert panel report were launched together at a press conference in Dalgety Memorial Hall on 29 March 1996. Miners rewrote Stuart Hood's speech in a hurry, to soften unkind references to the NSW Land and Water Resources Minister, Kim Yeadon, who was on radio in the morning making cautiously positive noises.

The Alliance was a new beast, created to carry the campaign into a new phase. Notwithstanding the broader country community's instinctive dislike for greenies, the Alliance committee members recognised the campaign needed help from the professionals. Groups such as the Total Environment Centre in Sydney and the Australian Conservation Foundation had the expertise, experience and political contacts to make sure the Alliance's voice was heard loud and clear in the whispering halls of Parliament in Sydney, Melbourne and Canberra.

Paul Leete and Harry Moss duly drove to Sydney a few days after the Alliance formed, for an appointment with Jeff Angel, the Total Environment Centre's chief executive officer. They tried to persuade Jo Garland to join them, but she demurred, nervous about alienating the Dalgety community. Instead, she remained on the periphery of the Alliance, working in tandem with Leete to make the Dalgety and District Community Association a good strong local voice back up the Alliance.

Jeff Angel remembers Paul Leete coming in his door with a small presentation in a yellow folder and a message. Leete is a slight man with soft, dark curly hair and beard, gentle eyes and a penchant for thorough research. Before he moved to Dalgety, he did not do anything remotely political, and has not since he left the town. He seems altogether rather too shy and certainly unassuming, but the Snowy River's plight offended his sense of natural justice. As he warmed to his topic in Angel's office, he sat on the edge of his seat, using his arms expansively for emphasis, highly sprung and ready to leap up and grab more supporting documentation to prove the case.

But 'they weren't getting anywhere', said Jeff Angel later. 'The Snowy Mountains Authority was neutering their campaign with the politicians, and they needed our help.' The Snowy River Alliance contacted the Total Environment Centre just when it was discussing which campaigns to support in the coming year. 'There is any number of campaigns that you can fall in love with — there is no lack of those — but we cannot support them all,' said Angel. 'It could have been another forest for all we knew, but Paul Leete turned up at the right time.'

Jeff Angel is not a romantic man. He is a hard-nosed political strategist, and he saw at once the potential to use the iconic Snowy River to popularise the concept of environmental flows. An added bonus was the hydro scheme's iconography as a symbol of outdated technology and attitudes. 'When you look at most environmental conflicts, it is our vision of technology that has got us into a lot of trouble,' Angel said. 'When you look at the Snowy Mountains Scheme, it's 110 per cent engineering. It is a particularly extreme example, dramatised by the fact they diverted everything they could find and left just 1 per cent of the river and no alpine streams. It had a special rarity in that sense. I thought these few lone voices saying look at what we are losing deserved to have their concerns amplified in an era where they could be heard.'

Jeff Angel explained that the TEC was committed to long-running campaigns where persistence paid off. 'It usually takes two election cycles to get a result,' he told Leete. 'And that is after all the groundwork has been laid by the community groups.'

The secret of success was staying the distance.

THREE

Rough and Tumble

What people had was the iconic status of the Snowy River, but so had the scheme — which is more or less the icon?

PETER STAVELEY, NSW CABINET OFFICE

Cottage 16 can be found on the banks of Lake Jindabyne, surrounded by water, gum trees and a big blue sky. Officially, it is the staff research facility at the end of the road at Waste Point, the housing estate for Kosciuszko National Park rangers, but Cottage 16 is also a state of mind. Colin Steele, Brett Miners and Graeme Enders met there every two or three months for years. It was their space to dream and to plot, far away from office emails, phones and managers from the Sir Humphrey Appleby school of public service.

Steele worked for the Department of Planning and Urban Affairs in Queanbeyan. He met Enders briefly at university and then again when Enders came to work in Mt Kosciuszko National Park. The colleagues then met Miners in 1996, when the Snowy-Genoa Catchment Management Committee coordinator was invited to meetings convened to ease tensions between the local council, the community and National Parks. Steele was also involved in corporatising the hydro scheme. His job was trying to fit the anomalous federal body into the state planning system.

Steele, Enders and Miners quickly discovered they had something in common. 'None of us were very good bureaucrats,' Steele said. 'We didn't really follow the line. We all worked on the basis of what is the best outcome we can achieve for the communities of the south-east, then we figured out how to achieve it. I don't know what the line from above was, but our objective was restoring the Snowy River. We did what was best for the community.'

None of them were in influential positions, so they did what they could on a small scale within a wider network of like-minded public servants also working for a good outcome for the Snowy River. They encouraged an open dialogue with the community and local stakeholders, and making the most of their limited access to important people further up the bureaucratic food chain. And they met regularly to compare notes in Cottage 16 on the banks of Lake Jindabyne.

They asked each other, 'What if?' They tried to work out where the Snowy River fitted into the big picture in government, and how to make sure community messages were not lost in the fog in head office. 'Cottage 16 was based on an understanding that government is clumsy,' said Miners. 'Governments are very rarely malign: they usually have good intentions but a poor ability to implement them. They receive thousands of mixed messages every day and it can be hard to see the broader context. Cottage 16 was about recognising that a lot of success and momentum is about getting to the right people at the right time with the right bits of information, so governments know why they have to fix it.'

⌒

The pilot was in a cold sweat. So was Brett Miners. A gale was shearing over the snow-capped mountains to the west, pushing the plane this way then that as the pilot wrestled with the controls on the approach into Cooma Airport. It was going to be touch and go. Miners glanced back at Marie Tehan and Kim Yeadon. Their knuckles were almost as white as the pilot's. Miners looked out the window and contemplated whether inflicting damage on two state ministers in a light plane crash was a smart career move. He had his doubts.

They probably shouldn't have gone flying in such weather, but it was so hard to get two ministers together that Miners was keen to make the most of the opportunity. The ministers had visited Dalgety for a cup of tea, some cake, a chat with the locals and a look at the weed-choked Snowy River from the Dalgety bridge. Then they were taken to other spots to see how low flows affected the Snowy. It was the standard tour, including the 'burst water main' from which the Snowy River sprang from Jindabyne dam. But there was nothing like a bird's-eye view to really appreciate the scale of degradation.

Miners held on as the pilot got one wheel down on the tarmac, just as a gust of wind caught and lifted the opposite wing. The plane skidded at a crazy angle on one wheel, teetered, then righted itself and came down on the other wheel with a bump. Excellent: Tehan, Victoria's Conservation and Natural Resources Minister, and Yeadon, NSW Land and Water Resources Minister, would live to tell the tale of the Snowy River to their colleagues in Cabinet.

The Snowy River Alliance and the Total Environment Centre were working overtime lobbying for a public water inquiry before Parliament approved corporatising the Snowy Mountains scheme. They also wanted flows written into the legislation. A federal election on 2 March 1996, followed by a Victorian election on 30 March, pushed the nominal corporatisation deadline from June 1996 to September, giving the campaign more time.

The elections threw other spanners in the works. The Commonwealth Government changed hands from Labor to a Liberal/National coalition under John Howard as Prime Minister. Liberal Premier Jeff Kennett romped home again in Victoria, but reshuffled his Cabinet. It meant two lots of new state and federal ministers to persuade. It became the pattern over the years. Just as one group of ministers got their heads around the issues and began making progress, another election caused more delays and delivered more new ministers. It was as frustrating for the corporatisation committee as the community. NSW Treasurer Michael Egan appointed David Crossley, an experienced energy bureaucrat, as paramount Snowy project manager in May 1996. Crossley said that after four years of six-month deadlines came and went, the committee sensibly stopped setting deadlines because no one knew how long the corporatisation process would take.

The Snowy River Alliance and its affiliates left no stone unturned, no opportunity wasted, no politician untouched. 'We were bending any ear we could find,' said Stuart Hood. The community kept up a steady stream of letter writing. The Whites, Gil Richardson, Ian Moon and East Gippsland Shire's feisty councillor Brenda Murray traipsed to Melbourne to brief the new Conservation Minister, Marie Tehan, after the election. Then they traipsed to Canberra with Paul Leete to do the rounds of the Labor Party, the Democrats and advisors to the Environment and Energy ministers. Then they went back again a month later to see the ministers themselves. 'One politician told us we had as much chance as a snowflake in hell of getting water in the Snowy,' said Gil Richardson.

Richardson is solid like a tree trunk, with burnished skin from a lifetime outdoors on tractors and a remarkably young face for his seventy-plus years. He wears a suit and tie like a straitjacket, but Roddy Kleinitz, who has worked for years on Richardson's farm, watched his boss bear the discomfort time and again for the sake of the Snowy River. 'Gil is someone who likes to go in and get the job done. It frustrated him that he couldn't just go out and fix the Snowy,' said Kleinitz. 'There were all these meetings, and he would come back and it was like a debrief, unloading what had happened over a coffee. We were both passionate about the river, but I had to work. But I would think, "This is what I am doing for the Snowy River, so that Gil can go to these meetings."'

Leete and Harry Moss did the political rounds in Sydney. Their local member, Peter Cochran, introduced them to his National Party colleagues. Jeff Angel opened doors into the Labor Party, the Greens and independents, and drafted a private member's bill for the Greens' Ian Cohen or independent Richard Jones to put before Parliament, asking for a water inquiry. He assigned a campaign manager, Fran Kelly, to coordinate publicity and seek celebrity support. Paul Leete and Dalgety Association member David Glasson even talked with irrigation representatives and the Snowy Mountains Council in Cooma, at a meeting arranged by the Environment Protection Authority. No one disputed the environmental case for more water in the Snowy River, but Leete and Glasson were bombarded with financial arguments as to why 28 per cent was impossible to achieve.

Miners made the most of his role as the Snowy-Genoa Catchment Management Committee coordinator. He went to Sydney to brief ministers and their advisors on the expert panel report. If he heard through the grapevine that a minister or advisor was coming anywhere near the Monaro, he called their office to squeeze a Snowy River tour onto the itinerary. The National Parks helicopter was usually available for ministerial briefings on corporatisation, and its 'whoppa-whoppa' became a familiar sound in Dalgety, setting down and flying off from the oval below the pub.

Indeed, Brett Miners pushed the issue so hard internally throughout 1996 and into 1997 that a departmental supervisor, Warren Martin, asked Stuart Hood to pull Miners back from advocacy. The campaign's increasingly political focus caused some committee members to question whether its role was appropriate. With Hood as chairman of both the Snowy-Genoa Catchment Management Committee and the Snowy River Alliance, the line was blurred between the advisory body and its advocacy offshoot. 'None of us were political people, but I suppose we were pretty political,' Hood said later. 'We were outside our fence. I guess we would get down there and rattle our bucket, but I felt if we had sat back and sent in report after report, it would never have got to the minister. It would have been shelved three or four levels down, and that was no use.'

As the campaign became more and more overtly political, however, Hood stepped down as Alliance chairman and was replaced by Leete. Hood remained active via the Snowy-Genoa Catchment Management Committee. Miners resigned as coordinator in July 1997 and took up a new position as the Snowy-Genoa Water Resources Manager with the Department of Land and Water Conservation in Cooma; the role was created in response to the Snowy issue. It was a step away from the catchment committee's community focus, but somewhat closer to the action inside government. Mike Gooey, another public servant in the Cottage 16 mould, took Miners' old job in September 1997. An agricultural scientist by training, Gooey's motto is 'Healthy landscapes enable sustainable communities'. The committee could not believe it was lucky enough to get another coordinator out of the box, after its good fortune with Miners. 'Mike did what he thought was right, stretched the envelope and was willing to go out on a limb,' said Hood.

The Alliance won some, it lost some. Federal Environment Minister Senator Robert Hill was not in the least bit interested in the Snowy River's plight. Neither was John Anderson, the Deputy Prime Minister and National Party leader, who met Stuart Hood and Alliance members in Bombala in June 1996. Later the same month, federal Energy Minister Senator Warwick Parer emphasised in a meeting he called with the Alliance that corporatisation would not change the way the scheme's water was managed — ie, no more water for the Snowy.[1]

Others were receptive. Max White and Gil Richardson came away from Marie Tehan, Victoria's Conservation and Natural Resources Minister, with her in-principle support for a public inquiry first, and a promise to visit the Snowy. The Alliance then killed two birds with one stone when Kim Yeadon, NSW Land and Water Resources Minister, agreed to visit the same day as Tehan, on 1 August 1996. Yeadon found the Alliance courteous and reasonable compared with the strident irrigation interests he dealt with out west. The NSW Agriculture Minister, Richard Amery, made the trip a couple of weeks later. A succession of advisors passed through, including a junior called Matthew Strassberg. He came with Sandra Nori, then parliamentary secretary to Michael Egan, who wore three hats as Treasurer, Energy Minister and Minister for Regional Development. Nori and Strassberg were in Cooma to talk about the jail closing, but the Dalgety Association persuaded them to swing by the Snowy River as well.

The visit left a strong impression on Strassberg. He remembered his sunburnt pate because there was no room left to stand under the shade of the trees, and he recalled the sight of 'this town with the arse hanging out of its pants and not much of a river'. But he was most struck by the collective passion. 'It was not like they held the power in a hung parliament, or they had the majesty of the Snowy River either,' he said. 'It did not look like particularly good farming country, it was a struggling town, but still, everyone turned out to show us the river. I thought, "Gee, we can do better than this with this river" — but it was not a top of mind issue at the time.'

It was a top of mind issue for a government backbencher called Ian Macdonald. He met Paul Leete on one of Leete's forays to Sydney, and became a regular visitor to Dalgety. Macdonald was secretary in the Left faction, which opposed NSW Labor's privatisation policy. He was also involved in environmental issues. Macdonald walked along the banks of the Snowy with Leete, and drank many cups of tea in Leete's home with its sad view over the river. He also got to know Graeme Enders, Brett Miners and Carl Drury on those trips.

Drury was keeping the Alliance on its toes. He shivered with nervous energy and kept odd hours. The others dubbed him 'Cosmic', because he was 'way out there'. 'He was very upfront and confrontational,' said Stuart Hood. 'You never quite knew what Carl would come out with if you had a minister there. But you have to have people like Carl because they serve their purpose and are passionate about the issue. You just have to try to control and direct their energy, and not have it scatter all over the countryside.'

The white-water rafter intimately understood the hydro scheme's technical aspects and appreciated its engineering excellence. At the same time, he regarded himself as living in enemy territory, waging a war of subversion. Drury believed the Snowy required at least 44 per cent of its original flow. When it was pointed out that such a high flow would render Jindabyne redundant for the purposes of the hydro scheme, Drury would retort, 'Tell someone who cares!' He sold campaign stickers to his white-water rafting clients, telling them, 'When it is time to stand in front of bulldozers, we will get in touch with you all!' He was only half-joking.

Drury's intensity did not frighten off Macdonald, who was convinced the claim for 28 per cent was right. He said later it was a political judgment untouched by romance. 'I did not have the sense of the Snowy River as charging round looking for brumbies — which shouldn't be there — or rounding up cattle in the highlands — which shouldn't be there either,' Macdonald said. 'I just took the view that it was a very little bit of water coming out of the dam, and agreed with Paul and Carl. I had a sceptical view of the romantic image because what was it about? It was not about environmental sustainability.'

Macdonald championed the cause in Sydney, taking ministers aside and talking at length to the crossbenchers. The issue, as he saw it, was twofold: the Snowy needed at least 28 per cent returned, and corporatisation had to be stopped because it would likely lead to privatisation. It was the perfect issue: both his main political interests neatly dovetailed into one campaign.

I worked for the scheme as a summer job in 1991. I came from Queensland in winter to do some snowboarding, met my wife, Lindy, and never left. When I went to work, I'd cross over the dam wall at Jindabyne and try to peer over the edge to see where the Snowy River was, because I could only ever see a sign. It is one of those great Australian rivers, like the Murray, and I wanted to see it. In the end, I thought this was just one of the valleys they had to dam, and the river wound around somewhere else.

Then we moved to Dalgety in 1993, and the Snowy was the talk of the town. When I saw this swampy mess, I thought it was only temporary and, come spring, there would be more flow. It was only after talking to the Dalgety and District Community Association that I found out this was not the case, and I was disgusted. I don't think it would have mattered whether it was the Snowy River or the Murray or what it was — I just could not believe that anyone could be allowed to do that to a river.

PAUL LEETE

The Snowy Mountains Authority was also busy in 1996. John Harrowell and Charles Halton's truce dissolved after Murray Jackson took over as commissioner. Jackson had no qualms about being a political player, and he played hard.

Jackson could be a charming and persuasive man. He turned it on when I rang him in New Zealand for an interview; he works there now for Genesis, the state-owned power company. He said he became aware of the Snowy River campaign in December 1993, when he met the Dalgety and District Community Association. The meeting was arranged after Jackson announced prematurely in the local media that the scheme would be corporatised. The association wanted to know what he was talking about, but also asked him to release the Mowamba River as an interim measure.

The new commissioner asked his staff if it was possible to open the Mowamba weir during the snowmelt, to give the Snowy a bit of a flush at least. 'I thought that was the way to go, but I was reminded we could not, because we would leave ourselves open to negotiations with the community outside the formal Commonwealth–state relationship,' he said later. Only the three governments could change the 1958 formula for allocating water, and they said they would deal with the issue after the scheme was corporatised.

The Snowy Mountains Authority began to argue the Snowy River was not as badly off as the Alliance claimed. It said the river also got an average

24 extra gigalitres a year in spills over the Mowamba weir, bringing its flow up to 3 per cent of the original. It is hard to know on what basis it made this claim: Snowy Hydro's information officer, Lesley Barlee, told me in an email that flows in the tributary and spills over the weir were not recorded; local knowledge says the weir has only very occasionally spilled, in exceptionally wet seasons.

Jackson wondered whether increased flows really would transform Dalgety into a vibrant township. He called for a balanced approach and said the issue was too narrowly focused. 'You can't ignore the impact of land use upon the Snowy River since 1835, and people are taking a simplistic approach if they think that simply flushing more water down the river is the solution to all of the problems,' Murray told the *South-East Magazine* in May 1996.

Just as the National Parks helicopter became a familiar sight on the Dalgety oval, so too did the sight of the Snowy Mountains Authority helicopter. It flew along the Snowy River from Jindabyne and turned left just before Dalgety to fly up the Wullwye Creek, a small tributary. Politicians, their advisors, Snowy Mountains Council members, corporatisation committee members, and Jackson would be inside.

The commissioner would explain how the Snowy River was a victim not of low flows, but of erosion, weeds, septic tanks, township effluent and livestock pollution. Persistent drought in the 1990s also played a role, reducing water from tributaries below the dam. The left turn up the Wullwye was intended to prove the point. The creek was also badly silted up, weed infested and polluted, yet it did not lose any water to the scheme.

The Dalgety Association was outraged. All these pressures were there before the scheme was built too — the difference was the river's inability to cope as a direct consequence of losing its headwaters. Adding insult to injury, treated effluent from Jindabyne's sewage plant was discharged into the river below the dam and counted as part of the Snowy's flow. In theory, the treated effluent was safe to drink, but the sewage plant was nonetheless moved from the edge of the lake across from Jindabyne town to the other side of the dam wall following complaints about discharging effluent into the lake's crystal clear waters. In peak tourist periods, the water under Dalgety bridge was as much as 10 per cent effluent.

Jackson figured he could mollify Dalgety if he did something about the effluent. He reasoned that releasing more water would only push the effluent further downstream, so he proposed removing it, using the effluent instead to water a proposed 18-hole golf course at Jindabyne. Dalgety was not impressed. The town did not want Jindabyne flushing its toilet in the

Snowy, but it rankled that Jindabyne did so well from the hydro scheme — a new town, a lake, a booming tourism industry and now apparently a world-class golf course — while Dalgety got nothing but a ruined river.

Jindabyne was not especially sympathetic. The rumour got around that restoring water to the Snowy River would lower the lake's level, leaving an ugly rim of bare dirt. The opposite was true. The hydro scheme's executive officer (water), Barry Dunn, explained at a departmental forum that a 28 per cent flow in the Snowy actually meant higher lake levels,[2] because the Snowy Mountains Authority had to keep more water in storage so it could meet the increased flow rates and keep the lake level high enough for the offtake station to pump water up to the tunnel under the mountain to feed the Murray power station turbines. This simple technical fact was not widely publicised, however, and so Jindabyne's support for Dalgety's campaign wobbled.

Aesthetics were also an issue in Dalgety. The town looked over a weedy, scummy mess. Soon after moving to Dalgety to manage the caravan park, Paul Leete and his wife, Lindy Johansen went for a swim in the Snowy. The water was knee deep and the bottom, which used to be clean gravel and sand, was inches deep in slime and fine silt. It was disgusting.

Murray Jackson figured he could do something about that too. He announced the authority would spend $100,000 building a new weir, removing weeds, landscaping and dredging to create a semi-decent swimming hole. The works would create the illusion of a broad river upstream from the bridge. Downstream, the trickle would no longer completely disappear under the sand, blackberries and willows. Jackson also persuaded the Snowy River Shire to seal the steep, twisting back road from Dalgety to Jindabyne, ostensibly to attract more tourists.

It was a naked attempt to buy off Dalgety. 'We had this bizarre meeting on the banks where Murray Jackson said this river was all fine, all it needed was electric barbeques and nice grass to the edge,' said Miners. 'Stuart Hood and I were the only ones standing there trying to get the point through to them that it was a broader issue.'

The Dalgety Association was divided on the offer. Harry Moss argued that the works would rob the campaign of its greatest asset — the visual impact of greasy water trickling through willows in the big, ancient river channel. There are few points of easy access to the Snowy River, and none quite so easy and graphic for the television cameras as standing on the Dalgety bridge.

Paul Leete was in two minds. The mess was literally in his face every day when he looked out his kitchen window, and it was not much of an advertisement for campers. But he was also determined that neither the authority nor the three governments should think they were off the hook for the price of some cosmetic improvement. The association debated what to do. It decided to take the money, but on condition the governments and the authority understood the works were not a substitute for more water.

Jackson could charm, but he was also rather a volatile character. Many people found him difficult and abrasive. One infamous day he was invited to speak to the Snowy-Genoa Catchment Management Committee. He gave the usual spiel, about how the Snowy River's problems were due to poor land management. The committee comprised mostly conscientious farmers involved in LandCare. They resented being made scapegoats. When Jackson finished, Derek Rutherford from the EPA put up his hand and began asking questions along the lines that poor land management was not the sole reason for the Snowy's woes. Jackson, sick to death of this issue that would not go away, lost it.

'Who are you?' he shouted from the podium. 'Where are you from? Give me your name — I am going to report you!'

Alison Gimbert, a Bombala landholder on the committee, leapt to Derek's defence. She was furious about what looked like an attempt to intimidate and bully the community.

'How dare you!' Gimbert shot back. 'We have a right to ask these questions, and we have a right to know these things, and who the hell do you fucking well think you are, speaking to us like this?'

Jackson went red in the face and walked out. The committee resolved never to have him return, yet the hydro's representatives on the Snowy-Genoa Catchment Management Committee later said they thought the meeting went really well and the Snowy Mountains Authority had got all its points across. 'They had not changed, but the world was changing,' said Brett Miners. 'They thought they could just go there as Snowy Hydro and say the line, and it would be accepted.'[3]

In a perverse way, Jackson's antics helped the Snowy River's supporters. He aggravated them no end, but was so extreme that he lent credibility to their case. The corporatisation committee also found Jackson difficult. Towards the end, some said Jackson was cut out of the loop in favour of the finance manager, Vin Good, and the operations manager, Clive Perrett. Jackson left the authority in March 1998 and Good was appointed transition commissioner to see the authority through its corporatisation. He was instructed not to rock the boat.

Good loved the scheme and, by his own admission, was not the easiest person to deal with when he perceived proposals that might be detrimental to its long-term viability. 'No one fought harder that I did all the way through the corporatisation process to retain the value of the scheme,' he said. 'I did accept the three governments' rights as shareholders to determine the level of environmental flows to the many rivers, but constantly pointed out the potential loss of value and the requirement for Snowy to be a viable on-going business.'

However, Good also respected his instructions to stay out of the politics of water and just provide the facts. Snowy Hydro Trading, a provisional entity created to trade the scheme's power in the new national electricity market, would do the lobbying. For the authority, it was full circle back to Halton and Harrowell's truce six years earlier.

〜

The community had the potential to stuff things up, but they did not have the inside running with the NSW ministers. Still, their nuisance factor was very large.

DAVID CROSSLEY, NSW PROJECT MANAGER,
SNOWY CORPORATISATION, 1996–2002

Victoria was the first to break ranks. David Downie assistant corporatisation manager for DJG Projects, consultants for the Snowy Mountains Authority corporatisation project, was surprised. He knew New South Wales was vulnerable to pressure because the Carr Government depended on a handful of Greens, Democrats and independents in the upper house to retain office. The Victorian Premier, Jeff Kennett, on the other hand, had commanding majorities in both houses and didn't care about public opinion. Victoria had been consistent about maximising the scheme's commercial return, yet now it was announcing it had a political problem on water.

The trouble started after Marie Tehan and Kim Yeadon visited Dalgety in August 1996. They decided to push for a water inquiry on Snowy River and other flows before corporatisation. Yeadon got nowhere with the NSW Cabinet. 'We met brick walls with the bean counters,' he said. In Victoria, however, water became a stumbling block inside the intra-agency working party on corporatisation. Victoria's project manager, Paul Dunn, said the group was working through the many and complex issues, but when it came to water, an insurmountable divide emerged between the Victorian Treasury and the Department of Natural Resources and Environment.

'We were saying that you cannot resolve this without resolving the water issue,' the then Environment Minister, Marie Tehan, said later. 'We had to keep coming back to Treasury and saying that we cannot get a sale, or sign up to anything, without dealing with water. We kept insisting that water was integral to this deal.'

Tehan agitated in Cabinet, clashing with the Treasurer, Alan Stockdale. 'Political tensions were rising and the issue was proving intractable even within government departments,' said Dunn. 'Getting a united government position was difficult enough without then having to try and get inter-jurisdictional agreement.' The Victorian agencies compromised, and told the corporatisation committee in September 1996 that the state wanted an inquiry to address water and environmental issues before the scheme was corporatised.

The committee was taken aback. The process had proved more labyrinthine than anyone had imagined, but after nearly eighteen months it had progressed to the point legislation could finally be submitted into the NSW Parliament by June 1997. Now Victoria wanted a public inquiry first. The project manager, David Crossley, was dismayed at the thought of more delays. He could see the years stretching out before him, lost in a grey fog of never-ending inter- and intra-governmental wrangling in a nondescript meeting room in Sydney's Governor Macquarie Tower. Crossley had only been in the job a few months, and his boss, the Treasurer, Michael Egan, was already asking why it was taking so long!

The committee debated what to do over the next few months. One school of thought argued an explicit decision had been made fifty years ago to kill the Snowy River as the price of progress. 'Was it too late to breathe life into the corpse?' Peter Staveley wondered. 'It does not mean I was opposed, but it is the difference between being driven emotionally and philosophically, as opposed to rationally.' The committee did not want to deal with this issue but it was not going to go away. Greens member Ian Cohen and other NSW upper house crossbenchers were signalling they too wanted a water inquiry first.

David Crossley was torn. Appearances can be deceiving. Crossley looks like the archetypal grey 'suit', but some say he was something of a bearded eco-warrior in his youth. 'I was in a difficult position,' he said. 'I am basically an environmentalist and I was contracted to work for Treasury, and they were not exactly in favour of environmentalists. I had to be careful. I could not let my personal views get in the way.'

He acted as an independent mediator in negotiations; his brief was to get the job done as quickly and cheaply as possible and make sure New South Wales was not diddled in the process. 'I personally felt the Snowy was stuffed, and to make it unstuffed would require a level of water beyond what anyone would have accepted,' Crossley said later. 'Why spend the money on the

Snowy River when you get a bigger bang for your buck in other rivers? Why spend lots of money on a flow too low to do anything good? The difficulty was working out how real were the claims for 28 per cent, given the river had 1 per cent at the top and 50 per cent by the time it went out to sea. It was beyond the committee's ability to sort this out, so there was agreement that a separate inquiry was needed to put this issue to bed.'

The committee eventually agreed that the inquiry should take place *after* the three Parliaments approved corporatisation. That way, the flows would require only ministerial approval, without running the gauntlet of Parliament. 'If you had the inquiry first, you would never get the legislation,' said David Downie. 'They would never agree on the flows because there were too many shades of opinion. If just one house in all those governments said no, then you don't get corporatisation.'

Crossley went to the NSW Treasurer in March 1997 with the committee's proposal. The corporatisation legislation would be drafted to include an independent public water inquiry into all rivers affected by the scheme, including the Snowy River. The inquiry would take place within six months after Parliament approved corporatisation. The relevant ministers would then make a decision on flows and corporatisation would proceed on that basis. Michael Egan gave the plan the nod. The legislation was scheduled to go through NSW Parliament in June.

∽

The flows issue began to surface publicly in Parliament in the weeks counting down to June 1997. The Greens' Ian Cohen addressed the Legislative Council, urging water be restored to the Snowy River before the scheme was corporatised.[4] Independent Richard Jones questioned the Treasurer, Michael Egan, about the timing of a water inquiry. The Treasurer said the legislation to corporatise the scheme would not be proclaimed until the relevant ministers resolved the water issues.[5] That way, a decision on flows would not be put off into the never-never while the governments went ahead with corporatisation.

The Alliance and its affiliate organisations were not appeased. The lobbying effort redoubled. Letters sent to key politicians and officials were followed up with persistent phone calls. Paul Leete, his father-in-law, Norman Johansen, and Carl Drury haunted the halls of Parliament in Sydney for days on end, working out of Cohen and Jones's office. 'We didn't come in as ALP apparatchiks or greenies, but as people who have lost their whole river. We were not greedy, we did not want the lot, but this legislation was not looking after anyone's interests,' said Drury. 'We would go from one mob to the next. We would go from Labor in the upper house, where they were circumspect, to Labor in the lower house, where they were arrogant because they had the numbers to get it through.'

Ian Macdonald meanwhile stoked internal dissent. As convenor of the Left's taskforce against privatising state energy utilities, he clashed with Egan back in April, when the NSW Treasurer pushed through caucus an agreement to corporatise the hydro scheme. The Left attempted to insert a policy undertaking that the scheme could not be sold and that the Snowy be guaranteed at least 20 per cent of its original flow at Jindabyne, but Egan dismissed the anti-privatisation bid without debate. Macdonald continued to argue vehemently in the party room against corporatising the Snowy Mountains Scheme, on the grounds that it would lead to privatisation and a poor environmental outcome for the Snowy River.

Egan was fairly confident the legislation would get through Parliament, however. The Liberal/National coalition as a rule supported privatising government bodies, so it was a reasonable bet the Opposition would not play party politics over corporatising the Snowy Mountains Scheme. The coalition, as it happened, had not given the matter much thought, despite Peter Cochran's best efforts. Parliamentarians are incredibly busy people. At any one time, especially when Parliament is sitting, they are trying to get their heads around dozens of bills and associated issues. The Snowy River did not strike most as much of an issue: the government said it would hold a water inquiry, so there seemed little reason to block the legislation.

Peter Cochran made a last-ditch appeal to Duncan Gay, the National Party's deputy president, to meet the Alliance and hear what they had to say. 'Peter, who is not a friend of environmentalists, came to me and said, "Dunc, you should listen to these blokes",' Gay recalled. The coalition did not want to hang Cochran out to dry with his constituents, so Gay arranged a time and a room for the Alliance to address coalition parliamentarians.

About twenty turned up. Cochran had barely shown Leete, Drury and Norm Johansen into the room before one National Party politician stepped up, too close to Leete's face. 'Where I come from, there's a lot of irrigators,' he said. 'We don't care about your river and how much water you have in it. We have salinity problems, and fish problems, and blue-green algae. We have enough of our own environmental issues and we don't give a toss about your river.'

Leete was taken aback. 'I said nothing, because I was not getting into a fight before we even started. But I was thinking, holy shit — are they all going to be like that?'

They sat down to wait for some latecomers, and Drury leaned over to whisper in Leete's ear. 'You are going to have to pull a rabbit out of your hat because I don't know how we are going to get these guys to follow us.'

〜

We would laugh at some of the get-togethers, where there would be the ladies in their twin sets and pearls, and groups from the communes in their kaftans and sandals — but they were all speaking for the river. The river symbolises the environmental concerns we all had, and it transcended politics and social allegiances. It was much bigger than we realised.

BRENDA AND KEITH MURRAY, PAYNESVILLE

'It is one minute to midnight for the Snowy River,' wrote Genevieve Fitzgerald in her very first press release for the Snowy River. The date was 1 June 1997. It was all happening inside NSW Parliament, but you would hardly know it outside, even in Orbost.

Fitzgerald met Max White in June 1996, when Fitzgerald and her husband, Richard Owen, won the tender to design a revegetation field guide for the lower Snowy River. It was part of a joint project between the Snowy River Improvement Trust and the Department of Conservation and Natural Resources. Having won the tender, Fitzgerald and Owen rapidly realised the Victorian government really wanted to know how much revegetation works might cost within a 30-kilometre radius of Orbost, and what it might take to quieten down people in Orbost for when corporatisation went ahead.

Fitzgerald was 'gob-smacked' at the first briefing meeting to learn that 99 per cent of the Snowy pumped across the Great Divide. Neither she nor her husband had known that before. With only a 1 per cent headflow in the river, the whole concept of a revegetation strategy to solve its problems was ludicrous. 'In defence of the government's position, this guy had responded to Max's insistence that there needed to be a 28 per cent flow by saying, in a bit of a fluster, "We can't possibly let that much money — er, I mean water — go down the Snowy!"'

The joint project gave Max White no joy. After all these years of asking the state government for more water, the best it could offer was a few willows removed and the banks revegetated. The Trust was also about to lose its voice to protest. It was being disbanded and its responsibilities and funding transferred to the new East Gippsland Catchment Management

Authority, being set up in Bairnsdale 90 kilometres away. The Snowy would become just one of many badly degraded rivers, crying out for attention and funds from an authority based in a town preoccupied by the deteriorating Gippsland Lakes.

And so Fitzgerald encountered a despondent man. 'No one cares about the Snowy River,' White said, every time Genevieve Fitzgerald came to Orbost. 'No, Max — no one knows,' Fitzgerald replied. 'If people only knew, they would care.'

Fitzgerald and Owen ran an indigenous horticulture consultancy and native nursery at Nungurner, midway between Bairnsdale and Orbost. Incredibly, they (and everyone else they knew) had not heard about the Snowy River campaign. It consumed those involved, but was not a broad movement engaging Orbost and surrounds in the way the Dalgety Association had emerged.

The Snowy River worked its spell on Fitzgerald when she realised the land they were studying was her great-grandmother's old farm. Grace Jennings Carmichael had been a poet and writer whose work was regularly published in *The Argus* and *The Bulletin*. Fitzgerald discovered the family link in a frustrated discussion with her mother about the difficulties of clarifying the native plant profile before Orbost was established. Her mother reminded Fitzgerald that she had a Melbourne University researcher's thesis on Jennings that included transcripts of the poet's work; she'd given it to Fitzgerald years earlier when her daughter undertook a professional writing degree. 'I thought it was a bit of a weird suggestion, but nonetheless hunted around until I found the document,' Fitzgerald said. 'When I sat down to read it, I felt the most incredible wave of emotion because my great-grandmother had described the landscape in great detail.

'I actually forced my youngest daughter and her best friend, who were about six at time, to come and listen to what I was reading. It was a particular story called "My Station Home" in which Jennings was lamenting the loss of her childhood haunts whilst she watched the first settlement pegs being hammered in to make way for the township of Orbost in the farm's south-west corner.

'She was very sad, and wondered what the land would be like 100 years from now. She was particularly upset because the trees and mosses that were her playground were being torn asunder. I couldn't believe it — she wrote that in 1894, and here I was in 1996 trying to figure out how and what was needed to restore the landscape. That was it for me — I was bewitched.'

Fitzgerald offered to help the Alliance with publicity. Having worked as a grant seeker, she suggested philanthropy might be the answer to the

Alliance's funding problems once the Snowy River Improvement Trust was disbanded. A former journalist, Fitzgerald also knew the fight would not be won on the strength of the argument alone, nor would private meetings with power brokers give the campaign the momentum it needed to succeed. A mass movement was the only way, in her opinion, that the Victorian Government would take the campaign seriously, while something was definitely needed to stiffen political backbones in Sydney where an extraordinary game of brinksmanship was being played out.

For Paul Leete had indeed pulled a rabbit out of a hat. He won over the coalition — not to a 28 per cent flow in the Snowy, but to the principle that water was too important a decision to be made behind closed doors by the government alone. Leete achieved it by doing the last thing anyone in the room expected: he agreed that the scheme was vitally important for irrigation, especially in dry times. 'So, are you going to let the government decide on what terms you get your water after the scheme is corporatised and sold?' Leete said.

'But Murray [Jackson] said there will be no change in the current water arrangements — everything will stay the same,' said Don Page, the National Party member for Ballina and Shadow Minister for Land and Water Conservation.

'Well, Murray is not the government, and corporatisation will lock up the water completely,' Leete replied. 'You will have a private company managing it all under a licence that will last for 125 years. Are you going to let through this legislation without knowing what that licence says? The company will want to keep it for power generation. You want water for the irrigators and we want it for the Snowy, and you are going to let the government make the decision for both of us? They might even turn around and give us half the water in the scheme, and you won't have a say in it. You have to have the water inquiry and settle these issues first, before you approve corporatisation.'

Leete was holding the rabbit by the ears and waving it for all it was worth.

'You are right!' said Jim Small, the member for Murray. Virtually all his constituents depended on irrigation, and he was concerned about losing control of the water if the scheme was corporatised. 'Everyone has this idea that we were being wasteful and getting too much water, but, over time, industries have grown up and we have become very dependent on the water for our produce,' Small said later. 'We weren't against increased flow in the Snowy — our problem was the 28 per cent because that would have very telling effects on the Murray.'

Small invited Leete to tour his electorate to see the other side of the debate, an invitation Leete took up a few weeks later. Small's colleagues persuaded others that the coalition should demand a water inquiry before Parliament voted on corporatisation. It was mid-May and less than two weeks to go before the legislation lobbed in the Legislative Assembly. 'I remember it was one of those unusual situations where, once we were persuaded, we were standing with these odd fellows from this community group against their natural allies, the Labor Government,' recalled Duncan Gay. 'But then it was really the NSW Right we were up against here, and they are pretty tough cookies.'

The government was jolted out of its complacency. Until then, the Snowy River had hardly registered on its radar amid the myriad other issues jostling for attention. The agitation seemed confined to a handful of zealots from two small and rather obscure towns, plus the usual suspects in the environment movement. 'They were not taking it seriously because they were getting the conventional arguments from Treasury that it would cost too much and would affect revenue,' said Jeff Angel.

The Premier, Bob Carr, played good cop. He appealed to Paul Leete in a letter on 15 May 1997, explaining corporatisation was essential, otherwise the governments could not legally resolve the flows issue. Leete doubted this was the case. Carr pointed out that the government was committed to environmental flows in all rivers: the EPA was talking about a universal 10 per cent target, but Leete said that would not be enough for the Snowy River.

The Treasurer, Michael Egan, played bad cop. He introduced the bill into the lower house on 29 May, then called Leete, Carl Drury and Jeff Angel into his office to tell them the only way the Snowy River would ever get any water was if they supported corporatisation. Egan said if the legislation was blocked, then the community, the coalition and the crossbenchers could blame themselves for missing an historic opportunity.

The three men were unmoved. So the government offered the Greens' Ian Cohen and independent Richard Jones some deals on other issues close to their hearts, but they had had their fingers burnt too often. 'We had been let down a number of times and hadn't got things we were promised,' said Jones. 'You can't live on trust, but they are hard nuts to deal with. They will twist your arm to support something. Still, the Snowy became a very passionate issue for the upper house members, including the coalition. We felt very strongly that we wanted the river to flow again. We all had slightly different reasons but we all felt very emotional about the Snowy.'

The legislation passed the lower house on government numbers, but the coalition voted with the crossbenchers in the upper house to refer the corporatisation bill to the Legislative Council environment committee. It was a delaying tactic, to wind up pressure on the government. It was also a chance to grill the Environment Minister, Pam Allan, and the Land and Water Resources Minister, Kim Yeadon, on whether the government had done flow studies for the Snowy River. The coalition also drafted alternative legislation, with a water inquiry before Parliament voted on corporatisation. Egan's office rang Cohen, Jones and Angel, threatening to call off everything and then the Snowy would get nothing.

'Tough,' Angel replied.

'Well, you are the ones who are going to be embarrassed, losing a once-in-a-generation chance to save the Snowy,' shot back the staffer on the other end of the line.[6]

Down in Orbost, Fitzgerald was a dynamo, rallying heads for the politicians to count. Her husband and two daughters barely saw her at home, and when she was there, she was on the phone, arranging two big public rallies to coincide with the legislation coming back into the NSW Parliament for debate in the second last sitting week, starting Monday 16 June 1997.

The first event was the Save Our Snowy rally, on Saturday 14 June. Fitzgerald arranged live music, free food and a sandcastle competition on a

The people of Orbost rally on the banks of the Snowy River on 14 June 1997, appealing to New South Wales and Victorian politicians to 'Save Our Snowy'.
Photo: Glenn Hooper.

river bend. The community responded enthusiastically. Barely 2500 people live in Orbost, but more than 1500 gathered on the sand, proving they did care once they knew. They came from everywhere — farmers, shopkeepers, school children, timber workers, the Indigenous community, the alternative lifestylers from up in Goongerah, and the local arts community. They formed a big SOS; everyone got to know each other well, standing in position, chatting while they waited for two hours for the plane to show up with the photographer. The picture made the front page of most of the region's papers.

The rally had barely ended before Fitzgerald and others drove to Sydney for the second rally on the steps of Parliament House on Monday 16 June. Fitzgerald blitzed the media outlets. 'This is the community's last attempt to get the politicians to hear what we're saying,' she wrote. 'Getting a fair deal for the Snowy River may well be Australia's first real litmus test on the allocation of water for environmental flows.'

A friendly ABC journalist had advised Fitzgerald to go for the Hollywood approach and capitalise on the potent Man from Snowy River legend. She duly announced in her media alert that the Snowy's supporters were bringing their horses, their Akubra hats and their hearts to Sydney. There was not enough time to organise trucking local horses, so she rang the Sydney police to borrow a few nags. 'Is this a joke?' said the cop on the other end. 'No,' replied Fitzgerald. 'We need some crowd-control horses that are used to the city.' The police promised to turn up to keep law and order, but no more. Fitzgerald hired horses from a stable in the Blue Mountains instead.

She also tracked down Gus Mercurio, one of the stars from the box office hit movie from 1982, *The Man from Snowy River*. Gus was in his seventies, but willing to help a good cause. Fitzgerald picked him up in a taxi on the morning of the rally. 'He had done his back, and his wife was angry about him taking on this job because he shouldn't be riding a horse,' she said. 'He asked me if these were good horses, and used to crowds, and I said "Yes".'

They saddled up a few blocks from Parliament House. Little boys from the Snowy River country gaped at Gus Mercurio, the movie star of their dreams, as he put his foot in the stirrup, swung his leg over the horse — and was unceremoniously dumped on his back on the pavement on the other side, the victim of a loose girth strap. It dented his fans' hero worship somewhat and Fitzgerald could hear his wife going crook at her for not looking after him. 'But he just got up, tightened the girth and got back on,' Fitzgerald said. 'It was so kind of him to do this — he didn't even charge us an appearance fee.'

Got the message? Protestors rally outside New South Wales Parliament on 16 June 1997, where the Government was resisting pressure to hold a water inquiry before corporatising the Snowy Mountains Hydro-Electric Authority. *Source: Snowy River Alliance.*

Fitzgerald and Carl Drury scouted Parliament House just before the ride started. They found to their dismay another mob of protesters there with placards about an altogether different environmental issue. 'We should join them!' shouted Drury. He was rather overexcited. The day before, he had raised eyebrows among several conservative Alliance supporters when he jumped out into the traffic to stop cars and lobby the occupants.

'We can't do that — just go and join some other protest,' Fitzgerald told Drury. She went up to the protesters and asked if they would mind moving on. 'We have a gig at noon and we need to set up,' she explained. They were surprised but obliging. When the riders and horses arrived outside Parliament House, there was a hurried negotiation with the security staff to get some chairs for elderly supporters during the speeches.

Gus Mercurio told the fifty or so people assembled that the river had become an embarrassment to Australia. 'It is a shrivelling little meaningless creek held together by pools of water,' he declared. The Sydney media loved the spectacle, but it was knocked off the front pages in Melbourne by the unfolding saga of Jaidyn Leskie, a toddler murdered in the central Gippsland town of Moe under bizarre circumstances. 'It was all insane really,' recalls Fitzgerald. 'We were running on endorphins. We barely slept for two-and-a-half weeks.'

Two days later, on 18 June 1997, the NSW lower house began to debate the legislation. One after another, the Opposition members stood up and said they did not trust the government. At 11.30 pm, Peter Cochran was still talking, saying a water inquiry first was the honourable thing to do. Drury watched from the public gallery, and wondered why Cochran bothered given there were only four people in the house to listen, and one was asleep. The government used its numbers the next day to push the legislation through, and it was scheduled for debate in the upper house the following week, the last before Parliament rose for its winter recess.

The bill was not listed for debate on the Monday so all was quiet in the Legislative Council. But behind the scenes, there was frantic lobbying. Leete and Drury spent all day Monday and half the night in Ian Cohen's office, haggling with Cohen and Jeff Angel over proposed amendments. Down in Orbost, Max and Glenice White struggled to keep up with the stream of legal documents coming through their fax late at night, with Leete on the phone, wanting their opinion. Cohen and Angel in turn haggled with the Treasurer, but Egan refused to blink: if Parliament did not approve corporatisation, then the Snowy River got nothing, ever.

Finally, Angel proposed a compromise: the corporatisation legislation could go through with an inquiry afterwards, but Parliament would have the power to veto the ministerial decision on flows before legislation was proclaimed. The regulations would also be reviewed every ten rather than every thirty years. Egan agreed. There was a quick midnight phone consultation with Victoria's Paul Dunn and Margaret Sewell, who had replaced Russell Higgins as the Commonwealth's Snowy corporatisation project manager. They agreed. But Leete, Drury and the Whites did not. Neither did Ian Cohen, and his was the deciding vote. They decided to hold out.

Egan withdrew the legislation rather than have corporatisation voted down, telling Parliament there was no point spending days debating amendments when there was no chance the House would pass the bill in any acceptable form.[7] In the dying hours of the last day of the last session, Michael Egan slipped the bill into a packed legislative schedule, but withdrew it again after Ian Cohen accused him of trying to get it through unnoticed. Egan blamed the coalition for not supporting him. 'Three governments have been working together on this for four years, which is a bit like having a three-dimensional chess game, and now it has been bombed by the Opposition,' Egan's spokesman told the media. 'As far as we are concerned, the plan is dead in the water.'[8]

Well, not quite dead, just postponed until Parliament came back for the spring session in September. The reprieve was the Alliance's first major victory, and a turning point in the campaign. The Snowy River at last was driving the corporatisation agenda.

⌒

If a company of that size destroyed 500 kilometres of coast, which is the length of the Snowy River, do you think people would just be sitting back and saying that that is okay? But because it was hidden behind the hills, they thought could get away with it.

PAUL LEETE

A few days after the dramas in Sydney, Drury rang Leete in a state of high excitement. A threat to bomb the Jindabyne dam was leading the radio news, and the federal police had just been to see Drury. Leete had not heard the news, but he was puzzled as to why the police had come straight to the Alliance. 'Maybe we're making too much trouble for the hydro, and they are trying to shut us up,' said Drury. 'Anyway, mate, you might be getting a visit yourself.'

Leete had hardly hung up before there was a knock on the door. The two detectives sat down at the kitchen table. They explained, over cups of tea, that a Snowy Mountains Authority employee had overheard a suspicious conversation in a pub in Cooma. A couple of blokes were apparently talking about putting a bomb under the dam wall, to let the water out.

'Why are you asking me about this?' Leete said. 'I wasn't in the pub. Why aren't you talking to the employee and tracking down the person involved based on his information?'

'Why would we want to blow up the dam?' added his mother-in-law, Beau. 'We live downstream from it. We would be swept away in the flood.'

Leete's mind was buzzing. Painting Alliance members as greenie extremists was a sure way of undermining local support. 'People say that all the time, that we should just blow the bloody thing up,' he told the police. 'No one means it. It is just a silly joke. It wouldn't surprise me if the authority has done this to try to quieten the Alliance down and discredit us.'

'Do you think so?' asked the detective, suddenly alert.

Leete thought he had better be careful. 'Well, no — I am on good terms with the people at the authority, and I would like to think they did not, but it is possible.'

The next morning, the media was crawling all over the story, giving the Alliance priceless publicity to talk about the Snowy River's plight. Leete even did a live-to-air cross to the *Today Show* in Sydney, standing on the banks of Jindabyne Lake.[9] The camera crew wanted to film on the other side of the dam wall, where the Snowy flows out of its small concrete pipe, but the Snowy Mountains Authority had blocked off vehicular access to deter would-be bombers.

Leete told *Today Show* host Steve Liebmann that the investigation seemed to be a bit of public mischief-making, based on a rumour coming from the Snowy Mountains Authority. 'I suppose obviously the detectives have to follow right through, but we see it as nothing more than a rumour blown out of proportion. Obviously we don't support such actions like this. The community has invested hundreds of thousands of dollars and years of time in this campaign and we are not about to discredit our campaign by making any threats on the Jindabyne dam.'

Liebmann interrupted Leete, asking incredulously if he was suggesting the Snowy Mountains Authority might be responsible. 'There are all possibilities and questions were asked by the detectives on that line,' Leete replied cautiously. 'I did have a call from the authority basically apologising for any inconvenience that it has caused us and the Snowy River Alliance, because it understands we are honourable people.'

The police soon dropped their inquiries, leaving the Snowy Mountains Authority looking rather paranoid. Talking to senior executives past and present for this book, the incident seemed forgotten. 'No information available,' said Snowy Hydro information officer Lesley Barlee in an email, responding to my email asking what happened and how the Snowy Mountains Authority responded to the perceived threat. Vin Good vaguely remembers something about a phone call threatening to blow up the dam as the easy solution to the environmental flows debate. 'There was some concern for a few days that it was a hoax, or we hoped to God it was a hoax,' he said. That was all.

⌒

In the list of government priorities, the Snowy River was not in anyone's top five, including the environment movement.

ROBERT WEBSTER, 1998 SNOWY WATER INQUIRY COMMISSIONER

The Alliance assumed New South Wales would pass its legislation first, then Victoria and the Commonwealth would follow suit with mirror bills. Leete was chatting on the phone to a friendly senator early on the morning of

26 June 1997 — in the midst of the dramas in Sydney — when he got a terrible shock. The senator mentioned in passing that the Commonwealth's corporatisation bill was scheduled for debate and a vote later that afternoon in the Senate. The bill, which did not acknowledge water issues at all, had quietly slipped through the House of Representatives while the Alliance was preoccupied with the shenanigans in Sydney.

The Alliance had got nowhere with the Commonwealth Government. The Energy Minister, Senator Warwick Parer, maintained water was a state issue and therefore the government had no role in determining the Snowy River's fate. 'We felt that they had abrogated their responsibility in that they set up the scheme to begin with,' said Leete. 'They said the states would sort it out, and we said what if they don't, what if they want the status quo? You would have no power to intervene. The Commonwealth were ready to sign an agreement on water that had not been agreed!'

Leete typed a letter in big bold capitals, asking whether the Senate was prepared to let the states do whatever they wanted with such an important national resource as water. He faxed the letter to all the senators with a request that they block the legislation. Many rang back for more information; it was the first most had heard about the Snowy River's plight. They delayed voting by referring the bill to the Senate Finance and Public Administration Legislation Committee for more information. The committee scheduled what Leete later described as a 'one-day, quick and dirty' public inquiry for Friday 26 September.

The Whites and two new Alliance recruits from Orbost — George Collis and Craig Ingram, representing Native Fish Australia — were up before dawn and drove four hours to be in Canberra by 8.30 am when the inquiry began. Irrigation authorities, the Murray Darling Basin Commission and a barrage of lawyers, corporatisation consultants and bureaucrats were waiting for them.

Andrew Martin from DJG Projects, Snowy's corporatisation consultants, opened proceedings by questioning the appropriateness of the inquiry. He told the senators they should not be talking about water, because the legislation dealt only with electricity generation and the Commonwealth did not have the constitutional power to pass laws concerning rivers. Senator Parer concurred, telling the committee that his responsibilities as a federal minister extended no further than saying yes or no to the states' decision on flows. The community, he said, ought to be restricting itself to lobbying the NSW and Victorian governments.

The Alliance and its supporters were appalled that the minister and officials were trying to shut down the inquiry on a legal technicality. George

Collis pointed out that the Snowy River was in trouble only because the Commonwealth built the scheme in the first place. Paul Leete pointed out that water could not be separated from electricity generation, and that the Commonwealth had a broader legal responsibility to operate the scheme in the community interest. Nick Thorne, also representing Native Fish Australia at the inquiry, asked to amend the bill to acknowledge at least that there were water issues that must be addressed.

It was no use. The damage was done. The senators on the committee clearly did not have a clue what the problem was, and the officials gave them an excuse not to try too hard to find out. Labor Senator Kate Lundy was the only one to ask probing questions, but was satisfied when Senator Parer said there would be opportunities — albeit limited — to review flows down the track. When the Snowy River people persisted, Senator Robert Ray explained that water was beyond the committee's jurisdiction. 'Strictly, we should be examining only the merits of the clauses of the bill,' he said. 'But while we are here, we might as well let it all hang out and let everyone ask the other questions. We find it very valuable.'[10]

Valuable maybe, but ultimately pointless. The hearing adjourned just before 11 am. It was a Friday after a tough sitting week, and the senators were keen to catch planes and get home. Two and a half hours was all it took for the major parties to wash their hands of the issue. About a month after the inquiry, both Houses of Federal Parliament approved corporatising the hydro scheme. Labor was content with Senator Parer's assurance that he would not sign off on corporatisation unless he was satisfied with the outcome of the states' water inquiry. The Shadow Energy Minister, Stephen Smith, put out a press release claiming this clause would ensure the environment's needs were taken into account — despite Senator Parer being on record saying he would not agree to anything that reduced the scheme's commercial viability.

The Victorian Government, too, was deaf to the Alliance. Max White wrote to Premier Jeff Kennett, suggesting Victoria could not trust New South Wales to draft legislation looking after Victoria's power and water interests. He did not get an answer. Glenice White wrote to the Treasurer, Alan Stockdale, complaining that public servants were saying the Snowy River's fate depended on how additional water affected the scheme's commercial operation. 'It would appear most of the Treasury officers both in Victoria and NSW who are formulating the new NSW Snowy Corporatisation Bill have never seen the state of the river below the dam wall, or the state of the economy along its length, either,' White said.[11] She was right.

Geoff Chambers, who took over from Paul Dunn as Victoria's Snowy project manager in mid-1997, said maximising the commercial returns remained Victoria's priority. The Department of Natural Resources and Environment also advised the corporatisation working party that it was managing the Alliance and representing its interests. The bureaucratic filter effectively neutered the Alliance's direct appeals to ministers. 'We carried what we believed we could carry from a government point of view, and where we thought we could carry the Snowy River Alliance without it becoming out of control,' said Chambers.

When the Alliance finally succeeded in persuading the Treasurer, Alan Stockdale, to leave his office and see for himself what they were talking about, the tour was a disaster. The weather on 14 November 1997 was appalling, and the flight to Dalgety was by all accounts terrifying. Stockdale looked around the top end of the Snowy, but his pilot abandoned the planned flight down its length to Orbost and flew instead to Lakes Entrance. 'We had a good discussion with him there instead, but again, you would not know what he thought. He just nodded his head,' said Stuart Hood, the chair of the Snowy-Genoa Catchment Management Committee. 'You could never tell how much the politicians took on board, but at least they knew what people on the ground thought.'

Ian Cohen, Richard Jones and Jeff Angel resumed negotiating with Michael Egan when the NSW Parliament resumed in September 1997. The winter recess did not soften the Treasurer's attitude. He was impervious to arguments that the government's green credentials were on the line. 'A couple of times Egan sent them away with a flea in their ear, saying if that is the way you feel, we have nothing to talk about,' said Peter Staveley. 'He was attempting to put the onus back onto Cohen and Angel to be a little more realistic in what they were seeking.'

As the year drew to a close, the political ground shifted. The Commonwealth, having passed its legislation, wanted its $800 million debt repaid. Victoria was also keen to get the show on the road. 'New South Wales could not just say we can't get it through,' said Richard Jones. The government had to sort out its political problem.

Peter Staveley said his attempts to engage the Opposition to do a deal were rebuffed. 'The attitude was, "Here is a stew — let the government work its own way out of it". They were not going to help us.'

However, there was a whisper around Parliament that the irrigation lobby might settle for a flow of 3–7 per cent down the Snowy River. The crossbenchers and Jeff Angel began to fear the Opposition would grab this, and the government would sell out the Alliance altogether for a token flow.

One of the Alliance's best allies in government, Ian Macdonald, had also mellowed. The NSW Labor Party overwhelmingly rejected privatisation policy at its state conference in October 1997 and, without the threat that the scheme would be sold, Macdonald came to see corporatisation as an opportunity. 'In November 1997, I was more comfortable about corporatisation because I could look at what other issues could be resolved in the process, including environmental issues,' he said. 'Corporatisation, in fact, was needed to change the Act sufficiently to get environmental flows.'

Jeff Angel, Ian Cohen and Richard Jones made a hard-nosed judgment. 'You see the work of people like Jo Garland and Paul Leete, slaving away to get something for the Snowy River, and you always had a feeling the whole thing could unravel,' said Ian Cohen. 'The Greens having a bargaining chip with the government is reliant on the coalition being obstinately opposed. The government can easily sideline us. So you have to make decisions about whether to take an in-principle stand, and get nowhere, or make a start, to get something. In the end, I thought the legislation would lead to the Snowy River flowing again — even if we did take it on trust.'

In mid-November, Treasurer Egan called a meeting with Jones, Cohen and Angel, with Peter Staveley and David Crossley in attendance, to thrash something out. Angel, Cohen and Jones dropped the demand for the inquiry before the Parliament approved corporatising the scheme. In return, the government agreed to write environmental flows into the water licence, and reduce the licence period from 125 to 75 years. It meant the Snowy now had a legal right to more water; the only question would be how much.

The other important amendment was that the NSW Legislative Council got the right of veto over the ministerial decision on flows, before the corporatisation legislation could be proclaimed. At least it was only one House of Parliament, David Downie thought. The legislation was duly passed in the last week of November, with the coalition parties crying foul about the Greens selling out with a 'shonky deal'.

Carl Drury was not easy about the deal, 'but we trusted our environmental brothers'. He assumed the water inquiry would resolve the issue in the Snowy's favour. Leete and the Whites were not entirely comfortable either, but it was not, ultimately, their decision. 'I don't think we agreed to the final outcome, but the government got it through with the Greens and independents,' said Leete. 'I think the TEC believed it was a better chance of getting water into the river. I think the Greens thought if they just kept blocking it, there was no progress, and it did not get us anywhere to keep stopping it.'

'We could have been tougher,' Richard Jones acknowledged in hindsight. 'But at the time you don't know how far you can push. You push as far as you think we can go — but you do not want to push it off the edge.'

For Jeff Angel, there was more than just the Snowy River at stake. He wanted to preserve the Total Environment Centre's reputation as greenies that governments could do business with. 'The major environment groups are not mere servants of the local groups,' he said bluntly, years later. 'Carl got paranoid and suspicious of the deals as backtracking. They wanted the decision right now so they could get on with it — people can't understand that you don't always win the battle immediately. We were confident the public campaign would continue to be strong, and you can take the optimistic view that you can bring the government along rather than continue being their complete enemy. The compromise was an acknowledgement of the strength of their position and the need for a certain amount of face-saving.'

Many inside government were wondering if corporatisation was worth all this trouble. 'Why are we doing this?' Egan asked David Crossley, not for the first or the last time. Crossley went through it all again: the scheme would pay substantial rent for using state land, contaminated sites in the National Park would be fixed up, the rivers would be improved, New South Wales would get sovereign control, and reap millions of dollars in dividends from the power sales as the majority shareholder. Why am I doing this? Crossley thought to himself, not for the first or last time. I was brought in to do it, not justify it! It was not my idea!

FOUR

The Snowy Water Inquiry

*I say there are two rivers dying in this country. One is the Snowy
because it hasn't got any water, and the other is the Murray because
it has too much.*

LADY MARIGOLD SOUTHEY, 1999

It rained the second day of the Snowy Water Inquiry's Orbost hearing. It rained as if God was sitting up there with a perverse sense of humour, tipping buckets of water through the clouds. 'I was saturated just getting out of the car,' said East Gippsland Shire councillor Brenda Murray. Minutes earlier, as she went over the bridge at Orbost, she noticed brown froth eddying down the Snowy River and knew it meant a flood on its way.

'I said to the commissioner and his staff that if they wanted to get out of Orbost that night, then they had better leave now. I had my turn speaking and took off straightaway because I did not want to be caught.' But the hearing continued as one citizen after another stood up to explain to the commissioner, Robert Webster, how the Snowy River was dying for lack of water, while the rain hammered down so hard on the roof of the Orbost Men's Club that it almost drowned out their voices.

'I can't remember anyone making the glib comment, "What are you talking about — look at it outside!" — but it must have run through their minds,' said Eric Sjerp, East Gippsland Shire's environmental planner who presented the council's submission.

The irony was not lost on the commissioner, but he was no fool. Michael Egan chose wisely when he appointed Robert Webster to the inquiry. Egan was friendly with Webster, a moderate Liberal parliamentarian who retired in the 1995 election. Webster was also Energy Minister way back in 1993, when corporatisation was first mooted, so was familiar with the issues. As a Liberal, Webster would be acceptable to the irrigation lobby. He'd also had a good working relationship with his interstate ministerial counterparts, Victorian Treasurer Alan Stockdale and Commonwealth Energy and Resources Minister, Senator Warwick Parer.

The inquiry would run for six months, from April to October 1998. Its budget was $2.8 million. Webster was to come up with costed options for improving the health of all rivers that the scheme affected, taking into account the impacts on commercial viability and stakeholders such as farmers. Significantly, Webster was not asked to make any recommendations, because this might limit the ultimate position adopted.

Webster was determined to conduct an independent, objective and transparent inquiry. Six weeks before the inquiry officially started, he spent two days in a helicopter looking around the hydro scheme. He finished the tour by flying with Paul Leete down the Snowy River to the coast, where he stopped for a chat with the Snowy River Alliance and an old political friend, Peter Nixon. 'It was beautiful weather and hot, and it gave me a perspective of the scale of the scheme,' Webster said. 'I would have loved to restore all of the river as it was before 1949, which some of the old people in Orbost wanted. The reality was it wasn't going to happen, but my goal was to get something good.'

Webster also visited the irrigation districts, to establish rapport there. His terms of reference stipulated the irrigators must not be disadvantaged, but, equally, 'I made it clear I would do everything I could to find as much water as I could for the rivers. I had a big enough understanding to know we could achieve some water savings because I knew how inefficient and wasteful the irrigation system was. We weren't empowered to opine on irrigation practices, but anyone with an open mind could see the huge wastage, like flood irrigation to grow pasture to fatten lambs.'

Public participation and consultation were a priority. Six formal public hearings were scheduled for Cooma, Orbost, Deniliquin, Griffith, Cobram and Swan Hill. Informal meetings and contacts complemented the formal hearings by constantly taking the temperature of community. Webster was particularly alert to disillusionment with the inquiry's approach. 'I wanted absolute transparency — to get out among the people so that they could have a say, and present their submissions, and no one felt like they couldn't make their point,' he said.

He also assembled specialist teams to analyse environmental, social and economic factors. These were then synthesised to model what might be expected from different flow regimes. The teams were drawn from various bodies, including the University of NSW, Australian National University, the NSW Department of Land and Water Conservation, and economic consultants, ACIL. Geoff Chambers, Victoria's Snowy project manager, was seconded to work as operations manager for the inquiry. Derek Rutherford from the NSW EPA was also seconded to work for Webster.

Webster quickly identified several possible water sources: reducing the water available to irrigators; recovering lost and wasted water; changing how water was managed within the scheme; and, finally, using water from the 1000-gigalitre 'above-target' reserve.

As the inquiry progressed, Webster came to see his task as making fundamental trade-offs in a clash of national icons: the Snowy River, the Snowy Mountains scheme and the inland irrigation miracle.

⟿

The Snowy River is a good example of how people's sense of place and landscape can drive conservation works. It was a kitchen table revolution in that most difficult decisions are made by people sitting around tables with a cup of tea. In terms of fundamental change, you do have to sit around a table and decide what to do.

MIKE GOOEY, EXECUTIVE OFFICER, SNOWY-GENOA
CATCHMENT MANAGEMENT COMMITTEE

The Snowy River campaign was officially launched at a rally in Dalgety on 14 March 1998. Actually, it was at least the fourth time the campaign was launched but luckily the media has a short memory and loves a spectacle, especially on a slow news weekend.

The launch took place on the International Day of Action for Rivers. Fran Kelly from the Total Environment Centre struck gold in drumming up celebrity support: Tom Burlinson, the actor who played Jim Craig, *the* Man from Snowy River, agreed to be guest speaker. 'I implore the New South Wales, Victorian and Commonwealth governments to bring the river back,' he told more than 250 people on the banks of the Snowy. 'It's a shameful legacy to leave to our children and grandchildren. Now is the time to listen to the experts — the Snowy River must flow again!'

He shouted the slogan again and again, echoed by the crowd holding a huge blue banner with the words in large white letters. Carl Drury, ever resourceful, found the banner at the Jindabyne tip; it was an old roadside advertising strip from one of the ski resorts. He bought it for $25 and took it down to the Dalgety caravan park, where he and Paul Leete painted it. The banner was a familiar backdrop in media events over the next few years.

Tom Burlinson made his speech sitting astride a fine dun pony, flanked by real horsemen and women from the Snowy River country. One of them was Dick Suthern. He spoke about the irony of being forced to buy winter fodder from the Riverina, where it was cultivated with water diverted from

Actor Tom Burlinson reprising his role as Jim Craig, the movie Man from
Snowy River, during the March 1998 rally at Dalgety to launch the campaign.
Source: Total Environment Centre, Sydney.

the Snowy. Suthern used to grow his own fodder, but water tables had
dropped too far since the hydro scheme was built. In a symbolic
reclamation of the Snowy River, Burlinson and Native Fish Australia
representative John Johnstone released baby bass, a native species in decline
due to the low flows.

It was a great day, but behind the scenes the Alliance was suffering some
growing pains. They were the inevitable side effect of the campaign
ramping up into a full-blown national affair, with many more voices at the
strategy table. A typical phone hook-up included Alliance committee
members from Dalgety and Orbost, plus affiliates such as the Total
Environment Centre; Environment Victoria; Native Fish Australia; the
South Eastern Conservation Council, Mike Gooey from the Snowy-Genoa
Catchment Management Committee; Eric Sjerp from the East Gippsland
Shire; Chris Barry, CEO of the East Gippsland Catchment Management
Authority; and Tim Fisher from the Australian Conservation Foundation.

New faces like Genevieve Fitzgerald, George Collis and Craig Ingram
breathed fresh life and energy into the Alliance committee, but inevitably
increased the potential for clashes of personality and opinion. Diversity
made the Alliance dynamic, but it also made for lively meetings. An
underlying interstate jealousy added tang to the volatile mix. In late 1997,

each side was suspicious enough of the other that they changed the constitution to stipulate the Alliance executive must have half and half New South Wales and Victorian representatives, so that neither state could make a power grab and take over the campaign. 'The Alliance was an interesting beast,' said Craig Ingram. 'Everyone had the same goal but lots of people had different ideas of how to get there.'

The broadening community and institutional support base created the critical mass needed to give the campaign momentum, but Paul Leete and Max White were anxious to maintain local ownership and control. Environment Victoria's water policy coordinator, Freya Merrick, said White made it clear, without spelling it out, that this campaign was run out of Orbost and Dalgety, with the city-based groups primarily a vehicle for taking the message state-wide.

Leete and White also insisted the message not be diluted by taking on other causes, such as the Tumut River's deterioration. Up high, the hydro scheme left the Tumut riverbed virtually dry. Further down, the riverbed and banks were torn to pieces because state authorities released the water in a torrent from Blowering dam for irrigation. But when Carl Drury said the Tumut landholders wanted to join the campaign, the attitude was, 'Okay — so long as they only support the Snowy River rather than push their own agenda.'

Nor would Leete, Max White or Jo Garland compromise for the sake of other dying rivers. The Australian Conservation Foundation's Tim Fisher got involved in the Snowy campaign primarily to ensure the Snowy River did not get water at the expense of hard-won environmental allocations proposed for the Murray. 'I was struck by the audacity and naïvety of the campaign,' he said. 'They had this idea the irrigators had plenty of water and they would not miss it — they couldn't grasp the reality of tradeable rights and market competition, that all the water was allocated, and there was not nearly enough left over for the environment.' Fisher believed the Snowy water could only come from irrigators or the Murray.

But the Alliance did not want to hear about the Murray's problems. Its single-mindedness was probably its greatest strength. 'We don't want to take water from the irrigators — we want the water that is wasted,' Garland would reply. Fisher doubted much could be recovered and the costs would be prohibitive. The Alliance did not believe him. 'The Snowy River Alliance is exclusively interested in the Snowy,' Max White would say tartly. Leete backed him up. 'The people on the Snowy River Alliance have got their issues together because they have been working on it for so many years. People with other issues concerning other rivers and creeks should bring up their issues in the same way,' he said.[1]

Money was another rub. Campaigning is expensive and resources were limited. The Alliance and the Dalgety Association raised money from membership dues, selling stickers, running cake stalls and the like, but the few thousand dollars raised went nowhere near covering costs. The Snowy River Improvement Trust and the Snowy-Genoa Catchment Management Committee had helped where possible, but there were limits. Max White nearly had a pink fit when a bill for $2500 arrived for hiring horses for the June 1997 rally in Sydney. He told Genevieve Fitzgerald she should not have spent so much. She was taken aback. While the Trust had not committed to financing the event, Fitzgerald was under the impression White was happy to go along with it for the sake of the publicity. She explained there had not been time to prepare detailed budgets beforehand — the rallies were organised in just two weeks. She said the horses' owner supported the cause and was prepared to wait until the Alliance raised the funds, but White was not mollified. He and Glenice were uncomfortable about the Alliance running up debts on promises.

As often as not, Alliance members covered expenses from their own pocket. Fitzgerald's husband was not impressed when phone bills for $1500 and $1800 began arriving. 'That bloody river,' he would mutter as he pulled the accounts from the envelope and surveyed the quarterly damage. It was the same story in almost every household involved. 'We struggle to pay phone bills, no one gets paid, we beg and borrow as we can — free photocopying from the Lakes and Wilderness Board, and businesses that absorb phone and postage into their accounts,' Fitzgerald wrote to Fran Kelly at the Total Environment Centre when the pair were working out the resources available for the Snowy Water Inquiry.[2]

The NSW Government gave the TEC a grant to counterbalance the deep pockets of the irrigation lobby during the inquiry. The grant paid for a part-time project officer, Leigh Martin, to coordinate the work and research conducted by the Alliance and its affiliates. His job was to gather expert reports, analyse the issues and liaise between the stakeholders. The Alliance also got a $3000 rural grant from the Lance Reichstein Foundation in late 1997 for community education. The grant paid for advertising and a shop display linked to a summer festival in Lakes Entrance in January 1998.

There was plenty of help in kind: the owner of the Surf Dive 'n' Ski chain grew up by the Snowy, and was so moved by the river's plight when contacted by Environment Victoria that he paid for printing 30,000 stickers. The stickers were left on counters in all his stores. The brother of Gil Richardson's wife Heather owned a bus company in the northern suburbs of Melbourne; he put stickers on every bus and got his clients to leave brochures in amenity blocks as they travelled across the country. Walking clubs, field naturalist groups, service clubs and so many others happily distributed brochures among their memberships.

But big money was needed to pay for scientific experts to back up the Alliance in the Snowy Water Inquiry. The Snowy River Improvement Trust helped pay for the 1996 expert panel report, but the Trust was no more by 1998. In June 1997, it was disbanded and its budget subsumed into the larger East Gippsland Catchment Management Authority, based in Bairnsdale. The chief executive officer, Chris Barry, provided some assistance, but the Alliance was in desperate need of a benefactor. In late 1997, Fitzgerald drew up a list of philanthropic foundations and began writing funding applications. She sent one to Michael Liffman, an executive officer with The Myer Foundation, which had its genesis in the philanthropic legacy of Sidney Myer, the patriarch of one of Melbourne's foremost establishment families.

The Myer Foundation is committed to community development. 'Part of our work is not just to write cheques, but we like to visit and follow up the organisations we support,' said Lady Marigold Southey, Sidney Myer's youngest daughter. In that capacity, the Foundation was already active in Orbost through the Women of the Snowy River. This group formed in April 1997 in a bid to lift the sullen mood gripping the town. At the time, Orbost was a divided, suspicious community. Unemployment was rife, with jobs falling victim to the inexorable decline of the town's two main industries, agriculture

Melbourne buses take the cause to the city streets. *Source: Snowy River Alliance.*

and timber. Violent clashes between timber workers and greenies had been in the headlines for too long, giving the region an ugly reputation. The Kennett Government's ruthless cutbacks in health, education, social services and local government exacerbated the town's sense of hopelessness and helplessness.

The Women of the Snowy River arose out of a regional workshop for rural women. The workshop was aimed at developing a sense of communal unity. One of the movers and shakers was artist and musician, the late Therese Shead. She had a gift for bringing disparate people together and healing rifts. She also loved her town and hated the angry undercurrents eating at its heart. She was not alone. Women flocked to the group. 'One of the most important things for me in this group was the breakdown of barriers, because it did not matter who you were — a greenie, a timber worker, a vegetable grower, or Indigenous. Everyone put in and made some effort, and we knew if we pulled together, we would be flying,' said one member, Lorraine Craigie.

The group decided to do an arts project highlighting an issue of concern to all. They chose the Snowy River. Thirty women designed and constructed a mosaic pathway depicting past, present and future ideals for the river. The path is a beautiful thing, winding up the hill in Forest Park on the edge of town. 'People just came in and laid some tiles whenever they had a spare hour or so,' said Ruth Hanson, a bright-eyed woman who overcame local suspicions about her green leanings to win respect for her devotion to reviving Orbost.

'The river is why we are all here and why the area was settled in the first place,' said dairy farmer Mary McDonald. 'If we can't have a healthy river, then the town won't be here for long.' McDonald and Hanson both went on to represent the Women of the Snowy River on the Alliance executive; the group became integral in the campaign, organising events and rallying the broader East Gippsland community to the cause.

The Myer Foundation provided a grant for the pathway under its community leadership program. Its program director, Helen Morris, came to Orbost for the official opening on a Saturday in November 1997. Max White and Gil Richardson went to the event, and McDonald introduced them to Morris. White returned home with Morris's card and an appointment in her office in Melbourne a few days later.

Morris said she was flat-out busy and did not really have the time to see the Whites, but she found the pair irresistible. Max's sometimes gruff exterior belies his dry sense of humour, while Morris was impressed by Glenice's gentle, firm way of talking. Their half-hour meeting stretched into two hours. Morris said she was bowled over by the Whites' stories about the Snowy Mountains scheme, the plight of the Snowy River, the years and years they had spent writing letters, making phone calls, traipsing to meetings and just trying to be heard. 'I thought, these are amazing people — I just could not ignore them. They weren't tearful, but there was this sense of despair about them.'

Morris explained The Myer Foundation was a non-partisan organisation. It could not be seen to be involved in political issues, but it could support communities in a way that gave them a voice. Fitzgerald's submission went through an exhaustive approval process, and $24,000 was granted for a scientific study in March 1998. The grant was channelled through Environment Victoria as an umbrella organisation because the Alliance did not have the tax status most philanthropic organisations require.

Some of the Myers were uneasy about the foundation being associated with such a political hot potato, but the convenor of the Science Committee, Phillip Myer, was supportive. He suggested to his aunt, Lady Southey, the Foundation president, that she join him on a flight to look at what they were spending their money on. They took off on 15 May 1998.

Lady Southey was horrified by what she saw. She knew the Snowy from 1956, when she and her first husband enjoyed a camping holiday travelling from Bairnsdale to Jindabyne. 'I remember the roaring river, and I can remember stopping many times to look at it on the way up. One fell in love with the Snowy River right there and then. It moved out of my life for a long, long time, until this day when we flew from the top and followed the river down. I am one of those people who, if I get interested in something, I like to get involved. I think I was personally touched by the fact this magnificent river was dying, it was almost dead, and that just seemed so wrong. I was so utterly shocked this day, I decided we had to do anything we could to help this wonderful group of people who had been working on this for years.'

Lady Southey organised and personally paid for a lunch at Melbourne Town Hall in June 1988, so the Alliance could present its message to 100 of the city's business, community, academic and political leaders. She arranged for Craig Ingram, Genevieve Fitzgerald, Glenice and Max White, and another Alliance member, Ian Moon, to fly from East Gippsland to Melbourne for the event. Paul Leete came down separately from Dalgety.

Fitzgerald said chauffeur-driven limousines met them at the airport. 'We felt like royalty! It was delicious — it was done with such style. We felt we were getting a bit beaten up at that point, and Lady Southey helped us to feel positive.'

The Purple Sage project was being launched at the Town Hall that same day. The project was a joint initiative of the Victorian Women's Trust, the Stegley Foundation, the Brotherhood of St Laurence, the People Together Project, the Victorian Local Governance Association, and YWCA. It sought to repair the gaping rents Jeff Kennett's radical policies had torn in the fabric of community. Purple Sage was active in community building in East Gippsland, and Fitzgerald had had a lot of contact with its organisers. She took it as a good omen to see them there at the Town Hall on this day. 'Another good omen was that it was exactly one year to the day after the horseback rally in Sydney,' she said.

The room upstairs for the Snowy River lunch was plastered with posters, and brochures were placed on every seat. Fitzgerald spoke, followed by Mike Gooey from the Snowy-Genoa Catchment Management Committee, and then Paul Leete against the backdrop of a video showing the Snowy in its glory days and as it was now. 'People who live in the city do not always know what is going on in the bush,' Lady Southey explained. 'Paul Leete spoke very passionately and got everyone so stirred up at the lunch that the people went away all determined to do what they could do. I was surprised what an impact it had.'

Over the next two years, Lady Southey was a staunch supporter. She drove around with a 'Snowy must flow again' sticker on her Mercedes, and took part in media events such as a horseback rally on the steps of Victoria's Parliament House in April 1999. 'This is not about politics, this is about the river,' she said at the time. 'And the science is on the side of the river.'[3]

⌒

On 28 July 1998, at the height of the Snowy Water Inquiry, John Harrowell passed away at his home in Oberon, aged eighty.

⌒

> *I am a brownie, not a greenie. I think when you build hydro schemes and large dams, poor countries go from hand-to-mouth feeding themselves to being able to develop industry and agriculture. But as they become richer, they become obliged to pay back to the environment. Only rich countries can afford to do the right thing by the environment as a matter of course. On that basis, we are a rich country and we are in a position where we have to do the payback.*
>
> Vin Good, Snowy Mountains Authority commissioner/associate commissioner, 1998–2002

David Glasson, from Jimenbuen homestead and a member of the Dalgety and District Community Association, was eloquent in his presentation to the Snowy Water Inquiry hearing in Cooma. 'The Snowy River is part of Australia's heritage,' he said. 'It is a river that is recognised throughout the world as truly "Australian" … We have had visitors from many parts of the world, and all have been excited that we have access to, and a love of, the Snowy River. But all of them, be they from Asia, Europe or the Americas, are horrified that the Snowy River, this image of Australia, this supposedly wild and magnificent river, is barely a trickle consisting of stagnant pools and low-flowing rapids.

'… But even if we ignore the rest of the world — isn't it important that the river be restored to some of its former glory for the people who know the Snowy, the people who love the Snowy, the people who live on the Snowy, the people who farm the country by the Snowy and for the people of Australia? These people are not asking for much — only a "fair go" … We owe it to our children and their children and the following generations that they may have some pleasure in this once mighty river. If we don't do it, who will?'

Glasson detailed how Dalgety, having lost its river, was now losing itself. The town once supported two general stores, a butcher, market gardener, service station, police station, school and a thriving hotel with the highest sales of Red Crown Rum in NSW. It was a mecca for recreational trout fishermen, with the hotel booked out a year in advance. But almost all these facilities were now gone, for sale or under-utilised. Farmers' fortunes reflected Dalgety's decline. Landholders used to be self-sufficient, growing their own hay and winter grain to get livestock through droughts, but the regional water table had dropped since the Snowy was dammed, making it impossible to grow fodder. Over the same thirty years, 60 per cent of winters had been drought-declared. Farmers were now paying $7000 for a truckload of hay and $6000 for a load of grain, imported from inland areas irrigated with the water that used to run past their properties. 'Where will the decline stop?' Glasson asked.[4]

At the Orbost hearing, Heather Richardson told the inquiry that landholders faced considerable expense trying to cope with saltwater creeping up from the estuary. Eroded riverbanks had to be stabilised and revegetated, and farmers were forced to pipe water long distances to replace water from now saline sources. Richardson was a former school teacher from Melbourne who came to Orbost in 1956 and fell in love, first with Gil, and then with the river. Like her husband, the Snowy ran in her veins. 'There is a personal sense of both grief and shame in the community, as we watch the death of this once majestic and powerful river,' she wrote in a submission from the Orbost Women's Awareness Group. 'Its decline in health has added to the social depression pervading the area due to the general rural decline.'[5]

Chris Allen, representing the Moogji Aboriginal Council, told the Snowy Water Inquiry the region needed new industries, but ones based on a healthy river. 'It may cost the government many millions of dollars in support for our declining timber and agricultural industries, but with a healthy flow, it may be possible to boost our tourism, recreational and agricultural industries, with possibly a much reduced monetary outlay from Government,' he said.[6]

Instead, the potentially lucrative tourism industry was going backwards. Mike O'Neill, president of the Snowy River Country Business Tourism and Community Association, said adventure tourism operators and schools were abandoning rafting and canoeing tours. In an economic analysis, one operator with accommodation on the river reported refusing business worth $40,000 in 1998 due to lack of water. Other rafting businesses earned up to $20,000 a week when there was sufficient flow. While persistent drought in the late 1990s took its toll, restoring a flow mimicking the spring snowmelt flush would at least guarantee three months white water a year[7]. In another study, Gillespie Economics estimated visitor days could increase by 136,000, worth up to $4 million in annual business turnover and 82 local jobs.[8]

Robert Webster heard equally impassioned pleas from New South Wales communities along the Murray and Murrumbidgee rivers. One after another, they pleaded they had developed their farms and created prosperous communities on the back of guaranteed water volumes. They argued governments could not now pull the rug from under industries supporting tens of thousands of people, compared with the barely 8000 people living in the Snowy catchment.

Rob Brown represented Murray Valley Voice, a broad alliance of farmers, industry, business and local government. Brown told Webster at the Deniliquin hearing that robbing Peter to pay Paul was poor policy. He said the Snowy scheme's water diluted salt and pollutants in the Murray River, and degradation should not be shifted from one region to another. He said farmers must be compensated if resources were transferred and there must be grassroots community support for any changes.[9]

Change, however, was vigorously resisted. In early 1998, the NSW Government began trying to implement a policy to reduce diversions by 10 per cent in all river basins, to restore environmental flows. The Murrumbidgee basin was an exception, due to over-allocation, chronic water shortages and the Snowy River campaign. Irrigation representatives instead agreed to reduce diversions by 8.5 per cent: 4.5 per cent for the

Murrumbidgee and 4 per cent for the Snowy, in anticipation of the Snowy inquiry's outcome.[10] Unfortunately this in-principle arrangement was lost in the fray before it could be ratified. The NSW irrigation lobby instead exploited the Snowy Water Inquiry to avoid giving up any water at all.

On the ground, attitudes ranged from indifference to hostility. Victorian irrigators enjoyed good water security and so were relatively relaxed about the Snowy Water Inquiry. They displayed so little interest, in fact, that Webster cancelled the Swan Hill hearing, and held just the one in Victoria in Cobram. It was a different story in New South Wales, where more water licences have been issued than there is water in the rivers. Irrigators there are far more insecure and therefore militant. Craig Ingram's wife, Ann-Maree, got into a heated discussion at a store in Deniliquin when the owner realised she and Craig were in town for the inquiry hearing. In another incident, some officials had their car tyres slashed.

Yet privately the Snowy River people found the irrigators by and large to be decent people doing their best. A year later, in 1999, Stuart Hood, Mike Gooey and the rest of the Snowy-Genoa Catchment Management Committee toured the irrigation districts and were impressed by the rice growers' sincere efforts to grow rice using less water. 'We always had good relations with the Murrumbidgee Catchment Management Committee, and we got on very well with them,' said Hood. 'They were very good, very hospitable people and they wanted to show us they were trying to be very efficient. They did not want to lose any water, but they could see we should have an environmental flow. I said we were looking for a win–win outcome.'

The irrigators had an ally in the Murray Darling Basin Commission, the intergovernmental body established to manage land and water in Australia's vast food bowl. The commission did not want the scheme corporatised at all. It said the Snowy Mountains Council historically balanced water security and flexibility for power generation. The council adjusted releases to take account of dry and wet years, and irrigators could 'forward borrow' from the above-target reserve if necessary.[11] As if to illustrate the point, the Commonwealth Energy Minister, Senator Warwick Parer, announced during the Snowy Inquiry an extra 200 gigalitres from the scheme to help farmers struggling to plant crops in the dry conditions.

The commission argued that a corporatised scheme would have an unfair market advantage, because it was in a monopoly position to set prices for water over and above the irrigators' statutory entitlements. The commission also cast doubt on finding water for the Snowy River by recovering water lost through evaporation, seepage and waste. It said reducing diversions to farms or reducing environmental flows in the

Murray Darling Basin were the only sources of water — and both options were unacceptable.

The Snowy Mountains Authority and its new commercial arm, Snowy Hydro Trading, suggested it would be economically and environmentally irresponsible to restore too much water to the Snowy and other montane rivers. 'The impacts of reducing the amount of water available for power generation and irrigation extends beyond simply lost electricity and agriculture revenues,' said Snowy Hydro's chief executive officer, Dr Phil Williams. He claimed, among other things, that more water inevitably meant higher greenhouse emissions, when Australia already risked breaching its obligations under the Kyoto Protocol.[12]

The hydro bodies also claimed consumers would face less choice and higher power prices; irrigators would suffer reduced drought security and higher water prices; jobs and tourism based around the scheme's lakes would be lost; and governments would be stuck with an ongoing burden of management and costs. The authority calculated a maximum 11–13 per cent flow in the Snowy as the best environmental and economic outcome.[13] 'After that the environmental benefits flattened out, but the costs continued to rise through water lost to the scheme,' said Vin Good.

In person, Robert Webster found Snowy Hydro's representatives 'very bureaucratic, putting it kindly'. He did not hide his frustration at the Cooma hearing, at one point taking Good to task. Webster had the impression there was rather a lot of water sitting in reserve, *just in case.* 'In case of what?' he asked Good. The point was whether there might be water to spare for the Snowy River if the above-target water was managed in such a way it did not jeopardise the scheme's commercial potential. Webster said he never got a straight answer.

Good said neither Webster nor the environmentalists wanted to accept the true value of above-target water for the corporatised scheme's viability. 'Above-target water was, and still is, the most valuable water in the scheme because it can be retained across water years, does not have to be released in a specific time period, and underwrites much of the financial contracting and insurance derivatives sold by Snowy Hydro Limited,' Good said. 'The greens and Webster saw the release of this water as an easy fix to the environmental flow problems.'

Webster said he accepted the authority had to keep a certain proportion of water in storage at all times, 'but I wanted to know how often in the past had we ever come near to needing that amount in reserve. They never really answered that to my satisfaction, because I think they had been so used to being a law unto themselves. It was the same with their management plan

— they had essentially a blank piece of paper to run things. So they fudged around.' Webster, however, concluded from the inquiry's own analysis that drawing down the reserve would seriously compromise the scheme's commercial potential. He switched his attention to options for recovering water from the inland irrigation districts.

It is worth unpicking some of the hydro's claims, such as the scheme being vital to Australia's efforts to control greenhouse emissions. This is based on the scheme theoretically displacing 5 million tonnes of greenhouse emissions that would otherwise be released from coal-fired power stations. It sounds like a lot, but actually equates to only about 0.9 per cent of national emissions, which are in the order of 550 million tonnes.[14] Proportionately, 28 per cent flow in the Snowy River would therefore translate to a 0.1 per cent increase in emissions. In other words, if the scheme shut down tomorrow — much less generated slightly less electricity on account of the Snowy River — the difference in national emissions would barely register. This is especially so against a backdrop of surging emissions in the late 1990s caused by the deregulated electricity market favouring coal-fired power.

It is also wrong to assume coal-fired power is the only alternative to hydro-electricity, and therefore would fill the supposed gap in supply. The scheme's main value is its capacity to be switched on and off quickly to meet spikes in demand, whereas coal power stations take twenty-four hours to come on line. It is doubtful coal would fill this important niche if the scheme's capacity were diminished. The deregulated national electricity market has seen the advent of new, low-polluting, quick-start sources such as gas turbines. It can also be expected that, with appropriate government support, wind, solar and other clean power technologies will continue to expand and offset the need for more coal-fired power.[15]

Another debateable point is whether environmental flows would render the scheme commercially unviable. Various estimates were made over the years, and often exaggerated. For example, the Commonwealth claimed in 2000 that a 28 per cent flow in the Snowy River would reduce the value of the scheme in the order of $1.5 billion. However, this figure assumed the worst: that the water would come from the above-target reserve, the most valuable in the scheme. By comparison, reducing assured releases for irrigation would only cost $250–400 million over the forseeable future.[16]

A 28 per cent flow would reduce average power production by about 11.5 per cent,[17] but the amount of water the scheme has at its disposal does not alone determine profitability. Other factors come into play, such as the ability of managers to read the market to sell power at premium prices and to capitalise on the asset value of above-target water in the ways described above by Vin Good. Snowy Hydro's excellent net profits since corporatisation — $158.8 million in 2004 — rather prove this point.[18]

The starting point for corporatisation is its real problem: the determination to maintain the status quo and repay the construction debt. It was generally accepted even in the early 1990s that the scheme would never be built today, in more environmentally enlightened times, so why perpetuate the mistakes of the past by maintaining the status quo? Why not scale the scheme down to something more environmentally sustainable, but still commercially viable? But these questions were not even repeated in the central halls of government, much less answered. Instead, financial imperatives related to power production drove the process, and the opportunity to investigate the sustainability of the more valuable, scarce resource — water — was lost.

⌒

A couple of us met some government workers in the foyer of this plush hotel on our way into the stakeholder meetings Marie Tehan organised for the Snowy Water Inquiry. The workers were having a chat, and we stopped to say hi and have a bit of a yarn. One of the Natural Resources workers, a bureaucrat, but a friendly one, shook her head, saying: 'You guys are mad. You're taking on Goliath. It's impossible.' I remember laughing and saying, 'But didn't David win?'

GENEVIEVE FITZGERALD

Not everyone engaged in the Snowy Water Inquiry as might be expected. Robert Webster was surprised not to see or hear from David Treasure, the National Party member for the state seat of Gippsland East. Treasure put his name to a joint submission supporting 28 per cent with Phil Davis and Peter Hall, his coalition colleagues in Gippsland, but that was the limit of his advocacy. 'Most of the National Party MPs and Libs turned up and gave evidence,' Webster said. 'The one who did not was David Treasure. I never saw him. He never uttered a word. I still would not know him. Craig Ingram and his wife came to all the hearings, and I got to know them, but I never saw this guy David Treasure — and he had the greatest to lose out of it.'

The Victorian Government was also notable by its absence. New South Wales' inter-agency working party was too divided to submit an all-of-government position. Instead, each agency was free to make its own submission, provided it made no recommendations that might be interpreted as where the government stood. Treasury subsequently made a submission focused on the scheme's financial viability, while Brett Miners, Derek Rutherford and Graeme Enders pulled together a submission for New South Wales' natural resource agencies, with contributions from many colleagues, including Lorraine Oliver, Alistair Grinbergs, Mark Adams, Robyn Bevill and a Canadian in the New South Wales EPA, Catherine Lipsett.

They drew heavily on the 1996 expert panel report, but sensing that a 28 per cent flow was a 'bridge too far' for the NSW Government, Miners convened a two-day lock-up with Dr Sam Lake from Monash University and Dr John Harris at the Fisheries Research Centre in Cronulla. They reviewed the expert panel recommendations and determined that 22 per cent was the absolute minimum critical threshold to restore the Snowy to a semblance of its former self — but every percentage point drop below 28 per cent greatly increased the risk the river would not recover.

Victoria, on the other hand, decided on an all-of-government submission. The Environment and Natural Resources Minister, Marie Tehan, wanted a government position that reflected community as well as bureaucratic views, so she invited the Snowy River people to join irrigation representatives in consultative stakeholder meetings.

The Whites, Gil Richardson, Genevieve Fitzgerald and Craig Ingram attended the meetings, on 1 and 18 May 1998. Chris Barry from the East Gippsland Catchment Management Authority and Eric Sjerp from the East Gippsland Shire also attended. All were shocked to discover that as far as the state water officials and irrigation representatives were concerned, the Snowy was a done deal.

Unknown to the Alliance, the Victorian Government had convened a multi-stakeholder committee to examine how to implement the 1994 COAG water reforms. The Murray Water Entitlements Committee, chaired by National Party MP for Swan Hill, Barry Steggall, included Tim Fisher from the Australian Conservation Foundation as well as irrigation interests. Its job was to work out bulk entitlements for all water users, including the environment.

After two and a half years of information gathering, analysis and negotiation, the committee released a report called *Sharing the Murray* in October 1997. It proposed allocating water for environmental flows, including a token 33 gigalitres a year to the Snowy River. This meant a flow of about 5 per cent. If New South Wales contributed in the same proportions as its three-quarter share of the scheme's irrigation water, then the flow could be brought up to 15 per cent. The Victorian Farmers Federation supported 15 per cent in its submission to the Snowy Water Inquiry.

Sharing the Murray assumed no water could be gained through plugging leaks in the system and more efficient irrigation practices. Instead, it proposed shaving 8 per cent from irrigators' entitlements, and creating fewer floods in the ecologically stressed Barmah Forest. Steggall said the Snowy's allocation was based on what could be 'reasonably' spared from the Murray River. He saw it as a generous gesture by communities that legally did not have to give any water back.

'It was always recognised that the Snowy got a bit overdrawn,' Steggall said later. 'We always had trouble with the Snowy people's 1 per cent claim, because the river still had 50 per cent going out to sea compared with the Murray's 15 or 20. But we also felt something should be done to help the people at the top of the Snowy, where there is not much flow.'

The Alliance felt ambushed. Max White wrote to Marie Tehan to complain about the irrigators' antagonism when the Alliance refused to accept the *Sharing the Murray* outcome. 'It could have been a more fruitful meeting had we prior access to documents and been invited to attend prior to discussions,' he wrote.[19]

Relations were further strained at the Snowy Water Inquiry's Cobram hearing. Barry Steggall showed Robert Webster the *Sharing the Murray* report, and told the commissioner in so many words that this was all the Snowy River was ever going to get, so there was no point considering anything else. Ingram was at the hearing and accused Steggall of bullying Webster and the Alliance. Steggall said he was the injured party, enduring ridicule and abuse for not giving the Snowy River more water. 'We were hurt because, without being asked, we put up a proposition to include the Snowy River. It put back the sincerity of what we were trying to do in the Murray, and then the anti-feeling to the Snowy River people grew.'

The Victorian Department of Natural Resources and Environment drafted a submission out of the meetings, but it never saw the light of day. According to rumour, the submission recommended a 15 per cent flow, but was blocked in Cabinet by the Deputy Premier, Pat McNamara, who said it was too much. Truth is, the report never made it as far as Cabinet. It landed on Marie Tehan's desk and stayed there. She said she did not take it further because she was appalled that it looked no further into the issues than *Sharing the Murray*.

'I knew the Snowy was an iconic issue potentially — it had the potential to become another Franklin in time,' Tehan said. 'I had had a meeting with a group of people from East Gippsland who spoke terribly convincingly and passionately about the river and the problems it was going through. It led to me flying up there, and I had been holding the line for something substantial in negotiations with Treasury. It would have been appalling for me to then put up 6 per cent in the submission when the people wanted 28 per cent.'

But in the vacuum, the Snowy River Alliance got the impression that East Gippsland's view counted for nothing with the Victorian Government.

⌒

Other mums run away with other men. My mum ran away with a river.

TANZY OWEN, GENEVIEVE FITZGERALD'S DAUGHTER

In the closing months of the Snowy Water Inquiry, Fran Kelly at the Total Environment Centre devised a detailed strategy with Genevieve Fitzgerald to build up public pressure.[20] Webster's final report was due in October 1998, and the NSW Government had signalled it wanted a decision through Parliament in November. Kelly and Fitzgerald wanted to persuade politicians there was strong community support for a meaningful environmental flow. The plan included recruiting talkback radio volunteers; letter writing; calling on MPs; drumming up funding from recreation groups, the major parties and corporations; finding outlets for brochures and posters; stalls in major suburban centres; and celebrity endorsements from the likes of Clean-Up Australia's Ian Kiernan and actress Sigrid Thornton.

The campaign would culminate in a media blitz in the last four weeks, maximising exposure with separate press releases from the TEC, the Alliance, the Dalgety Association and Environment Victoria. Mike Gooey scored a media coup when he arranged a visit by renowned British ecologist David Bellamy. Professor Bellamy, a media favourite, would tour the Snowy and attend one of Lady Southey's high-powered Town Hall lunches just days before Robert Webster handed down his final report. *60 Minutes* also screened an exclusive report on Bellamy and the Snowy River on the Sunday night before.

It was a great strategy, but the campaign's limited resources were running out. The Total Environment Centre spent $3000 it did not have on printing 27,500 leaflets, which it gave away to recreation groups, universities, unions and Rotary clubs. The Alliance still had a few thousand dollars in the kitty, but not nearly enough to cover all the demands. The committee was exhausted. The pace had hardly let up since early 1996. Members were working on the campaign virtually full-time while trying to hold down jobs and manage families, but so much was happening it was still hard to keep track of it all. Strong personalities rubbed raw against each other under the strain.

Money was always a contentious issue, particularly between Genevieve Fitzgerald and Max White. Fitzgerald was incandescent with energy and fabulous publicity ideas; the others dubbed her the V8, powerful but expensive to run. Max and Glenice White appreciated Fitzgerald's talent for fundraising, for writing submissions to philanthropic organisations and her great ideas, but they also felt she was inclined to spend money too freely and to rush off getting things done off her own bat.

'We have tried to work ever since the Alliance started on a consensus basis, but you get people doing their own thing and that makes things difficult,' said Glenice White. 'It is the same on every committee. It is very unusual to have people involved in a voluntary capacity on a committee last as long as the Alliance. Most fizzle out because it is too hard to cope with the issues and the people. But you have to keep the organisation credible, and to do that you can't have people going off and doing their own thing. The argument as far as the Alliance was concerned was that we did not have a lot of money to play with.'

Fitzgerald, on the other hand, felt the Alliance could do more to amplify its message and engage the broader public, using more direct action along the lines devised with Kelly. 'I just kept encouraging them to let the rest of Australia know — using the media and community events,' she said. Fitzgerald also believed the Alliance could do a lot more to help itself raise more money. She identified twenty foundations as potential friendly sources, and said many organisations offered help, especially after Lady Southey's Town Hall lunch in June 1998. The catch was the Alliance had to register with the Tax Office, but Max and the Alliance's Treasurer at the time, Rob Melville, were reluctant for obscure reasons. The Myer Foundation got around the problem by channelling its grants through Environment Victoria, but some Alliance members were not comfortable about Environment Victoria taking a small administrative commission.

The arguments over money and strategy got a little out of hand. Max White, a stickler for due process, warned Paul Leete that his authority as chairman was being undermined. Leete was sick of turmoil in Orbost, and wondered if relative newcomers like Fitzgerald, George Collis and Craig Ingram appreciated how much effort he had put in over the years. He called a crisis meeting at the Orbost United Church hall on 1 September 1998. Max White, Gil Richardson, Ingram, Collis, Chris Allen and Orbost farmer David Adams attended. Fitzgerald learned of the meeting afterwards.

Leete announced he was resigning, saying, 'If you want me to continue, then you have to re-elect me, and if you do, I do not want any more of this shit.' He was re-elected as chairman unanimously. They then discussed the protocol for expenditure. Leete thought the matter was settled without ambiguity. 'So, we are all clear that no one, bar no one, is to spend any money without prior agreement of an Alliance meeting?' he said. The others all nodded and the discussion moved on to the Fishing Show and Great Outdoors Expo coming up in Melbourne on 15–18 October 1998. It promised the campaign priceless public exposure.

A few weeks later, Craig Ingram rang Leete to let him know all hell had broken loose in Orbost again. Fitzgerald had ordered 40,000 pamphlets to hand out at the Expo. She discussed it with Collis and Ingram first, while the three were working on posters for the stall. The two men thought it was a good idea, but Ingram did not expect her to order so many. Christ, where are we going to get the money for this? he thought, as he called Max White and Leete to tell them what had happened.

White was very upset. 'We didn't even get to see them first, Paul! You have got to kick her out,' he told Leete over the telephone. Leete was stunned. He called another crisis committee meeting on 24 October 1998. 'I thought we made this clear,' he said. 'No one is to spend any money without the approval of the rest of the committee.'

Fitzgerald said in her defence that the brochures were needed in a hurry for the Expo. The Total Environment Centre had only 900 of its 27,500 leaflets left, and they did not include the Alliance or any Victorians as a contact. She said she was offered a good deal on bulk printing for $1600, with a promise to accept payment whenever the Alliance could afford it. Max White said the Alliance had to be able to pay bills to maintain credibility, and Collis and Ingram were out of order giving Fitzgerald the nod because they knew the rules. Collis thought too much was being made of a minor transgression. 'It would have been a disaster if we had nothing to hand out at the Expo,' he said later. 'We got thousands of signatures and gave away thousands of brochures. It was one of the most successful things we ever did, with national and international exposure. To me it was not a big deal, and we had to do it anyway.'

When Fitzgerald escaped with a roasting, White was so frustrated he went home and resigned. Fitzgerald had had enough. Bruised and burnt out, she began to withdraw, retreating to her family whom she had barely seen in eighteen months. One condition for reconciling with her estranged husband was giving up the Snowy River Alliance. White was coaxed back into the Alliance after Fitzgerald resigned in mid-November 1998.[21]

It was the beginning of the end for Paul Leete, too — he just took longer to realise it.

They all knew the impact of the Snowy River's water for the people of Australia, but they have no idea of its importance to the people of the Snowy River. Why shouldn't the water be as important to us as it is to the people of western New South Wales? What gives them the right? The people of western New South Wales had no water rights because lots of them had no river running near them. The people on the Snowy River lost their riparian right to water so these people in western New South Wales could have riparian rights. It was crazy to think they couldn't let some go — it has been only forty years, which is nothing.

GLENICE WHITE

When Robert Webster submitted his final report to the NSW and Victorian governments on 23 October 1998, he was satisfied his team had explored every nook and cranny in a tangle of complex issues. The inquiry examined twenty-four flow options for all montane rivers affected by the scheme, including flow regimes from 0 to 40 per cent in the Snowy River below Jindabyne. It received 489 submissions, listened to more than 100 presentations at public hearings, and did some innovative modelling to predict how different flow scenarios would affect the scheme, its rivers and the communities who lived by them.

The final report had seven composite options, with flows in the Snowy River ranging from 6 per cent to 25 per cent. The former would stop the river deteriorating any further; the latter would deliver ecological benefits right down to the Orbost flats. The costs ranged from $45 million to $343 million. The benefits ranged from none to $61 million.

The Snowy River Alliance and environment groups were devastated that all seven options stopped short of 28 per cent, but the real shock was Webster's recommendation of one above all others. He recommended Option D, which would add 140 gigalitres to the Snowy River and bring its flow up to 15 per cent.

The estimated cost was $194 million. This included $42 million to find the water, $41 million in works to offset an assumed increase in greenhouse emissions, $54 million for coal-fired power to replace the lost hydro-electricity, and $27 million to enlarge the outlet at Jindabyne dam. This compared with an estimated $45 million in benefits, mainly through increased canoeing/rafting opportunities and recreational fishing.

This option was attractive because potentially it did not affect irrigators at all. The inquiry identified 135 gigalitres that might be recovered by plugging leaks in irrigation channels in the Murray/Murrumbidgee system. There were substantial uncertainties — no one had ever tried to recover water on this scale before — so as an extra safeguard, Webster recommended that flows in the Snowy only be increased once savings were verified. Ecologically, 15 per cent was the point where additional benefits began to level out, but it also meant perpetuating a degree of degradation.

Webster's report warned that if the savings could not be achieved, and irrigation diversions were reduced instead, the economic impact would be $25 million per 50 gigalitres. It also warned that competition for the savings would be intense, 'with strong efforts made to keep the water to the west in order to ease pressure to reduce diversions to meet environmental needs or to expand irrigation developments'.[22] It predicted the necessary infrastructure works would take three to five years.

Webster said he took the key factors into account: a significant environmental gain for the rivers; a significant reduction in wasted irrigation water; minimal impacts on agriculture; a manageable impact on power generation; and a reasonable capital cost to government.

He said later he took it upon himself to make a recommendation, even though he was not asked, because he thought if he did not, the governments would not be getting the full benefit of the inquiry's groundbreaking research and analysis. 'I informed the minister, but no one tried to talk me out of it,' he said. 'It was really me as an ex-politician and someone who has always been known to see positive solutions. We got so close to this issue — we did some exciting work, and we came up with a recommendation that was reasonably cost efficient and really could change the health of the river. But at the time, I don't think my recommendation of 15 per cent pleased anyone.'

That is an understatement.

Christ, he's put a ceiling on the most we can hope to get, thought Paul Leete in frustrated consternation. He had put his heart and soul into writing the Alliance's comprehensive submission, and thought its case inarguable.

Damn, he wasn't supposed to do that! thought David Crossley, dismayed that Webster had effectively put a floor under the least the Snowy might get. Personally, he thought it was quite a good recommendation — 'It gave everyone something' — but the NSW Treasury was appalled. 'I don't think that anyone would eventually have accepted to have no flow. It was accepted that there would have to be some, although the preference was for none from Treasury. They just wanted to keep it as low as possible,' said Crossley.

The Snowy River Alliance rallies on horseback through the streets of Melbourne in January 1999, appealing to the Victorian Premier Jeff Kennett to oppose the 15 per cent flow recommended in the 1998 Snowy Water Inquiry. *Source: Snowy River Alliance.*

The Premier, Bob Carr, on the other hand, said when interviewed six years later that Webster's recommendation was disappointing — 'a bit on the low side'.

The NSW land and water agencies and the Snowy River Alliance struggled with how to respond. The Alliance felt Webster had treated its claim for 28 per cent as an ambit rather than a carefully considered position based on good science. Even the inquiry's own scientific reference panel concluded at least 25 per cent was needed to restore the river's length. The Alliance and its affiliates were encouraged by reports that the NSW Environment Minister, Pam Allen, was trying to stop the government setting its position before December, when Parliament rose. Her Victorian counterpart, Marie Tehan, reportedly still supported 28 per cent, but Eric Sjerp, from the East Gippsland Shire also pointed out that unfortunately, 'this is not a whole-of-government position'.[23]

Tim Fisher from the Australian Conservation Foundation argued that the Alliance should adopt a fallback position. Mike Gooey from the Snowy-Genoa Catchment Management Committee said they should hold the line on 28 per cent because it had ecological integrity, being the figure supported in three scientific studies. Max White agreed the Alliance should not get caught in the trap of horse-trading on flows. White and Gooey prevailed and the Alliance began to work out what it might do next. 'The [NSW] election in March offers a lot of possibilities,' Fran Kelly from the Total Environment Centre suggested. 'Peter Cochran has resigned, which turns Monaro into a potential marginal seat.'[24]

The NSW Government formed an inter-agency taskforce to thrash out a common position. 'After months of meetings and arguments it became obvious to everyone, as Webster said at the start, that we had a political problem here,' said Brett Miners. 'We would never resolve it at agency level — it had to be resolved politically. It was time to look at the politics and see where everyone was sitting.'

A couple of weeks before Christmas 1998, the taskforce had a fiery meeting. Senior representatives for Treasury and the Department of Land and Water Conservation argued that 15 per cent was the ceiling, and advocated 6 per cent. Miners was devastated; he had briefed the advisor to his minister, Richard Amery, and so had hoped his department would take the environmental line. Representatives for National Parks and the Environment Protection Authority argued 15 per cent was the floor, and the government could not go lower. 'It was a depressing meeting, with everyone trying to read the politics, and Treasury just rolling everything. We were battered and bruised because our best environmental arguments were shot down because they would all cost New South Wales x-squillion dollars,' said Miners.

Laurie Brown, an advisor to Premier Bob Carr, came in late and sat listening for a few minutes. 'The Premier is thinking something like 22 per cent,' he said as soon as he could get a word in. The meeting fell silent. 'I've got to go — I have another meeting,' said Brown, and he was gone as suddenly and mysteriously as he had appeared.

Where did this position come from? Bob Carr was, of course, regularly briefed on the slow progress of corporatising the scheme, but as far as anyone in the room knew, the Premier had not taken a personal interest in flows. Bob Carr himself cannot remember ever being told that 22 per cent was the absolute lowest threshold identified in the natural resource agencies' submission, but the message obviously got through. It might have been a memo from Pam Allan, a casual chat with Ian Macdonald in the halls of Parliament, or somehow filtered up through the bureaucracy from the regional offices. It did not matter. Miners and other Snowy sympathisers in the room knew then that the political game was about to begin.

FIVE

Getting Political

Craig, you are going to have to start wearing a tie, mate.

GRAHAM PIKE, ORBOST, 1999

'Pat McNamara is coming to open the new water treatment plant on Friday,' Chris Allen said. It was Tuesday, 18 May 1999.

'If Pat McNamara is coming here on Friday, then we should have a protest,' said Heather Richardson. Heather and her husband, Gil, usually eschewed anything that remotely smacked of activism, but after battling for more than a decade and getting nowhere, they were open to trying anything. 'If you have a case and really believe in it, then you do what you have to do, don't you?' she said later. 'We believed in this.'

Allen was delighted with Richardson's desire to stir things up. He was tired of being nice and well behaved, writing letters and sending delegations to fruitless meetings with politicians and public servants. A visit by the Deputy Premier and leader of the National Party would be a rare opportunity to get close to a senior minister inside Premier Jeff Kennett's ivory tower.

Richardson put out the call, and rallied the troops with the help of the Women of the Snowy River. They called it a community breakfast rather than a protest rally, so as not to put people off. More than 200 managed to turn up despite the extremely short notice. They were a mixed bunch: farmers, loggers, greenies from Goongerah, school students and business people. Everyone pitched in to make it a memorable occasion. Lynette Greenwood, one of the Women of the Snowy River group, remembers being up at dawn on 21 May 1999, taping posters on every second tree lining the road from the airport at Marlo into Orbost. '28%' in dark blue print on white paper must have flashed past Pat McNamara 200 times before he reached the gates to the water treatment plant.

The Snowy River Alliance pressed East Gippsland's Member of Parliament, David Treasure, to arrange a meeting with the Deputy Premier. The only times free were in the car to and from the airport. Craig Ingram and Max White duly met McNamara at the plane, and rode with him in the car to Orbost. 'Craig was in his black suit and shiny shoes, and so was I,' said White. 'We were both done up to the nines and looking very important, and so different from usual.'

They barely got past the pleasantries before arriving at the water treatment plant. McNamara's visit was supposed to be low-key. Just the unveiling of a plaque, a short speech and some small talk with a handful of local dignitaries before flying back to the city. The last thing the organisers expected was a noisy crowd blocking the gates into the plant, waving handwritten placards. They read 'No water, no fish', 'Snowy River — Our National Treasure Must Flow Again' and 'We could become marginal too!' — a reference to independents Russell Savage and Susan Davies wresting Mildura and Gippsland West from the government. Jeff Kennett had dismissed the results as an aberration.

McNamara's minders offered to rush him in the back way to avoid running the gauntlet of the protesters. The Deputy Premier thought that was a bit over the top, and they drove through the front gates. The VIPs inside nearly shook the hands off Ingram and White, mistaking them for part of McNamara's entourage. 'They were so pleased to meet us, kept saying what a wonderful day it was,' White said. 'We were flabbergasted — they did not even ask who we were!' Meanwhile, the 200 people outside the wire chain-link fence sang and made speeches, drowning out the official proceedings. Eventually, McNamara invited the crowd to join the twenty-five official and two unofficial invitees inside for a friendly natter over a cup of tea and cake.

The people said they wanted good news on the Snowy River. Therese Shead and the other singers moved over to give McNamara the microphone on the back of Gil Richardson's tray truck. McNamara gave no commitments, saying Victoria was waiting for advice from New South Wales as the majority shareholder. 'There was a general feeling that the minister was no friend of the lower Snowy River,' reported the *Snowy River Mail*. 'However, the gathering continued in good spirits and the Deputy Premier mingled with the crowd and answered many questions.'[1]

McNamara's good spirits evaporated in the car driving back to Marlo airport. David Treasure was driving. In the back seat were Ingram, Mary McDonald from the Women of the Snowy River, and Brenda Murray, now the mayor of East Gippsland Shire.

Ingram cut to the chase after going through the scientific basis for the claim. 'We want 28 per cent, and we want the government to push that position with New South Wales.'

'No,' McNamara replied. 'We support improved health in the Snowy, but we don't think 28 per cent is feasible.' He said the starting point was 15 per

Victorian deputy Premier, Pat McNamara, addressing an impromptu protest staged in Orbost in May 1999. Thirty minutes later, he scoffed at Snowy River Alliance threats to run an independent candidate if the government did not commit to a 28 per cent flow. *Photo: George Collis.*

cent, based on the 1997 *Sharing the Murray* report, the Snowy Water Inquiry and consulting irrigators. The government believed that was a balanced outcome. It was the first time a minister had said where the government stood.

'We are not talking about taking water from irrigators,' Ingram replied. 'We think there is more than enough water being wasted to put 28 per cent back in the Snowy River.'

'What happens if we don't agree with you? What will you do?' McNamara said.

'Well, we can go legal or political,' said Ingram. 'We can lodge a legal challenge to the hydro scheme, or take you on politically and run an independent candidate in East Gippsland.'

'If you want to achieve anything, you have to be in government,' the Deputy Premier snapped. 'David Treasure is a part of the government and he is putting your view. Independents cut no ice in Parliament. You'll get nothing if you don't have a member in government.'

'You won't achieve anything if you start losing safe National seats,' snapped back Ingram, as Treasure turned the car into Marlo airport. Ingram winked at McDonald sitting beside him. 'He had the biggest grin on his face — Craig was having a great time, but you could have cut the air inside the car with a knife — it was icy,' recalled McDonald.

'McNamara just laughed at us,' Murray said. 'I told him we would never let this drop, we would never give in. But he was scornful and wrote us off.'

In retrospect, McNamara thinks he may have been too blunt and dismissive, but then, 'this was all in the climate where TabCorp had [Opposition Leader] Steve Bracks at 50/1 odds to win office. I thought I should put $1000 on it, but the minders did not think that would be a good headline, that the Deputy Premier backed Labor to win'.

The paramount corporatisation project manager, David Crossley, remembers Victoria maintaining a fairly consistent position over the years: just corporatise the scheme as cheaply as possible without giving any water to the Snowy River. After the Snowy Water Inquiry, 'the Victorian bureaucrats reluctantly supported 15 per cent', Crossley said.

Fifteen per cent was relatively easy for Victoria to support. On the basis that the state was entitled to one-quarter of the irrigation water released from the scheme, then Victoria was responsible for coming up with one-quarter of an environmental flow in the Snowy. Victoria's one-quarter share of 15 per cent equated to roughly the 33 gigalitres already earmarked in the 1997 *Sharing the Murray* report. Whether or not New South Wales could, or would, come up with its share was not Victoria's political problem: it could claim it had upheld its side of the bargain.

Kevin Love was the senior officer involved in the Snowy corporatisation project in the Victorian Department of Premier and Cabinet. He said the 1996 expert panel's 28 per cent was viewed internally as a nice ideal, but 'it was too much of a push to try to achieve, and in any case, Webster had recommended 15 per cent. So 15 per cent became the position we were working to. It was New South Wales that was reticent to sign on to that outcome, and Premier Kennett began to push it because he wanted to keep corporatisation moving.'

New South Wales, however, was still nowhere near a consensus among its agencies or ministers. 'The lull was because the government did not want to do 15 per cent and could not see how it could get out of it because the SWI had said 15 per cent,' said David Crossley.

That might have been Treasury's take on the situation, but it was not shared across government. Pushing the other way was the new Environment Minister, Bob Debus, who was appointed after the March 1999 election. He was convinced of the case for something more than 15 per cent when he toured the Snowy River with Brett Miners and Graeme Enders in May 1999.

Miners was by now the south-east regional manager for the Department of Land and Water Conservation, while Enders was acting manager of

Kosciuszko National Park. Colin Steele had been appointed south-east regional coordinator for the Premier's Department and it was his job to know what was going on and work out innovative ways to solve problems before they became major political conflagrations. He saw himself as effectively the Premier's eyes and ears on the ground on everything from health and education to law and order. Naturally, Steele thought the Snowy was an important local matter, and made sure he brought it to the government's attention. 'The vast majority of people in Sydney didn't have a clue about the situation here, about the Snowy River or what it means to the people,' he said. He worked closely with Miners and Enders, who arranged ministerial tours including a good day out for Bob Debus, with Miners and Enders background-briefing the new minister on the natural resource agencies' position in their Snowy Water Inquiry submission.

'We saw the full splendour of the landscape,' Debus said later. 'It was very dispiriting to see photos of the river in the 1940s and see instead this weed-choked channel with a listless trickle of water down one side.'

In Dalgety, Paul Leete drew pictures with a stick in the sand to illustrate his points. As he warmed to his subject, he began waving the stick in the minister's face. Debus gently backed away until he was teetering on the edge of the river with Leete still standing toe to toe. Miners was never so relieved to hear the chattering blades of the National Parks' helicopter coming over the hill. 'Time to go!' he said, and snatched Debus from an inadvertent dunking.

They flew down the river and alighted on a sandbank in a remote area. Debus, a rather bookish character, sat down on a rock and took off his spectacles. 'My, my, what a passionate fellow that Paul Leete is,' he observed, polishing his glasses. Enders wondered whether Leete had done the Alliance's cause any good or not. Luckily, Debus was impressed by the public servants' intimate knowledge and the community's enthusiasm and commitment.

The minister returned to Sydney and got involved in the inter-agency meetings, where he championed the EPA and National Parks position. 'I maintained an attitude of resistance within the government to any attempt to dismiss higher flows as being too hard,' Debus said. 'Treasury was very concerned about the financial implications, but I was being advised there were no significant environmental thresholds between 6 and 15 per cent, that we had to go to 22 to 28 per cent to achieve a permanent restoration of significant habitat.'

Debus had Premier Bob Carr's tacit support for an outcome at the higher end of the scale, but Treasury still hoped for something in the order of 6–10 per cent. Treasury and the Department of Land and Water Conservation nitpicked over whether the Snowy Water Inquiry's proposed water savings were feasible. Treasury commissioned Bewsher Consulting to review their validity. Drew Bewsher found that not only were Webster's estimates sound, but even more savings might be achieved. His report said at least 154 gigalitres — more than half the 290-odd gigalitres needed to make up 28 per cent — could be saved in New South Wales alone at an estimated cost of $199 million. This estimate did not include potential savings from two irrigation districts that refused to participate in the analysis, or potential savings in Victoria. Bewsher concluded the savings would take ten years to realise.

The meetings went round and round, getting nowhere. 'There was concern after the Snowy Water Inquiry about what 15 per cent meant,' said Peter Staveley, policy manager for economic development in the NSW Cabinet Office. 'It seemed that every time advice came in, it was different — especially from DLWC — as to what it meant.'

At the same time, Vin Good, the Snowy Mountains Authority commissioner, came to meetings with a host of reasons why everything proposed was impossible. 'They held the data and we were totally dependent on them about the effect the various flows would have on the scheme. I don't think they exaggerated but they were always looking to put a particular view,' said David Crossley. 'After four years, we decided we had to allocate Vin time to do his block for half an hour at the beginning of each meeting. Once he did that, we could move forward. He would do his block about how it was all awful, and the world would end. He had to be allowed to have his say. It usually happened on average 15.3 seconds into a meeting.'

Victoria got impatient waiting for New South Wales to work through the tangle. The government was keen to get this troublesome issue out of the way because it had been dragging on so long. A few days before Pat McNamara went to Orbost, Jeff Kennett wrote to Bob Carr saying Victoria supported 15 per cent, and he wanted to see substantial agreement on flows and corporatisation by the end of June 1999. 'If this cannot be achieved then, rather than consider a future extension of time and financial outlay on a struggling project, we should make a realistic appraisal as to whether corporatisation can be achieved in the form contemplated.'[2]

It was an empty threat and Bob Carr ignored it. 'I did not think it was a serious proposition for us — the 15 per cent supported by Jeff Kennett,' Carr said later. 'I think he was just covering himself, to say he had written to New South Wales. We would have liked more detail on how they thought they were going to do that.'

The deadline was duly extended to 31 December 1999. McNamara was in no hurry. 'I had this mega portfolio, with agriculture, fishing, plantation forestry, water supply, mining and petroleum,' he said. 'The Snowy was one of maybe twenty issues I was dealing with. So I thought, we will get past the election — that is a distraction for four weeks — and then I will get back to my office and tidy up a few of these loose ends, like 15 per cent into the Snowy River.'

As for the Alliance's threat to run a candidate, McNamara took it with a grain of salt. The National Party had held Gippsland East for near enough a century. It was one of the safest in the state, with a 15.2 per cent margin. It was also only one electorate against many that the National Party held in irrigation districts, including McNamara's own electorate of Goulburn. Vote for vote inside the party room, irrigation interests were always going to hold sway.

〜

I was married to the Snowy River. You could call Lindy the campaign widow. It took its toll toward the end. I would be on the phone for hours.

PAUL LEETE

Craig Ingram, Mary McDonald and Brenda Murray drove back to the Moogji Aboriginal Council boardroom, where the rest of the Alliance was waiting to hear what McNamara had said. His response was a red rag to a bull. George Collis and Chris Allen had always thought standing candidates was the way to go. 'My strategy all the way along was political,' said Allen, whose laid-back persona belies the political fire in his belly. 'Being nice to politicians, meeting with them and talking nicely wasn't going to get us anywhere.' Standing a candidate, on the other hand, would generate heaps of free publicity the Alliance could not otherwise afford.

The NSW election in March 1999 was the Alliance's first opportunity to get directly involved in politics following the Snowy Water Inquiry. Allen tried to persuade Paul Leete to stand in the seat of Monaro, where National Party incumbent Peter Cochran was retiring. Cochran had a 16 per cent margin, but about 13 per cent was considered his personal following. It was therefore possible that the preferences of a good independent might decide the seat between the major parties. But Leete did not want to get down and dirty in the political swamp, preferring to hold the moral high ground. So the Alliance instead ran a mild campaign with press releases to raise public awareness and lobbying of candidates. The Total Environment Centre helped out, as did high-profile supporters like actor Tom Burlinson, who issued a statement calling on Labor and the coalition to publicly commit to 28 per cent. The idea was merely to persuade the major parties they could lose votes over the Snowy.

Leete and Jo Garland lobbied the five candidates standing for Monaro. The pair worked well together as a tag team, Leete representing the Alliance and Garland representing the Dalgety and District Community Association; that way, they could amplify the small community's voice. The candidates all supported 28 per cent, except the Liberal bloke. 'He had never heard of the Snowy River, I think,' said Garland. The Labor and National Party candidates, however, only made personal commitments; 28 per cent was not party policy. At the last moment, a couple of days before the poll, Leete and Garland made a flyer on the politics of the situation and distributed it to Dalgety and District Community Association members.

In retrospect, Leete said he and Garland were naïve. 'We thought people would be interested to know what the candidates' positions were if they wanted to vote for the river,' he said. 'It was done as a factual thing. We did not tell people how to vote — I was sensitive to that — but I did say the upper house was the crucial area, and if you wanted to vote for the river, you would vote Green or independent.'

Leete's ears were nearly blown off when he picked up the phone a day after the election. It was one of the more irascible local graziers. 'So now you're trying to tell us how to vote too,' the diehard National Party supporter shouted. 'You're just a bloody blow-in — who do you think you are, telling us we should be voting Green! You don't speak for all of us in Dalgety. I want a retraction.'

Leete apologised profusely and tried to explain it was never intended as a 'how to vote' card. The grazier could not be placated. I'm sick of this, Leete thought. This is my thanks.

Leete was at the time chairman of both the Alliance and the Dalgety Association. Like all community groups, the Dalgety Association had a small core that did most of the work. Most of these were relative newcomers to the district. Leete said he got on well with Dalgety's old-timers, like Pip Cogan. They would sit together by the river, Pip reminiscing about its glory days. The old man inspired Leete to keep going whenever he felt like giving up. 'The old-timers supported what we were doing without reservations,' Leete said. 'But there were some other issues that got me offside with some of other locals.'

They were things like fencing off the caravan park after some local lads threatened campers they would drive through their tents after a good night at the pub. Locals resented the fence blocking access to where they parked their cars in the shade by the river. Others muttered Leete did not do enough to keep them informed on what was happening with the campaign.

Leete said so much was happening it was impossible to keep everyone up to date, and he did not have the time to write detailed reports. Still, the campaign was getting widespread media and everyone had his phone number if they wanted a briefing. 'But when that bloke rang and abused me, I thought you guys do bugger all,' said Leete. 'Here we are trying to save the river, and this is all they can think about. I was very hurt. Even if we made a mistake, we are not perfect. We are country people trying to make a difference, but we will never be accepted here. We will always be blow-ins.'

He called Garland. She was furious that one person had carried on like that, and threatened to walk away from the whole campaign. She didn't — the row blew over and ruffled feathers were smoothed — but Leete had had enough. He was burnt out and he knew it. 'I felt the campaign had got to the point of no return. Even in March, I felt it was in the bag, and it was just a matter of people keeping up the momentum. I was sure that the Snowy was going to get something, and I could just walk away.' He began looking around for a new job, a new town and a new life with Lindy and their family.

The Alliance and its affiliates held a post-mortem in Bombala in April 1999. It was a low point. 'There had been the Snowy Water Inquiry, and we did all the work we thought we had to do, and in the end it was down to politics. It was disappointing,' said Craig Ingram. 'Then we didn't achieve anything in New South Wales except cause problems for a key Snowy River Alliance member. Paul was ostracised and there were vicious personal attacks afterward because he took a political position. We failed. A National Party member was re-elected and we got no commitment from the major parties. They hate people taking a political position and are vicious if you don't win. The last thing you can do is take them on and lose.'

The Victorian contingent stopped in Cann River for a coffee on the way back to Orbost. They talked about the upcoming Victorian election. Jeff Kennett was not due at the polls until July 2000, but he was widely expected to go before the end of 1999. 'We have to run a candidate,' said David Adams, an Orbost dairy farmer and Alliance executive stalwart. It was a radical idea, coming from a dyed-in-the-wool National Party supporter, as were most people around the table. 'We think it should be you,' Adams said to Craig Ingram.

Everyone looked at Ingram, who suspected he had been set up. 'I deflected it, and said it should be a good woman like Mary McDonald.' McDonald started when everyone looked at her expectantly. 'I realised they were serious, and suddenly I was terribly busy and flicked it back to Ingram!'

Actually, the idea Ingram might stand had been kicking around for a few months. A few days after the Snowy Water Inquiry was handed down in October 1998, an Alliance delegation led by National Party elder Peter Nixon went to see Peter McGauran, the federal member for Gippsland, at his office in Sale. Phil Davis, state member for Gippsland Province, was also there. David Treasure, the state member for Gippsland East, could not make it, as was often the case.

The meeting did not go well. The Alliance wanted their local members to speak out in support of 28 per cent, push the issue harder inside government, and defend the campaign publicly against the irrigation lobby's vitriolic attacks in the rural media. Nixon asked the two men why they were so quiet in their advocacy while their colleagues over the divide were so vocal in backing the irrigators. Davis explained he was too busy, being not only a local MP but also parliamentary secretary to McNamara.

Nixon thumped his fist on the table. 'Enough,' he roared, jabbing his finger at Davis. 'Don't you tell me your excuses, sonny Jim, because I've had more parliamentary secretaries than you could poke a stick at!'

The delegation left McGauran's office soon after, and went for a coffee. 'We haven't got a hope in hell without someone standing against Treasure,' Nixon said. 'It's the only way they will take us seriously.'

The Alliance members played with Nixon's idea. 'Who would stand if we did put up a candidate?' asked Genevieve Fitzgerald. Everyone did a quick mental assessment, going around the table. Max White was too old. George Collis looked like the Godfather. Peter Nixon growled, 'Don't even think about it!' Fitzgerald was something of a greenie and, well, a girl, so that definitely ruled her out. That left Ingram.

'Why are you all looking at me?' he said.

'Because you only work a few days a year. You're the only one who can afford it and has the time!' laughed the others, before the conversation moved on to other things.

It was true. Ingram was an abalone diver. He only had to dive about fifty days to reach his quota and make his money for the year. He was young — just thirty-four years old — and good-looking, a big, loose-limbed country boy with a wicked grin. Ingram was also Peter Nixon's second cousin on his mother's side, in an electorate where family pedigrees count for a lot although his mother Julie and father Joe say there was nothing in their son's upbringing to suggest he might one day follow Nixon into politics. But Ingram was also a raw, fresh face at a time when rural voters were disenchanted with the major parties. The sense that Labor, the Liberals and Nationals were out of touch had translated into the phenomena of One Nation and record levels of support for 'real' independents in the late 1990s. Ingram was as 'real' as they come. He voted National, like most other people in East Gippsland, but that was the extent of his political activity. Ingram's passions lay elsewhere.

As a child, Ingram first lived on the Snowy River flats out of Orbost, on his maternal grandfather Jim Nixon's dairy farm. After his father, Joe, took up an abalone diving licence, the family moved around, living variously at Marlo, Point Hicks, Cape Conran, Mallacoota and, finally, Cabbage Tree Creek during Ingram's last years at high school.

Ingram loved his sport. He played football for the Snowy Rovers and the Mallacoota/Cann River Tiger Sharks, coached a couple of seasons and served on club committees. He played competitive pool and in the Orbost volleyball league. Ingram was also known as a bit of a wild boy, who rarely wore shoes and liked a good party with lots of beer. 'Cowboy' his friends called him. When he left school, he worked as a deckhand on his father's abalone boat. When two strong-willed personalities on one small boat proved too much, Ingram went to work at a sawmill.

'I didn't see a lot of future in that,' he said. 'It's not a demanding or rewarding occupation, stacking timber in an oven, so I went to Tasmania and put myself through the Australian Maritime College at Beauty Point.' He came out with a certificate in fisheries management and an interest in environmental sustainability. Eventually, with his father looking to retire after thirty-seven years' diving, Ingram took over a third of the licence and worked the boat again.

Abalone diving left Ingram plenty of time to pursue his passions: recreational fishing, horse riding and canoeing. He was especially interested in native fish like the Australian bass, a native sport species renowned for its ill temper and fighting attitude. Just like his 'Pa', Jim Nixon, Ingram liked to know what was under the surface. He would often put on a face-mask and dive under for a look. That's how he noticed the Snowy was unlike other rivers in the region. 'There were no small fish down along the flats, like there are in other rivers. It was the same up at McKillops Bridge, so then I started searching for a reason they were not spawning or recruiting. It drove me to a crusade.'

Ingram formed the East Gippsland branch of Native Fish Australia with a new friend and equally keen angler, George Collis. Collis had recently moved back to Orbost after forty years away. He was in the process of retiring from Telstra, and thinking about how he was going to spend his leisure. His business card, thanks to a prank by Gippsland media magnate

Bob Yeates, advertises Collis as 'noted canoeist'. The other Snowy River campaigners called him, variously, 'the senator', 'generalissimo', and 'pinko George'. He wore the badges with pride.

'I was buying a boat, so I made it my business to meet this bloke,' said Collis. 'He had a reputation as being an extremely good angler, and I knew his parents; I am closer to their generation. I wanted the boat to explore the Snowy, because it is so shallow, and I heard that Craig had a boat that would go up the river.'

Collis said the Native Fish Australia branch was not set up for any political purpose. 'It was common knowledge around here that there was something wrong with the Australian bass. The Marine and Freshwater Research Institute just said they could use people who liked catching things to help collect data.'

Gradually, however, Ingram and the Labor-leaning Collis were drawn into politics through the Snowy River Alliance. 'Pa was pretty actively involved in the Snowy River campaign and arranging the expert panel,' said Ingram. 'At that stage, he was considered an expert on fish of the Snowy, but because I had spent time studying, Jim Nixon and the Alliance started coming to me to answer questions. I started to get invited to the meetings and slowly got involved.' By late 1997, Collis and Ingram were on the Alliance executive committee, and Ingram was firm friends with Brett Miners. The pair met when Ingram acted as guide for Miners when the NSW Department of Land and Water Conservation was looking for Victorian sites to monitor the ecological response if and when the Snowy got more water. 'Ever since that time, we have shared our passion for the river by being close bass fishing mates and we fish the river together each year,' Miners said.

One of Ingram's great advantages, apart from his knowledge, was time to attend the constant meetings and inquiries when many of the others in the Alliance had day jobs to hold down. He found he enjoyed the rough and tumble. Everyone laughed that day in the café in Sale, but the seed was sown. Over the next few months, it grew, took root and blossomed.

Ingram talked it over with his wife, Ann-Maree. 'It was a bit of a shock but exciting at the same time,' she said. 'We did not know what was in front of us, but hopefully we were going to do some good and there was no looking back.' It would mean a huge change in lifestyle for a couple with four very young children used to a quiet life in the country. The deciding factor for Ingram, though, was the day Pat McNamara came to town and threw down the gauntlet. Ingram, backed by the Alliance, rose to the challenge.

*From our reading, the Snowy River is not a significant icon. The
Man from Snowy River was. The story was about a man who chased
cattle on a horse. It was not about the river, which is no more
significant than if it was the Murray or the Murrumbidgee, and look
what happened to them.*

DAVID DOWNIE, ASSISTANT CORPORATISATION MANAGER, DJG PROJECTS,
CONSULTANTS TO SNOWY MOUNTAINS HYDRO-ELECTRIC AUTHORITY
CORPORATISATION PROJECT

Victoria's Labor Opposition was doing it tough. It was routinely ignored in
the metropolitan media and derided as irrelevant in Parliament. Opinion
polls consistently pointed to Labor being soundly beaten again in the
upcoming election, but the Opposition leader, John Brumby, was not so
sure.

Brumby and his private secretary, Ben Hubbard, did some number
crunching and some lateral thinking. Rural and regional Victorians were
not happy campers under the thumb of the Liberal/National Coalition
Government. Premier Jeff Kennett's radical 'reforms' had brought small
communities to their knees. They'd lost schools and health services, which
were centralised in regional cities. They lost local councils in
amalgamations that left many feeling they had lost their democratic voice.
Agricultural programs were wound down, while market reforms jacked up
the price of water. Privatisation of utilities led to massive job losses,
particularly in Gippsland's La Trobe Valley, home to the state's coal-fired
power generators.

The government justified the harsh measures as necessary to get the
state out of the budgetary black hole dug by the previous Labor
Government. Yet Jeff Kennett had plenty of money to spend on pet projects
in Melbourne, such as the heavily subsidised Grand Prix in Albert Park. The
Premier often bumped into Peter Nixon, the former federal minister and
Country Party member for Gippsland, at Radio 3AW, where Nixon was
chairman and Kennett had a weekly talkback session with broadcaster Neil
Mitchell. Their conversation ran on well-worn lines.

'So what is the problem of today, Peter?'

'The problem is Victoria does not stop at Dandenong, Jeff.'

Nixon would list the reasons for rural unrest, including the Snowy River,
and warn Kennett he should take these issues seriously. But the Premier
shrugged off complaints about his city-centric largesse, memorably

describing country communities as 'the toenails of the Victorian body politic while Melbourne was the beating heart'.[3] Indeed, by 1999, after six years in office, Kennett did not seem especially interested in state affairs. Instead, he dabbled in interstate and national matters. He lectured his NSW and federal colleagues for being weak, penned preambles to the Constitution and spoke out on population policy, superannuation and corporate tax reform. Little wonder he was perceived as out of touch with the aspirations of ordinary Victorians.

Rural dwellers blamed their local members, especially National Party members, for not defending their interests. 'Looking back on it, we had been returning the Nationals faithfully to government and yet they had achieved very little for East Gippsland for seventy years,' Gil Richardson said. But the Nationals had negligible bargaining power in a coalition where the senior partner had enough seats to form government in its own right. Even Liberal party members were sidelined in what was essentially Kennett's one-man band. Both coalition parties took their rural supporters for granted, assuming they would never, ever vote Labor.

John Brumby and Ben Hubbard read the situation rather differently. The 1996 election saw a substantial swing against the government in the country — as high as 8 per cent in some electorates. Voters did not necessarily switch to Labor, but to independents and minor parties. One independent candidate, a former policeman, Russell Savage, got enough primary votes and preferences to wrest Mildura from the Liberal Party. Leftist independent Susan Davies followed suit in a by-election in Gippsland West in 1997, taking the seat from the Liberal Party. If the Labor Opposition was smart, it could capitalise on this trend.

Labor needed to hold its existing seats and win another fourteen to take office. Brumby and Hubbard identified a dozen rural electorates where Labor had a chance. They then identified another half-dozen or so where a good independent might knock off a coalition member with Labor preferences. This group included Mildura, Gippsland West, Swan Hill, Portland and Gippsland East, where Labor branch member, Bill Bolitho Jnr, thought a young bloke called Craig Ingram had a good shot.

'So we put a huge effort into taking the ALP to the country,' said Brumby. 'Linking into the concerns and aspirations of country Victoria was crucial to where I saw the future of the state, and where I saw the prospects for Labor making gains. My view was we were well positioned to win seats, so I was always proceeding on that basis. We thought we had a 50:50 chance.'

Brumby was well aware of the Snowy River issue, and favourably disposed. He had been a ministerial advisor in Canberra when corporatisation was first discussed. Years later, he met Max White and George Collis at a community Shadow Cabinet meeting in Bairnsdale in 1997. White and Collis asked Labor to commit to 28 per cent. Brumby said he would think about it. He came across the Alliance again in mid-1998, during a visit to the Tambo River valley in the wake of devastating floods.

There he sensed the discontent in East Gippsland. Pat McNamara earlier made a flying visit for half an hour, but Brumby spent the afternoon with the flood-affected communities. 'It means a lot to country people that you make the effort to go out and see them and spend the time for a chat,' he said. 'People were saying how they wished they got the same concern and respect from the government, and how much they appreciated it. There was so much animosity towards Jeff Kennett, and towards the Nationals for not standing up to Jeff Kennett.'

In November 1998, the Shadow Environment Minister, Sherryl Garbutt, spent three days in Orbost on a fact-finding tour as a guest of the Women's Awareness Group. She came back recommending Labor support a 28 per cent flow. 'This will establish our environmental credibility and has little political risk since Murray River irrigators don't vote for us anyway,' she reported. 'Costs would be shared by three or four governments and spread over three to five years. The decision may be made before we come to power anyway.'

All signs pointed to a labor victory being some years away, whatever Brumby thought. Labor was trailing 11 percentage points behind when Shadow Treasurer Steve Bracks took over as Leader of the Opposition on 22 March 1999. 'Improving our position is a big challenge,' Bracks said at his first press conference. 'But that will be done coherently and patiently between now and the next election. If we do everything right — and that's my intention and plan — I believe we can win.' It sounded like wishful thinking.

Brumby stayed on as Shadow Treasurer and continued to mastermind Labor's re-election strategy. Bracks met Ingram, Collis, Max White, Gil Richardson and Mary McDonald in late April, a month after taking the leadership, to discuss where Labor stood on the Snowy River. Bracks did not need convincing, after camping by the Snowy River at McKillops Bridge years earlier with his wife. 'We walked around in the National Park in that great landscape and in the rainshadow,' he told me. 'It is beautiful — the water is warm with sandy beaches. Terri and I were aware when we were camping that there were environmental flow issues and that it was not the great wild river it used to be. I was not even in politics then. It was an outrage that this river was reduced to 2 per cent. It was an iconic river, a great landscape and a legend in Australian history and it was very poor environmental practice to let it become a trickle. It was something that should be restored.'

Bracks gave the Alliance delegation a commitment to restore 28 per cent as part of Labor's election platform. At the end of the meeting, McDonald wished him good luck as leader. 'I think you are going to need it,' she said. A few weeks later, impatient for Labor to commit publicly, McDonald got through to Bracks on talkback on rural radio and put him on the spot. Bracks replied that Labor would negotiate with New South Wales and the Commonwealth to restore 28 per cent.

Bracks was the first leader of a major political party to publicly state a position. It was an easy commitment in one sense, since Labor was unlikely to win office, but Brumby said that as Opposition leader and Shadow Treasurer, he would not have supported the policy if he did not think it was possible, at least in principle. He had examined the Snowy Water Inquiry findings, and seen for himself the extent of water wasted. The Woorinen pipeline, near Swan Hill, stuck in his mind. 'It was built in the Depression and was full of holes. For every 10 litres put into the channel, only one made it to the farms; the rest were lost through leaks. I had seen a few instances like that, where water could be saved for agricultural expansion and the environment. So we knew the water savings were there.'

In a further show of good faith, Bracks wrote to NSW Premier Bob Carr, asking for a meeting between ministers and shadow ministers to discuss ways to achieve a 28 per cent flow. It was a calculated risk. Bracks' policy advisor, Rob Hudson, said the letter's main value was political, to show Labor was serious, but its credibility would have been damaged if Carr wrote back and said he was not interested.

Carr did not write back, but only because the letter got lost in the system. David Crossley came across it a few weeks later, after the Victorian election campaign had started. 'I thought we should do something about this, but by then they had come out with their policy. If the letter had not been lost, New South Wales would have written back and said this is a bad idea. But then again, if it had been obvious the ALP stood a chance of being elected, we would have paid more attention to the letter,' he said.

It was time for a change. We had been neglected by the Kennett Government and how else do you send a message that you won't put up with that?

CRAIG INGRAM

Once Ingram said he would definitely run, the Alliance faced the task of devising an election strategy. No one had been involved in anything remotely like this before except Chris Allen. Allen is laid-back, a good communicator and mediator. In his youth, he was president of the Student Union in Gippsland and on the National Student Union executive, where he worked with Julia Gillard and Lindsay Tanner who are now senior federal Labor parliamentarians. He also cut his political teeth alongside Michael O'Connor, who went on to lead the militant timber-workers union and become a major factional player in the Labor Party. 'I used to be very active in the Labor Party, and helped form the Socialist Left in the La Trobe Valley,' Allen said. 'I was active in launching Keith Hamilton's political career. He was a lecturer in physics in college and we got him elected to the local council. He went on from there to become a state MP.'

This was not something to boast about in Orbost, and Allen generally kept quiet about his former life. Now, though, his experience could come in useful. He was not sure how it would go down when he told the others in the Alliance, but they were delighted to have someone in their midst who knew how to mount a political campaign.

Allen was nominated campaign manager. Max White was treasurer. Collis was personal assistant to Ingram and worked closely with Allen. Collis quietly recruited Genevieve Fitzgerald to help him with media advice. Ingram, Max and Glenice White went to others for campaign advice. They attended an independents forum in Moe, convened by Russell Savage, Susan Davies and Peter McLellan, a Liberal who resigned from the party in protest in 1998 over Kennett's plans to diminish the independence of the Auditor-General's office. The three independents talked about what it took to run a successful campaign outside the major parties.

'People do not understand how incredibly difficult it is to get yourself known enough, to get enough people who to help you do all the work that has to be done,' said Davies later. 'When people appear at these forums, you have no idea about their community or the support systems they have, but I would have to say that Craig and his group were organised — that was pretty obvious pretty fast. They had a lot going for them. They had money and a cause and they knew what they were doing in a way most of the others did not.'

George Collis talked long and often to Graham Pike, Native Fish Australia's representative on the national recreational fishing body, RecFish. Pike is a retired journalist-turned-public-servant in Canberra; he was well schooled in the internal workings of government and politicians. He, Ingram and Collis looked into the federal Environment Minister, Senator Robert Hill's legal obligations to protect endangered species, and got some good publicity in July 1999, threatening court action if Senator Hill did not protect native fish in the Snowy River.

Collis also developed a close, if extremely discreet working relationship with the Labor Party. He was in his element. 'I have always had an interest in politics and I am an enthusiastic unionist,' Collis said. 'I know many people in politics, and people call me Pinko George. I was always known as an ALP man. Ingram and Bill Bolitho and I had often sat around over red wine talking politics. Bill was an astute politician, and Ingram was not, but Bill was always sitting there as a friend and not a Labor representative. Still, he perceived there were benefits to the party if we did something up here.'

It suited Labor's strategy to have a strong independent running in East Gippsland, and so it assisted with advice on preparing candidates and a decision to direct first preferences to Ingram. The Alliance gave Labor nothing in return but the prospect of taking a seat off the government. Chris Allen in particular was wary of Labor after his student experiences. 'They offered people to help us with research and the campaign, but I said, "No, we know what we are doing,"' Allen said. 'I understand the Labor machine — I didn't want their spies hanging around.'

Subsequent events inspired all kinds of conspiracy theories, but John Brumby insisted there were no deals struck before the election. He doubted it would have been possible. 'You would be hard put to describe Craig as a stooge,' Brumby said. 'He is one of the strong characters from East Gippsland. Had he been in a party, it would not have been ours.' Anyway, depending on preferences, the Labor Party did not think it needed a deal. Bill Bolitho Jnr was its candidate, and 'there were no secret plans because Bill was in it to win it'.

Bill Bolitho Jnr told George Collis that a local real estate agent, Bruce Ellett, stood at the last minute as an independent in Gippsland East in the 1996 election and managed to pick up 17.3 per cent of the primary vote. Ellett's message was simple: East Gippsland deserved a 'clear, honest, unbiased voice' in Parliament that put the region first, rather than toeing the party line. Collis was impressed. 'Ellett had three weeks' preparation and did virtually nothing, and he got 17 per cent of the primary vote,' he said. 'I was astounded when I found that out. Then I researched his tickets and I saw that indirectly he got ALP preferences. Seventeen per cent became a 'We can do it' figure. All we had to do was get another 8 per cent and we were in.'

Collis said his relationship with Labor was strategic. 'A large part of the association with Bill Bolitho in the months running up to the election was simply learning how the ALP worked, who were the powerful people and how to get to them. We tried to do all the same things with the Liberals, but we were not taken very seriously. We sent them letters, but there was no interest at all.'

⤳

It was a classic example of where philanthropy can play a role. You support the community to raise an issue, find out if it has legs and then form a partnership to see it through. We supported the science to find something out, then backed the community body with the broadest consensus and we stayed with the Alliance throughout, including the period of high political tensions.

CHARLES LANE, CHIEF EXECUTIVE DIRECTOR, THE MYER FOUNDATION, 1999–2004

The Alliance was, of course, mighty pleased with Labor's policy commitment, but Jeff Kennett was the man it had to convince. Kennett had not formally announced a position, but the Alliance was tipped off about his letter to Bob Carr on 17 May 1999 supporting 15 per cent. His office refused to confirm or deny, and deflected requests for a meeting. Ingram and Lady Southey from The Myer Foundation went to see the Environment and Natural Resources Minister, Marie Tehan, but, as far as she knew, the government had not settled on a preferred flow. 'You have to talk to the Premier and Treasurer and get them on side,' she advised. 'You have me on side for 28 per cent, you have to get them.'[4]

Unfortunately, having Tehan on side was not a lot of help. She was retiring at the election and so far out of the loop that Jeff Kennett, Treasurer Alan Stockdale and Pat McNamara did not bother telling her they had already settled on 15 per cent. Tehan, in turn, did not confront Kennett after meeting Lady Southey and Ingram. 'There was not that much point being angry,' Tehan said to me. 'I would have rationalised it, that he was thinking 15 per cent was sufficient and maybe it was just a starting point, and it would bring the issue to some fruition. This had been going since 1996 and, like many things in politics, something is better than nothing.'

Lady Southey and Charles Lane, The Myer Foundation's new executive director, made an appointment to talk to Kennett on 1 July 1999. Lady Southey knew the Premier personally, having gone to school with his mother, and from attending functions with her husband, the late Sir Robert Southey, a former state and federal Liberal Party president.

The meeting went well. The Premier listened and made positive noises as Lady Southey and Lane went through the scientific case for 28 per cent. Two weeks later, he wrote to Lady Southey to assure her that discussions were ongoing, but that morning, Lady Southey read in *The Age* that the campaign for 28 per cent had failed to win State Government support. Kennett was quoted in the article, confirming publicly for the first time that Victoria was pushing New South Wales to agree to 15 per cent. 'It's not as much as anyone would like, but I just don't know if we're going to get much more than that because of what is already out there for the irrigators,' he said.[5]

Lady Southey was bitterly disappointed. Until this point The Myer Foundation had been very much behind the scenes. Now, Lane and Lady Southey took the unusual step of approaching *The Age* to express their disappointment publicly. I interviewed Lady Southey a few days before the election was called on 24 August 1999. The political atmosphere was highly charged, yet Lady Southey seemed genuinely unaware that going public might be interpreted as a political act.

The article ran on Saturday 4 September, at the height of the election campaign. Lady Southey said Kennett had not come clean with her on the day his position became public, and that she was considering a personal appeal to the NSW Premier, Bob Carr. 'I don't think we are being political in this,' she said. 'I think our interest is environmental and we care about the environment.'[6] A week earlier, another influential Melbournite, retired auditor-general Ches Baragwanath, attacked the Kennett Government over its secrecy and lack of accountability in a headline-grabbing speech at Melbourne University. In context, it appeared as if the Melbourne establishment was turning on Jeff Kennett.

Four years later, when I interviewed her for this book, Lady Southey said she was older and wiser from that experience. 'We were always very conscious not to be politically involved,' she said. 'It never occurred to me that it might be seen as political. My only aim was to rescue a dying river, and we did everything we could to aid the cause. I got involved out of a genuine love of the river, my memories, and simple respect for the people fighting hard to save it.'

⤶

I was extremely uncomfortable about not being behind the National Party, but I saw it as an opportunity to further our ambitions to get a living river back.

GIL RICHARDSON

Greta Nettleton had her head full of white dresses, flowers and romance in August 1999. Her wedding day was drawing near. The invitations had been sent, the clubhouse at the Orbost Golf Course was booked for the reception, and there were only a few loose ends to be tied up when her sister, Ann-Maree Ingram, arrived for a bridesmaid's dress fitting.

'I don't suppose there is any chance you might be able to put the wedding back a week or two, is there?' Ann-Maree asked, standing in the front of the mirror while the dressmaker fiddled with pins and hemlines.

'Why?' Greta was not sure if her sister was joking. She and her fiancé, Peter, knew it was risky picking 18 September. It was Grand Final day for the local footy and netball leagues, but they banked on Orbost not making the cut. (The town did, which made things a bit difficult with her brother, Royston, who was on the footy team, and for the photographer, whose daughter was in the netball finals.) Already, there had been a fair bit of mucking around with the best time to hold the ceremony so most everyone could get there. 'What now?' Greta took her sister's bait.

'They've just set the election date today — same day as the wedding,' said Ann-Maree. 'It is just the election is going to be such a busy day anyway, we thought maybe you could have the wedding on a different day, just to make things a bit easier.'

Greta was dimly aware that her brother-in-law, Craig Ingram, was standing, but she knew her priorities too. 'No way were we changing the date,' Greta told me later. 'We picked it because it was the only one that suited us around that time, and it was my wedding day long before it was the state election. My wedding was first!'

The wedding was set for 4.30 pm at the Uniting Church and Ingram was down to be master of ceremonies at the reception in the evening. 'It should be okay,' he told Chris Allen. 'I can vote first thing, spend a bit of time at the polling booth here in Orbost, and then go home and get ready for the wedding.'

Allen laughed. 'You're not going to any fucking wedding, mate,' he said. 'You are going to be spending the day driving around the electorate handing out how to vote cards and kissing babies. If you're lucky, you might make the reception.'

Ingram, by his own admission, did not have a clue about election campaigning. 'We had this bloke who had the look, the money and the time, but no idea what to do,' said Allen. Ingram's rawness was his biggest advantage, but there were limits. 'We had to polish Craig,' said George Collis. 'We would have him standing in the corner of my kitchen to practise public speaking, and he'd be there all loose limbed and waggling his arms. We put shoes on him and I lent him a tie. He had to borrow my car to get around because his was not respectable, and I fined him a dollar for every "um".' One particularly profitable speech later hooked Collis $43.

Allen and Collis masterminded the campaign. A key issue was preferences. 'Do we want to win or do we just want to give the National Party a scare and make the seat marginal so they never take us for granted again?' Allen asked Collis and Ingram. They were standing on the rickety back steps behind the Orbost campaign office. 'If we run a split ticket, we have a good chance because we will get the disaffected voters from both sides.' The others were unanimous: 'We want to win.' With a split ticket, the Alliance could not be accused of being Labor or Green stooges. 'We were running for the Snowy River,' said Allen.

The strategy was maximum exposure, in contrast with David Treasure's low profile. One of their first stops was the office of Bob Yeates, East Gippsland's media magnate. Yeates owns all the newspapers in the district and is heavily involved in everything going on. It perturbed him to watch the once prosperous region sink under Kennett's policies into one of the state's most depressed corners. He had not in the past showed much interest in the Snowy River story, but he took an instant liking to Ingram and could see the benefits of making the seat marginal.

As Ingram, Allen and Collis were leaving, Yeates said, 'Let's get a picture of you then.' He took off his suit jacket and tie, put them on Ingram, propped him in a corner of the office, and took the kind of mugshot we are all familiar with in our passports, except Ingram is grinning. That grin ended up plastered everywhere throughout East Gippsland, on posters, in brochures, on advertisements deliberately printed in Liberal blue.

Allen aimed to get at least one poster in a shop window in every town, village and hamlet in the electorate. He also broadened Ingram's platform so he could not be dismissed as a single-issue candidate. Ingram promised he would fight for city-standard telecommunications services, better employment opportunities, rail services to Bairnsdale reinstated, more health professionals and police, support for value-adding in the timber industry, no dams on Bairnsdale's Mitchell River and programs to address the ecological deterioration of the Gippsland Lakes. Oh yes, and the restoration of the Snowy River.

In some towns, especially in the Tambo Valley, there was hardly a shop window without Ingram's face smiling out into the street. 'Vote for a fresh approach' the posters said. 'Independents can deliver.' 'Young, enthusiastic, hardworking for East Gippsland.' 'Craig will put East Gippsland first.' 'A voice for the people of Gippsland East in the Victorian Parliament.'

The messages resonated in a community that felt neglected and ignored. Its discontent found eloquent embodiment in the 'Lone Rider', a high-country cattleman named Derek Manning. The Lone Rider rode 800 kilometres around East Gippsland during the election campaign, collecting thousands of statements of rural concern. A coalition of church and community organisations called A Future For Rural Australia (AFFRA) coordinated the ride to draw attention to rural decline and the community's sense of hopelessness and isolation.

'In an age of high technology, and because our Members of Parliament no longer represent us, country people have been reduced to sending messages of concern and despair to Parliament via the saddlebags of a lone rider,' said Bill Bolitho Snr, an AFFRA organiser and father of the Labor candidate for Gippsland East.[7] Manning delivered East Gippsland's messages to the steps of Parliament House two days before the election. In the minds of many voters, Ingram became the man who could make those messages resonate inside government.

Ingram was everywhere in the flesh. 'We got Bob to find out everything that was going on in the district,' said Collis. 'Every book launch, every public meeting — we got Craig to everything that was going on, and we sold him as the independent candidate.' The Alliance also advertised Ingram's weekly schedule of appearances so that voters could meet him. He was backed by a small army of volunteers who letterboxed brochures, posted out letters appealing for financial and other support, and manned the two campaign offices, one in Orbost and one in Bairnsdale's Main Street. The latter was not easy to find, as the Alliance came up against Main Street resistance to anyone rocking the boat for the National Party. 'When we went looking for offices in Bairnsdale, all we could see were 'For Lease signs, but when we went to see the real estate agents, they said, "No, we haven't got anything for you",' said Ingram. 'But Bob Yeates told us someone we could go to, who rented us an office.'

The buzz was infectious. Chris Allen's wife, Lynette Greenwood, worked in the Orbost campaign office. She typed letters, took phone calls and gave people forms to ask questions, which Ingram would personally answer. 'It was the heart of the campaign,' she said. 'People would be coming in to sign up, and we had balloons, and posters and brochures with that bloody awful photo Bob Yeates took of Craig. If it was very quiet, I would go out on the pavement and spruik! You always knew everyone, and I'd be asking, "Are you going to vote for Craig?" Everyone had the stickers on their cars. There was lots of energy and excitement.'

So many supporters came out of the woodwork that Max White could roster 132 people to hand out how to vote cards at every poll booth in Gippsland East, all day — even the small booths with perhaps twenty or thirty voters registered. It was unprecedented. 'I think we ran a professional campaign that surprised a lot of people,' said Ingram. 'We were pretty brash and in people's faces with our ads.'

The incumbent, David Treasure, was discomforted. He found it difficult to get the government's message out there because Bob Yeates decided he would not run any political stories. That left advertising as the only option, but the party gave Treasure only $13,000 for his campaign — not nearly enough to counter the Alliance's publicity blitz. Rumours circulated that the Alliance had a war chest of $65,000 and David Treasure still wonders where the money came from.

The truth is rather mundane. The Alliance had nothing like $65,000 at its disposal. Gil Richardson kicked off fundraising by finding 'ten good men' to put in $500 each. Max White wrote to more than 2000 businesses in the electorate. None replied, but a few businesses and many individuals later responded to personal appeals for financial support; the donations were in the order of tens and hundreds rather than thousands of dollars. Most importantly, the Alliance received a lot of help in kind and discounts on its bills. 'We gave the impression of being big spenders but we had things that never cost us anything,' said Collis.

David Treasure was also uneasy about the coalition campaign statewide. 'I felt it was too quiet, too few controversial issues to get our teeth into.' This was not for want of matters voters wanted addressed, however, but the fact that Kennett put a gag on coalition members speaking anywhere but in their local media. It meant the Premier was effectively the sole voice of government, and he refused to engage with controversial issues raised on talkback radio or by journalists. 'It was a frustrating campaign,' said Treasure. 'Up to the day before the election, all polling was saying the coalition would walk back with a large majority, but we did one poll that showed many people were undecided, and the worry was where would they go?'

Poor David Treasure. His constituents widely referred to him as 'Hidden' or 'Buried Treasure', on account of his low profile. He was considered a nice enough fellow, but weak. He was criticised for failing to speak out publicly against Kennett's local depredations, such as shutting the train line to Bairnsdale and gutting services in remote communities, particularly in the high country. The nickname really took hold after the devastating 1998 floods in the Tambo River valley. David was overseas in Europe on a Commonwealth Parliamentary Association trip. The party asked him to come back, but he did not return for five weeks. He was not popular, and the party executive was implicated in an attempted preselection coup to replace Treasure with a prominent and outspoken East Gippsland Shire councillor, Shaun Beasley, for the 1999 election.

Beasley was a staunch supporter of 28 per cent in the Snowy River. Beasley and Councillor Brenda Murray, assisted by the shire environmental planner, Eric Sjerp, commissioned an expensive economic study that found the dying river was costing the region $7 million in lost tourism alone. As mayor, Beasley led a well-publicised shire delegation to Canberra in March 1999 to push the case for 28 per cent. 'Irrigators don't have [the water] as [a]

'**Don't send a boy to do a man's job.**' The National Party cartoon warning East Gippsland voters against supporting Craig Ingram. The ad backfired, as it served to remind voters why they were dissatisfied with the Nationals as the near-silent partners in Jeff Kennett's coalition government. *The cartoon was published in* The Bairnsdale Advertiser.

right,' he later told *The Age*. 'It is not theirs to give back. It is the Snowy River's water.'[8] David Treasure survived the coup, thanks to the local National Party branch, but it is likely that had Beasley won instead, the Alliance might not have put up its own candidate.

Treasure, in his defence, said he discussed the Snowy River with Pat McNamara and Jeff Kennett on several occasions, but the consensus was it was not achievable. 'We had to look at this from all angles and get the balance right,' Treasure said. 'People outside politics think the world is black and white. In reality it is so many shades of grey once you get in there. If one group wants something on one side, there are equally large groups on the other side. People say "You should represent us", but for heaven's sake — which group and how do you represent them all? That is why there has to be consensus and negotiation.' He feels it was easy for the Alliance to be the good guys pushing for 28 per cent — they were not in government. He also believes he did as much as could be expected of a local member.

A few days before the election, the National Party branch realised Treasure might be in trouble and decided to run some ads. They were full-page, with the headline 'Don't send a boy on a man's job … an independent won't be heard by the Government', and a cartoon of a schoolboy with a satchel saying 'IND' on his tiptoes trying to reach the door handle into the Premier's office. The ads backfired, serving only to raise Ingram's profile and remind voters why they were unhappy with Treasure's performance. Treasure and his party only dug their own hole deeper.

﹏

I don't think you could ever say the voters wanted David Treasure out — they just wanted Craig Ingram in.

GEORGE COLLIS

Greta Nettleton's wedding day — Victorian election day, 18 September 1999 — dawned cold, wet, windy and miserable. There was plenty of pre-wedding excitement, with her brother, Richard, breaking his collarbone riding a racehorse two days earlier. Nettleton just wanted the day to go quietly and smoothly. Ingram's wife, Ann-Maree, got up early to get her hair and make-up done for her sister's 4.30 pm wedding. Ingram got in the car with Chris Allen and drove to the biggest polling booth, at West Bairnsdale Secondary College. They spent the day there, handing out how-to-vote cards. 'It was a good feeling — everyone saying "good on ya", and lots taking only our card,' Ingram said.

He and Allen left Bairnsdale about 4 pm and drove back via Lakes Entrance, where they spent another ninety minutes at the poll booth until it closed. Glenice White handed out how-to-vote cards for much of the day at Paynesville. 'I was standing next to the Bairnsdale National Party representative, and they were getting so upset because people were just taking our cards,' said White. Heather Richardson handed out in Orbost, giving cards to Greta Nettleton's wedding guests on their way to the church. Ingram got to the golf club just as the wedding reception was getting underway; Orbost had won the Grand Final, so spirits were especially high. Chris Allen went to the campaign office, where the Whites, the Richardsons, Lynette Greenwood and other Alliance stalwarts had gathered for post-poll drinks. Collis arrived a little later, from the Bairnsdale office where he had coordinated the poll-day logistics.

'I had the telephone on, and as I came into town, the first parcel of votes from Orbost had been counted and the figures were astounding — 70 per cent of the primary vote,' Collis said. 'People were calling wanting to know who would get his preferences. But I though he would win. I walked into the Orbost office and the place had a ring to it — it was electrical.'

It was to be expected Ingram would do well in Orbost, but supporters scrutineering other booths soon rang in healthy primary votes elsewhere too. 'He has Bruthen!' Ian Moon told Collis, ringing from the town's tiny counting room. The excitement mounted as it became clear Ingram would force David Treasure to preferences. It was a better result than most had expected in their wildest dreams.

Something else amazing was happening. From early in the night, it was apparent there was a huge swing against the unbeatable Jeff Kennett. Coalition members were losing rural seats one after another to the Labor Party, and several were on a knife-edge. Russell Savage and Susan Davies were returned with increased primary votes. Independents in Portland and Swan Hill were, like Ingram, taking 'safe' rural coalition seats to the wire. A tragedy in the outer-suburban electorate of Frankston East heightened the drama. Former Liberal Party member Peter McLellan was standing as an independent, but on the morning of the election he was found dead of a heart attack in his apartment. The voting was declared void in Frankston East, and a supplementary election announced to be held in four weeks.

The ABC TV commentators paid little attention to Gippsland East, except when Labor Party numbers man Graeme Richardson predicted that not only would Ingram snatch the seat, but he would hold the balance of power in a hung Parliament. That was going too far. 'I could not believe that,' said Glenice White. Gil Richardson just stared incredulously at the television, saying over and over, 'What have we done?' He said later he did not realise that by voting for Ingram, he might have been voting for a change in government. Ingram's father, Joe, was watching at home and woke his wife, Julie, to tell her what Graeme Richardson had said. 'I was pretty excited, but at that stage I could not see how it could be right, because he was the lowest on the graph,' Julie said.

The party in Ingram's campaign office piled into cars and headed up to the golf clubhouse to share the moment with Ingram. 'We went in, and everyone was dancing and we joined in,' said Chris Allen. 'Greta's mother, Bonnie, gave us a lecture about it being Greta's wedding and not taking the focus away from that, but then someone put on the TV in the bar.' Half the wedding crowded in. Some guests were bluebloods from the state's aristocratic western district and convinced the voters of Victoria had lost their minds. Glenice White still could not believe Craig would take the seat, whatever Richo thought, while Collis fielded calls from Labor strategists and former Labor minister Robert Fordham, all saying Ingram would win.

Greta was gracious about sharing her wedding celebrations with the Alliance. 'I knew most of them anyway, and the more the merrier!' she said later. 'We were very excited about Craig doing so well, but my husband and I were not taking that much notice — it was our wedding day and I was a bit oblivious to everything else.' Her aunty, Margaret Joyce, was not. Eventually she went into the bar, turned off the television, and reminded the Alliance why everyone was there. 'I think we have all seen enough,' she said firmly. 'Don't forget — this was Greta's wedding day first.'

SIX

Ingram's Choice

*This was a group of disparate and desperate people. Party politics
did not come into it except for us to say that we will give these
bastards a fright if we can. We went as far as putting up a candidate
— the rest was pure chance. But if Craig had not become a Member
of Parliament, and Jeff Kennett had not been kicked out, we would
still be struggling along. We never got any traction until Craig got in.
Sometimes the stars line up.*

GLENICE WHITE

Sunday lunch was well underway at Joe and Julie Ingram's house when
the phone rang again. Julie heard it above the hubbub of the barbeque
organised to thank her son's campaign team. 'Whether we won or lost or
drew, we were going to celebrate anyway because we had made a difference
in East Gippsland,' Craig Ingram said. 'We had made the point that we
would not be stuffed around.' It was the day after the election and the phone
had been ringing hot with congratulations from friends and supporters.
Julie went in to answer this latest call, and came running back out to get
Ingram. 'It's Steve Bracks,' she said. 'He wants to talk to you.' Everyone knew
then that this was for real.

'Hello, Craig, I just wanted to call you to say congratulations and well
done,' said Bracks.

'Thanks, Steve, but I think it might be a bit too soon to say that,' Ingram
replied.

'Well, we think you have the numbers to win the seat. The scrutineers are
saying you have the numbers and even if you haven't, you have done very
well — but we would like to talk to you because we think there is a potential
the Parliament might be hung.'

Everyone was stunned. 'We were not 100 per cent sure Craig had won the
seat, but when Steve Bracks rang, I thought they must know what is going
on,' said Joe Ingram. It would have been exciting enough for the Alliance
just to get their man in, but who would have thought Ingram might hold
the balance of power? The Snowy was not the reason rural voters thrashed

133

the Kennett Government to within an inch of its political life, but it might now determine who governed Victoria.

'Everybody was mesmerised and no one could believe it,' said Glenice. 'We were nonplussed. We were all very pleased to see Craig had been elected, but Craig was stunned. This result, for people who had had little to do with politics! We just thought we wanted to get people to listen to the Snowy. George's smile never left his face all day. It was totally unexpected. Someone must have been looking down on us — it was time that the Snowy River had its day, I think. But of course, no one was more surprised than Steve Bracks and David Treasure.'

Jeff Kennett took another twenty-four hours to call Ingram. His government was on a knife-edge. Four seats remained undecided: Mitcham, Carrum, Geelong and East Gippsland. The coalition needed all four to form government. Without them, the result hinged on the independent members and the supplementary poll in Frankston East on 16 October following the death of Peter McLellan. The National Party was claiming it could win East Gippsland, but Kennett did not share their optimism. Instead, he called Ingram. 'It looks as if you will get home and we want to be sure you do not make any decisions until you talk to us first,' he said.

'There is no chance of that — if we have the balance of power, we will be talking to everyone,' Ingram replied.

Late that night, Ingram was having a celebratory red wine with Ann-Maree and his sister, Gaye, at home in Cabbage Tree Creek. Amid much mirth, the phone rang. Ingram did not quite catch who was on the line and hushed the laughter. It was Kennett again. 'We had been trying to talk to him for three years and never got closer than talkback radio to throw questions at him — so to have him actually calling me at home was amazing,' Ingram said. 'He had obviously worked out by then what one of my issues was. He said it was the Snowy and tried to tell me everything that the government had been doing for the river.'

Kennett told Ingram his government had always supported 28 per cent, and blamed New South Wales for not coming to the party. He said the policy commitment to 15 per cent before the election was meant only as a starting point to get New South Wales to the negotiating table, but New South Wales had refused for more than a year to discuss even that. 'We have been fighting very hard for this,' he told Ingram.

Ingram interrupted. 'Just wait a minute there, will you, Jeff,' he said. He rummaged through some files and came back to the phone. 'Jeff, with the greatest respect, could I quote something to you?' He began to read:

'Dear Bob, I am writing to encourage early resolution of two critical issues related to the corporatisation of the Snowy Mountains Scheme … The first issue is agreement on an outcome to the Snowy Water Inquiry. The commissioner recommended Option D, which included an increase in flows of 15 per cent for the Snowy below Jindabyne … Victoria favours this option.'

Kennett went quiet. It was his letter to Bob Carr, written back in May. 'Look, your position is not and has not been 28 per cent — this was your position,' Ingram told him. 'It might not be your position now, but don't try to bullshit me on this. Don't come and tell me what is going on and how you are doing great things for the Snowy when we have been battling for years to get you to concede anything.'

'I don't know how you got that,' Kennett said. 'But it is no good going down that line now — things have changed. Just promise me you won't make any decisions until we can talk to you.'

Ingram would not speak to anyone — not even the media — until he was sure he had the seat. Over the next couple of days, Labor picked up three of the four seats hanging in the balance. The fourth, East Gippsland, was declared on Wednesday afternoon, four days after the election. A crumpled David Treasure did not go to the Australian Electoral Office in Bairnsdale for the announcement. He was too busy cleaning out his office around the corner, ready for Ingram to take possession. Members of the Snowy River Alliance heading up to the pub later saw Treasure driving past with his trailer piled high with all his gear. He barely left so much as a paper clip behind. Ingram was on the road too, driving his beaten-up Toyota ute to Melbourne. It was time to talk.

His first conversation was with independents Susan Davies and Russell Savage. They met early Thursday morning, before their first meetings with Jeff Kennett and Steve Bracks. The party that won the independents over would form government, so the pressure on them was intense. Davies had drawn up a draft Charter of Independents. It was largely based on advice from Peter Wellington, the Queensland independent who had found himself in a similar situation in 1998; his vote enabled Labor leader Peter Beattie to form a minority government.

The charter was a blueprint for good governance. It included restoring the Office of the Auditor-General, electoral reform of the upper house to end the coalition's dominance, public access to all government contracts, and strengthening Freedom of Information laws. The charter sought to undo many of Jeff Kennett's controversial 'reforms' that had allowed his

Reluctant kingmakers: independents Craig Ingram, Susan Davies and Russell Savage pose for the media before their first meeting with Jeff Kennett after the shock result in the state election. *Photo: Wayne Taylor,* The Age, *24 September 1999, p.6.*

government to operate almost free from public accountability and independent scrutiny. Ingram approved, saying, 'You must have been reading my campaign material.' The independents agreed they would decide which party to support separately, but their decisions would be guided by the major parties' response to the charter and the outcome in the Frankston East supplementary election; the supplementary election would become, in effect, a litmus test of the public desire for change.

The three independents then walked to Treasury Place through the inevitable media scrum. First up they talked to the National Party. Russell Savage remembers the leader and Deputy Premier, Pat McNamara, criticising Kennett while a colleague enthused that the Nationals could get six Cabinet positions now that the Liberals needed their junior coalition partner to stay in office. 'That was all they were interested in,' said Savage. 'We independents said we are here for the people of Victoria, not the National Party.'

The next meeting was with Jeff Kennett and deputy Liberal Party leader, Mark Birrell. The Premier had not long returned from his weekly radio stint on radio 3AW. The media was bursting with letters and talkback gloating over Kennett's predicament. The Premier answered on air with an astoundingly patronising poem. 'People are unreasonable, illogical and self-centred. Love them anyway' was the opening line, and it went on in similar vein: '… The biggest person with the biggest ideas can be shot down by the smallest people with the smallest minds. Think big anyway …'[1]

Kennett singled out Ingram as soon as the independents were shown into his office.

'G'day, Craig — so you're an abalone diver,' he said, as they shook hands.

'Yeah, Jeff, that's right.'

'So do you own your own licence?'

'I have a share of a licence.'

'Ah, well, so I guess you won't be wanting your parliamentary superannuation then.'

Ingram was taken aback. 'He wanted to know what made me tick. They knew then that if I got voted out next time, it wouldn't matter to me as long as I had achieved what I wanted to achieve. That is unsettling for politicians, because most come for the golden handshake.'

The independents told Kennett and Birrell their decision depended on the response to the charter and the Frankston East supplementary election in three weeks. They delivered the same message later the same day to Steve Bracks and his deputy Labor leader, John Thwaites.

Susan Davies and Russell Savage, as sitting members, resisted the temptation to take advantage of the situation with a shopping list of personal demands. 'The first thing I could have said was put back the train [to Mildura] and build the courthouse you have been promising for the last twenty years — but none of us did that as conditions for supporting the government,' said Savage. 'The discussions were all about good governance for the benefit of Victoria. There was nothing personal in it for us as sitting members, or we would have been as bad as everyone else on this hill of opportunity.' Davies agrees: 'It would have looked pretty sleazy. But Craig could make demands because that is what he was put in to do.'

Davies' natural inclination was to support Labor. After she told Jeff Kennett on the phone the day after the election that he should resign, the coalition did not make much of an effort to woo her. Russell Savage, on the other hand, is a conservative man representing a conservative electorate. His natural inclination to support the coalition was tempered only by his disgust at the vitriolic personal abuse he had endured from Kennett and his cronies since Savage had knocked off the Liberal Party in Mildura. That left Ingram seemingly as the dark horse. He was not an existing Member of Parliament, and had run for office right from the start with the specific demand to restore a 28 per cent flow in the Snowy River. So his decision would also depend on which of the major parties seemed best placed to deliver on the Snowy.

Labor had much in its favour. It had gone into the election with an explicit 28 per cent policy. Steve Bracks, unlike Jeff Kennett, had taken the trouble to meet the Snowy River Alliance and listen to their case. However, seeing a Labor Party in government went against Ingram's grain. Personally, he is conservative and uncomfortable with some of Labor's social and workplace policies. He comes from a staunchly National Party family, just like most of the electorate and key members of the Snowy River Alliance.

Gil Richardson, like many other National Party supporters in Gippsland East, changed his vote for the first time in his life to back Ingram. During the interregnum between the 18 September poll and the 16 October Frankston East supplementary election, Richardson said many locals who voted as he did would be horrified to think they might be helping a Labor government get into office. Asked if there would be less anger if Ingram supported the coalition, Richardson replied, 'My assessment would be yes.' He said the fact that Ingram had received such resounding support indicated most people agreed with what he was trying to do, but at the same time, Gippsland East had traditionally been a National Party seat for ninety years. 'Some of our constituents will feel that they have been betrayed, I would suggest,' Richardson said of the possibility Ingram might go with Labor.[2]

Ingram drove from Melbourne back to East Gippsland feeling confused and overwhelmed. 'I expected to be a backbencher independent in a reasonably large majority Liberal Government, with fairly feral members opposed to the idea that I could knock off the National Party,' he said. 'It was absolutely gut-wrenching. The whole thing was just, "Arrggghh! What have I done? What have I got myself in for here?"'

⌒

Between the poll and Frankston East, we just watched and waited. We recognised Craig was an independent politician, and although we were on his campaign committee, we were not going to be the sort of people who said, 'You owe us.' He had to make his own decision.

GLENICE WHITE

Graham Pike watched a familiar pair of large bare feet with the trousers rolled up walk past the venetian blinds. It was Cowboy, finally arrived at George Collis's house for a strategy meeting. A week ago, he had been an obscure independent candidate in a remote corner of the state; now the whole nation watching his every move.

Collis was anxious. The Alliance had a once-in-a-lifetime chance, but the window of opportunity would be brief. Ingram had to be smart about how he played the game to get the best possible deal for the Snowy before he lost his advantage — and that included not giving his political enemies ammunition. The Cowboy, as Pike put it, was going to have to hang up his dungarees and grow up.

'You just did not know what could come out of the woodwork,' Pike said. 'So I went through everything, like pulling your coat down when doing a television interview so it does not ride up. And wearing white shirts, not blue, because blue would disappear if they had chromakey backgrounds. And then we got serious. We told Craig he could not associate with anyone using drugs. One beer was okay, but drink in moderation. No more speeding in motor vehicles. When he went to receptions, he should not be left on his own at the end in any room with a woman or women other than his wife. He could not be in any situation where he might be compromised or there was a chance that compromises could be made.'

Ingram listened intently. It made a deep impression, as had his conversation earlier in the week with Peter Nixon's son, Mark. Nixon rang to offer his congratulations and a warning. 'Don't forget your family. I never saw enough of my dad when I was kid.'

Collis, Pike and Ingram then considered the political situation. The coalition had forty-three seats, Labor forty-one, with three independents and Frankston East undecided. 'We went through all the pros and cons, all the different scenarios that might play out, without any pressure on Craig because it had to be his decision as to which way he would go,' said Pike. Ingram said he listened, but came to his own conclusions. 'It was not something you could really take counsel on,' he said. 'I had to make my own decision, and it was very hard.'

In Labor's favour was a better relationship to the NSW Government, their long-standing policy supporting 28 per cent, and the fact they needed Ingram, Davies, Russell and Frankston East to form a minority government with a one-seat majority. It gave Ingram more leverage, but then his electorate would be more comfortable with a coalition government, as would Ingram. The coalition could also potentially enlist its federal colleagues in government in Canberra to pressure New South Wales — except that Kennett had antagonised those colleagues by meddling in national issues. The Commonwealth had also kept out of the Snowy flows debate, leaving the decision to the states.

'I was also not certain that Kennett did not think the poll result was just an aberration,' Ingram said. 'He could form government, stabilise the situation and then go back to the polls and I would end up holding nothing. I knew a solution for the Snowy would not be easy and we needed full term, and so we needed a party that needed us totally and who wanted to go full term.'

After several hours of weighing up, it seemed clear to Ingram that Labor was the best bet. He made the decision with deep misgivings, knowing it would not go down well with his family, much less the electorate. The three men wrote a mock press release, explaining to the East Gippsland electorate the reasons for Ingram's decision; Ingram said it helped to focus his mind on what he had to get out of Labor. 'The first week, I don't think I had a huge amount of control over what was going on. It was very stressful, but after we sat down and worked out some clear objectives and strategies, it was pretty hectic but I knew what I had to do. I felt comfortable then that we were in reasonable control of the negotiations, and everything went according to plan.'

The plan was simple: ask both parties for a written commitment to restore 28 per cent to the Snowy River by July 2001. Then keep them both guessing as to which one Ingram would support, in order to keep the pressure on Labor to come up with the best possible deal.

Despite this, Ingram said Kennett was still in with a chance if the Premier played his cards right. The Snowy was Ingram's pivotal issue, but he also wanted satisfactory responses on other issues like rural services and fixing the degraded Gippsland Lakes. Bracks also had to address Ingram's concerns about Labor's approach to other issues, such as logging. 'I think I made it clear I was open to support either side. It was obvious that the Snowy was a passion — but there were other considerations as well, like would my in-laws ever speak to me again if I supported Labor.'

Secrecy was paramount with so much at stake. 'That was an essential part of it, keeping the cards well and truly to ourselves until we played the bastards off on each other, to be brutally frank,' Ingram said. Collis, Ingram and Pike resolved only to discuss the negotiations between themselves, and only face-to-face, to avoid leaks that might ruin the game plan. It was also essential that Ingram give nothing away in his meetings with the parties and the other two independents. As it happens, he has a good poker face.

I was completely and fully aware of how difficult it was for him because of his National Party background, with immediate relatives who were National Members of Parliament. As he moved around East Gippsland, he would have had a lot of people who had long voted National Party meeting him in supermarkets and telling him he should stick with the status quo.

STEVE BRACKS, MELBOURNE 2003

Steve Bracks had been playing his cards for all they were worth since the polls closed. Ingram was quickly identified as the potential weak link. Labor preferences might have delivered Ingram the seat, but he owed Labor nothing and his political pedigree put him firmly in the coalition's camp. If he stayed there, it would be more difficult to persuade Russell Savage and Susan Davies to support Labor. Both disliked and distrusted Kennett but neither wanted a hung parliament. Labor was going to have to jump through hoops with triple twists to prove it could deliver what Ingram wanted. Bracks' policy advisor, Rob Hudson, got the daunting job of working out whether 28 per cent was feasible.

'My first thought was, oh my God, how do you actually do this? Find the water and get the flow?' Hudson said. 'I knew nothing about it, absolutely nothing. I had to find out about water markets, irrigation allocations, pricing and what megalitres and gigalitres actually were. I had to find out the potential for water savings in Victoria and New South Wales. The irrigators were starting to crank up about the implications of Craig being elected, yet we could not alienate Russell.'

Hudson tracked down a bureaucrat willing to give him a crash course. He learned about the intricacies of the water market, which state got what power and water from the Snowy Mountains scheme, and the potential for saving water wasted in Victoria's irrigation districts. He then spent days with the phone glued to his ear, holed up in one of the shabby broom closets they called offices in the ALP campaign headquarters in King Street, West Melbourne. Hudson talked to anyone and everyone with a perspective. He talked to Treasury officials in Victoria and New South Wales, independent economists, environmental experts, the water authorities, irrigation industry groups and activists of all hues.

Politics ruled out the cheapest and easiest solution: buying the water on the open market. Government purchasing on such a scale could inflate prices, and affect small communities reliant on irrigators continuing to farm rather than selling their entitlements. Labor's campaign mantra about caring for rural Victorians would soon start sounding hollow if people perceived the party wanted to take away something as vital as water. It was doubtful New South Wales would agree to entering the market, anyway. Its irrigation districts were a hotbed of discontent over rising water prices, market reforms and poor security of supply. In Victoria, irrigators were assured of getting 100 per cent of their licensed entitlement in 97 out of 100 years; in NSW, it was only one in two years in the Murray irrigation districts, and one in three on the Murrumbidgee. Taking more water away by buying up big in the market would inflame an already volatile political situation.

Hudson needed some sort of commitment from New South Wales, however, although the signs were not encouraging. Victoria's shadow environment spokeswoman, Sherryl Garbutt, advised Bracks that New South Wales was non-committal when she sent letters before the election, but it was well known that the NSW Treasurer, Michael Egan, was implacably opposed to 28 per cent. His department maintained that the state could not afford the costs of infrastructure to recover lost and wasted water; that not enough could be recovered in any case; and that the state would lose millions of dollars in income from reduced power generation. NSW Treasury's preferred option was 6 per cent in the Snowy; at most, it might accept Webster's 15 per cent.

Garbutt, however, also advised that the NSW Premier, Bob Carr, was rumoured to want a good outcome, in the order of 22 per cent. So Steve Bracks called Carr and asked if he would be prepared to meet Ingram and Paul Leete from the Snowy River Alliance. Carr agreed. He did not know Steve Bracks well, but Bracks had produced a hung parliament against the odds, putting him in a position comparable to Carr in 1991. 'I could not form government then, and I wanted to help Bracks get over the line, having been there myself,' Carr said.

There was also more than a touch of *Schandenfreude*, or taking pleasure in others' misfortune. Carr laboured in the shadow of Kennett's flamboyant, can-do, crash or crash through persona. He endured unfavourable comparisons in the media and occasional barbs about his personal style from Kennett himself. Six months earlier, when New South Wales was going to the polls in March 1999, Kennett derided Carr as a weak leader who did not deserve to be re-elected. But now it seemed Kennett was not the consummate politician after all. He'd crashed and burned while Carr was still there. 'There was never any chance of us doing a deal to reinforce Jeff Kennett's position,' Carr said. 'I rather like Jeff, but he was a bit of a showoff and a smartarse.'

Bob Carr's office on the thirty-ninth floor of Governor Macquarie Tower in Sydney, has floor to ceiling windows on two sides. The view is spectacular: a sweeping panorama east and north over the harbour. It was lost on Steve Bracks' chief of staff, Tim Pallas, Paul Leete and Craig Ingram. The three men sat in Carr's office on 28 September 1999, ten days after the Victorian election, with eyes only for the NSW Premier, trying to read his intentions. Bracks told Ingram before Ingram flew to Sydney to meet Carr: 'I give you my word on this — it will be very difficult for Jeff to get Bob Carr to commit to this.'

Leete played the Alliance's video with its graphic before and after images of the Snowy River. He gave his spiel about the huge volumes of water wasted in the irrigation system. The men discussed the potential impacts on irrigators and the commercial viability of the hydro-electric scheme; Leete got agitated over what he regarded as distorted information from Carr's advisors, inflating the costs. Carr assured Leete the public servants did not have the last word. 'We don't take much notice of Treasury!' the Premier said, tongue in cheek.

Then Craig Ingram took over, questioning Carr on his commitment to increased flows in the Snowy. The Premier gave nothing away other than that New South Wales supported increased flows down the Snowy River, but he would not commit to an actual figure. Ingram and Leete were disappointed, but they appreciated the chance to put their case at last: they had never been able to get near Bob Carr before in all the years of campaigning. Crucially for Ingram, the access proved that New South Wales would have a better working relationship with Labor rather than the coalition in Victoria.

Hudson, however, was dealing with the NSW Treasurer's office, and he got no comfort there. Egan's staff intimated that while New South Wales might say publicly it was willing to work with Victoria for the sake of helping Bracks, it would play hardball on the Snowy. 'I have driven through Orbost — it is a godforsaken place and the only thing to do is keep on driving,' one staffer told Rob Hudson. 'Why would you want to waste water through there? There is nothing there but a fish and chip shop, a servo and a dirty café.'

'They did not think it was achievable and thought of the Snowy as a Victorian river,' said Hudson. 'I would say to them that half of it is in New South Wales and most of the improvement will be up there, and they replied, "We don't care, it is not an issue up here."'

It was a nail-biting few weeks. Bracks said later he had no idea what Ingram was thinking. It was not for lack of trying. The Labor Party had its feelers out. Glenice and Max White fielded calls from mysterious strangers who mumbled their names and then asked all sorts of personal questions about Ingram. 'They really tried to scare up any information that could be made into gossip,' said Glenice. Some of them were Labor hacks, some of them from the coalition and the media. Glenice and Max told them all firmly 'No comment' and hung up. Bill Bolitho, who was back on his farm catching up after the mad six weeks of the election campaign, was interrogated; he was an old mate of Ingram's — surely he knew his mind? 'I have no idea what he is thinking,' Bolitho told the party. 'All I can tell you is one thing — Craig is pretty straight. Don't lie to him or feed him any bullshit.'

So there was no relief to the suspense. Steve Bracks and John Thwaites continued to meet once or twice a week with Ingram, sometimes alone, sometimes together with Russell Savage and Susan Davies. They talked about the Charter of Independents; it was not difficult for Labor to agree to it since most of the requests were in their policy platform anyway. They discussed Ingram's other concerns, such as rural neglect and rescuing the degraded Gippsland Lakes. 'We had a good story to tell and our whole emphasis was on restoring infrastructure and services to regional Victoria, so we had a good starting point,' Bracks said.

They also assured Ingram that Labor had a plan for the Snowy River — while crossing their fingers that Rob Hudson would come up with the goods. Hudson is not easily daunted but he was under the hammer. 'There was a big question mark over it and I was being asked if we could do it. People just thought it was beyond possibility.'

Helpful as always, NSW Treasury sent Hudson the figures to show why 28 per cent was impossible. It claimed farm income in the Murray irrigation district would drop by 10 or 11 per cent, or an average $4280 per farm. In the Murrumbidgee, income would drop 3.5 to 5.5 per cent, or an average $3200 a year per farm. Security of supply, already a contentious issue, would be even more tenuous: Murray irrigators would receive their full entitlement in only one out of five years, instead of one in two. In the Murrumbidgee, it would be one in ten years, instead of one in three. In Victoria, 100 per cent security would drop from 97 years out of 100 down to 91. All up, NSW Treasury claimed a 28 per cent flow would cost between $378 million and $630 million in lost agricultural production.

The figures were inflated because they assumed returning water to the Snowy meant taking water away from irrigators. By the same token, NSW Treasury and Victoria's public servants advised Hudson that 28 per cent could not be achieved by plugging leaks in the system alone. Hudson's challenge was working out if the naysayers were right or wrong.

‿

In all those meetings with the coalition, I didn't feel there was a genuine commitment to be responsible in the sense they wanted to change — they were doing it because they were desperate to stay in power. I felt a bit sorry for them because I could see they did not relish the process they were put in. They had been in conflict with us, and here they had to sit around in the Premier's office and be nice to us.

RUSSELL SAVAGE, MELBOURNE, 2000

It was a confused and confusing three weeks. Kennett was in overdrive to win the independents' favour. One after another, he backtracked on controversial decisions he had previously imposed on the state with scant regard for public opinion and due process. He promised to reinstate the powers of the Auditor-General after championing their dismantling. He promised to pump millions of dollars into the Frankston East hospital after gutting the state health system in the name of 'efficiency'. He caved in to the National Party demands for more Cabinet positions after years of promoting smaller government.

The Premier said his willingness to adopt most of the Charter of Independents and change his policy priorities did not constitute a backdown, but Ewan Hannan, state political editor for *The Age*, wondered if there was anything Kennett would not do to stay in power. 'Even in these novel times, his apparent preparedness to cut a deal must be confusing, if not disillusioning, to the hordes of Kennett supporters who religiously applauded him "for getting things done",' Hannan wrote.[3]

The independents, too, wondered if there was anything the Premier would not do to stay in office. 'It felt like Jeff Kennett would rip up the fabric of society to get what he wanted,' said Davies. In one private meeting, Kennett offered Russell Savage the job as Speaker of the House; another day the Premier and his deputy, Mark Birrell, told Savage that the Treasurer, Alan Stockdale, wanted to take a job in the private sector immediately, which meant appointing an interim Treasurer until the electoral mess was resolved. 'I know you don't want anything from me, but I want to swear in all my ministers now, with you as Treasurer,' Jeff told Savage.

'But if you go to Government House and swear in the ministers, you are saying to the Governor that you are the Premier, and you have the numbers,' Savage replied. 'And then if we don't support you, there will be a motion of no confidence and we will go back to the polls.'

'No, no, I give you my word that I will hand over to Bracks, if that is what you all decide. I have spoken to Craig about this, and he agrees.'

Savage left the meeting and called Ingram. 'No, that's all news to me,' Ingram said. 'But Jeff did ask me if I wanted to be Speaker.'

Kennett put immense pressure on Ingram and Savage in other ways. He told them they had a duty to support the coalition because they represented traditionally non-Labor seats. He set up a 'telephone tree' of supporters who rang the independents constantly to urge them 'to do the right thing' and back the coalition. He alternately cajoled and bullied. At one point, he threatened retribution if the independents backed Labor. He told them if they supported Labor, he would force a vote in Parliament and video-tape them voting down the coalition. Then he would use the footage against them in the next election. Russell Savage had serious doubts about Labor's readiness to govern, but Kennett was his own worst enemy.

~

I think the campaign to save the Snowy River was an absolute disaster. We are reversing one of the most important engineering feats in our national history, pouring water down a river and denying it to irrigation, which is the basis of our agriculture. It is the snowmelt, too, the beautiful water. Beyond that, we are turning back the potential for the best form of electricity generation. The same people are claiming to be saving the environment, and here they are turning hydro-power into brown coal. I remember being aghast about the claims about the Snowy River only being 1 per cent. That was only at the foot of the dam, and what else would you expect? The Snowy River had more water out its mouth than the Murray River, and on that criteria, Ingram should have been riding up and down in his oilskin trying to get more water for the Murray. I think it was a public relations exercise and lots of well-meaning people were misled by it.

ROGER HALLAM, FORMER NATIONAL PARTY FINANCE MINISTER

One week after the election, Melbourne's *Sunday Herald Sun* reported Kennett would make saving the Snowy River his personal crusade. The same day, the Premier rang Peter Nixon. The former federal National Party minister and Gippsland MP was in Noosa, on his way to the airport to pick up his granddaughter, when his mobile phone rang. He was so surprised to hear Kennett on the other end that he missed his freeway exit.

After months of ignoring Nixon's warnings about the Snowy River, Kennett now wanted his help. 'What would it take to get Craig Ingram to support the government?' he asked Nixon.

'You will have to promise him you will get the water for the Snowy River, and he will need it in black and white.'

'Would you be prepared to talk to him for us?'

'No,' Peter was firm. 'I am not the one to talk to Craig. You'll have to do it yourself. I have no influence over him and I have stayed right out of all of this. I have just let it take its course. If you want Craig to support you, you will have to do the talking.'

Jeff Kennett was going to have to play the game on his own. Nine days later, he had a proposal. Sitting deep in the comfy cushions of the white brocade couch in his office, Kennett explained to Ingram that the government had several million dollars in a bank account from the proceeds of selling power from the Snowy Mountains scheme. He would use that money and future proceeds to set up a $100 million infrastructure investment fund to fix leaks in the irrigation system.

Kennett said his government was taking the flows issue seriously before the election, when it commissioned the consultants Sinclair Knight Mertz to report on how much water might be saved, where, and at what cost. Preliminary investigations by the Department of Natural Resources and Environment, however, suggested Victoria would be able to find 75 gigalitres, which was roughly its one-quarter share of the 28 per cent flow. The government would try to persuade New South Wales to come up with its three-quarter share, but if worst came to the worst, Victoria would aim to find the whole 28 per cent by buying water in the market as well as finding more savings within the state. Ingram was not sure how the plan might go down with the National Party, but Kennett assured him the junior coalition party would do what he told them.

Kennett had first run the proposal past Barry Steggall, the National Party member for Swan Hill. Steggall thought it was a bad idea. The Murray Water Entitlement Committee, which he had chaired in the mid-1990s, had recommended that Victoria allocate 33 gigalitres to the Snowy River. This was roughly the state's one-quarter share of a 15 per cent flow. He doubted New South Wales could find its share of 15 per cent, much less more — and if there was more water to spare, then the Murray was in greater need. Steggall was also very nearly a casualty of rural discontent with the Kennett Government, almost losing his seat to former footballer Carl Dietrich, running as an independent. With many irrigators among his constituents, Steggall was disturbed to see the Snowy River emerging as a key issue driving Jeff Kennett's efforts to retain office.

'I told Kennett his plan was not a good idea because it was going too far for the acceptance of people in northern Victoria,' Steggall said. 'I was greatly concerned because sensible outcomes were going by the side. It was one of those things that sounds good and looks good, but we could not deliver it, and that is bad policy. Kennett would not have got what he offered because there was no way he would have got it through the coalition.'

Ingram had Kennett's offer in his head when he met later the same day with the National Party's Pat McNamara and Finance Minister, Roger Hallam. Ingram wanted to know what the Nationals could do for the Snowy. He mentioned he had been offered a $100 million infrastructure fund created over five years with earnings from the hydro scheme. McNamara and Hallam promised they would look into what was feasible and get back to Ingram as soon as possible.

Before the election, McNamara supported Kennett's decision to pursue the 15 per cent flow as realistic and achievable. Now he made a pragmatic decision for the sake of retaining office. 'I said we could support the 28 per cent; it would just cost us money and we had to weigh that against things like schools and hospitals,' McNamara told me. 'But for us to survive, we had to find that money — and you tend to do this when you want to stay in government! It would not be a problem with the other members politically if the flow was achieved through savings — as long as it did not affect existing entitlements.'

But Roger Hallam, like Barry Steggall, was dismayed. 'If it seems like I was out of step, it is because I was out of step,' he said. 'We took an executive decision and that was to support the 28 per cent target, but I thought it was illogical and unrealistic and I have not changed my view on it.' He was determined that Ingram, too, should know what was realistic. 'I always kept my feet on the ground.'

The next day, the three independents met with the leaders of the coalition parties together, for detailed negotiations on the Charter of Independents. Roger Hallam slipped a sheet of paper to Ingram as he was leaving. It was an analysis, detailing why the proposed infrastructure fund would not work. Hallam's figures showed the revenue from the scheme's power sales was about half what Kennett had claimed. Ingram wondered why the National Party would be trying to white-ant its coalition partner's idea. Then he realised the Finance Minister had assumed the plan came from Steve Bracks, not Jeff Kennett.

Hallam told me he had a close working relationship with Kennett and would not knowingly have undermined him. Yet his analysis revealed at this crucial time that the lines of communication between the coalition partners were down. That set off the alarm bells for Ingram. 'It proved the relationship was pretty rocky,' Ingram said. 'They weren't talking to each other. The coalition was unstable. It relied on me, and Russell Savage — and to get my support, they would potentially have to sell out the irrigators. I thought there was a good chance some of the Nationals, especially up along the Murray, would not stand for that.'

&

Carr would be more likely to work constructively with the Victorian ALP, and this will help in the intergovernmental power relations during negotiations. I'm not sure how far Carr will go for us if he is outnumbered on important aspects of the environmental flow decision. In general, 'new' governments, after having spent some time in Opposition, keep their promises longer and are more vigorous in implementation and administration than parties that have been in power some time.

JEFF ANGEL, TOTAL ENVIRONMENT CENTRE,
UNSOLICITED ADVICE TO CRAIG INGRAM

Ingram barely had the chance to cogitate on the implications of poor communication within coalition ranks before the media found out about his 'secret' meeting with Bob Carr on 28 September. Some reports claimed Carr had given the independent encouraging signals. The NSW Premier happened to be in Melbourne that day. Journalists collared him to ask if he

Mark Knight's take on New South Wales Premier Bob Carr's role in determining whether Jeff Kennett retained office. *Photo: Mark Knight/Newspix,* The Herald Sun, *7 October 1999.*

was Victoria's kingmaker, brokering deals with Ingram to ensure Steve Bracks won office.

Carr said he had promised Ingram nothing more than that New South Wales would take his position into account. Then he added that Victorians had voted for change in government, and if he could help Bracks become Premier by doing 'the right thing', then he would. 'I support Steve Bracks but I don't get a vote,' he said.[4]

Kennett was furious at what he saw as Carr meddling on his turf. There was only a week to go before the Frankston East supplementary election, and the can-do Premier was desperate to show what he could do for Ingram. A couple of weeks earlier, New South Wales had asked Victoria to agree to releasing an extra 300 gigalitres from the Snowy Mountains scheme to help drought-stricken irrigators. Otherwise, New South Wales farmers would get just 11 per cent of their licensed entitlement, which was not enough to plant crops. The water had to be released by the end of October or it would be too late to sow seed. As it happened, 300 gigalitres was also close to 28 per cent in the Snowy for one year. Jeff Kennett saw his chance to force Bob Carr's hand.

He wrote to Carr, saying he found it 'difficult to see how we could agree to your Government's urgent request' given New South Wales' stance on the Snowy River. Kennett castigated Bob Carr for failing to respond to his request in May for 'at least a 15 per cent increase in Snowy flow'. Kennett also claimed Victoria really wanted 28 per cent back then, but asked for less only because of New South Wales' reluctance to negotiate.[5]

Kennett then went on the attack in the media, blaming the NSW Government for the irrigators' predicament. He said New South Wales had failed to provide security of supply, unlike Victoria, which always held back some water in reserve in case the following season was dry. He said if New South Wales did not have enough water to meet its irrigators' entitlements, then clearly it did not have water to spare for the Snowy River — so Carr was not in a position to be making promises to Craig Ingram or Steve Bracks. He also intimated it was a bit rich for New South Wales to expect Victoria to come to its rescue at the drop of a hat when it had continually deferred a decision on the Snowy. 'You can't on the one hand refuse to conclude contracts and then ask us to agree to others at your whim,' Kennett told Radio CO-FM in Albury-Wodonga. 'We're saying, we can give approval for 300 tomorrow. Right? We're not opposed to the water being released. What we are saying is sign off on Webster. You've had it since last year. Surely the two can go hand in hand.'[6]

Ingram privately applauded Kennett's hardline stand. The irrigation lobby applied the blowtorch. More than 1500 farmers attended a fiery meeting in Deniliquin, and threatened to sue the Victorian, NSW and Commonwealth governments for $500 million damages if they could not plant crops. The NSW member for Murrumbidgee, Adrian Piccoli, said the battle between environmentalists and farmers over water had become a massive propaganda war. 'The environmental lobbies are kicking our bums in terms of public relations — that's why we are losing!' he said.[7]

Piccoli was only one of many stoking the passions. The president of the Rice Growers Association of Australia, Mr Ian Douglas said it was inconceivable that the Victorian and NSW governments would consider increasing flows to the Snowy River when the future of up to 3000 farmers and dozens of rural communities was at stake.[8] Warren Elsbury, the secretary of Murray Irrigation Ltd, predicted the world would end. 'Hundreds of farms will fail, town businesses will fail, export markets will be lost, economic indicators will be hit — and no one in government is listening to us,' he said. 'We're talking about $300 million, half the Australian rice crop and risking a further $150 million from dairy farms producing 20 per cent of NSW's milk. It is madness.'[9]

The NSW Government also hit back at Kennett. The Victorian Premier's letter to Bob Carr was barely out of the fax machine before the Agriculture Minister, Richard Amery, responded with a press release. 'Mr Kennett has chosen to sacrifice NSW rice growers in a last ditched [sic] effort to salvage his political career … This proves Mr Kennett has learnt nothing from his rebuff by rural Victoria.' Amery said the extra 300 gigalitres was a one-off commercial request that had nothing to do with negotiations on the Snowy flow. He accused Kennett of misrepresenting his government's position for political advantage. 'In today's letter to Mr Carr, Mr Kennett refers to a May letter in which he referred to "at least a 15 per cent increase" in the flow of Snowy … His May letter, however, refers to a 15 per cent only flow as Victoria's favoured option.'[10]

It was embarrassing, but Kennett was defiant. By the time Ingram went to Sydney for a horseback rally on 12 October, the irrigators were threatening to blockade the Hume Highway between Sydney and Melbourne. The Prime Minister, John Howard, entered the fray. He told Federal Parliament that the water resources of the Snowy Mountains were too precious to become a pawn in the contest for government in Victoria. Behind the scenes, his ministers were leaning hard on Kennett to quit playing games.

The Alliance, the Total Environment Centre, Chris Barry from the East Gippsland Catchment Management Authority and Charles Lane from The Myer Foundation had organised the horseback rally weeks earlier, when it was thought the Victorian election result was a no-brainer and New South Wales the only government worth pressuring. The Myer Foundation made two last grants in September 1999: $15,000 each to Environment Victoria and the Total Environment Centre in New South Wales to pay for advertising and other forms of community education. 'We needed to stay with them,' said Lane. 'It was clear the campaign had run a good course, but it was flagging a little and the opportunity to do something about it was diminishing. We were on the eve of a decision. We had to make the best possible push on influencing decision-makers in Victoria, New South Wales and the Commonwealth.' The unexpected Victorian cliffhanger was manna from publicity heaven as the Alliance prepared for the rally.

'We traipsed up to Sydney, two cars of us, with Craig and Jo and Paul and The Myer Foundation,' said Glenice White. 'We were staying in Liverpool and had to get the train into the city. We had these banners and T-shirts, "Save the Snowy", and we were giving them to people on the train as it got packed and before we got out of the carriage, almost all said in one voice, "Hope you win! Hope you get the water!"'

It was a nice warm day in Sydney and the hired horses behaved beautifully. Craig Ingram and actor Tom Burlinson rode up Macquarie Street to Parliament House: the parliamentary and the cinematic Men from Snowy River together. Behind them rode Mike Gooey from the Snowy-Genoa Catchment Management Committee on a spare horse that needed a rider. Caught on TV, Gooey raised bureaucratic eyebrows, and he was later asked whose side he was on. 'He was there obviously on his lunch break,' said one of his defenders.

The Women of the Snowy River sang another song penned by the indefatigable Therese Shead, to the tune of 'We shall not be moved'.

New South Wales and Bob Carr,
Please listen to our plan.
The once mighty Snowy River has a brand new man.
Become a legend as the one who lent a hand,
Come on, please make a stand.
We want at least 28 per cent,
We will not, we will not relent,
We want to see the Snowy River flow again
To a healthy extent.

'No Australian wants to see it die!' Tom Burlinson told the assembled journalists. 'This once wild and majestic river of the deepest blue colour now has virtually no flow. It is infested with weeds and in many areas is nothing more than a series of stagnating pools filled with toxic algae. If water is not returned, the river will slowly but surely die.'

Ingram read a poem: 'Should nature write a message in the dust where there were pools/it would be one simple sentence/Mankind is led by fools.' He told the Sydney media he was looking for a government that had the best interests of rural Victoria at heart, and one of the key issues was the Snowy was a key issue.

The media lapped it up, but not everyone was positive. Glenice White happened to stand next to a grumbling, well-dressed onlooker. 'If they bloody knew what they were talking about and got jobs, they might do better!' the man was muttering.

'You know, the Snowy does need the water, and who are you?' Glenice said. The man was from one of the rice-grower groups.

'Oh well, everyone is entitled to some water, you know,' Glenice said.

'Stupid bloody woman,' he replied, and moved away.

Glenice shrugged. 'We got that all the time,' she said later.

The last hurrah of the mild-mannered caravan park manager turned savvy political campaigner. Paul Leete addresses the Sydney horseback rally on 12 October 1999, making the most of media attention on the political drama in Victoria. A week later, a burnt-out Leete turned his back on the campaign and moved with his family to Coff's Harbour. *Source: Total Environment Centre, Sydney.*

Gary Donovan from the NSW Irrigators Council told the journalists: 'If you take away the water that the Snowy provides to the food bowl of the west, then you turn it back into a dust bowl. If you take away the water, you take away the food.' He said the wider population would not be fooled 'by romantic imagery or scientific trickery'.[11] On radio, Sydney shock jock John Laws tore strips off Ingram, accusing him of being a home wrecker among farm families in the irrigation districts. Paul Leete characteristically and colourfully retorted that some Murray River irrigators were 'right-wing greedy heads about water'. It was his last hurrah. Two weeks later, he and Lindy packed up their house and their children and went to Coffs Harbour to run a banana farm. It would be five years before Leete returned to Dalgety to see what they did with his beloved Snowy River.

⤳

The day after the rally, the Commonwealth met representatives from Murray Irrigation Ltd to discuss the water crisis. Kennett was still holding out on rural radio in the morning. A few hours later, he caved in. He wrote a conciliatory letter to Bob Carr, agreeing to the 300 gigalitres, but asking that it be paid back to the scheme by the end of 2001. That was not difficult for New South Wales to agree to since it had asked for the water as a loan right from the start.

The water also was not a 'gift' to irrigators, as Kennett had portrayed it, but a commercial proposition. As it transpired, few farmers bought the water because it was too expensive. As for the Snowy River, Kennett said, 'We do not want to see further deferrals by NSW of its decision on environmental flows and in your response to the Webster Report. We support full environmental flows and seek a clear statement from your Government of your intentions by next week's meeting of the MDBMC [Murray Darling Basin Ministerial Council].'[12]

Ingram found out in the afternoon that Kennett had given in. Playing hardball over the water was Kennett's last chance and, as far as Ingram was concerned, the Premier blew it. 'It was a bargaining chip and Kennett seized it to blackmail New South Wales. It backfired. Jeff had no leverage over New South Wales and the one thing he did have he did not use well enough,' Ingram said later.

Ingram was left with the impression that the coalition was not totally committed to saving the legendary river. He also suspected Kennett had buckled under pressure from the Commonwealth, which confirmed in his mind that the Premier would have trouble persuading his federal colleagues to come to the party on the Snowy River. Annoyed, Ingram told the media he would hate to have Kennett selling his house. Annoyed in turn, Kennett told Ingram in their next meeting, on 15 October that he was not comfortable with that comment.

'Well, you've announced an agreement which, a few days before, you said you wouldn't,' Ingram retorted. 'Without any communication with me, you've just gone and basically sold out one of our major bargaining chips.'

This was not a good conversation to be having the day before the Frankston East supplementary election. Ingram's confidence in the coalition eroded further when Kennett revealed that private polling suggested it had little chance of winning Frankston East. That meant the coalition would need both Ingram and Russell Savage to form government. Jeff Kennett and his deputy, Mark Birrell, worked hard on persuading Ingram, homing in at one point on Ingram's misgivings about Labor's policies on natural resource management, such as forests and fisheries. They queried whether he could have confidence in Sherryl Garbutt, if she became minister. Ingram was even more discomfited — it seemed they had somehow learned the gist of what he had thought was a private conversation with some constituents a week or two earlier. 'I had made some off-the-cuff remarks about issues that would potentially influence my decision,' he explained. 'When they raised this, I thought, now how do they know that? And basically it was because they had sent someone off to find out stuff about me.'

The discussions were long and protracted; Ingram had to leave midway through to go to his next meeting, with Steve Bracks and John Thwaites. He promised he would come back to the Premier's office afterwards to resume negotiations.

〜

> By the end of the last week, I had just presumed that Craig would go
> with Labor, but he did not say anything to me. Susan Davies asked
> me what I thought Craig would do, and I said I did not know. In
> that last week we had a discussion round the kitchen table, my wife
> Gay and my son. I asked my son what I should do, and he said 'Go,
> Bracksy!' That was his assessment, made in the last week after
> listening to all our discussions.
>
> RUSSELL SAVAGE, MELBOURNE, 2004

It was showtime in the Opposition rooms at Parliament House. but Ingram had played his cards well over the past few weeks. Bracks said he still had no idea that afternoon which way Ingram was leaning. Bracks and John Thwaites had put Labor's case to Craig Ingram; they felt it was a good case, Labor could not give the Gippsland East independent what he wanted: 28 per cent in the Snowy River by July 2001. The NSW Treasurer, Michael Egan, would not promise anything more concrete than a final round of discussions on flows 'with interested parties', in light of 'new information that had emerged in the year since the Snowy Water Inquiry'.[13] It was like getting blood from a stone to persuade Egan to put even just that in writing. Rob Hudson made several pleading phone calls before Egan's office finally released a statement the day before Bracks was due to meet Ingram for this crucial final meeting. When Hudson called Sydney to thank the Treasurer and his staff, the advisor who took the call said, 'We're happy to help you out with words, but don't think this means you're going to get anything in the negotiations. It's the fiftieth anniversary of the Snowy Mountains scheme this weekend, and we're going down there with the river killers for the celebrations. We're going to get up on the edge of Jindabyne dam and piss over the edge. That'll give you your environmental flow.'

Bracks made much of the fact that he had already laid the groundwork for the negotiations via his letter to Bob Carr before the election, and his facilitation of the meeting between Carr and the Snowy River Alliance afterwards. Then he called Hudson in to show Ingram exactly how Labor in Victoria would achieve the 28 per cent flow.

The silver bullet was details of the 'new information' New South Wales would consider. It was the additional potential savings identified in the Bewsher Consulting report to NSW Treasury, which identified at least 154 gigalitres that could be recovered from irrigation areas along the Murray and Darling rivers. Hudson was sure more savings could be found given that Bewsher's assessment did not include two large irrigation districts that refused to cooperate. His investigations also led him to believe Victoria would have little trouble coming up with its one-quarter share.

His confidence had been boosted in a formal briefing from the Department of Premier and Cabinet, which he attended with Bracks' chief of staff, Tim Pallas. The department advised that the potential for savings was limited, but the public servants seemed unfamiliar with Bewsher's report. Instead, they were still working from a default position of returning a maximum 15 per cent flow, notwithstanding Kennett's change of heart since the election. 'You know more about the Snowy than they do,' Tim Pallas said to Hudson as they left. 'And if that is the advice Kennett is getting from the bureaucracy, then he is in trouble.'

Hudson was able to demonstrate to Ingram the costs and location of likely water savings in New South Wales as well as in Victoria's irrigation districts. He explained that Victoria would invest $100 million in funding its one-quarter share of the water savings. Importantly, a Labor Government would also spend $20 million on environmental repair works to arrest the degradation of the Gippsland Lakes, another of Ingram's priority issues. Then Hudson went back to his cramped office, leaving the leaders to further discussions with Ingram.

Within minutes, Steve Bracks came rushing in. 'Quick, bring the charter here — Craig is going to sign now!' Except the charter was not there — it was in the briefcase of another advisor, James Higgins. He answered Hudson's phone call in a pub near Labor campaign headquarters at the other end of town. It was the night before the Frankston East supplementary election, all that could be done to secure the seat had been done, and there was not much else for the staff to do but contemplate their futures over a few beers.

'James, quick, bring the charter up here — Craig is going to sign!' said Hudson.

'Well, I haven't got it with me, and I've had a few drinks,' replied James. 'Do you have to get it there right now?'

'Get in a taxi then — we need it now!'

So Ingram signed the charter, supporting Labor to form office. His only conditions were that Labor must win Frankston East the next day, and say nothing before Ingram announced his decision on Monday. Even though Labor was not promising everything he wanted, Ingram backed them for the reasons articulated on that first Saturday with Collis and Pike: Labor was the best bet to get water for the Snowy.

Bracks stood up and shook Ingram's hand as the independent put down the pen. 'You've made the right decision — you won't regret it,' he said.

Ingram went back to resume his discussions with Jeff Kennett and Mark Birrell. He told them he would consider his options over the weekend and would make his announcement on Monday. Then Ingram jumped into his old ute and drove four and a half hours back home. He packed up his wife and four young children and went fishing for the weekend on the Snowy River, far beyond the reach of mobile telephones and the media. Jeff Kennett, meanwhile, made a bet with his chief of staff, Anna Cronin, that he would be forming government on Monday morning.[14]

I was the only one the coalition could have persuaded, I think,
because they had misled Craig on what they were preparing to do
with the Snowy River. But the real problem I had with Kennett was I
could not trust him, and you can't go into a minority arrangement if
you can't trust the person who is the Premier. I said later that if he
had resigned, things might have been different. People in the Liberal
Party afterwards asked why didn't I tell them that, and I said
because it is not my job to determine the leadership, and if they
couldn't work it out for themselves, that is their call. You would have
to be dumb to think I would support Kennett.

RUSSELL SAVAGE, MELBOURNE, 2004

Steve Bracks and John Thwaites have the same birthday, 16 October, which in 1999 also happened to be the day of the Frankston East supplementary election. The day before, a lunchtime barbeque was organised at Labor campaign headquarters to celebrate. The birthday boys, Tim Pallas and Rob Hudson were late getting there due to the unexpected developments with Ingram at Parliament House, but their mood was especially festive. Tim Pallas wandered around introducing Hudson to everyone as 'the man who helped deliver us Craig Ingram'.

The next day, the voters in Frankston East resoundingly endorsed the Labor candidate Matt Viney; Bracks and Thwaites could not have asked for a better birthday present. Tim Pallas hopped in a plane and flew to West Gippsland, where Susan Davies had the charter. She signed it, and Pallas flew to Mildura for the third and final signature, Russell Savage's. Pallas arrived late at John Thwaites' Albert Park home on the Sunday, where another birthday barbeque was in full swing. 'Mr Premier, I deliver you government,' Pallas said as he laid the charter down before Bracks with three signatures. Photos of the occasion hang now on the walls of the Premier's office. Bracks is seated, staring at the document on the table before him and grinning like the cat that got the cream, surrounded by a deliriously happy mob of soon-to-be ministers.

Jeff Kennett conceded defeat two days later, on Tuesday. He said he had decided it was not in Victoria's best interests for the coalition to contest the independents' decision. At the same time, he announced he would step down as Liberal Party leader and return to the backbench. In his farewell speech, he said his government had worked to restore a sense of pride, dignity and employment to Victoria, but he acknowledged that some Victorians had not appreciated his style, nor the outcome of his policies.

He went out in typical Jeff style, with a spray of invective against the three independents for making it possible for Labor to fall into office in an 'extraordinary way ... It is not that they [Labor] have won government, they have no mandate, they are a minority Labor government supported by three individuals, one of whom hasn't even been sworn in as a parliamentarian; one of whom, of course, would do us all a better service perhaps if she just rejoined the Labor Party; and the third who has indicated that he didn't believe the Labor Party had the experience to govern. So be it.'[15]

⌒

My view was that I would cop more flak supporting Labor than the Liberals, but I was not in this to become completely well liked — I was here to achieve some of the things I set out to achieve.

CRAIG INGRAM, MELBOURNE, 2003

Tony Meade was driving home from work along Bairnsdale's Main Street late on the day Craig Ingram had made public his decision to support Labor. One of his constituents left Ingram a message: 'Labor scab' they sprayed across his electoral office window in 30-centimetre-high iridescent green letters. Odd use of the word scab, thought Meade as he cruised past. It looked awful, graffiti scrawled like that across a prominent shop front, so he collected some paper towel and a can of cleaner from home, drove back and washed away the first spray of vitriol from some very angry Gippsland East voters.

Ingram was always going to make an unpopular decision. Gippsland East felt neglected by the coalition, but that did not mean the people wanted a Labor government instead. When Ingram first told his wife, Ann-Maree, he intended to support Labor, she blurted, 'No, you can't do that! You just can't!' She couldn't believe what she was hearing. 'My family is very strong National Party and we have always, Craig and I, voted National Party,' she said later. 'But looking back, we wouldn't have had it any other way. I think it was the right decision as far as the Snowy goes and getting the water. We would never have got it otherwise, not in a million years.'

In announcing his decision, Craig Ingram stressed his independence. He said he had only guaranteed Labor supply so that it could govern, but everything else that came before Parliament was up for negotiation. Less than one hour later, the first of many disgruntled letters came through the fax. 'I believe most strongly that you have gravely misrepresented the Gippsland East electorate,' the woman wrote. 'The majority of this electorate did not vote Labor ... It goes without saying that your political career will be short-lived, irrespective of whether you achieve your aims for the Snowy.'[16]

On the other hand, the majority of the electorate — 64 per cent — did not vote for the coalition either. They voted for Ingram, Labor, One Nation and two other independents, and gave Ingram their preferences. 'I owe a lot of people,' he joked at the time. Ingram, who had never voted Labor in his life, knew he was in an impossible position. 'I am basically a conservative person,' he told me at the time in an interview for *The Age*. 'This is a conservative electorate. It was a very tough decision to have to make ... I was very uncomfortable supporting the coalition for a number of reasons. I am also slightly uncomfortable with this decision, but I believe they are the best team to provide a transparent, stable government ... I find it easy to accept that if I am voted out next time, then I haven't done a good job.'[17]

Ingram told his constituents he was happy to discuss the reasons for his decision with anyone who wanted to come to his office. Only one person took up the offer. Two weeks later, a newspaper poll found a clear majority of voters in East Gippsland supported Ingram's decision to back Labor.[18]

When first elected, Ingram said he would be a one-hit wonder, and get out when he had achieved what he set out to achieve. Something changed. Three years later, in the next election, Ingram was returned as the independent member for East Gippsland with an increased primary vote, up from 24.8 per cent in 1999 to 41.3 per cent in 2002. The National Party's Darren Chester limped in a poor second with 24 per cent. Ingram's Pygmalion-like transformation from unknown abalone diver to polished politician was complete.

SEVEN

A Tale of Two Rivers

Jim Small, the Member for Murray, invited me on a fact-finding tour
of the irrigation areas after we met in Sydney in 1997. Most of the
people I met were very reasonable, and not aggressive. One of their
leaders said, 'We can't oppose what you are doing because we are
seeking the same thing with the Murray and it would be very
hypocritical.' They were just concerned about where and when the
water would come from, and how it would affect them.

But the light went off when we were standing at the off-take pipe
for the Mulwala Canal at Yarrawonga. We are looking at all this
water gushing out into the canal, and one of the irrigators said, 'I bet
you are thinking that all that water coming out of there could be
going down the Snowy.' And I said, 'No.' I was looking at the waste,
at the water leaking from under the gates. I realised they lived in
such a water environment, with so much of the stuff in the canals
and rivers and dams, that they could not even see the waste, the little
bits, whereas in Dalgety we lived in a drought environment and we
saw every little bit of water lying around the place. I could see the
mindset. I pointed the waste out, but the irrigator shrugged his
shoulders — he could not see it.

Paul Leete

There is a hill near Griffith, in New South Wales, a rocky, scrubby outcrop, the kind of place where bored teenagers hang out amid a rubble of beer cans and dead campfires. But the view from the top is impressive: a panorama of orange groves, vineyards and rice paddies. In the distance, shimmering in the heat, is the line between this green oasis and the dry heartbreak country from which it emerged. Irrigation made this desert mirage real, and the locals are rightly proud of the results.

Griffith is the largest town in the Murrumbidgee Irrigation Area (MIA), which supports more than 35,000 people. Unemployment is practically non-existent. Murrumbidgee Irrigation, the agency responsible for delivering water, claims the gross value of farm production in the area is $700 million a year. It is a similar story elsewhere in the Murray/Murrumbidgee river valley. Coleambally, to the south of the MIA, is a community of 1800 people created in 1959 specifically to make use of water from the Snowy Mountains Hydro-Electric Scheme. It values its farm production at $50 million a year.

Even further south is the Murray Irrigation District, centred on Deniliquin. Murray Irrigation says its produce has an annual farm-gate value of $300 million, and supports a population of 25,000 people. 'Irrigated agriculture is vital to the local economy and community,' the company says in its corporate brochures. Victoria, too, champions the social and economic benefits of irrigation. According to the Victorian Farmers Federation, the gross value of irrigated agriculture in the Murray-Goulburn valley and the Sunraysia district around Mildura is $1.8 billion, or 25 per cent of the state's total agricultural output, and increasing at 1 per cent a year. Taken together, these irrigation districts are the most productive areas in Australia's food bowl, the Murray Darling Basin, which generates 40 per cent of the nation's agricultural wealth from an area that makes up one-seventh of the continent.

A 28 per cent flow in the Snowy River could not be achieved without sacrificing these lands of milk and honey, and robbing Australia and the world of their bounty. At least, that was how the irrigation lobby responded to the Snowy River campaign. Opposition began to build during the Snowy Water Inquiry in 1998, when it was clear the campaign was gaining political traction. In principle, the irrigation lobby supported the need for an environmental flow in the Snowy River, but it was sceptical that 140 gigalitres could be recovered by plugging off-farm leaks to deliver Webster's 15 per cent flow. But if the water *was* there, the irrigators wanted most of it for their own stressed rivers, to avoid having to reduce their consumption.[1]

The scaremongering about Snowy flows being the supposed ruination of inland Australia began in earnest when Labor won office in Victoria. 'The biggest threat to our area is uninformed comment and emotive untruths regarding our industries,' Jon Cobden, chairman of Coleambally Community Action, wrote in The Weekly Times. 'I don't believe that any environmentalists or politicians (even Mr Ingram) would like to see our irrigation communities disappear. I'm sure they all like to eat.'[2]

Gary Donovan, chief executive of the NSW Irrigators Association, dismissed 28 per cent as 'fairyland stuff' harking back to a 'prehistoric' past. Mr Dean Bortoli, spokesman for a Murrumbidgee committee formed to raise money for a publicity counter-assault, said irrigators would only accept an 8 per cent flow in the Snowy River, provided they did not lose any water.[3]

Bill Hetherington, chairman of Murray Irrigation, gave Steve Bracks a glossy brochure when they met in Melbourne on 20 December 1999. Entitled *The Other Side of the Snowy*, it called for a balanced assessment and recognition of mutual responsibilities. 'Amidst the emotion of the current debate over the Snowy River, it is vitally important we do not lose sight of the environmental and economic costs associated with any changes, including the potential for devastating impact [sic] on the Murray and Murrumbidgee rivers and inland communities,' said an accompanying statement.[4]

The brochure was produced by the Murrumbidgee, Coleambally and Murray Irrigation agencies, the Rice Growers Association of Australia and the MIA Council of Horticultural Associations. It argued against returning water to the Snowy on the grounds the river still has 55 per cent of its natural flow out its mouth; that a 15 per cent flow from Jindabyne would cost $4 for every $1 benefit; and that removing just 10 per cent of water from irrigation regions would cause a net farm-gate loss of $70 million, decommission up to 500 farms and lose regional jobs. 'The romantic notion of letting the Snowy River run free does little to help the Government on behalf of the Australian people reconcile what is an inherently complex issue,' the brochure says.

The issues were indeed very complex, but not the way the irrigation lobby presented them. In the politics of perception, its case boiled down to a simple choice between the welfare of people living along the Murray and Murrumbidgee, and the dreams of those on the Snowy. The irrigation lobby is very powerful politically, and does not pull its punches, but the hard evidence supporting its case was, to put it kindly, rather thin on the ground.

Take the oft-quoted comparison that the Snowy has 55 per cent of its original flow out its mouth, compared with the Murray's 21 per cent. This is a selective use of statistics. Before white settlement, only 54 per cent of the total inflow into the Murray River ever made it to sea. The rest evaporated or was soaked up by vegetation. Now the Murray has 110 per cent of its historic inflow, thanks to the Snowy Mountains scheme, and 21 per cent of that flows out to sea. This means the flow out the mouth is actually 40 per cent of its historic level,[5] compared with the Snowy's 55 per cent. These figures include major floods, however, which distort the averages. Median flows — those occurring in most years — are more accurate. The Murray's median flow out the mouth is now 27 per cent of its original level, compared with the Snowy's 39 per cent.

Flows out a river's mouth are, in any case, a crude and ecologically meaningless comparison. Two-thirds the way along the Snowy, for instance, at Willis on the New South Wales border, the median flow is only 12 per cent of its pre-scheme level. A river's health must be judged by what is happening along its length, and by that measure both the Murray and Snowy are dying for want of the right amount of water at the right times of the year.

The irrigation lobby insinuated that increasing flows in the Snowy would inevitably accelerate deteriorating conditions in the Murray and impoverish irrigators. But the Victorian and NSW governments agreed from the start that their negotiations would proceed on the principle that restoring the Snowy would come at no cost to the inland rivers or the irrigators. The Snowy would only flow again if water lost in leaky, uncovered irrigation delivery channels could be recovered. In theory, thousands of gigalitres are lost through evaporation, waste and seepage; in practice, no one knows how much can realistically be recovered and at what financial cost until the authorities give it a go. With that in mind, Victoria and New South Wales also agreed savings had to be achieved and verified before the Snowy got any more water. Only as a last resort would the governments buy water from irrigators through the market to top up the Snowy's allocation.

Even if the water did come from irrigation allocations, returning 28 per cent to the Snowy would barely be noticed inland. The Snowy River and the Snowy Mountains Hydro-Electric Scheme are often used interchangeably, as if 28 per cent in the Snowy River translates directly to a 28 per cent reduction in water released into the Murray and Murrumbidgee. This is not the case. The Snowy River accounts for just under half the water captured by the scheme; the rest comes by diverting and regulating rivers such as the Geehi, Tumut, Tooma and Murrumbidgee, which all flow inland eventually in any case.

The calculation is complex, but, essentially, a 28 per cent flow in the Snowy River translates to about a 1.4 per cent decrease in Murray River flows, and about 6 per cent in the Murrumbidgee. In severe drought years, this would rise to 4.5 per cent and 8.4 per cent respectively.[6] In a different analysis, the Australian Bureau of Agricultural and Resource Economics estimated a 28 per cent flow represented 1 per cent of water consumed in the Murray irrigation areas, and 2 per cent of irrigation water consumed along the Murrumbidgee. In severe one-in-thirty-year droughts, this would rise to a collective 11.7 per cent.[7] This assumes that 1 gigalitre more going down the Snowy River at Jindabyne equals 1 gigalitre less available to farmers. In truth, 65 per cent of the latter is lost in transmission through evaporation or flowing out to sea.[8]

These small fractions compare with the estimated 20–30 per cent of water lost inland due to seepage, leakage, evaporation, escapes, theft and spills.[9] A study released in December 2004 by the federal Deputy Prime Minister John Anderson estimated a massive 900 gigalitres a year could be saved in the Murrumbidgee alone at a cost of $824 million in pipes and new technology. The study found 1334 gigalitres or a third of the river's flow, was lost through leaks, evaporation and overuse, or unaccounted for due to inadequate control.[10] The Murray Darling Basin Commission earlier estimated 3036 gigalitres were lost through leaky channels, evaporation and inefficient on-farm practices across the lower basin. Much of that water would be extremely expensive to recover, if in fact it was possible or even desirable; some, for instance, runs off farms and back into parched waterways and wetlands that otherwise would go without. However, the commission estimated a mere 10 per cent improvement in efficiency on and off farms would free up 1000 gigalitres of water.[11]

Economic impacts are similarly marginal. The Australian Bureau of Agricultural and Resource Economics estimates a 25 per cent flow in the Snowy River would cost irrigators $6.6 million in reduced production. This is less than 1 per cent of the estimated $750 million worth of agricultural production in the New South Wales irrigation areas that get water from the Snowy Mountains scheme.[12] These costs could be more than offset by switching from low-value crops like rice to high-value horticultural crops, which have a far higher dollar return per megalitre of water used.

Virtually all of Australia's rice is grown in the Murray/Murrumbidgee irrigation areas. The reliance on this crop reveals a deeper problem with water security. Irrigation development was driven in large part by a desire to 'drought-proof' inland Australia. Victoria has largely achieved this goal, because its agencies hold back water in reserve every year as insurance against dry seasons. It means that its irrigators can rely on getting their full entitlement in 97 out of 100 years, with the chance to buy another 100 per cent of their entitlement from excess 'sales' water in 67 out of 100 years.

New South Wales, however, has been rather cavalier in its approach. It holds nothing in reserve from one year to the next, with the result that farmers get practically nothing in droughts. On average, New South Wales irrigators along the Murray get their full entitlement in only one out of two years; along the Murrumbidgee, it is only one in three. The insecurity of supply encourages opportunistic behaviour. Farmers rely on annual crops like rice, and they plant as much as the water available allows. They also rely on top-ups from the Snowy Mountains scheme in a big dry like 1999. In that year, there was only enough water to allocate 11 per cent of irrigators' entitlements, but the Commonwealth, Victorian and NSW governments helped them out with an additional 300 gigalitres from the hydro scheme.

An historic over-allocation of licences exacerbates the water shortage. Over the years New South Wales has issued more licences for more water than flows in the rivers. It did not matter so much when many licences gathered dust in a bottom drawer because irrigation channels did not reach all properties, or landholders combined dryland farming with intermittent cropping. However, water rights were detached from property titles with the advent of the water market in the 1990s. Suddenly all these 'sleeper' and 'dozer' licences were worth something. It was money for jam for landholders, but the piece of paper represented real water that had to come from somewhere. Even before the market, water consumption was steadily rising as irrigation expanded and intensified in the Murray Darling Basin. Consumption rose from 3000 gigalitres in 1930 to almost 12,000 gigalitres in the 1990s. More than two-thirds of the Basin's water resources are now being diverted, mostly for irrigation.

The rising trend in water use was clearly unsustainable, so, in 1995, the Murray Darling Basin Commission introduced the controversial 'cap'. The cap holds total diversions at 1993/94 levels. Newly active licences have to be supplied from this pool, and farmers whose entitlements fall short as a result have to buy someone else's to make up the difference. The result is rising water prices, compounded by corporatised and privatised state water agencies charging more to cover operation and maintenance costs traditionally subsidised by government.

On top of all these changes, the Murray Darling Basin is in the early stages of an environmental crisis of Biblical proportions. Rampant land clearing and inappropriate agricultural practices, particularly since 1950, have left the landscape susceptible to erosion, salinisation, acidification and soil structure decline.[13] The Murray Darling Basin is basically the floor of an ancient inland sea. Its soils are naturally high in salt. Removing its trees causes water tables to rise, bringing the salt to the surface. Irrigation compounds the problem by adding water to the landscape. Up to 80 per cent of the Murrumbidgee Irrigation Area is now affected by shallow water tables, with up to 5 per cent of the area having gone out of production because of waterlogging and salinity. By 2100, an estimated 10 million tonnes of salt a year will be moving through the land and water.

The salinity threat cannot be overstated. It cost the nation an estimated $187 million in reduced agricultural productivity in 2000, and rising. It is destroying already severely diminished habitat for native flora and fauna.

Saline water damages bitumen and concrete. An estimated 1600 kilometres of rail, 19,900 kilometres of roads and 68 towns are thought to be at risk. This is expected to rise to 5100 kilometres of rail, 67,400 kilometres of roads and 219 towns by 2050, along with a tripling in the area of salt-threatened land to 17 million hectares. By 2020, Adelaide's water, which comes from the Murray, will no longer be fit to drink, and the annual costs of poor water quality and damaged infrastructure could be as high as $700 million.[14]

The irrigation lobby, South Australia and some Commonwealth ministers argued against increasing flows to the Snowy River on the grounds that its water was needed to dilute the rising salt load in the Murray River. But the salt tide rising across inland Australia is so great that scientists say the Snowy's fresh water amounts to no more than a drop in the ocean.[15]

Irrigation is one of Australia's holy cows. A thorough cost-benefit analysis is beyond the scope of this book, but suffice to say, its self-proclaimed success is debateable. Historically, Australia's irrigation schemes have failed to operate profitably. Governments moved towards user pays during the 1990s, but operational subsidies late in the decade were still in the order of $300 million a year — without accounting for high infrastructure costs, or remedial work (projected at $900 million in Victoria over the next thirty years).[16] Water even now is still so cheap there is little incentive for farmers to stop squandering it on wasteful, low-return activities such as flood irrigation to grow rice in a desert and grass for dairy cows and fat lambs. A persuasive case can be made that Australia would have been better off economically and environmentally had the area of irrigated land been much smaller, and governments had invested taxpayers' money in something other than the grandiose but ultimately destructive dreams of the Snowy Mountains scheme and political obsessions with greening the desert.[17]

All of the above serves to illustrate that saving the Snowy River would not spark famine in Australia, or the world. Saving the Snowy would not condemn the Murray to a salty death — in fact, aggressive measures to save water and boost efficiency of use will help arrest salt moving into rivers. Communities will not collapse and jobs disappear en masse. A 28 per cent flow in the Snowy River would not even be the straw that broke the inland camel's back. Its burden was too heavy long before the Snowy campaign started. The campaign was just a convenient scapegoat for all the irrigators' fears and insecurities about the advent of a deregulated water market and reforms to address waste, inefficiency and environmental degradation.

People living in irrigation districts are defensive. Most have never seen the Snowy River; like most other Australians, they sustain a mental picture of the raging torrent of old. In January 2000, I received a letter from Sue Morgan at Deniliquin. It was polite, but she clearly felt my coverage of the Snowy River campaign did not give enough credit to irrigators. 'Farmers have an appalling reputation as being rapers of the land,' she wrote. 'This may have been the way for previous generations, but the farmers of today know they cannot afford to abuse their land ... Farmers on the whole are greener than green as their livelihood depends on it.'

It is true that Australian farmers have come a hell of a long way. When they don't do the right thing today, it is more likely because they cannot afford to, rather than ignorance or indifference. I took up Sue Morgan's invitation to visit Griffith and Coleambally. The striking thing was not the sincere effort at better land husbandry, but the sense of entitlement. In Coleambally, young farmers complained that the Snowy River people did not really care about the environment, but only wanted to develop their own irrigated industries. 'Even if that was the case,' I said, 'what is wrong with that? Why shouldn't they be able to benefit from their river, just like you do?' They shrugged. 'I'd never really thought of it like that before,' said one bloke.

A couple of months later, Brett Miners' colleague, Colin Steele had his biggest coup. As part of a Cabinet meeting in Bombala, the south-east regional coordinator for the Premier's Department negotiated some time spare for Bob Carr to undertake a low-key inspection of the Snowy River. It was just before Labor held a conference in Griffith to discuss the problems caused by the region's chronic labour shortages; questions about the Snowy River were bound to come up there. The wind was howling and snow was falling and Carr got airsick, so the helicopter pilot set down in a paddock by the Snowy. 'What would you say to the communities out west, if you were proposing they were going to lose water?' Carr asked Brett Miners as they walked around, chatting about the relative merits of different flow rates. 'I would make the comparison that Griffith has over-employment problems and people in Dalgety are saying their general store is about to shut, and the servo closed five years ago,' Miners replied. 'They need access to water to revive the community as much as people out west have had the water to power their prosperity and wealth.' Carr is a visual thinker. Brett Miners hoped the image would stick in the Premier's mind.

I am a city girl. I have not spent time on the Snowy, I just knew it was important to save it and it was something good to do.

ROBYN MCLEOD

Robyn McLeod heard about the Snowy River's plight for the first time at a public meeting in Mordialloc in mid-1999. McLeod was representing Labor at a forum for the upcoming election. A questioner wanted to know what Labor had in mind for the Snowy. 'I had no knowledge about the issue,' McLeod said. 'I had been talking about roads and health care. Luckily I remembered about the Labor policy and could answer the question correctly. Then I thought nothing more about it.'

Little did McLeod suspect she was about to eat, breathe, drink and dream the Snowy River for the next three years. Neither did Candy Broad, who was appointed Minister for Energy, Resources and Ports after the election. She was still getting over the shock of entering Parliament as a minister when Steve Bracks called her into his office. 'There was a whole bunch of us — me, Justin Madden, Marsha Thompson, Bronwyn Pike — who were elected and sworn in as ministers before we were sworn in as MPs,' Broad said. 'We went into Parliament and faced the first question time before we had actually given our maiden speeches. It was a wee bit stressful. At least after those years working as an advisor, I knew enough how to stay out of trouble.'

Broad had been chief of staff to Victorian Labor Premier Joan Kirner, and then Labor's assistant national secretary in Canberra during the Keating years. In that job, she worked closely with John Della Bosca, the NSW State Labor Secretary. Now 'Della', as NSW Special Minister of State and Assistant Treasurer, would be negotiating the Snowy deal with Victoria. 'Steve had the view that if New South Wales was putting one of their sharpest political operatives onto the case, he would do the same,' said Robyn McLeod. 'Candy is one of the strongest negotiators in the Victorian ALP, and these would be tough negotiations.'

Steve Bracks learned just how tough when he went to Sydney a month after he took office. A media report quoted 'senior government sources' claiming that four senior ministers had all but settled on 11–13 per cent for the Snowy, because any more would be too damaging for irrigators.[18] A spokeswoman for Premier Bob Carr told *The Age* the report was 'a bit suspicious', but Carr played his cards close to his chest. Bracks' policy advisor, Rob Hudson, said the NSW Premier was positive about a good outcome without saying what he thought the outcome ought to be. The Treasurer, Michael Egan, however, was cool. 'The issue was clearly not the highest priority for NSW Treasury, which felt it was hard to justify the amount of expenditure,' Bracks said later.

Whatever the outcome, New South Wales wanted to go 50:50 in finding the water savings, and share the costs equally with Victoria and the Commonwealth. 'We wanted to get the balance right,' said Carr later. 'We were aware the water had to come from somewhere and aware it could be costly, and anything we committed ourselves to could cut the value of the hydro.' Further, a 28 per cent flow only benefited Victoria; a mere 15 per cent would improve the Dalgety stretch.

Bracks said no. Victoria got a quarter of the scheme's water for irrigation, so he said the state would find, and pay for, a quarter of the savings. Victoria's share of 28 per cent amounted to roughly 70 gigalitres[19] at an estimated cost of $60 million. The state's water officials were fairly confident this could be achieved. However, Victoria's costs would rise dramatically in a 50:50 arrangement. Finding another 80 gigalitres would cost $80 million to $160 million, if indeed the savings were possible. 'Any change to the sharing arrangement would need to be accompanied by a change in the share of irrigation water,' Bracks told journalists. 'This would be difficult to achieve unless you have plans to withdraw water allocations from irrigators.'[20]

Consultants Sinclair Knight Mertz warned Victoria it might not be practically possible for New South Wales to find the other 220 gigalitres required. Consultant Drew Bewsher identified 154 gigalitres in potential savings, but that included 30 gigalitres in the Darling River catchment. These savings could not be transferred to the Murray/Murrumbidgee irrigation areas to offset increased flows in the Snowy. The costs also rose exponentially, and soon passed the point where it was cheaper for governments simply to enter the market and buy water. The governments, however, said they would only buy water as the absolute last resort. They promised the irrigators every effort would be made to find the water through off-farm efficiencies first.

Bracks was prepared to go equal thirds in the costs if the Commonwealth came to the party. He told the media on 25 October 1999 he was confident he could get Commonwealth support for 28 per cent, but the signs were not encouraging. The day before, the federal Environment Minister, Senator Robert Hill, said he doubted there was enough water to spare without exacerbating environmental problems in the inland rivers.[21] He was later overheard at a function in Melbourne saying the Snowy was a dead river, and should be left to rest in peace. Peter Staveley from the NSW Cabinet office also warned Bracks the Commonwealth would be forced to veto 28 per cent because it eroded the hydro scheme's commercial value for power generation.

Steve Bracks came back from Sydney thinking his government would have to work at several levels. 'I knew I had support from Bob Carr, and I knew that NSW Treasury would be advising against it,' he said. 'So we would have to work at a departmental level as well as ministerial, because we had to get some consistency in the advice to the Treasurer and Premier. I sensed there was a roadblock we had to remove, but the complexity was mind boggling — the amount of agreements in place with the Snowy scheme, and the different levels of government involved, and then the Commonwealth as well.' South Australia could not be ignored, either. The state had no say in the hydro scheme, but it could veto a deal affecting the water flow in the Murray Darling Basin and minimum flows through South Australia.

Bracks called in Candy Broad, and gave her the job of picking a path through the tangle. She admits to mixed feelings. 'This was a terrific opportunity. There was never a question, but that I would be happy to do it — but there was also this sinking feeling, too, that this was something very high profile and everyone would know if I did not manage to deliver it.'

Broad assigned Robyn McLeod, her chief of staff, to be her right-hand woman in the negotiations. Both women are strong-minded, savvy negotiators, but temperamentally quite unalike. Whereas McLeod is, by her own description, blond, bold and brassy, Broad is dark-haired, reserved and thoughtful. Broad is also outdoorsy and interested in environmental issues — a passion dating back to her university days in Western Australia, when she entered the Labor Party via the green and women's movements. She, at least, had set eyes on the Snowy on trips through East Gippsland. 'I was not searching for the Snowy — it was just something that was pointed out to me and I thought it didn't look like what I imagined it would from the mythology,' she said.

Neither woman knew much about the intricacies of corporatisation. Their first briefing with the public servants did not get off to a good start. 'A bloke from Treasury and Finance, a Kennett appointee, walked in and said to Robyn and I, "Don't you little ladies worry about anything. We will fix this up for you,"' said Broad. 'It was like a red rag to a bull. He left soon after Christmas — I think he realised that this was not a government he wanted to work for.' The other public servants — Kevin Love and Kate Streets from the Department of Premier and Cabinet, David Fickling from Treasury, and Campbell Fitzpatrick and Terry Healy from the Department of Natural Resources and Environment — were more constructive.

'They had all been working on this for a long time, and were frustrated at not being able to get it fixed,' said McLeod. She had the impression they were focused on a flow of 10 to 15 per cent, based on the messages they got from the Kennett Government and New South Wales. 'Fifteen per cent was seen as challenging, as the most you could really deliver without really pushing the boundaries of practicality, whereas 28 per cent is certainly a large task,' said Kevin Love later.

Looking at the complexity of the issues, McLeod was inclined to agree that 28 per cent was just too hard. The minister refused to countenance anything less. 'Candy was determined. The election policy was 28 per cent, and so she would find a way to get that,' said McLeod. 'Once that was clear to the officials after a couple of months, they went ahead to achieve it. It was amazing what that leadership gave them.' Love shrugged. It is the public servant's lot in life to adjust to changing goalposts. 'We act professionally in these things,' he said. 'We were given a task to do this thing, and so we said, "These are the quantities, and what does this mean in money and the practicality of achieving the outcome?"'

The NSW officials also took a little while to realise the new Victorian Government was serious about 28 per cent. David Crossley thought often of that letter from Steve Bracks before the election, and wished the idea had been knocked on the head then. 'On election night, we realised that if he got in, we would have to do something about this. But at the time there was such euphoria in the ALP in New South Wales that the Victorians had got in, that they were prepared to do anything to help them set up government. At that stage they were not bothered about the 28 per cent idea — but once it began to be costed out, they were not happy at all.'

John Della Bosca and Candy Broad's first meeting was 15 December 1999. New South Wales 'sources' were at it again, with the media reporting Victoria would be offered between 10 and 19 per cent. 'Twenty-eight per cent is not feasible, it is not realistic and it is not going to happen,' the sources said.[22] Della Bosca said later he brought positive and negative personal biases to the table: on the one hand, he admired the bold vision that created the hydro scheme; on the other, he enjoyed the alpine beauty and its heritage, and was sorry the Snowy was dying. But he did not bring riding instructions from the Premier. 'I got more explicit instructions from the Treasurer: that the government wanted a water agreement, that it was not a zero sum game, but we wanted it to be sustainable from a policy point of view. The Premier's attitude was just "Make it happen". Michael Egan's attitude was, "Let's make it happen, but in a sustainable way".'

After a frank and vigorous exchange, the ministers came out having decided only to share technical, economic and scientific information so all parties knew what was realistic. They also put the corporatisation deadline back from 31 December 1999 to 30 June 2000. 'Obviously the Victorian

Government has put to us a very tough position,' Della Bosca told journalists. 'They are sticking to the 28 per cent target. We have said we are not prepared to sign up to any particular target. Rather we want to focus on the whole environmental and economic question.'[23]

The ministers also agreed to seek urgent talks with the Commonwealth. The Natural Resources and Energy Minister, Senator Nick Minchin, who had replaced Senator Warwick Parer in the portfolio in 1998, had already asked to be included in the negotiations. Broad wrote back on 17 December 1999 to say she would be pleased to meet him, with Della Bosca, as soon as their schedules allowed.

She wrote similar letters to the federal Environment Minister, Senator Robert Hill, and South Australia's Environment Minister, Dorothy Kotz. Kotz had expressed her misgivings about Victoria's stance in a letter to Steve Bracks in early November. She complained that South Australia had already invested in works to offset water quality problems caused by increased irrigation development upstream due to the hydro scheme. 'Diversion of more water to the Snowy River will reduce the opportunity for dilution flows to this state, jeopardising our ability to provide suitable quality water for both irrigators and urban supplies,' she wrote.[24]

Broad assured Kotz and Senator Hill that 'any solution for the Snowy River should not compromise the quality of water available to South Australia'. Senator Hill, a South Australian, replied a few days later with a public attack dashing hopes of Commonwealth cooperation. 'If that water can be saved, I think the question then is, "What's the best use for it in the national interest?"' he said in an ABC Radio interview on 20 December 1999.[25] 'Is it to return it to the Snowy for some form of romantic connotation, or is it to return it to the Murray which is in a state of serious ecological health?' He announced he wanted a study on how corporatising the hydro scheme affected the Murray's environment. Senator Hill said it was necessary to help the Commonwealth make a rational decision. 'Unfortunately, we have recently seen that politics rather than good science and good sense is still the strongest driving force,' he said.

Senator Hill's intervention was part genuine concern, part political mischief-making. The Murray Darling Basin Commission had long been in his ear, casting doubt on the wisdom of corporatising the hydro scheme. The commission was critical of the focus on energy reforms before resolving the water issues. It argued that water, not energy, was the scarce resource that should take priority.

Hill was also playing to his home audience. South Australia's Coalition Government was facing a tough election within a year, with water quality in

Adelaide a perennial issue. Concerned that restoring 28 per cent to the Snowy would concentrate rising salinity in the Murray, the SA Premier, John Olsen, told journalists the state's future was at stake for the sake of political expediency. 'What we see with the election of the Bracks Labor Government is a capitulation to independents, which will be to the very significant long-term detriment of the River Murray system and South Australia,' Olsen said.[26]

An all-out, inter-government brawl was exactly what Victoria and New South Wales had hoped to avoid. Steve Bracks returned fire. 'This is not something Labor has come to lightly,' he told journalists in Melbourne. 'It was our policy position from six months ago, well before anyone knew there was an independent that stood on this matter.' He accused Senator Hill of parochialism, and reminded him he was Environment Minister for all Australia, not just his home state. 'His view is ill-founded. I urge him to read reports from the Snowy Water Inquiry, which say the Murray will not be affected in pursuit of a 28 per cent flow for the Snowy River.'[27]

Internally, Victoria was worried that a federal environmental impact study could provoke a lengthy dispute about who got the water savings, derailing the Snowy negotiations and therefore corporatisation. Victoria believed corporatisation was realistically the only way to get water back into the Snowy River, but its bargaining power rested on the goodwill of New South Wales and the Commonwealth's desire for its $800 million construction debt to be repaid.

Steve Bracks complained to the Prime Minister, John Howard, in a letter just before New Year. He pointed out that the Commonwealth had passed legislation to corporatise the scheme pending the outcome of the Snowy Water Inquiry, which had thoroughly considered impacts on the Murray as well as the Snowy. Senator Hill answered that the Murray Darling Basin Commission's 1999 Salinity Audit raised the issue as to 'whether the current guaranteed minimum flow down the Murray is going to be adequate in the medium to long term to maintain its environmental health'. He claimed the Snowy Water Inquiry did not adequately address this issue.

Most of Hill's Cabinet colleagues did not care about the Snowy River, but there were several who cared deeply about the salinity crisis in the Murray Darling Basin. They included the Agriculture Minister, Warren Truss, and Deputy Prime Minister and National Party leader, John Anderson. The latter entered the fray in January 2000, offering the states a 'compromise' 15 per cent with a vague promise to review the flow if the amount proved ecologically inadequate.

This offer — similar to Jeff Kennett's before the 1999 state election — was not so much a reasonable compromise as an attempt to find a political solution to the environmental tragedy apparent on both sides of the Great Divide. But the compromise, if one was to be made, was already on the table. The 28 per cent, or an average 330 gigalitres a year, was not an ambit claim but the minimum required to restore the river down to its mouth. Anything less could be a waste of water for all the environmental good it would do — not to mention a waste of money to modify the Jindabyne dam and capture the water by plugging leaks in the irrigation system. The compromise would have only achieved partial ecological recovery in the Snowy's upper reaches, and maybe kept South Australia and the irrigators happy for another election.

It was not, however, a long-term solution. Victoria and New South Wales' Snowy agreement would stand for seventy-five years. Having spent many millions of dollars modifying the Jindabyne dam to release 15 per cent, and hundreds of millions of dollars more on irrigation infrastructure works to find the extra water, it was unlikely future governments would revisit the Snowy issue as Anderson claimed. The political attention would more likely be on the Murray's salinity crisis, requiring billions of dollars and decades of investment in infrastructure, agricultural transition and revegetation. In January 2000, the Commonwealth wanted to settle for a compromise that would make no difference to the Murray River, nor help the Snowy.[28]

But politics is politics — and Steve Bracks was not on the same team as the coalition government in Canberra. 'There was a view inside the coalition — a minority view, but I had to contend with it — that, "Why are we going out of our way to help the newly elected Bracks Government with its political problems, and give it a free kick if that was going to be at the expense of a conservative constituency along the Murray?"' said Senator Nick Minchin later.

Senator Minchin the federal minister was responsible for the corporatisation process, so it was up to him to decide whether Hill's environmental impact study should happen. Senator Minchin is no friend of Senator Hill. The two men are from different Liberal Party factions. They clashed repeatedly in Cabinet, with Senator Minchin rolling Senator Hill on Commonwealth responses to key issues such as the Kyoto Protocol on climate change. But both men also represent South Australia. Politics at home in Adelaide and in Canberra dictated Senator Minchin's response on the Snowy.

So Senators Hill and Minchin announced a six-month environmental impact study on 20 January 2000. Senator Minchin said it would be one of the final steps in corporatising the scheme. 'This EIS will be an important part of gaining agreement between the Commonwealth, New South Wales, Victoria and South Australia about the level of environmental flows from the system,' he said.[29]

A key component would be a cost-benefit comparison between alternative uses for water savings, effectively pitting the economic and social worth of the Snowy River against the Murray. Craig Ingram accused Senator Hill of trying to play East Gippsland off against South Australia on the eve of the SA election. 'He believes it is OK for the Snowy River to provide environmental flows for the Murray but it is not OK for the Snowy River to provide environmental flows for itself,' he told journalists.[30] The SA Premier, John Olsen, had no problem with that. He said the Murray was in worse condition than the Snowy, and the study would allow his state to argue that at least some of the water savings should be used to improve the Murray.

The Victorian and NSW governments received the news with sinking hearts — another spanner in the works that would inevitably delay a decision on flows even longer.

⤸

I think once Craig was elected, there was a feeling the worst was over, and in reality, the worst was probably still to come. Getting the policy in place with Labor and then them being in power was really the easy bit. Keeping tabs on what was written into the laws and agreements and having some influence over that has been really hard. We lost total control and input. We were not really connected to the process any more.

MARY MCDONALD, WOMEN OF THE SNOWY RIVER

The Snowy River Alliance members were unhappy campers in the months following Ingram's election. The committee assumed everything would continue as before, but when the euphoria of the victory died down, they felt sidelined in what they saw as the Craig-and-George show.

George Collis took over from Paul Leete as Alliance president. He ran a tight disciplined ship in which he was the sole spokesman. He was also the intermediary between the Alliance and Ingram, who came to fewer and fewer meetings. 'The only information we got about what Craig was thinking was from George, not from Craig,' said Max White.

It was also a difficult time for Ingram. He was on a very steep learning curve. His constituents elsewhere in Gippsland East were claiming his attention, and he was trying to get his head around parliamentary process and the broader state issues thrown up in the House. His young family was also adjusting to a new life, with Ingram away in Melbourne for long periods.

Ingram literally widened his distance from the Alliance when he moved his family from Cabbage Tree Creek to Bairnsdale after three months. It was ninety minutes closer to Melbourne, but Alliance members were miffed he did not open an Orbost electorate office. 'The core of the campaign was in Orbost and its surroundings, and we never saw him,' said Lynette Greenwood.

'You had to make an appointment almost to see Craig,' added his former campaign manager, Chris Allen. 'You couldn't meet him in a café or the pub, but he would come up and go over to George's for a beer. Craig was George's protégé, and he kept Craig away from us. The rest of us had to go back to work and earn some money, and George was working out of Craig's office in Bairnsdale. There was lots of backroom wheeling and dealing with Steve Bracks that we were not a part of. George would say, "I know what we are doing — just trust us."'

Hindsight is a wonderful thing. Collis admits now he went too far, but says he was anxious that the Alliance presented as a professional group the government felt it could deal with. 'I thought we would only get one shot at this,' he said. 'What are the chances — how many hung parliaments have we had in history, and what have independents achieved? It was a once-in-a-lifetime chance, and we would never have these circumstances again. The push from me was "let's negotiate while we are in a position of strength", and the longer we went, the weaker we got.'

That was true. In December 1999, Labor picked up Jeff Kennett's seat when the former Premier resigned from Parliament. In May 2000, it picked up another seat when National Party leader Pat McNamara resigned. Ingram's vote was then no longer essential to Labor staying in office; the government only needed one, at most two, of the three independent votes to pass legislation. Collis fretted that another election could be called at any time to secure Labor's position. 'If we lost the seat, or it was no longer a hung Parliament — then where would we be?' he said. 'We would have nothing.'

Broad, McLeod and the Victorian public servants met the Alliance members several times in Orbost, to keep them abreast of progress. Della Bosca, Matthew Strassberg and David Crossley similarly kept the Dalgety and District Community Association in the loop as much as possible. Ingram became an important alternate conduit of information. 'There were times I could not provide all the information to the Alliance because of

Cabinet procedures or things still being negotiated,' said Candy Broad. 'So it came down to trust. At one end of the spectrum was the Alliance and at the other end were the irrigators — and we were trying to keep people's trust, which is partly about the information they get. So lots of times I would give Craig a higher level of detail about what was going on, that I could not provide publicly. He had gone through documents and would have assessed the situation, or been present for legal briefings.'

But Ingram often found himself in a delicate position, where he and his parliamentary advisor, Helen Foard, had access to documents they should not have had. 'We knew what was going on but we could not tell the Alliance,' he said. 'I think that frustrated them a bit — we would ask them to do things to put on the pressure, but could not say exactly what was going on.'

The Whites and others in the Alliance wanted more. They wanted to be players inside the process. 'We were on the outside during the negotiations with New South Wales,' says Glenice White. 'We relied on Craig to know what was going on, but he did not tell us everything. I thought the government would have included us more, because we had done so much research and we know the river. I thought the government agencies would have consulted with us for local knowledge, but they never did. They would have meetings with us, but it was just a token gesture. Tim Fisher [Australian Conservation Foundation river campaigner] was used as a consultant, but his knowledge of the Snowy did not compare with ours.'

As time dragged on, disillusion crept in. In March 2000, the Victorian Government announced a ten-year, $25 million rehabilitation program for the lower Snowy. It included works to recreate deep pools and reinstate the original rainforest vegetation on the banks. The program would begin with a two-year, $1.8 million trial to test the effectiveness of different measures. The trial was intended to send a positive signal about the government's commitment to flows, but the gesture was greeted with suspicion. Alliance members feared it was just a sop to keep them and Ingram on side, while the Snowy would never get its water. They also suspected Ingram, accusing him of being too friendly with the government and not pushing the issue hard enough.

Ingram is philosophical. He says he kept the Alliance at arm's length because, 'as a Member of Parliament, I had to represent the whole electorate. I was not the Alliance's Member of Parliament. While I might personally have agreed that something was a bad thing, I had to think about the stability of government. The Alliance would speak on its behalf and I would speak on mine. The separation was important for the credibility of me and them.'

Max White thinks Ingram forgot too quickly how he came to be there in the first place. 'We though we were just going to give the National Party a fright, and Craig was just the one in the Alliance who put up his hand to run. He was our candidate. He was elected because of the work and money of the Snowy River Alliance, because Native Fish Australia did not have the money. It was the Snowy River Alliance who manned the polling booths and created him.'

～

Ian Macdonald and I went to a footy match in Melbourne one time. Ian is a rabid Essendon fan, and he is always lining up to go see them. This time we were in Victoria and I think we were going to see Candy Broad and there was an evening match — the first one in the Colonial Stadium. We walked down there and it was an extremely hot night. We had club seats so we are sitting there, and so was Peter Costello. They were both wearing Essendon scarves, and it is like the old days of the Catholics and the masons — these fans speak their own secret language and can relate to each other. So there they were, talking footy for ten minutes, and then Costello asked, 'Why are you two here?' And we said, 'We are here for Snowy negotiations,' and Costello put his fist in the air and said, 'Let the Snowy flow! I am on your side!' He was only half-joking and, to be fair, quite a few people in the Commonwealth that we came across were prepared to support it because they thought it was a good idea. But the general attitude of the Commonwealth seemed to be 'Piss in the pot or get off it, we are sick of mucking around.'

JOHN DELLA BOSCA, NSW SPECIAL MINISTER OF STATE

It was like pulling teeth, but on 8 March 2000, Rob Hudson reported to Steve Bracks that New South Wales finally appeared to be 'moving away from its Treasury position of around 7–11 per cent flows'. It was now talking about 16.5 per cent, with the possibility of a further 3.5 per cent.

It was a baby step forward. New South Wales was still insisting on a 50:50 split on finding and paying for water savings. Under New South Wales' formula for a 20 per cent flow, Victoria would have to find another 20 gigalitres on top of its committed 70. Glumly, Hudson advised no Victorian officials could tell him where Victoria might find another 20 gigalitres — and a 20 per cent flow fell far short of the government's committed 28 per cent target.

'I think you would find it hard to sell an outcome that is anything less than 20 per cent, given our repeated policy statement,' Hudson told Bracks on 8 March. 'A 16.5 per cent outcome would be regarded as only marginally better than what the Kennett Government promised and would be impossible to sell to Craig Ingram.' He complained that New South Wales was not offering all its potential savings. The Bewsher report, for instance, identified 154 gigalitres, and did not include Coleambally or the Western Murray irrigation districts. 'Both could presumably yield some savings,' Rob said. 'There is no reason New South Wales cannot find 130 gigalitres overall.'

There were other sticking points. NSW Treasury insisted that any flows over 15 per cent meant compensating Snowy Hydro for lost generating capacity. Victoria's modelling suggested negligible difference in revenue between 15 and 28 per cent flows. New South Wales also talked about returning flows over fifteen years; Victoria wanted a seven-year time frame. The Premier told Candy Broad not to give ground when she saw Della Bosca the next day.

Victoria's attitude in turn frustrated New South Wales. 'They were coming to the table saying, "We want you to pay a whole heap of money to solve our political problem", and, "We have a commitment, we have to do this!"' said Peter Staveley, from the NSW Cabinet office. 'And we would say, "Yes, but we haven't — your problem is not our problem. You show us why it is in our interests." They would get frustrated because we were not just folding over to solve their problem for them.'

Della Bosca said Victoria was unrealistic in those early days. 'It was not physically possible to use some of Bewsher's savings for the Snowy because they were on the Darling River,' he said. 'So we had to get rid of a lot of dross arguments on both sides, to work out what water was actually there on a permanent basis. We always thought Victoria had more water than they were 'fessing up to.'

Candy Broad and John Della Bosca found an unexpected ally in Senator Minchin when they all met for the first time in Adelaide on 9 March 2000. Della Bosca, Broad, their advisors and officials had a quick conference in a café around the corner from Minchin's office, to paper over their differences. 'We had to present a united front because we would have to ask for a national vote, and Minchin had the option politically of just poking holes in our discussion,' said Della Bosca. Broad agreed. 'The last thing I wanted was a position where the Commonwealth was arbitrating between New South Wales and Victoria. I thought that would be hopeless.'

The café became a regular if rather uninspiring haunt over the next few months. 'There were no seats inside,' said Della Bosca's advisor, Matthew

Strassberg. 'It was not a pleasant, big coffee shop — more of a milk bar — and we would be sitting outside with the street fumes, and the noise, and people trying to get their lunch.' It was not easy getting everyone together though, and so the ministers and their staff held meetings whenever and wherever possible.

One morning in Adelaide, Broad and Della Bosca hadn't had a chance to talk first before they met Minchin. 'So we thought we would be really clever and book a stretch limo for me, Della, the officials and advisors, and do it in private on the way from the airport,' said Broad. Della Bosca, however, did not think the luxury was a good media look. 'So we all squashed into a cab and put all the staff into the limo,' Broad said. 'The driver was listening very hard to what we would be saying to Minchin, so we would have had trouble explaining if it had been in the news in the morning. Then we arrived in front of the Commonwealth office in Adelaide, with no media and no one interested in us. All the officers got out of the limo, while Della, me, Robyn and Matthew peeled ourselves out of the taxi.'

The states found Senator Minchin and his staff positive and constructive, and appreciated their willingness to work through sticking points. 'There was a genuine recognition of each other's problems,' Senator Minchin said in turn. 'That was the key when, at any stage, the whole thing could fall apart if anyone fell apart.' The federal minister had little interest in the Snowy River, but he did want to be done with corporatising the scheme as quickly and painlessly as possible. If returning water to the Snowy was the means to that end, then he was prepared to talk.

'Although Minchin was playing it cool, I was confident that at end of the day, if New South Wales and Victoria put a proposition to him, it would be accepted,' said Broad.

But first the states had to come up with a proposition. One of Bob Carr's staff might have mentioned 22 per cent internally as the Premier's favoured outcome way back in 1998, but there was no hint of this in the negotiations. 'It would have come as a major surprise,' said Kevin Love, from Victoria's Department of Premier and Cabinet. 'We had to keep chipping away at them.'

The Total Environment Centre and the Australia Conservation Foundation's Tim Fisher pressured Della Bosca to seize the initiative. Fisher cornered the minister at a salinity summit in mid-March 2000 and warned that the Commonwealth environmental impact study was a major threat. He said the two states were vulnerable to Commonwealth delays and a pitched battle over whether the Murray or Snowy should benefit from water savings. 'Both the federal and South Australian governments may be expected to use this issue prior to state and federal elections next year should the issue fail to be resolved quickly. Hence there is some urgency,' he wrote to Della Bosca afterwards. He urged New South Wales to abandon its 50:50 position and expedite a resolution with Victoria. 'In this way, the federal environmental impact statement will lose impact, and claims that allocating water to the Snowy will have negative impact on the Murray and South Australia can be more effectively countered. Only by regaining the initiative, can NSW and Victoria put pressure back on the feds.'[31]

The negotiations needed a circuit breaker. Steve Bracks raised the Snowy in a meeting with Bob Carr on 4 April 2000 in Sydney. He said New South Wales must move away from its insistence on a 50:50 split in finding the water, towards something closer to a 75:25 split reflecting its irrigation water share. If New South Wales did that, then Victoria could consider financial assistance to help New South Wales find its share. Bracks said the negotiations should resume on this basis, and that at least a 21 per cent flow was possible without imperilling the hydro's commercial returns. Bob Carr agreed in general terms that if Victoria was prepared to find more money, then he was prepared to find more water. 'It was a big breakthrough,' said Rob Hudson. 'It was a base to work from, to get up to 28 per cent.'

Two steps forward, one back. A week later, NSW officials sent Victoria a 'joint proposal' for Broad and Della Bosca to take to a meeting with Senator Minchin the next day. It did not reflect the Premiers' implicit understanding. Much to Victoria's irritation, the proposal still had the states going halves in finding, as well as paying for, the water, and 15 per cent as the compensation trigger for Snowy Hydro. 'I think the document indicated the empire still fighting back, notwithstanding the agreement with Bob Carr at the highest level,' said Hudson. 'The bureaucracy was going to fight tooth and nail over the justifications for every drop of water.'

Victoria's mood did not improve the next day, on 19 April 2004, when Senator Minchin said the Commonwealth favoured a 15 per cent flow, but would not give any money towards achieving it. Bracks replied there was no deal unless the Commonwealth opened the purse strings. Victoria initially estimated the state would be up for $60 million to find its one-quarter share of the water; now the estimates were creeping over $100 million as Victoria looked for ways to sweeten the deal with New South Wales. Victoria's Treasurer, John Brumby, watched the prospective dollars mounting up with a resigned sigh. 'Treasurers would always prefer things cost less, rather than more,' he said later. 'But the commitment was given and we have not budged from it. It is an article of faith. The Snowy was a key element of our plan and policies.'

Victoria's advisors warned Bracks and Broad that the Commonwealth was getting impatient. So was Craig Ingram. Broad and McLeod kept Ingram and his advisor, Helen Foard, in the loop, but Ingram also had his own networks. 'Sometimes he would provide us with inside information that we wouldn't have known, particularly with different positions being adopted, and we could intervene,' said Broad. The Gippsland East independent was tirelessly vigilant. 'He was always on our tail, ringing us, hassling us, saying I heard a whisper, or how did that meeting go, or when are you going to meet Della Bosca next?' recalled McLeod. 'I was in London to attend the World Sustainable Energy Conference with Candy Broad in late May, early June, and the phone went at 3 am and it was Craig Ingram asking me "What are you doing? What is happening?"'

Senator Minchin was a key contact. Ingram and Minchin met three or four times before Ingram was elected, when the Snowy River Alliance sent delegations to Canberra. The two men got on well. 'He would always return calls, and he would call me to let me know things that were going on,' said Ingram. 'I don't know how much he believed in environmental flows but he was helpful. He was a reality check on the information I was getting from New South Wales and Victoria. He was another view, and he would say what was really going on. He did actually help and support what we were doing, and not a lot of people federally did.'

In April 2000, Ingram was worried the negotiations had stalled, with the Commonwealth environmental impact study months behind schedule. 'There was a lot of nonsense going on and it was time to up the ante,' he said. So he briefed a Melbourne lawyer, Steve Howells, to prepare a High Court challenge to the hydro scheme's legality, on the grounds the Commonwealth did not have the power to divert rivers back in 1949 under Section 100 of the Constitution. 'It was not an idle threat,' said Ingram. 'The injunction would say we want a real outcome, and if the governments can't get it, then the courts will. It would have put heavy pressure on the states and Commonwealth to get over the line on 28 per cent. The Victorian Government would not have liked it, but the timing was right.'

Ingram and Howells flagged the case in a meeting with the Victorian Attorney-General, Robert Hulls, in late May. Hulls' legal advice suggested that theoretically there might be a case, but practically it was unlikely to succeed given the scheme had existed for fifty years embedded in intergovernmental agreements. The Victorian Government asked Ingram not to proceed, warning it would be expensive and counter-productive. 'It was iffy it would succeed, and it would just delay things,' Robyn McLeod recalled. 'The case would just put corporatisation on hold. I just saw it as a distraction. The only way to change flows was to change the water licence, and only way to do that was through corporatisation.' Ingram was unmoved. He called on the states to decide whether they believed the scheme was legally valid, and said a High Court challenge would enable people living along the river to claim compensation for forty years of degradation.

Ingram thought a legal challenge was the Alliance's trump card, but the case did not go ahead in the end because the Alliance would not come to the party. Technically, the case had to be brought by someone living on or near the river, which ruled out Ingram. He and Howells had a meeting with the Alliance to ask for its help in finding plaintiffs to put their name to the challenge. Alliance members were cautious, not least about the risks of losing houses and property through legal costs if the case did not win. They wanted to wait and see if the governments could work it out first. Ingram considered it a lost opportunity. 'Many people in the Alliance are conservative, and they were unsure and felt it was a big risk. That is true — it was an all or nothing strategy. It would have been messy, but then we would have achieved the flow whether it was political or legal. The challenge was our trump card. It would have been a catalyst.'

As if to underline the risks of letting the matter drag on too long, the draft Commonwealth environmental impact report was released in early June. The report warned that rural communities on the Murray, as well as the environment, would suffer if the Snowy River got 28 per cent of its flow back at Jindabyne. 'If savings are used for the Snowy River, this may reduce the flexibility of the Murray Darling Basin Commission to implement environmental flow programs for the River Murray at a later date,' it said.[32]

South Australian Premier, John Olsen, and Senator Hill seized on the report to claim salinity in the Murray would increase if Snowy flows were lifted. Candy Broad responded by accusing Senator Hill of promoting the 'fallacy' that the Murray's problems would be solved by letting the Snowy River continue degrading. She pointed out that the report acknowledged that problems such as algal blooms and deteriorating wetlands were symptomatic of long-term water management practices, rather than flows per se.[33] The report also said it would make little difference to the inland rivers' environmental condition if less water was released from the scheme, because flows in the inland rivers were so highly regulated already.

The environmental impact study generated little public interest. Only 44 submissions were received, compared with the 489 flooding the Snowy Water Inquiry two years earlier. But the process stirred up angst in the irrigation areas, where NSW Parliamentary Secretary, Ian Macdonald, was working hard to keep the lid on the irrigators' simmering hostility.

Macdonald was promoted to assist Della Bosca after the March 1999 NSW election. Candy Broad and Robyn McLeod knew well what Macdonald was up against. In January 2000, they bounced around the NSW irrigation districts in a little plane in very hot weather to get a feel for the issues and to reassure the communities they would not be disadvantaged. Most received the overture civilly, but some did not. In one town, the two women were kept waiting in a corridor for fifteen minutes while an irrigation board finished its business inside in the air-conditioning. 'It was petty stuff — "Let them sweat out there in the heat before we talk to them", said Broad. 'Gradually as the NSW Government got more organised, they took over that work. But in the early days they were not there, so it was important not to let things get out of hand.'

Getting irrigation leaders on board was essential. It was not easy. The Rice Growers Association of Australia provocatively held its annual conference in Cooma in 1999, and voted that the Snowy River should get no more water at all. 'We could not have got an agreement without the irrigators. It had to be a win–win and have everyone in the cart,' Macdonald said. He focused on the fact that the infrastructure was falling apart and in dire need of upgrading. Della Bosca, who also visited the irrigation districts several times, made it clear the government would not spend $200 million on an upgrade for nothing. If the irrigators wanted public money for major works, their last best hope was via corporatising the hydro scheme, and that meant more water in the Snowy River.

'I think we did a good job to show them we would stick up for them, and there was an opportunity for them if they played their cards right,' Della Bosca said later. 'If they spat the dummy, they would get nothing. We said there was a big movement to restore the Snowy and there was a good chance sooner or later that someone was going to do it, because it was one of those things that kept coming up. Given the state of the Victorian Parliament, it would be sooner and so they sensibly attached themselves to our project.'

It was an uneasy truce, however, and the longer it took the states to work something out, the more likely it might fall over. The deadline for corporatisation was put back again, from 30 June 2000 to 31 December 2000. Still Victoria and New South Wales danced around a solution.

By mid-July, talks had barely progressed from a 6 June meeting, where Broad and Della Bosca had agreed to focus on savings achieving a 13 per cent flow, with NSW providing 75 gigalitres and Victoria 45. But Della Bosca only agreed on condition the Commonwealth fund 30 gigalitres of NSW's share, which Senator Minchin would never accept. And, as a frustrated Rob Hudson reported to Bracks, another 72 gigalitres was still needed just to get to a 21 per cent flow, much less 28.

Victoria offered a formula for finding water that amounted to a 2:1 ratio between the states and would deliver 21 per cent over ten years. This reflected the understanding reached between the Premiers at their meeting way back in April. It would mean Victoria and New South Wales contributing $159 million each, rather than $129 million and $223 million respectively. It also overcame the obstacle of the Commonwealth refusing to pay anything.

But New South Wales' needle was stuck in the groove of a 50:50 split in finding the water. Robyn McLeod dubbed David Crossley and Peter Staveley 'Dr No' and 'Dr No-no'. 'We would have meetings where Della was being conciliatory and saying to Candy, "I think we can do this, or this", and they would be sitting behind him shaking their heads.'

Della Bosca's advisor, Matthew Strassberg, however, appreciated having two men so steeped in the minutiae of corporatisation. 'David Crossley was a pedant, but most of the time he was right,' Strassberg said. 'If there was a problem, he was spot on about whether it could be done or would continue to be a problem if we went down this or that path.'

On 27 July 2000, Rob Hudson warned Steve Bracks that the window of opportunity to strike a deal was closing. The Commonwealth's supplementary EIS report was due for release as early as 26 August, and could be the means by which the federal bureaucracy dictated the Commonwealth's position. The report would be forwarded to Senator Hill to read and make recommendations to Senator Minchin. Federal officials said Senator Minchin would then likely take his decision to Cabinet around the first week of October. 'The officials say federal ministers are tired of waiting for a water solution and are supporting a harder Commonwealth line,' Hudson told the Victorian Premier.

Senator Minchin said later that as the months dragged on into the middle of 2000, walking away was increasingly attractive. 'There was a point where I felt we would never get a deal done because it was all too big, too hard to bring the parties together and resolve fifty separate papers,' said Minchin. 'I had the irrigators banging on my door, saying don't you dare destroy us for the Snowy River, and sometimes I wondered why we were doing this. It was nice for us to corporatise the Snowy, but it was not the end of the world if we did not. I don't like to walk away from things and I was genuinely concerned to try to get an outcome. I thought it worth the effort for corporatisation, although it was not like selling Telstra in terms of importance. We hung in there, but it would have been easy for the Commonwealth to walk away.'

This was about where things were sitting when John Della Bosca had lunch with veteran ABC political journalist, Maxine McKew.

Della Bosca has a restless intellect. Colleagues say he is a brilliant problem-solver when focused — the trick is to keep him focused on one thing for long enough. In 2000, Della had rather a lot on his plate, and he was not giving the Snowy his full attention. He was running for the ALP national presidency and in the thick of internal debate about the federal Goods and Services Tax (GST). Federal Labor opposed the GST, but it passed through Parliament with the help of the Australian Democrats and came into effect on 1 July 2000. Della Bosca was convenor of the national right faction and, as such, a leader of the view that Labor should drop its GST opposition. 'The GST had become inevitable and we were positioning ourselves as just being negative unless we had other things to say,' he recalled. 'But there was no intention to make it a public push.'

In early July, Della Bosca had lunch with Maxine McKew for her weekly interview column in *The Bulletin* magazine. McKew is married to Bob Hogg, a Labor colleague of Della Bosca's and former Victorian and National Labor Secretary. Towards the end of the lunch, Della Bosca kicked back for what he thought was a personal conversation speculating about how the embattled federal leader, Kim Beazley, might improve his chances of winning government. It included Labor's opposition to the GST. McKew maintained the conversation was on the record. It was published on 11 July 2000, and immediately interpreted by the Canberra press gallery as the powerful NSW Right faction white-anting Beazley's leadership.

The Victorians had decided the ALP national conference on 1–3 August in Hobart was too good an opportunity to miss for another round of Snowy negotiations, but they'd had trouble nailing down Della Bosca for a meeting — until *The Bulletin* article was published. Della Bosca withdrew his nomination for national president, but that did not calm the media storm. The ALP conference opened with Della Bosca trailing round the halls in the glare of television cameras while his political colleagues gave him a wide berth. He had gone from holding overwhelming factional support for national president to *persona non grata*. The Victorians were the only ones wanting to monopolise his time now. Della Bosca gladly seized the opportunity to, as he put it, 'concentrate on some political basics'.

Until Hobart, the ministers had managed only brief meetings on the phone and in person. Now they spent hours shut away in back rooms with their advisors and officials. 'By that stage, Premiers Bracks and Carr had recommitted, and they wanted to move ahead and get a resolution,' said Kevin Love, from Victoria's Department of Premier and Cabinet. The officials were often alone, trying to work out how to do what the politicians wanted. David Crossley remembers Kevin Love standing at a whiteboard, drawing up the costs and sources of water as they debated the figures. 'We from New South Wales were trying to pull it down as far as we could, and we could not go below 15 per cent because of bloody Webster,' said Crossley. 'We would have tried 12.5 per cent, but the politicians would have suffered such a backlash we could not have got away with it. And Kevin was trying to pull it up.'

Geoff Chambers, the former Victorian corporatisation manager who was now working for NSW Treasury, broke the deadlock by suggesting a joint government enterprise straddling the NSW/Victorian border. 'It would be left to its own devices to figure out the best way to achieve the water savings. It would not be fettered in the way that governments are,' Broad said. Chambers' idea removed the economic and political friction, reducing the flows problem to one of science alone. The parties then identified 212 gigalitres in prospective savings, enough to bring the Snowy flow up to 21 per cent over ten years at a total cost of $300 million split equally between the two states. The deal would reduce the hydro's power production by about 390 kilowatt/hours, or 8.5 per cent, but there was another breakthrough when Della Bosca accepted independent analysis concluding this would not require compensating Snowy Hydro for lost revenue. On 3 August, the last day of the ALP conference, Bracks and Carr gave the plan the nod over coffee with the ministers and advisors.

The states moved quickly to tie up loose ends and pre-empt the Commonwealth's environmental impact study final report. The deal's total cost to Victoria was estimated at $190 million over seven years: $150 million for finding the water savings and $40 million on environmental rehabilitation and monitoring along the Snowy. New South Wales' total bill would be more than $182 million, including $32 million for environmental remediation inside Kosciuszko National Park.

On 20 August 2000, after eight months of negotiations, Broad and Della Bosca signed a bilateral agreement. On 23 August, they met Senator Minchin and asked the Commonwealth for another $150 million for the Joint Government Enterprise, on top of the states' $300 million. Broad and Della Bosca proposed that $80 million go towards works for the Snowy and the Murray, and $70 million to find water for environmental flows in the Murray alone. Senator Minchin said the Commonwealth would not spend a cent on the Snowy River, and negotiated its contribution down from $150 million to $75 million, dedicated to finding an additional 70 gigalitres for the Murray alone. The agreement became trilateral on 1 September 2000.

By mid-September, the proposal was before federal Cabinet. Senator Hill had only just received a supplementary environmental impact report, following up on the June draft. He was yet to consider its findings and make his recommendations to Senator Minchin, but Cabinet was reluctant to agree to anything more than 15 per cent in the Snowy. Ministers argued that if three governments were going to spend $375 million on environmental flows, then the Murray was in much greater need. 'That is not the choice facing us,' Senator Minchin told them. 'Victoria and New South Wales want to put this money for flows into the Snowy, and the money is not available for anything else — so let's deal with the real issue before us.'

Craig Ingram was another troublesome loose end. His advisor, Helen Foard, said they went straight to the Premier's rooms after being tipped off a deal had been done. Waiting outside the doors, they could hear Bracks' chief of staff, Tim Pallas, inside.

'Oh, hang on, minister — Craig is on the warpath!' Pallas said, ending the phone call.

'Look, we helped you form government on 28 per cent, and we are hearing the deal is 21 and that is unsatisfactory!' Ingram and Foard told Pallas. Foard got the impression Pallas was not across the details and that this was possibly all news to him, but his bottom line was clear.

'Listen, mate, this is as good as you are going to get,' Pallas told Ingram.

Ingram eventually caught up with Robyn McLeod and Rob Hudson, and told them he would not accept the deal unless it included a mechanism to get the flow up to 28 per cent. Without that, there was a risk the announcement would be greeted with community protest rather than applause. The states came up with a plan to deliver the last 7 per cent through public/private partnerships after the first ten years. It assumes water will be worth so much in the future that private enterprise will invest in public infrastructure to recover savings for sale. McLeod acknowledged it was a 'blue sky' proposition, but believed such partnerships were inevitable as the new water market matured and the commodity became scarcer and more valuable.

'From our point of view, it was a big achievement to get to 21 per cent, and the commitment to 28 per cent, with New South Wales,' said Rob Hudson later. 'It was the outcome from nearly a year of full-blooded negotiations which relied on New South Wales' goodwill. It required a significant contribution from them of their water and money, and they started from a low base. Given this was as far as we could push it, Craig had to decide if he was going to go out and sell it as a great win that would deliver 28 per cent, or be seen as marginal and not having achieved what he wanted to achieve for his constituents. There always comes a point in the political process where it can go no further, and Victoria and New South Wales had reached that.'

Ingram argued that 21 per cent had no scientific foundation, and he was sceptical about the public/private partnerships idea. He was also disappointed water would be delivered only if and when savings were verified. Ingram had lobbied hard for a deal the other way around. He wanted the Snowy to get its 28 per cent guaranteed in stages over ten years, which meant the irrigators would lose water if they did not get serious about efficiencies. He felt that would better focus their minds. He was also unhappy that the last 7 per cent required compensating Snowy Hydro for foregone power generation capacity, which would be a disincentive for future governments.

On the positive side, Ingram got the Heads of Government agreement amended to recognise the legitimacy of environmental flows and identify ecological outcomes. The deal also provided for more water to be returned to other long-suffering montane rivers within the Kosciuszko National Park, to the equivalent of 150 gigawatt-hours of foregone electricity (roughly 120 gigalitres).

Ingram was faced with a hard choice. The deal fell short, but it was presented to him as a fait accompli. He considered rejecting it and withdrawing his support for the Bracks Government. 'But what would it have achieved if I had ditched the government?' he said later. 'It would not have brought them down. Sometimes the relationship was strained, but not because the government was not trying. It was, but it had to get agreement with New South Wales and Commonwealth. We pushed hard, and we won some, we lost some.'

In the politics of perception, the governments had a headline plan to restore 28 per cent. It would be embarrassing if Ingram and the Snowy River Alliance did not support the deal, but the states were determined to get the hydro scheme corporatised by the end of the year. They were also worried about word leaking out. They duly set the date for the big announcement on flows for Friday, 6 October 2000, at the foot of Jindabyne dam. Meantime, Ingram prepared to go out like a politician and sell the deal.

EIGHT

A Little Bit of History Undone

It is a river, and a river has an inalienable right to water. It is such
a simple premise. It is a river, it has a right to be a river and to flow.

GABRIELLE GELLY, LAKES AND WILDERNESS TOURISM, EAST GIPPSLAND

Bill Savory, the owner of Marshall's Commonwealth Hotel in Orbost, was a bit surprised to see Candy Broad and her entourage trooping through the door late on the night of 5 October 2000. 'These were not the kind of people you would usually see in a pub like this,' said Bill.

The Commonwealth Hotel was no-frills back then, before the Savorys did some renovations. The kind of people who usually stayed there were single men from the oil rigs, backpackers, and pensioners a step or two up from homelessness. 'These were fancy motel people, with the bottle of red wine,' said Bill of the ministerial party. 'They came in with their suits and ties, all prim and proper, but a few stayed down here in the bar for a few beers. They weren't prim by the end of the night when they straggled up to bed about 12.30 am, with their ties off and collars undone. People are not so different.'

Staying at the Commonwealth was not part of the government's carefully laid plans for announcing its historic the deal on the Snowy River. Candy Broad, Robyn MacLeod and their team of public servants went to Orbost to brief the Snowy River Alliance on the night before the big event in Jindabyne. They flew down, got into town late, and went straight to the meeting. When the meeting ended and they went to their motel to check in, the reception office was in darkness and the owner was not answering his phone. George Collis and Craig Ingram were beside themselves. They did not have enough couches to put everyone up at their homes. The Commonwealth Hotel was not the most salubrious of abodes, but it was the only place in town still with its lights on. Beggars at that late hour could not be choosers. Ingram rang Bill Savory to see if he had any rooms made up and available.

New South Wales and Victoria had gone to great lengths to keep their deal secret, and they rushed to organise the official announcement before word leaked out. They did a good job keeping it under wraps — the Total

Environment Centre in Sydney only found out on 28 September that a deal would be announced on 6 October. Jeff Angel sent an urgent letter to John Della Bosca's office asking for a briefing, saying he wanted to be in a position to applaud the deal. Ian Macdonald and David Crossley briefed Angel and Fran Kelly on the details on 4 October. Angel had been lobbying Della Bosca for 15 per cent in three to five years, and 28 per cent within six to ten years. The Government's ten-year deal for 21 per cent fell far short, but it was too late for Angel and Kelly to do anything about it.

Ingram, meanwhile, had told George Collis what was in the offing, but for most people in the room in Orbost on the evening of 5 October 2000, this was the first they had heard that a deal had even been done. Candy Broad explained that the governments were committed to a long-term target of 28 per cent. They had allocated $300 million towards water efficiency measures to recover 21 per cent, which would be restored to the Snowy River in stages over ten years after the scheme was corporatised early in 2001. The last 7 per cent for the Snowy River would be achieved through privately funded infrastructure projects sometime after the first decade. The deal also included increased flows in the upper Murrumbidgee and other montane rivers inside the Kosciuszko National Park.

The people at the meeting were delighted — although the public servants nearly fell off their chairs when someone asked, 'What if 28 per cent is not enough?' It had been hard enough just to get this much. But George Collis was a little uneasy that night. 'Up to the last moment, we thought it was the full 28 per cent,' he said later. 'It was not till Candy came up to explain to us the night before that we knew there was two parts of it. That was a surprise to all of us. I knew the 7 per cent was a separate issue and not funded, but I only became aware that night that it was privately funded and outside government influence. That was difficult for me because the government was offering 21 per cent, and saying now is the time to take it, but the expert panel called for 28 per cent, and if we wanted to maintain credibility then we had to back that figure. When it was not a cut-and-dried 28 per cent, I was more than disappointed.'

He decided to speak in favour of the deal, however, to support Ingram, and because he perceived the government would go ahead, regardless of the community reaction. 'I have often wondered what would have happened if the Alliance had said, no,' Collis recalled. 'The deal we got was the minimum to make Craig happy, and if this was what he supported, I would publicly support it.'

Glenice White was pleased, but troubled. She twigged that the last 7 per cent was far from guaranteed, despite the minister's assurances, and was frustrated that the Alliance had not had the opportunity to consider and comment on the deal before it was struck. 'We did not realise Craig had had the documents and kept them to himself,' White said later. 'I thought the Alliance had been the people pushing for this for so long that it would have been courteous of the government and the government departments to let us know what they were going to do. We should have been able to comment on it, before it was settled.'

Generally, the Alliance members went home a happy crew. The minister and her entourage went to the darkened motel. One of the party, Campbell Fitzpatrick, was staying in a different motel and had had the foresight to check in before he went to the meetings. There was a debate about whether to wake him up and kick him out so the minister at least had a room. Robyn McLeod said she would rather stay at the Commonwealth Hotel with everyone together than sleep on Craig Ingram's lounge room floor. Candy Broad decided in that case she would rather stay with the group, and so Fitzpatrick narrowly escaped a rude awakening.

Victorian officer, Kate Streets, climbed up the hotel stairs with their ruby red carpet, looked down the long narrow corridor painted pale toilet block green and lined with doors, and shivered. Her room — like the minister's, like everyone's — was a tiny, high-ceilinged box, virtually bare, with a single bed against one wall and a chipped enamel wash basin with a chrome towel rail opposite. The communal bathrooms and toilets were down the end of the hall. The others went downstairs for a beer in the public bar after dropping off their bags. Streets went into her room, locked the door and went to bed. The next day would be one of the biggest in her professional life, and she hardly got any sleep. 'The mattress had springs poking up everywhere and the bed creaked whenever I moved.' In the morning, she lay in bed for a while, trying to remember her Victorian code of conduct for public servants, and whether it said anything about communal showers and letting the minister go first. Luckily the minister was an early riser and got there first anyway.

Candy Broad took the Commonwealth Hotel in her stride. 'After growing up in the north-west of Western Australia, I was used to pubs like that,' she said. 'I was pleasantly surprised to find there was hot water the next morning as we were lining up for the bathroom.' The publican, Bill Savory, was more discombobulated when he was asked if the hotel had a hairdryer.

Kevin Love went down to settle the bill, which was less for all of them in total than a single room had they stayed at the motel. Candy Broad hoped it wouldn't give the Treasurer, John Brumby, any bright ideas for saving money on future country trips. One of the public servants went over the road to organise breakfast at the Snowy River Café, and came running back to the hotel to tell the minister the bad news before she stepped out into the street and saw the newspaper posters for herself. The secret deal the Premiers would be announcing later that morning at Jindabyne was all over the front page of *The Age*. This was not part of the plan. Bloody hell, Claire, thought Robyn McLeod when she saw it. How did you find out?

I had driven down to Orbost the night before with a photographer for a special treat: flying with Candy Broad and Craig Ingram in a helicopter up the Snowy River to Jindabyne. The rest of the media were going up in light planes from Melbourne and Sydney. The government rang to offer me a seat on the helicopter a couple of days earlier; it wasn't hard to put two and two together and work out a deal had been done on the Snowy River. It was tough getting the details — they certainly had this one under very tight wraps — but eventually a source came through while I was in the car to Orbost.

I was feeling pretty smug when I met the government party outside the café. They looked daggers at me. 'The minister's not very happy with you!' one said. Craig Ingram started half-joking that the minister wouldn't let me on the helicopter and I would be left behind. I pointed out the silver lining: the Snowy had been overtaken by events overseas overnight, with a coup in Croatia, and so at least they got the front page today. It was small comfort. Craig sat between the minister and me in the helicopter. The atmosphere was rather tense. Broad told me years later she was mostly worried she would get into trouble, as if she might have given too much away at the Orbost meeting and word had leaked out. 'Managing the media is always a challenge,' she said.

The media were not the only ones the governments were trying to keep in the dark. Political media minders can be a bit paranoid about their charges mixing with the great unwashed in situations they cannot control. Candy Broad had invited the Orbost Alliance members, but in Sydney the invitation list was restricted to state politicians, the media and a few officials. There was no controlling this event, though. Governments leak like sieves — a fact that, oddly, always seems to take minders by surprise. The bush telegraph out of Dalgety was running hot for a couple of days before the event. 'We waited for them at Jindabyne, and saw the media disappearing down this dirt track,' says Jo Garland. 'One of the Chapman girls was redirecting everyone to where it was, and we had all these old diggers and we walked for miles.'

By the time the official party arrived at the dam, more than 100 people were waiting in the bush for them. 'It was all supposed to be hush-hush, and

Victorian Premier Steve Bracks and New South Wales Premier Bob Carr crossing the Snowy River below the Jindabyne dam wall, to announce their plans to restore 21 per cent of the original flow – enough for the water to be well over their heads at this spot. *Photo: Newspix,* The Australian, *6 October 2000.*

then we get there and there are all these school children to greet us!' said Kate Streets.

It was a beautiful day: crisp, clear air and cloudless skies. NSW Premier, Bob Carr, and Victorian Premier, Steve Bracks, jumped across the thin stream 200 metres below the dam wall and stood on a small grassy patch surrounded by water to address their unexpected audience. Bracks said he was proud to leave behind a legacy of the Snowy River running again for future generations, while Carr told the crowd that where they were standing would be deep under fast white water within ten years. 'This is the way of the new, modern Australia,' he said. The Premiers said the first releases for a 6 per cent flow would be made early in 2001, as soon as the scheme was corporatised.

Craig Ingram thanked the people of East Gippsland for voting for him, and the people of Victoria for being undecided in the 1999 election, leaving three independents with the balance of power. 'Today is the first step in achieving what is an ecologically sustainable flow for the Snowy River,' Ingram said. Australian Conservation Foundation president and Midnight Oil rock singer Peter Garrett hailed the deal as 'a major shift in our nation's treatment of rivers'. He said the Snowy deal was a rare instance in which an environmental problem was afforded the level of financial commitment it deserved.[1] The NSW Irrigators Council accepted the deal, welcoming it as an 'innovative solution' to reconcile competing needs for water.[2]

The danger was always that the Commonwealth could skittle the states' agreement, using the environmental impact study as the excuse. But even that cloud evaporated on this sunny day in Jindabyne. Commonwealth representatives were not invited to the ceremony — Candy Broad was adamant that if they did not pay for flows in the Snowy, they did not get to bask in the glory — but the vibes out of Canberra were positive. The final report of the environmental impact study was due out in a couple of weeks, but the Prime Minister, John Howard, pre-empted its results by promising a 'constructive' approach to the states' deal. Senator Minchin backed that up with a statement flagging the Commonwealth was likely to come up with a complementary package for the Murray and Murrumbidgee rivers.

The mood deep down in the Beloka Gorge, however, was not, as my daughter Imogen might say, all sunshine and daisies. Many community onlookers preferred to wait until promises of water became guarantees before they celebrated. Up on the dam wall stood a lone protester with a cardboard placard: 'Talk's cheap — where's the water?'

'I think we are still holding our breath,' said Moina Hedger at the big event. Her property, Cave Creek, abuts the Snowy River just south of

Glenice and Max White at the Jindabyne dam outlet for the Snowy River, almost daring to believe their beloved river will flow again. *Picture:* The Herald and Weekly Times *Photographic Collection.*

Dalgety. 'The announcement came out of the blue.' Jo Garland said 21 per cent was 'positive, terrific', but 'we will continue lobbying for the 28 per cent to be guaranteed within the ten-year time frame'.[3]

The Orbost crew set aside their misgivings temporarily to enjoy what they were hearing. Max White could hardly believe the river would be getting substantially more water. 'We think this is the catalyst for wins for rivers throughout Australia, not just the Snowy. It will be the forerunner of many,' he said to me. Gil Richardson wondered if the deal might be too good to be true, but, 'If [they] can get started implementing it quickly, it would be a very brave person who tried to undo it.'

Senator Hill did not go down quietly. He criticised the states' deal a few days later, saying it would blow out the cost of fixing the salinity crisis in the Murray Darling Basin. 'If Victoria and NSW are going to fund $300 million to purchase water to send down the Snowy, so be it,' Senator Hill said. 'But from a national perspective we should understand that you buy the cheaper water now and if further water is going to be necessary for the Murray in the future, it will be more expensive.'

Few were listening outside South Australia. Behind the scenes, Senator Minchin had prevailed in Cabinet. The Commonwealth was just waiting for due process to run its course with the environmental impact study. A final report was never released, and Senator Hill's recommendations to Senator Minchin were a formality. On 6 December 2000, eight weeks after the Premiers raised their glasses below Jindabyne dam, Senator Minchin announced the Commonwealth would support the deal with $75 million to find an extra 70 gigalitres for the Murray. 'The Snowy River and the River Murray are both stressed rivers,' he said. 'The use of joint government funds to provide for an increased environmental flow in both rivers is a practical response to the difficulty of balancing competing needs for water.' Ecologically, 70 gigalitres was minuscule in relation to the scale of problems in the Murray, but politically it allowed the South Australian Liberal Government to claim a win.

At last the way was clear for the Snowy Mountains Hydro-Electric Scheme to be corporatised — just as soon as the broad outlines in the Heads of Government agreement on flows were translated into the detail required for the water licence and other documents. Premier Steve Bracks could hardly contain his excitement. 'It's a fantastic day for Victoria, a fantastic day for Australia,' he said. He predicted the scheme would be corporatised early in the New Year, and more water would be flowing in the Snowy by mid-2001 at the latest.

The difficulty for government was they were trying to set the water reform agenda on the back of corporatisation. It was like a set of tram tracks and everyone was trying to get it to turn left or right, but it kept going straight and government could not change the trajectory. There were all these hardliners who could have brought the whole thing undone whatever the political and community will, and the environmental necessity. The problem was that in New South Wales, Treasury was still the responsible body for interstate negotiations, and they had no interest in getting environmental flows over the line. They kept putting up obstacles. It was going nowhere fast and we were concerned that the momentum was being lost. It looked as if we would snatch defeat from the jaws of victory. We were bogged in the detail.

BRETT MINERS

The devil is always in the detail. Glenice White's misgivings on the night Candy Broad came to Orbost deepened into dismay when she finally received a copy of the Heads of Government agreement between the Commonwealth, Victoria and New South Wales. 'The problem was that it was all slanted in favour of the irrigators,' she said.

The agreement, signed on 6 December 2000, spelled out the timetable for returning water. The first release of 38 gigalitres a year would be from the Mowamba weir as soon as the scheme was corporatised. This would bring the flow up to 6 per cent. The second stage, two to seven years after corporatisation, included Snowy Hydro building an outlet at Jindabyne dam within three years, to enable a flow of at least 28 per cent. Releases would be progressively increased by 142 gigalitres during this period, to bring the flow up to 15 per cent. In the third stage, eight to ten years after corporatisation, the additional flow would rise from 142 to 212 gigalitres, or 21 per cent of the original. Any more beyond that depended on private enterprise investing in public infrastructure and the willingness of future governments to pay compensation to Snowy Hydro for foregone power generation.

The fine print also only guaranteed the Snowy River 15 per cent. The flow between 15 and 21 per cent would be allocated from one year to the next at the same reliability as irrigators received their entitlements. That meant in drier years inland, the Snowy River would get somewhat less, regardless of natural conditions prevailing in the mountains. The Snowy had also to wait until savings were achieved and verified on the other side of the Great Divide. The exception was the initial release from the Mowamba weir. The Snowy would get that water immediately — but on loan. It would have to be 'paid back' to the scheme after three years, once water savings began to be audited.

'We got overrun with the blarney of the bureaucracy about we have to do this, and that, but don't worry — we will get it done,' says Lynette Greenwood. 'I think people were happy we had got the 28 per cent, then they realised it was not really 28 per cent but 21 per cent. But I think our expectations might have been unrealistic about what we could achieve with all that energy.'

Gil and Heather Richardson agree. 'It was a first in the world, and I don't think we realised the difficulties of the negotiations, with the legalities and the interstate competition in husbanding the water,' says Gil. Max and Glenice White are less forgiving. They are pleased the governments are committed to substantially increasing the river's flow, but doubt it will ever make 28 per cent. Max mutters darkly that the Alliance was sold out.

Carl Drury's disappointment festers like an open wound. 'All the players just did it for their political career or to get awards,' he says. 'When push came to shove, no one was there for the river.' He is particularly scathing about the Alliance's 'middle-class politics' and Craig Ingram, who he says should have opposed the deal on principle, even if it meant condemning himself and the Alliance to the margins. Drury loathes compromise, and traces the rot back to 1997, when the Total Environment Centre agreed to the corporatisation legislation and the Snowy Water Inquiry. 'It was a series of glorious defeats after that,' Drury says. 'We haven't got an environmental flow, we have got a political flow. It all became just this percentage bidding game. And there is no incentive, no whip for the irrigators to find the water. I was devastated — we lost.'

There was also deep disquiet in Orbost and Dalgety that the agreement did not include dismantling the Mowamba weir. Demolition was important ecologically and psychologically: the community does not trust future governments or Snowy Hydro. As long as the infrastructure remains, the Snowy River can always be turned off again.

An unregulated flow from the Mowamba River is also important for the Snowy's ecology. The tributary would act as a much-needed substitute headwater, with daily variations in flow in response to natural conditions in the mountains. This daily variation is vital for proper ecological functioning in dynamic mountain rivers like the Snowy. Without the Mowamba as a proxy headwater, the Snowy's flow will be entirely human-controlled out of Jindabyne dam. At best, this can only ever be a poor approximation of seasonal and monthly variations worked out a year in advance with Snowy

Hydro. Demolishing the aqueduct would also allow fish to travel once again up into a montane headwater to breed, although a fish ladder would to some degree overcome this problem.

Demolition of the weir was in the draft Heads of Government agreement back in late August 2000, when the states took the document to Senator Minchin after the Hobart ALP national conference. Clause 8.8.1 said Snowy Hydro would be responsible for removing the Mowamba structures within three years of the aqueduct being decommissioned. Craig Ingram had wanted the structures demolished immediately, but was persuaded it was necessary to keep them for the first three years to keep the initial releases under a maximum 38 gigalitres per annum. Otherwise, if there was a very wet year and substantially more went down, the Snowy River's water debt to the scheme would blow out before it could be offset with savings.

However, this clause had disappeared when the Heads of Government agreement was signed and released on 6 December. Vin Good says it was removed because it was not consistent with the water licence under the *Snowy Hydro Corporatisation Act 1997*, which stipulates no infrastructure can be demolished. Kevin Love, from Victoria's Department of Premier and Cabinet, does not recall when and how the clause came to be removed from the draft. He recalls subsequent debate with the Snowy River Alliance about the decommissioning of the aqueduct but considered it an ambit claim that had to be balanced against the ability to regulate the flow in the long term. The south-east regional coordinator in the New South Wales Premier's Department, Colin Steele, said the clause dropped off unnoticed in the rush to get the agreement approved by all three governments. It did not seem like such a big deal at the time, but it would come back to haunt them all.

For Victoria, New South Wales and the Commonwealth, the Heads of Government agreement amounted to a statement of good intent. The outcome still had to be legally interpreted and incorporated into the corporatisation documents. The ministers and their advisors left it to the public servants to dot the i's and cross the t's. The Snowy had consumed their working lives for months, and it was time to devote attention to other issues and demands — although Candy Broad kept a close watch for potential obstacles.

The Murray Darling Basin Ministerial Council was always a worry. The council consists of land, water and environment ministers from the Commonwealth, Queensland, South Australia, Victoria, New South Wales and the Australian Capital Territory. Technically, South Australia did not have a say in matters relating to corporatising the Snowy Mountains scheme. But indirectly, the state had a say because the ministerial council had to approve any changes in releases from the scheme that affected the Murray Darling Basin.

As an energy minister, Candy Broad did not have a seat on the ministerial council, but she went to most of the meetings anyway. 'I knew the council had the potential to block things so it was important I managed that,' she said. 'There were so many points that required backing up. It got a little difficult at one point with Senator Hill and [federal Conservation Minister, Wilson] Tuckey criticising the Snowy deal, but I prevailed by drawing Minchin into the discussion and saying, "You are aware by this time that the Premiers and the Prime Minister have agreed this will happen. If you have a problem with that, then you should take it up with the Prime Minister."'

In the meantime, the corporatisation committee nitpicked and argued over every small detail. Any residual, low-level obstruction from the Snowy Mountains Authority dissipated entirely with the appointment of outsider, Terry Charlton, as commissioner in August 1999, with Vin Good as associate commissioner. Yet progress remained slow. The water licence was only one of forty-seven legal documents required to corporatise the scheme, and the lawyers and consultants were intent on going over every one with a fine-tooth comb. David Crossley sat at the head of the table, apparently dozing while the others argued. At critical moments, he startled everyone by rumbling into life to point out, 'No, that's not what we decided three meetings ago.' Other times, rather unnervingly, he suddenly said, 'David Crossley!' then muttered for a few minutes with his eyes still closed. After a while the others worked out that he was talking into an earpiece for his mobile phone.

Outside the interminable negotiations in Governor Macquarie Tower in Sydney, other news distracted public and political attention. In March 2001, Australian insurance giant HIH collapsed. Ansett Airlines began sounding its death rattle in August, the same month as the Tampa scandal. The tragedy of September 11 in New York followed, and then more scandals in the Commonwealth's Pacific Solution for Middle East asylum-seekers, and false claims some had thrown children overboard in October. The Commonwealth called a highly charged election in November 2001; the coalition was returned resoundingly, and there was a ministerial reshuffle. Ian Macfarlane replaced Senator Minchin as Energy and Resources Minister, and took the requisite few months to get across his new portfolio. Early in 2002, well down the list of things to do, he came across corporatising the Snowy Mountains scheme. 'By the time I knew anything about it, Snowy Hydro had been set up for six months but doing nothing and we inherited it,' he said to me. 'I am not sure if it was breathing, but it was certainly in a coma. Corporatisation seemed a small part of the portfolio, but it was doing nothing and it needed to be progressed.'

Macfarlane is a gravel-voiced farmer from Kingaroy in Queensland, with dust in his throat and a long face lined by years of gazing into cloudless skies. Personally, he was not enamoured of sending more water down the Snowy River. 'The question is what is the best use of water after you have got the savings?' he said. 'Is it to grow more crops or is it to create an environmental flow? I would say grow more crops, and if there is to be environmental flows, it has to have a tourist value and that means it has to be more than a trickle. The Snowy used to be a wild raging river and it will never be a wild raging river again. That was part of its mystique — the snowmelt and the thunderstorms, and the floods. It is never going to do that again, so it is not as if we are restoring it to be anything like it was.'

But he was not going to get into an argument over it; his job was to get the done deal. South Australia was still dragging its heels. Six months earlier, Bracks and the Prime Minister, John Howard, had threatened Liberal Premier, John Olsen, that they would make alternative arrangements and South Australia would get nothing if he did not approve the Snowy deal. Olsen dropped his opposition. Then South Australia went to the polls on 9 February 2002 and the government changed hands. The new Labor Premier, Michael Rann, also prevaricated. 'He was of the view that although I had a verbal agreement with the previous South Australian Government, he was going to re-examine it because he thought the Murray should get a better deal,' Steve Bracks said.

Overcoming that obstacle cost Victoria $15 million in a $25 million bilateral deal with South Australia to tackle salinity and water quality in the Murray River. Bracks and Rann announced on 15 April 2002 that the $25 million would be used to find another 30 gigalitres for the Murray. 'I was bloody annoyed,' said Bracks later. 'We had come so far, and still there were stumbling blocks. I had had an agreement with John Olsen, and then we had to get extra for Rann. But we judged it was worth a bilateral agreement because it was good environmentally, and the alternatives would have been more cumbersome because they would also involve altering myriad agreements involving South Australia.'

Macfarlane had the impression there was little trust and goodwill between the Commonwealth and state officials charged with finalising corporatisation. So his advisor, Andrew Blyth, got together with Robyn

McLeod and Matthew Strassberg to work out what they could do to hurry things up. They decided to hold a lock-up session in Parliament House in Canberra, where no one would be allowed to leave the room until every one of the scheme's forty-seven corporatisation documents was finalised.

The lock-up took place in April 2002. The sense of urgency was sharpened by Victoria receiving advice from Carr's office that the NSW Premier had set aside 10 May as the big day when the first 38 gigalitres of water would be released from the Mowamba weir. The three advisors took turns chairing the sessions, sitting together at the head table. The Commonwealth, Victorian and NSW corporatisation project teams were lined up at tables arranged around the other three sides of the square. Behind the public servants sat the lawyers and consultants. All up, about thirty people were in the room.

Matthew Strassberg planned on the session taking a day and a night, and duly flew home late the first evening. He got a phone call the next morning, asking him to come back. Robyn McLeod similarly flew up assuming it would take a day; she did not take a change of clothing and snuck out the second day to buy fresh underwear. The lock-up ended up lasting a gruelling three days. 'Normally ministerial chiefs-of-staff and advisors do not delve into documents and do the details — we just do the overviews,' said McLeod later. 'But we were there to get this resolved and finalised. If we had not done that, I think we would still be buggerising around. Some of these people had spent fifteen years of their lives trying to corporatise the Snowy scheme, and it needed someone with a clear set of eyes to say "Just sign off on this thing or you could just keeping playing with the legalities forever."'

The three advisors set a cracking pace. Each of the forty-seven documents was examined to work out areas of agreement and disagreement. Breakout groups were sent out to resolve differences, then the documents would be signed and not revisited as the meeting moved on to the next one. 'It was overwhelming to chair it and be looking at all these tax experts, but I was there to get a quick agreement,' says McLeod. 'We would start a document, I would say has anyone got an issue — they had been through them all a million times — and one would say "This clause here — I don't think I have an issue with it, but —" Then I would cut in and say, "Well, if you haven't got an issue, we will move on."'

They were nearly done on the third day when a Commonwealth tax lawyer ran in with an unforeseen problem: the Goods and Services Tax. Strassberg was furious. 'We were at the point of saying, "Is that it, then — is it final?", and then there was this question about the GST.'

The corporatisation process had taken so long that it was overtaken by the GST, introduced in July 2000. It meant every transaction related to corporatisation and flows would be taxed — adding millions and millions of dollars to the total cost. Everyone swore. Commonwealth lawyers clustered at the back of the room scoured the *GST Act*, looking for an exemption for the scheme. 'Something that holds water — oh, no, it has to be less than 50 megalitres!' one would say. 'What about a drainage line — does the Snowy count as that?' another would suggest. 'Sewerage? Oh, no, we can't say that because the exemption is only for infrastructure,' said another bright spark. 'Why don't you call the Snowy a sticky bun without icing and be done with it,' snapped a very frazzled Robyn McLeod. She straggled back to Melbourne about 10 o'clock that night and went straight into Parliament House to tell the Premier and Candy Broad of the last-minute hiccup.

A ragged Matthew Strassberg rang Carr's office to say everything was settled but the GST, and was it possible to delay the big day at Mowamba weir a couple of months, until this last hurdle was overcome? He was given till September.

David Crossley had to leave the lock-up early to go to Vietnam. He called Geoff Chambers, his offsider in the negotiations for New South Wales Treasury, when he got off the plane to make sure everything had gone through, and got the bad news about the GST. 'It hinged on who owned the asset,' Crossley said. 'It was on NSW land but paid for by the Commonwealth. So if it was being purchased by the states, then they had to pay GST on the transaction. That meant we had to get the Tax Office and the federal Treasury and Finance department involved — and not having been involved all along, they wanted to go back to the beginning!'

Ian Macfarlane was not going to see the whole thing tripped up so close to the finish line. He talked it over with the federal Treasurer, Peter Costello, who three weeks later solved the problem by granting the scheme a one-off exemption.

At last it was done. On 3 June 2002, Candy Broad and the Victorian Treasurer, John Brumby, walked from one document to another laid out in triplicate on tables around a room in Melbourne, signing corporatisation to come into effect on 28 June 2002. Robyn McLeod was travelling in the United States at the time, as a guest of the US Government. 'I was in Houston when I got a call to say it was all signed, and I opened a bottle of champagne and drank it in celebration.'

✍

Max and I, amongst many, many others, needed to see this river flowing again. The obvious fragmentation of its waterway over the years ... was something we could never get out of our heads or our hearts.

GLENICE WHITE, ORBOST, 2002

The first flush of extra water to bring the Snowy River back to life meant many things to many people. A crowd of about 400 gathered on the hillside above the Mowamba weir on Wednesday, 28 August 2002. They watched Steve Bracks and Bob Carr squeeze into a small concrete control room. At exactly 10.23 am, the Premiers pushed a button to close off the pipe diverting the river into Lake Jindabyne. The air was cold, but the late winter sunshine warm as everyone waited.

It seemed to take forever, but slowly, slowly, the water behind the weir rose. A dribble tinkled over the wall at the far end. The dribble built up into a trickle. The trickle spread across the weir and became a murmuring veil. The veil thickened into a heavy curtain of water cascading over the edge. The politicians had to shout over the splendid splashing.

Within half an hour, children were paddling in the water flowing down the river, throwing sticks into the current where before there were only

Steve Bracks and Bob Carr had to shout to be heard above the splendid splashing when the Mowamba diversion was closed off and water began flowing to begin slaking the Snowy River's 30-year-long thirst. *Source: Craig Chapman.*

stagnant pools among the reeds and rocks. More than a few onlookers had lumps in their throats and tears in their eyes; many had never imagined this happy day would come. 'I felt so emotional, seeing that water coming back, saying, "I am here, I am back, I am coming back to see you!"' said Moina Hedger, from Cave Creek station. 'The Snowy River was very popular and it brought a lot of tourists and fishing and campers over Christmas, and that all adds up to a little bit of money to keep Dalgety alive.'

'It's a historic day for Aboriginal people and non-Aboriginal people,' Ngarigo elder Aunty Rae Stewart told the assembled throng. She said the Snowy had nearly been strangled to death, but thanks to the 'governments of today' it would flow again and, in time, return home. 'Now my dead elders won't be thirsty any more,' she said. 'The spirits of the elders of this area will be free at last with the flowing of the river — but a little more water next time, guys!'

'You can't imagine what it feels like, to see something back in the river, knowing the way it was and what it became — this trickle, not even a creek,' her cousin, Ngarigo elder Aunty Rachel Mullett, said to me. 'Certainly our elders would have loved to have seen it, what is happening today. My mother was the youngest of the family. She passed on about six years ago. You could call this reconciliation for us. It is reconciliation and respect for all the community, especially the Aboriginal people.'

Aunty Rachel and her husband, Uncle Albert Mullett, a Gunai elder, saw the belated glimmerings of a new sensibility in the promise to restore some water to the Snowy River. 'White people are beginning to learn to care for country, and if it is not too late, they might learn something,' said Aunty Rachel.

Al Campbell, from Orange in New South Wales, thought the release meant a pleasant morning kayaking from the weir down the Mowamba into the Snowy and on to Dalgety. In an unscripted move, upstaging the Premiers' long-awaited photo opportunity, the kayaker appeared from nowhere, gliding across the weir's pond before the mystified crowd. They cheered as he bumped over the wall to ride the cascade, then winced as he hit the concrete splash tray at the bottom with a nasty thud. The Snowy may have increased its flow from 1 to a nominal 6 per cent on this day, but Al Campbell was about ten years too early for shooting the rapids.

'I came today because I heard they were going to let the water over,' he said ruefully after picking himself and his kayak up off the riverbed. 'I thought there would be enough water, but there wasn't. I should have rung up or done a bit more to find out.'

Kayaker Al Campbell steals the limelight going over the Mowamba weir – about 10 years too early for the legendary rapids. *Photo: Joe Armao, The Age, 29 August 2002, p.1.*

Al had kayaked all the Snowy except the stretch between Jindabyne and Dalgety where the river was too shallow and severely degraded. This section had been legendary for its wild rapids before the Snowy Mountains scheme took away the water. It would again offer some extreme kayaking once the flow was brought up to 21 per cent. Al could hardly wait. 'If they can get a bit more water down this little creek, it would be awesome,' he told me, breathless with anticipation and the pain of a bump to the head. 'It is a good section, nice wilderness. It's the full package.'

The officials were less than impressed with Campbell's stunt. One political advisor grumbled he could have broken his neck and spoiled the day — or at least the headlines, which would have been about tragedy rather than triumph on the Snowy River.

There were plenty who thought all that water going down the Mowamba River was tragedy enough. A carload of septuagenarians from Jindabyne pulled up by the Snowy River near Dalgety the day before, where the media scrum was watching Bracks and Carr get their pants wet wading among the reeds with Brett Miners. 'It's all politics, isn't it?' said one of them, Wal Weston, less than impressed by the scene. 'I'm sad to see the river reduced to this, but this isn't going to make that much difference, is it? It's my personal opinion, but there's water much needed in other places. The timing couldn't be worse, could it?'[4]

A small group of irrigators parked a truckload of hay near the Mowamba weir the next morning to underline the point. Glenice White thought someone generous must have donated the bales for a raffle; hay was nearly impossible to buy for love nor money in that severely drought-afflicted year. She was wrong. The rural press was editorialising that it was irresponsible to start releasing water down the Snowy during the worst Big Dry in a century.[5] The hay was a symbol of how farmers were being forced to drive hundreds of kilometres to buy feed at prohibitive prices, and they had yet to get their livestock through summer. (Monaro graziers along the Snowy River had endured the same expenses since persistent drought set in during the mid-1990s.) The bales were draped with banners: 'The Snowy can borrow — why can't we? Mr Carr and Mr Bracks, please release some water to farmers too.' 'That 38,000 megalitres down the Snowy could be used to grow fodder,' said Trevor Clark, chairman of the South Riverina Irrigation District Council. 'We are definitely not against the allocation of water for the Snowy River today, we are quite in favour of it. But we are in desperate need at the moment.'

Four weeks earlier, advisors from Victoria and New South Wales met officials from the Snowy Mountains Authority at the weir for a test run. Rob Hudson watched the water spilling over the edge, and turned to one of the men from the authority. 'What do you call that?' he asked, pointing to the cascade.

'What do you mean?' said the hydro official.

'Water going over a weir like that.'

'A fucking waste of water!'

In the corporatisation committee, Vin Good had joked he would pitch a tent beside the Jindabyne dam when it came time to do the spring flush flows. 'I said I would have little models of schools and hospitals, and throw them into the water. As they went down the Snowy, they would indicate how many schools and hospitals we were flushing down the river. It was my joke to get back at them. The governments committed $375 million and the hydro will lose at least $300 million in net present value[6] to make those releases, so the true cost is closer to $700 million. In my view, if the public knew those releases down the Snowy and other montane rivers was costing $700 million, they might opt to spend it on schools or hospitals or some other thing, but the politicians never explained this to the public.'

The politicians thought more important things were at stake than money. They welcomed the release as a symbol of a new era and proof that the democratic process can work. 'It's probably one of the proudest moment I've had as Premier,' Bracks said at that celebration of the first release of water on 28 August 2002. 'We have turned off the aqueduct and turned on the river. Fifty years ago, the Snowy scheme was a nation-building exercise — and this is one too, recognising that environmental flows and the environment are part of our future and a necessary part of balanced economic growth ... I will look back in ten or fifteen years on my time as Premier, that this was one of the best things we could ever have done.'

Carr said the release showed that the states and the Commonwealth could cooperate to solve environmental problems 'in this tired old land ... This is a good indication that cooperation at a ministerial level between governments can get a great environmental outcome, a very happy outcome. Young people shouldn't despair of politicians and shouldn't write politicians off. It was political change, a change of government in Victoria that delivered this result, with our support ... Politics does count, it can change things.'

Craig Ingram agreed. 'Small communities, when they're right, can stand up and say to government, "This is wrong", he said. Ingram thanked Bracks for committing to the Snowy River long before there was a vote in it, but said many people had fought long and hard for thirty-five years to make it happen. 'Listening to the sound behind us here, that is what has been turned off and that is the sound of the Snowy. Everyone who has contributed in any way — today is a celebration for them. I think when they dammed the Snowy River, they took away our pride in our river and faith in democratic institutions for those below Jindabyne dam ... This will go down in history as a great day for the Snowy.'

They were all there: the ministers, their advisors, the public servants and sundry celebrities. The politicians and the rock star, Peter Garrett, got to make the speeches, but unlike the Jindabyne event two years earlier, the day was organised first and foremost for the community. Because, when all was said and done, it was the community who really got the Snowy River flowing.

After the formalities, Dalgety did what it does best: a barbeque on the banks of the Snowy below the bridge. There were horses galloping through the water, bands, poets and lots of very excited children and even more excited dogs. The public hall was filled with photos, paintings and stories about the river.

Skipping stones
New water
Over the rocks
Water to swim
Yippee.

Jerrika Taylor,
Berridale Primary School

Students sang 'Waltzing Matilda' and other songs, a light breeze blowing their tunes all over the crowd. Jo Garland was all smiles, but doggedly focused, as always. A few days before the big event, Dalgety's self proclaimed endurance queen said the Mowamba release was only a start. 'They're finally going to double the trickle!' she said. 'At the moment the river's dead and getting worse all the time. Hopefully with this release, the deterioration will stop.'[7]

The party continued at the pub after the politicians and the city media went home and the shadows lengthened across the picnic ground. Graham Pike opened a book and took bets on when the Mowamba water would reach Dalgety and how much the river would rise. At midnight, Craig Ingram and Pike sat by the moonlit river and talked. 'There was a tremendous sense of satisfaction and peace,' said Pike. 'We ranged over a whole lot of things in that hour and a half. And I think we both realised anything was possible after this.'

The day before, I'd stood in a similar spot with John Eccleston, a sixty-nine year old who lives in the house his great-great-grandparents built in 1850 on their property, Coonghoongbula. Eccleston has seen the Snowy at its best and its worst, and he hated seeing it die. We talked about how the Mowamba release was undoing a little bit of national history in the hydro scheme. 'But gee, it is not a bad bit of history to be undone just the same,' he said with a chuckle.

NINE

A Long Time in Politics

*I did not mind the challenge. I don't mind being on the losing end
for a long time if there is sunshine at the other end.*

MAX WHITE

Was the Snowy River really saved? Only time will tell — and ten years
is a long time in politics. Circumstances, governments and ministers
change, as do priorities. Governments should be given the chance to do the
right thing before they are criticised for doing the wrong thing, but there is
a school of thought that the Mowamba weir release is all the extra water the
Snowy River will ever get. Then again, these cynics are probably the same
ones who said at the beginning there was no point trying to get any more
water at all.

However, the Snowy River faces daunting obstacles on its long journey
back to ecological health. There is no doubt the river will get more than the
nominal 6 per cent from the Mowamba tributary. Snowy Hydro Ltd has
started work on modifying the Jindabyne dam wall so that at least 28 per
cent can eventually be released. The $69 million works will be complete in
2005, and a big hole with no water coming out won't be a good look for the
NSW and Victorian governments. They will make sure there is water
available. The open question is, how much of the guaranteed 21 per cent
will be forthcoming — much less the promised 28 per cent — and how long
will it take to deliver?

Looking on the bright side, the NSW and Victorian Labor governments
did what they could to safeguard the deal. The flows deed is attached to the
Snowy Corporatisation Act 1997, and includes a section on legal intent and
remedies. The deed is intended as an interpretative document, which means
that in theory, if the flows do not materialise, the community can take
current and future governments to court. The deed can only be changed if
all three governments agree.

The Joint Government Enterprise, formally named 'Water for Rivers', is
another safeguard. Water for Rivers is a government-owned corporation,
with the Commonwealth, New South Wales and Victoria as its shareholders.

As a company, its operations should be less vulnerable to future changes in governments and their priorities than if bureaucracies undertook its work. The corporation, like most things associated with corporatising the Snowy Mountains scheme, took longer to set up than expected, but the board was finally approved in November 2003 and Water for Rivers began trading the following month, in December 2003.

In the meantime, the Victorian and NSW water bureaucracies set about finding water savings ready for transfer to Water for Rivers. In August 2004, Victoria had 74 gigalitres in the bag, of which 41 gigalitres will be available for the Snowy River in the second stage of releases. Stage two occurs two to seven years after corporatisation in June 2002, with releases progressively increased to 142 gigalitres, or 15 per cent of the original flow at Jindabyne. The Victorian Department of Sustainability and Environment is confident the volume will rapidly ramp up towards the end of stage two in 2009, as more savings come on line. The NSW Department of Infrastructure, Planning and Natural Resources, for its part, has identified 52 gigalitres in savings, to be shared between the Murray and the Snowy rivers. The water in both states comes from decommissioning shallow reservoirs such as Victoria's Lake Mokoan and New South Wales' Barrenbox Swamp; accurately metering water diverted for stock and domestic purposes on farms; introducing computerised distribution systems; and, in New South Wales, on-farm efficiencies.

Water for Rivers' chief executive officer, Neville Smith, said in August 2004 that the corporation had identified projects to yield 280 gigalitres, as required to return 210 gigalitres to the Snowy for a 21 per cent flow, and 70 gigalitres to the Murray. The enterprise's advent has had unforeseen benefits, with potential water sources expanding to include on-farm efficiencies. These were not counted during the government negotiations because irrigators insisted they keep any gains made on farm, but Smith said their attitude was changing. 'We have some farmers saying if they sell some water, they will talk to us rather than put it on the open market where another grower buys it,' Smith said. 'The farmer might get the money, but they get no enduring benefit. If they sell to the environmental reserve, then they are doing more to ensure their supply and quality in the long term.'

The Mowamba flow will, perversely, slow down the pace of releases in the second stage. According to the deed, the Snowy gets no water until savings are identified and audited — in other words, not for at least two or three years after corporatisation. However, the politicians wanted to release some water immediately as a show of good faith. So the Mowamba diversion was switched off to give the Snowy River up to 38 gigalitres a year, or a 6 per cent flow, for three years, until the hole in the dam wall was completed and savings materialised.

This water comes from the above-target reserve, and must be 'paid back' to Snowy Hydro Ltd. Once savings are audited and become available, they will be distributed a third each to the Murray, the Snowy and Snowy Hydro Ltd until the debt is repaid. The good news is only 22 gigalitres or so a year has flowed over the Mowamba weir since 2002, due to prevailing drought, so the water debt will be much lower than anticipated.

The bad news is that Snowy Hydro wants to recommission the Mowamba diversion in June 2005. This means the Snowy's flow will come from Jindabyne dam alone. The water deed is silent on whether Snowy Hydro can do this, and the Snowy River Alliance is campaigning to keep the tributary flowing for ecological reasons. The Mowamba River is a substitute headwater for the Snowy, providing small but important daily variations in flow in response to natural weather conditions. Scientists attribute much of the recovery already observed in the Snowy to this renewed natural dynamism. Human-controlled releases from the dam can only ever be a crude approximation.

Snowy Hydro, however, says the Mowamba flow must be diverted so that the Snowy River releases can be accurately regulated. Otherwise, the Snowy River might get more than its mandated flow through an unexpected wet spell in the Mowamba catchment. Alternately, Snowy Hydro says it needs the water from the Mowamba coming into Jindabyne dam so that it can release 'flushing' flows every three or so years to mimic the snowmelt flood. Snowy Hydro also claims that uncertainty over how much water might be lost to the Snowy down a free flowing Mowamba makes it difficult to plan for power generation and irrigation releases from one year to the next.

The arguments are nonsense. The fact is that a gauge can be placed in the Mowamba River measuring its flows on a daily basis. The releases from Jindabyne dam can then be adjusted accordingly from one day to the next, including the periodic flushing flows when a fixed amount will be sent downstream over several days. Overall, the water down the Mowamba also represents a tiny fraction of total inflows into the scheme and the total water held in storage; whether or not it is diverted into Jindabyne will not make or break the scheme's capacity to deliver water to the turbines or irrigators from one year to the next. Snowy Hydro, it seems, just can't bear the idea of letting a river under its control run free, much less give it up altogether and dismantle the weir.

Snowy Hydro's rigidity on this matter reveals that, culturally, the organisation has not much changed. Far from embracing the concept of environmental flows, the corporation still resents giving the Snowy River any water and shows itself reluctant to adopt the modern adaptive management required for environmental sustainability. The Snowy River's restoration gets only a passing mention in promotional material as something Snowy Hydro is doing only because the governments told it it had to. The corporation, however, makes a big deal of the engineering aspects of building the new outlets in Jindabyne dam wall, extolling the corporation's environmental credentials in its video.

The corporation also remains as secretive as ever. Its communications department was steadfastly unhelpful whenever I called looking for detailed information. Rather than letting me speak to a live person who could answer my queries, I was simply referred to the Snowy Hydro website and told to send an email with questions if I could not find what I was after there. The replies to written questions were monosyllabic. The three governments, as the hydro scheme shareholders, will determine the outcome of the tussle over the Mowamba weir. Their decision will reveal whether the Snowy's mandated flow really is only political in intent, or geared to achieving the best environmental outcome possible.

The worsening Murray River crisis is another obstacle. Scientists say the Murray River and its tributaries need at least another 1500 gigalitres a year simply to prevent further degradation. Ecologically, the system could need as much as 60 per cent of its natural mean flow of 12,300 gigalitres to achieve scientific sustainability; the Murray Darling now has only 20 to 30 per cent, even with additional water from the diverted Snowy River.[1] In June 2004, the Council of Australian Governments made a policy commitment to increase the Murray's flow by 500 gigalitres as a first step. The danger is the Murray's desperate need could swamp the efforts to deliver the Snowy River's guaranteed 212 gigalitres for a 21 per cent flow.

Considering how hard it was to find 212 gigalitres ostensibly through off-farm savings for the Snowy River, inevitably much of the Murray's water must come from consumers. Some states are more prepared than others to bite the bullet. Two days before the COAG announcement, Victoria revealed radical reforms in which, remarkably, irrigators agreed to reduce consumption to free up 169 gigalitres for the Murray River. An average 5 per cent levy will also be imposed to raise $225 million for environmental repair and efficiency works.

New South Wales irrigators, however, are still resisting such reforms. How all of this will play out over the next decade remains to be seen, but if the NSW Government is genuine in its rhetoric about saving waterways, it will have to weather a savage political storm first. Climate change in coming years will heighten the tensions. The CSIRO is predicting rainfall in the Murray Darling Basin will be 10 to 35 per cent lower than the long-term average by 2070, while higher temperatures will increase evaporation rates, making the land drier earlier in the season.

Added to all this is the uncertainty about how much water will do the trick in the Snowy River. The ten-year project is among the most ambitious river restorations attempted in the world, and scientists do not really know what to expect. 'No one has ever done this before — taken a big snowmelt river down to 1 per cent of its flow, degraded it for thirty-five years, and then said, "What do we put back in it?"' said Brett Miners.[2]

In theory, with 21 per cent and a flush in early spring to mimic the snowmelt surge, the Snowy will be strong enough to start carving a channel down through the sand to expose the original gravel bed. Within twenty-five to fifty years, with a 28 per cent flow, the Snowy should look like the Thredbo River: a cut-down but genuine version of its original lively self.

However, in practice, no one knows how much water it will take. It may be that 21 per cent is enough; it may be that 28 per cent is not enough. Scientists must wait and observe how the Snowy responds to progressively higher flows. The signs so far are promising. The Mowamba flow has raised the level perhaps only an inch, but it is enough to boost the growth of reeds, and seep in under previously dry sandbanks to germinate native seeds.

Brett Miners wades in the Snowy River, looking for signs of ecological recovery eight months after its flow was increased to six per cent.
Photo: Andrew De La Rue, The Age, 26 April 2003.

Small surges from thunderstorms in the Mowamba headwaters are helping the river to begin cleaning itself of silt and algae. 'We are starting to break it out of old sedentary habits, like someone who has been sitting in an armchair too long,' says Miners.

New South Wales and Victoria are also well on the way to removing willows, blackberries and other woody weeds along the length of the river. Without willow root mats choking the channel, the Snowy can flow more freely. Native species are being planted to replace the weeds. Down in Orbost, the Victorian Government is spending $1.7 million trialling measures to restore fish habitat and holes in the now desolate 14-kilometre sand plug. The trial will guide how the government spends $40 million on restoration works over the next decade, as increased flows begin to take effect downstream. The willow removal and other programs ensure the hard-won environmental flow amounts to more than just more water sloshing over sand and weeds.

Land-use changes will also have a bearing on the project's success. The company Willmott has bought the timber mill at Bombala, and is taking advantage of tax breaks to purchase farmland for pine plantations. Willmott has so far put 45,000 hectares under plantation in the region, but says it needs at least 65,000 hectares for the mill to be viable. But young trees drink up far more water than pasture or mature forests, which means reduced runoff into creeks and rivers that ultimately feed into the Snowy River. Skye Thain, who has land at Tubbut, says that just 10,000 hectares of plantation could reduce runoff into Snowy tributaries by 20 gigalitres a year. She cites Dr Rob Vertessy, a CSIRO expert on forest hydrology at the Cooperative Research Centre for Catchment Hydrology, who warns about the effects of large-scale pastoral afforestation. 'Principal among the consequences will be reduced water yield and reduced groundwater recharge,' he says.[3]

The community around Bombala, Delegate and down into the Deddick River valley is fighting to limit the amount of land put under plantation. They cite historic failures in plantation development in low rainfall areas, and point out the irreversible social consequences of losing farm families en masse. At the time of writing, the tiny Victorian communities of Tubbut, Dellicknora and Deddick had just won an injunction against more plantations in the Deddick River valley. The fight continues around Bombala and Delegate.

There is a lot riding on a successful river restoration. If the Snowy substantially recovers its health and character, it will bolster the case for bringing other stricken rivers back from the brink. It will also prove that environmental flows should be determined according to environmental outcomes, rather than what little water farmers and other bulk consumers feel they can spare. If the Snowy experiment is less than successful, sceptics will be hardened in their view that environmental flows are a waste of money and water.

Aboriginal attitudes remain ambivalent. Gunai elder, Uncle Albert Mullett, is pleased something is being done for the the Snowy River at last, but it rankles when scientists talk about how they will be taking better care of the environment now. 'I say that is all okay, but our people have been the real environmentalists of this country for thousands of years, and since you mob came, the impact has been devastating.'

Rod Mason, Mount Kosciuszko National Park's Indigenous liaison officer, is waiting for the day the river runs free again. 'The big boss made that big valley and the gorge, and he will come back and wash the dam away,' he said. 'They will lose big time, because they have gone against nature there. People think they can take on nature and win, that they must be some sort of god, but it is impossible. All we want to see is the poor old river flowing again, and everything associated from spiritual to material. That is all. That will make us happy. We want to see Nurrudjurum [a migratory black fish] on his way again. He has a job to do for us. It is his birthright. We have to watch out for him. The creator gave him that job, to go back to the ocean from the mountains and tell us everything is all right.'

The Snowy River Alliance continues to be active, although it has contracted back to a small core of people in Orbost and Dalgety. The Whites, the Richardsons and Jo Garland remain involved, and Chris Allen and Lynette Greenwood still attend meetings. 'We can't just sit back,' said Heather Richardson. 'We will have to be very vigilant to make sure that what they have promised is carried out.' The Whites and the Richardsons wish more young people would step up to the plate to take the fight into the future, and miss the camaraderie when the group was at its peak from 1997 to 1999. But George Collis feels that while groups may have a long life, individual participation is finite. 'I gave four to five years to that, and I thought at the end of it, when I did not stand as chairman again, "What else can I contribute to this campaign?" And there wasn't any better I could do. I have done my best.'

Happily, the Snowy River is proving a uniting force in a divided community. Orbost has shaken off its depression and feels more like a town with a positive outlook. The main street is spruced up, and new businesses and people are moving in. A mini real-estate boom is pushing up house and land prices. The eclectic Orbost Community Forum, formed in 2002, is

Sam Richardson's paddleboat, the *Curlip*, which transported people and produce along the Snowy and Brodribb rivers to the port at Marlo. *Source: Gil Richardson.*

cultivating new development ideas to offset the declines in timber and agriculture. Most ideas revolve around promoting the region's natural attractions, with the Snowy River as the centrepiece.

There are plans for a replica of the *Curlip*, the paddle steamer that Gil Richardson's great-grandfather, Sam, built in 1889 to transport agricultural produce down the rivers to the Marlo port. The Moogji Aboriginal Council is working with the Forum on feasibility plans for the East Gippsland Great Walk, a network of serviced trails encompassing the region's stunning rivers, coast, forests and mountains. Similar ventures, such as Cradle Mountain in Tasmania, have attracted thousands of tourists who support a strong local economy with jobs in eco-tourism, track maintenance, tour guides, transport and much more.

But Orbost's change in attitude is perhaps nowhere more apparent than on the highway outside town. Shrubs have been planted to hide the signs on giant logs welcoming visitors to Victoria's 'premier timber town', while new and prominent signs promote Orbost as the gateway to the Snowy River country.

Dalgety is still struggling to maintain a critical population mass, to keep open the pub, the school, its little café-cum-general store and recently

The Snowy River at Dalgety in November 2003: on the long road to recovery.
Photo: Claire Miller.

reopened servo. Dalgety, like Orbost, has experienced a mini real-estate boom since the turn of the century, but buyers are mostly city folk looking for weekenders near the snowfields. What Dalgety really wants is more families living there permanently. As Brett Miners says, Dalgety is a good idea before its time, but its time will come. One outsider I interviewed for this book said he could not for the life of him see what sustained Dalgety. The answer is an enduring sense of community and connection to the Snowy River.

The Snowy River campaign achieved many things. It put environmental flows on the national agenda, and gave the term scientific meaning. It raised issues and proposed solutions that seemed like lunacy at the time, but are now accepted as mainstream thinking. And it achieved the seemingly impossible. Governments started out adamant that the Snowy River would never get any more water because it was just too hard to achieve. In only nine years, a group of the ultimate underdogs turned government thinking around. As Jane Glasson from Jimenbuen says, 'It goes to show that people can still make a difference, ordinary people in a funny little place like Dalgety' — and Orbost, too. And that always has to be a good thing.

Stories from
The Men and Women of the
Snowy River

The Snowy River is a powerful presence in the Australian psyche. Australians carry a sense of the river with them everywhere in their pockets: the blue-green ten-dollar note features the likeness of A. B. 'Banjo' Paterson and the 'Man' chasing brumbies on his horse. Commercial variations abound in everything from motels to clothing; driving from Dalgety to Melbourne via Bombala, I was even stuck behind a removal lorry emblazoned with the company name, The Van from Snowy River. When researching this book, I typed 'Snowy River' into my newspaper's database, and found references in Australian newspapers at least once a week, usually as shorthand for all things Australian. I also came across a plethora of songs, poems and paintings. The best that can be said of most is that they are heartfelt, but that is precisely the point. The Snowy River is a seductive muse who somehow inspires sensible, rational people to do extraordinary things. She has wielded that power for a very long time. Australians all know the story of the Man from the Snowy River and his amazing horsemanship, but that story merely encapsulates the spirit of real-life stories told by the real men and women from the Snowy River over thousands of years. These stories arise from a rich local tradition of oral history describing these people to themselves and their often fraught relationship with the river. The stories reveal why so many think the Snowy is something special and worth fighting to keep. The campaign to restore the Snowy River arose out of this shared local history and passion — a passion shared with the rest of the nation thanks to Paterson's poem.

⌒

The moon took the water from the ocean, and travelled to the mountains to the north. The platypus followed, and busted the moon's waterbags when the moon fell asleep in the mountains. The water gushed out and made the Snowy River and all its children.

Creation story, as told by Rod Mason,
Kosciuszko Indigenous liaison officer

The Snowy River is an ancient river. It came to life 90 million years ago, as a stream carving its way across a drainage basin on the southern supercontinent, Gondwanaland. When Australia broke away to begin its slow drift north-east 55 million years ago, it brought an old, old river along for the ride.

The Snowy then, as now, seeped from springs and sphagnum moss bogs fed by a semi-permanent snowdrift under the eastern lip of Mount Kosciuszko. The river comes down from the Snowy Mountains to curl across the southern Monaro, a vast, undulating and largely treeless volcanic plain slung between the Great Dividing Range and the New South Wales coastal hills. Eventually the Snowy River turns back on itself in a wide loop, cutting an ever-deepening gorge before finally turning south towards Victoria. It then follows a winding and largely inaccessible course through a dry, rugged wilderness 700 metres below the surrounding plateaux. It

Stone Bridge, where the Snowy River runs beneath house-sized boulders intricately carved by fast flowing water over thousands of years. *Photo: Graeme Enders.*

comes out of the gorge country to finish its 380-kilometre journey to the Tasman Sea across an alluvial floodplain as fertile as the Nile.

When Aborigines came onto the Monaro plains from the west and the north, the Snowy was already deeply embedded in the landscape, as constant a presence as the sun, the stars and the mountains. Its ancient spirit was threaded into tribal story lines and sent weaving back along the Murray River deep into the red interior, and north to the rainforests on the wings of the migratory Bogong moths. The Snowy was a national life force describing Australians to themselves long before white people arrived and started writing poetry.

The Snowy River's Aboriginal story has barely been told. Historical records are incomplete. Many descendants themselves are not sure about the connections, with generations of white diseases and dispossession breaking and fraying the threads of their story lines.[1] In some cases elders have not passed on information, out of concern for their children in a white world as much as anything else. Those who do have the knowledge are wary of entrusting it to white people.

But the story is also not recorded because the Indigenous community in the area keeps to itself, and, until recently, few outsiders took an interest in their history.[2] The missing Aboriginal perspective leaves the Snowy flowing through an apparently empty landscape before white people came with their cattle and their dreams. In reality, the Snowy River country has always teemed with life and legends.

There is archaeological evidence from the Buchan Caves in Victoria indicating that Aborigines have lived in the Snowy River area for at least 20,000 years. Three tribal groups traditionally cared for the Snowy country: the Krowuntunkoolong of East Gippsland (a subgroup of Gippsland's Gunai/Kurnai), the Bidawal of far East Gippsland and the Ngarigo of the Monaro plains.

The Krowuntunkoolong were generally coastal people. Their country ranged from the Tambo River east across the Snowy River, sometimes as far as Cann River. The Bidawal were forest people. They lived in the dense, wet rainforests in a broad band straddling what is now the Victoria/New South Wales border inland as far as Deddick, Bonang and Delegate. The Ngarigo ranged across the Monaro plains and down along the Snowy River into Victoria. The Snowy remains a powerful totemic symbol uniting these three tribal groups' descendants.

The Snowy River country still contains an abundant record revealing how the Ngarigo, the Krowuntunkoolong and the Bidawal lived. There are shell middens, scar trees, camp sites, stone tool quarries, tools — once your eyes have been opened, the signs of Indigenous habitation are everywhere. They are often in places that appeal to us now for camping: sheltered, level, with shade, water and a good view. The Aborigines found them first. In Deddick, I ran my hands over the rounded edges of bark framing an oval of smooth inner trunk, exposed 150 years ago perhaps by a Bidawal woman in need of a food preparation board, or a warrior in need of a shield. I could see the distinctive first cuts to prise the bark away in a single sheet. Suddenly, the people who lived in this serene and beautiful valley were no longer in the shadows, but a very real presence.

There is an argument for keeping these sites out of the public eye: vandalism is a constant problem where sites are identified in the Snowy River National Park. Barry Kenny is a Gunai man and the culture and heritage officer at Moogji Aboriginal Council in Orbost. He said bollards had to be installed to deter campers driving over one site and crushing the stone tools — but they still found a way in. A park ranger ended up with stitches in his head another time when he confronted a man snooping around in a closed-off cave with artwork on the walls; the intruder took a swing at the ranger with an iron bar. 'Ninety per cent of people respect the sites — others just say, "stuff them!"' Kenny said. Luckily, most sites are in rough, remote country without vehicular access, or on private property.

Aboriginal Scar tree at Deddick.
Photo: Claire Miller.

Generally, landholders respect Aboriginal sites and cultural objects on their properties, but some are reluctant to admit sites exist for fear of native title claims. 'If ever you find any of these Koorie remnants, just bury them because you are just asking for trouble,' one local advised a new family when they bought land at Deddick, in the Snowy River's wilderness area a few years ago. It seems an unfounded fear: Native Title laws generally do not apply to freehold land.

The conspiracy of silence makes it difficult for indigenous descendants to record and reclaim their cultural heritage. In the vacuum, people are willing to believe anything. Just past the Jimenbuen homestead, south of Dalgety, is a former soldier settler block called 'Willdoo'. A large ring of boulders around a dead tree on a hillside overlooks the house. Jane Glasson from Jimenbuen station told me the property owner made the ring in the mid-1960s as part of his daughter's high school art project. Glasson, who taught at Berridale Primary School, chuckles as she recalls staff talking with reverence about the amazing Aboriginal 'stonehenge' years later.

'It just goes to show how people create things in their minds,' she said. 'They can't imagine anyone they know who would put stones in a ring, but they must have meaning so they think of all these myths.' A couple of nights later, I was having a beer in the Buckley's Crossing Hotel in Dalgety, and talking about my visit to Jimenbuen. 'I've heard there is an Aboriginal stonehenge down there — did you see it?' asked one of the other barflies in great excitement.

The Snowy River's Aboriginal spirit survives in place names, learned phonetically and then frequently disguised with anglicised spelling. They include Jindebein (Jindabyne), Soogan Boogan (Suggan Buggan), Buckin or Buckeen (Buchan), Batta Boulong (Bete Belong, near Orbost) and Mulloo/Murloo (Marlo, at the mouth of the Snowy). The *Curlip*, a famous paddleboat on the Snowy at Orbost, was apparently named for the Gunai word 'Kerlip', meaning Cape Conran; there is also a Lake Curlip on the Brodribb River, which enters the Snowy near Marlo.

The pitfalls of transliteration help explain a bitter local dispute over the river entering the Snowy about two kilometres downstream from the Jindabyne dam. It is the Mowamba River on most modern maps, but locals insist it is the Moonbah, named for the Moonbah homestead higher up in the catchment. Some historical accounts refer to it as the Mowenbah. The confusion is understandable: the name apparently comes from the Ngarigo 'moenbar'.[3]

A Manero-Ngarigo elder, 'Aunty' Rachel Mullett, said the Snowy River was literally 'Joona Mar Djumba' in her language: 'joona mar' for snow, and 'djumba' for river. However, the Indigenous liaison officer at Kosciuszko National Park, Rod Mason, a Ngarigo man, said his people named places, not specific natural features. 'You can't separate out anything — it is all part of that country,' he said. 'The Snowy River is a giant spiritual area — it is like a big church.'

Mason said Indigenous people all over Australia were interested in the Snowy River because it was connected to everything else along spirit lines. 'Over in South Australia, they say, "How is our family over there?" [Aborigines consider all creatures on land and in water, as well as the spirits residing in features like the Snowy, as family members with whom they have personal relations.] Right over Australia, all lakes, all rivers are connected. We have been caretakers of this river for hundreds of generations. It has become that way because we depend on the river. It is our lifeline from here to South Australia.'

White people began settling the Monaro in the 1820s. From there, they gradually spread south into East Gippsland, pushing the traditional owners before them. There was clearly a frontier conflict, with accounts of pioneers distributing poisoned flour and meat to Aborigines; whole groups of Bidawal were reputedly wiped out around Tubbut, on the Deddick River. The settlers set dogs on the Aborigines, shot them, or rounded them up and sent them to missions, as if their very presence was too uncomfortable a reminder that they had prior claims.

The Bidawal and Krowuntunkoolong retaliated, at least at first. The Bidawal had a warlike, aggressive reputation. 'They would make raids and steal and maim, and were a terror to everyone,' pioneer John O'Rourke wrote.[4] In 1841, persistent attacks by the 'Snowy River blacks' — probably Krowuntunkoolong — forced settlers John Stevenson and James Allen to retreat from a cattle run they tried to establish near modern-day Orbost. The following year, Peter Imlay took 800 cattle onto the Snowy flood plain where he 'had considerable trouble with the blacks, who frightened the cattle and made them very wild, besides spearing great numbers of them,' wrote Orbost old-timer John Cameron, in 1914. 'The men became very afraid and would seldom venture out except in twos and threes.'[5] The cattle run was abandoned when a stockman, Jack Wilson, was speared in the wrist. The settlers left with 500 cattle.

The Bidawal, however, fell victim early to diseases, alcohol, killing by settlers and intertribal warfare. By 1844, travellers observed that Bidawal country appeared very thinly populated with Aborigines. The last stragglers had 'come in' to the Delegate Aboriginal Reserve by 1877, where the Lake Tyers mission manager, John Bulmer, observed they were in a deplorable condition: 'They all smoke tobacco and 12 are opium addicts from mixing with the Chinese gold miners.'[6] Many Bidawal apparently also moved to the coast, where they became itinerant farm workers.[7]

The fighting spirit was eventually knocked out of the Snowy River blacks in a series of massacres after Norman and John McLeod took over the Orbost cattle run around 1843. The best documented was the Milly Creek Massacre, in May 1851. It was triggered by the violent death of a cook on Orbost Station, known variously as Dan Moylan, Little Dan, Dan the cook and Dan Dempsey. He was a nasty piece of work by any name, with a reputation for giving Aborigines flour laced with arsenic and throwing boiling water at them.

One day, Dan kidnapped a young Aboriginal girl. He held her captive in his hut for three days where he repeatedly raped her. Her relatives tried to rescue her, but were repelled by the hot coals Dan placed around his home and the gun with which he threatened all comers. The Aborigines hid in the bush and waited for him to leave his hut unarmed. He died in a volley of spears so thick his body could not fall to the ground. The Aborigines grabbed the girl and took off to a secluded camping spot far from the homestead.

John Cameron is sympathetic, saying the Aborigines were becoming 'civilised' and had they been treated fairly, the murder might never have occurred. 'However, in a small community, a murder was a serious matter,' he wrote. A punitive posse of white men and trackers from enemy tribes went out to 'clean up' the offenders. The Aborigines were taken by surprise; between fifteen and twenty were shot dead, including women and children.

After all these killings — and many more unrecorded deaths sparked by fear, misunderstanding or belligerence — a visitor to Orbost homestead in the 1850s was able to observe that the Snowy River Aborigines were 'a quiet lot of fellows; they have been by some means greatly decimated. After the establishment of the station, they were not more than 20 all told, and as they had a great love for their country, many of them never settled at Lake Tyers [mission].'[8] Instead, they stayed on the Snowy flood plain, living on the fringes of white society and working for the settlers.

The riverbank community grew up to 200-strong, and included people from many different tribal groups who intermarried. Gunai elder 'Uncle' Albert Mullett said the Snowy River remained his people's spiritual and material lifeline after they lost their tribal land. 'It provided us with employment and removed us from the missions into the wider community, and we did survive. We were one big family, and respect for our elders was very strong.'

It was a good life in many respects. The camps moved up and down the river, following the field work picking beans, peas and corn. The kids caught fish, collected mussels and picked blackberries. 'They were happy times as a kid,' said Uncle Albert. 'We had a mudslide into the river, and would swing off the willows into the deep holes. We collected food with spears, and we were not threatening people who thought they owned the river.'

Wholesale slaughters do not seem to have occurred on the Monaro plains, where the Ngarigo were described as shy and not dangerous. But there were killings, out of fear and guilt. Rod Mason said his people fled into the bush when they saw white people murdering each other; Mason's grandmother was 106 when she died in 1979, and she remembered her elders' stories well.

'The poor blackfellas got blamed, but it was the whitefellas killing each other,' Mason said. 'When it started to get out of hand, and they realised that the blacks could speak for themselves, and some had English and could report this stuff, they would hunt them down and kill them. We just took off into the bush and let them take it. A lot of the fellas around here illegally got their land by killing their neighbours and taking their land and papers. People were scared about what we had to say, so they left us alone for a long time. We are not liars when it comes to history. We have no word for lying but death.'

Early settlers on the Monaro spoke of seeing Aborigines in great numbers, but their ranks thinned rapidly as white diseases, alcohol and the loss of their hunting grounds took their toll. Polish explorer Dr John Lhotsky reported in 1834 that in certain parts the Aborigines were 'already very weak … indeed, not civilised but corrupted'.[9] Forty years later, white people recorded only a handful of Ngarigo men left; the last, Biggenhook, died in June 1914 at the age of sixty-two. 'With his death, the story of the once proud and virile Ngarigo tribe came to its last sad chapter,' wrote local historian Laurie Neal in 1976.[10]

But the Ngarigo did not die out. At the time they were recorded as extinct, many were living on the government reserve at Delegate on the southern edge of the Monaro plains. Several Ngarigo families worked on the Monaro properties. Edward (Ned) Solomon, the grandfather of Manero-Ngarigo elder Aunty Rachel Mullett and her cousin Aunty Rae Stewart, was a stockman up around Jindabyne about the time Biggenhook died.

In the early 1930s, the work on the Monaro dried up with the onset of the Depression and Ned Solomon moved his family south to Orbost, away from their ancestral country. They worked in the timber mills there and as domestic help. His granddaughter, Rae, was born on the banks of the Snowy River at Orbost, delivered by her aunt Kitty in the traditional way, 'on the lines connected to my grandparents' birthplace,' Aunty Rae said. 'They were hard-working folks. Ngubby [Ned] did not believe in living on a reserve. He said it was not the proper way to bring up children or to live. He wanted to live a free man. We lived a more traditional way off the mission because we were free. We lived from the bush — my favourite was wild bush honey.'

The Snowy River banks were a place of great laughter and entertainment. Almost every day, Rachel's many aunties set up camp there to wash clothes and children, cook and talk. 'The kids lived in the water — we swam every day,' said Rachel Mullett. 'Everyone would turn up down there. They just threw you into the water. Kids as little as three and four could swim like fish, and we would dive from the old bridge. The river was wide and fast and deep and clear then — you would get your head stuck in the sand if you did it now.'

At night, the Solomon children would gather around the campfires and listen to ghost stories with eyes so round they nearly popped — stories like the time their Aunty Alice walked home along the river road late one night, puzzled that the leaves of the trees kept falling as she passed. She looked up and saw a coffin floating, moving along with her as she walked. 'We don't know whose spirit it was — someone murdered or killed. If anyone is killed, their spirit never goes — it stays there even if they are buried somewhere else,' said Rae Stewart.

She herself ruined a smart pencil skirt returning home from the Orbost cinema with her brother Allen one night. As they reached the old bridge over the river, the light on the footbridge went out. 'So we walked in the middle of the road. I was in high heels and a tight skirt, and the next thing, I could hear creaking footsteps on the footbridge behind us. It was moonlight, and I looked back and saw a spirit man carrying his head. I asked my brother, 'Can you see it?' and he said, 'Yes', and we both took off as fast as we could. By the time we were on the other side, my skirt seams were split up to the waist!'

In the mai-mai shelters, Rachel, Rae and the other children also listened and learnt. Ngarigo women are custodians of the language and traditional knowledge. Their men had their sacred places and trails, but the Ngarigo country belonged to women — in contrast to the Gunai, whose country is primarily in the hearts of men. Aunt Alice was a medicine woman. 'She passed all that on,' said Aunty Rachel. 'She was very strong in her language and the culture. She was one of those people who was special. She carried the sacred stones. She was so strong in how she spoke — it was almost a whisper and you had to listen to hear her speak, but to hear her talk, it would scare the daylights out of you. You listened and did not move!'

Elders described the Snowy River country as a crowded land in which people could easily be lost, but were never alone. There were the Jiwawas, little people who stole wandering children. The Nyol lurked in the caves on the Murrindal River, a tributary of the Snowy. They would grasp the feet of unwary people and drag them underground. The Dulagars, strong, hairy, manlike spirits, lived in the mountains behind Suggan Buggan. They flew through the air to seize women wandering alone.[11]

Rod Mason described the Gurangatti, half-man, half-eel, with long hands and a long beard, who watched from the trees and slid into waterholes to lie in wait. 'That is why no one goes near the water holes alone,' said Mason. Gurangatti is the son of the rainmaker Dyilligamberra; his brother is Gurugulla, who lives in the clouds. 'They follow our people from the mountains, and the old men would ask Gurugulla for water on their journey. They would throw in a pebble and sing his name three times for all the water holes, and he would make sure everything was full. Sometimes, one fellow did it wrong and there would be a big flood.' And always, everywhere, there is family — the birds and animals and reptiles — to keep the Indigenous people company and their spirits high. The Snowy also wound through all their stories, past and present. 'The Snowy River is very sacred to the old people — they always spoke of it as a part of them,' Aunty Rae said.

As time went on, fewer and fewer elders returned to traditional country up the Snowy River from Orbost. It was too far for frail elders to walk, fences blocked traditional trails, and few Aborigines had motor transport. Aunty Rachel continues to care for her country, although some things are gone forever. 'Our time and their time do not mix, so we do not use the sites or touch them,' she said. 'We respect those places and never disturb them. We would not say we could dance there now. We wouldn't even walk on it. Otherwise our ancestors will leave.'

Contemporary Aborigines no longer use the sites because white settlement forced a break in cultural continuity. Concern for his children's welfare, for instance, persuaded Rachel and Rae's great-grandfather Billy Rutherford to keep traditional knowledge to himself. 'There was a farmer who got cancer, and the Sydney doctors told him he had six months to live,' Aunty Rae said. 'My great-grandfather Billy Rutherford and my uncle went out and got this plant, and they boiled it up and the farmer drank it, and he was cured. He went to Sydney to tell the doctors a black fella cured him of cancer, and they came to Deddick looking for my great-grandfather.

'The doctors found him up a tree digging out a possum, and poked him with their rifles to get down and show them where this plant was. He said it was too late and come back tomorrow. Then he took off into the bush when they went away. He came to my aunts and uncles at the camp fire and said, "That is it. I will not pass anything down to my family", because of the heartache he went through and the fright. It was not worth it, and he did not want his children to go through it. So he would just poke around in the bush on his own.'

Itinerant work gave the Aborigines living at Orbost freedom and autonomy. However, only Aborigines living in missions were counted in population censuses, and so the Snowy River people, like the Ngarigo and Bidawar, officially ceased to exist late in the nineteenth century — even though they were there for all to see camped by the Snowy River at Orbost. But living free was no protection against racism and harassment. Aunty Rae said three or four carloads of police regularly visited the camps during her childhood. 'If anything went wrong in town, they would blame all the poor old blackfellas,' she said.

Children were regularly seized and taken away, although the Orbost police respected Ned Solomon and, by and large, left his family alone. 'The only ones who were a danger to us were the missionaries, because they would dob us into the police or welfare,' said Aunty Rae. 'I would climb trees and have nothing to do with them. My mother and aunties protected us. One time, the police came to the riverbank where my Aunty Doris was looking after us. We were waiting in a tent for mum to come when the missionaries and police came. My mother somehow knew and left work. She heard the missionary telling my aunty they had to take us because our mother wasn't there. "You are supposed to be a Christian, and you are trying to take my kids away! Get out of here — you are not taking my kids!" my mother shouted, and kicked the missionary in the backside and down the riverbank. He took off. My mother was a gentle woman but when she got her temper up, she was the worst in the world!'

Uncle Albert Mullett's family was not so fortunate. His brothers were born at Lake Tyers mission. Two were taken away, and his mother only ever managed to trace one to the Burwood Boys Home in Melbourne. 'I could not understand why all these Koorie boys were living in this joint,' he said. His mother moved to Orbost to live with relatives on the Snowy River banks when Albert was four years old, the better to keep her children out of the authorities' clutches. Later she moved her family up onto the NSW south coast. Uncle Albert was one of the lucky ones.

Aborigines lived on the banks of the Snowy River until the late 1960s, when they began to disperse in search of work. Farmers were planting fewer crops, and machines were replacing humans on farms and in the timber industry. Indigenous workers were among the first laid off. Uncle Albert

Mullett said the 1967 referendum recognising Aborigines as Australian citizens was a turning point: once Aborigines were afforded the same rights as white Australians, employers figured they might as well hire white people. Governments also began to take an interest in the Aborigines' welfare, with funding for housing, health and education.

The Moogji Aboriginal Council was set up in 1992 to help local Koories find work, improve their health and education, and recover their lost heritage. The Snowy River looms large in its plans. 'We have to go back and connect with the land again,' said Uncle Albert Mullett. 'It is a slow process, but those who want to learn will sit and listen. I think Native Title has brought a change of thinking, with people asking, "Why can't we go to country and fish and hunt, and teach our children what was denied to us for so long?" We thought accessing the river for our cultural needs would always be available to us, but white laws stopped us.'

Indigenous families were moved into housing commission houses on the edge of Orbost — sometimes forcibly. Children mixed more with white kids instead of their elders. 'We just wanted to fit into the community and did not want to be called racist names,' said Christine Milliken, office manager at Moogji Aboriginal Council in Orbost. 'We just wanted to fit in, and it was not easy.' Parents concerned about their children living in the white world in town did not push the issue, either. Heritage officer Barry Kenny said his generation was not brought up with the culture and traditions. 'Our family still knew the language back then, but they never preached it into us,' he said. 'We are only just coming back into it now.'

The pace of life also picked up, and it seemed there was not the time any more to sit around a fire, yarning. Too many Aborigines in their middle age have scant knowledge of their heritage, yet endure the social disadvantages of being Aboriginal, with high unemployment, poor health, and educational difficulties. Christine Milliken regrets the lost opportunities keenly. 'They probably wanted us to live different lives, and better ourselves,' she said of her parents. 'But when our parents were alive, we should have asked them more questions — I would like to know more now.'

Of course, no one consulted the Ngarigo and the Krowuntunkoolong about building the Snowy Mountains Hydro-Electric Scheme. The dams blocked important spirit lines keeping the river alive. Mt Kosciuszko Indigenous liaison officer Rod Mason said the scheme stopped the black fish, Nurrudjurum, following the thunder, Merribi, from the coast to the mountains to find food before returning to the coast to breed. 'Our brothers on the coast sent word, asking us why we were not sending the Nurrudjurum back. They said Nurrudjurum was not there any more, and they blamed us, but it was the dam. The fish can't get past.'

Aunty Rachel said her elders would be so disappointed. 'They relied on the river more than we had to — it was their lifeline for food,' she said. 'Our people said the dam would cause problems for the Snowy. It was all nature to them and to change it was not what the elders wanted. But they just went ahead and did it and never asked anyone, let alone an Aboriginal person. The poor old Snowy — I always thought of it as the poor old Snowy because they nearly killed it. I visited Jindabyne just after it was built and to think that here is the Snowy coming out of a pipe — it was unbelievable. You just could not get your head around it. We all grieved in the years to come.'

Rod Mason and Aunty Rae Stewart say the scheme drowned ancestral burial sites, sacred sites and medicinal plants. 'We did not even know what was going on,' said Aunty Rae. 'They kept it a secret and did even not invite any of the original owners to work on it. They just got all these people from overseas.'

Indigenous people are ambivalent about restoring an environmental flow to the Snowy River unless a cultural benefit can also be obtained. Graeme Enders, working on the Snowy River's recovery for the NSW Premier's Department, said elders were distressed 'that white people could have shut off this life force and not understood what we were doing'.

'The landscape was not lonely for Aborigines,' said Enders. 'It was populated, it was full of the animals and plants and the spirits and the responsibilities to nurture the life force and connect and maintain the story lines across the nation. So when you bring people together and say we want you to be more involved in environmental flows, they say, "Well, you did not ask us about the dam — what do you mean environmental flows, when what about the dam itself?"'

⌒

The Snowy River has a vast catchment: 15,540 square kilometres, split roughly equally between New South Wales and Victoria. Only about 8000 people live here now, and the towns are tiny. There are only two towns actually right on the Snowy River: Dalgety at the top on the Monaro plains, and Orbost at the bottom on the floodplain. Both towns have a bridge over the Snowy with just one, McKillops Bridge, in all the long, lonely kilometres between.

There is no record of the first white settler to see the Snowy River, nor how it got its name. There are tantalising but unsubstantiated reports of white people in the area as early as 1816. In 1948, a Cooma grazier, D'Arcy Hixon, reported finding a roughly carved wooden cross on his snow lease in the high country. It marked the grave of a seventeen-year-old girl born in the late 1700s, but he could not decipher the last two figures.[12]

The Pendergasts of Jindabyne and Omeo claim their ancestor, Thomas Pendergast, was the first white man to cross the Snowy River in 1823, when he established the Moonbah station south of present-day Jindabyne. How the river got its name is anyone's guess though. The obvious answer is because it rises in the Snowy Mountains, but some Monaro people told me the Snowy was named for its frosted appearance during the spring snowmelt. In any case, by 1834, Polish explorer Dr Paul Lhotsky noted the name Snowy River was in common usage, although he fancied he was first to 'introduce the river into Geography'.[13]

Lhotsky stayed at Matong station, which means he likely used Buckley's Crossing, the site of present-day Dalgety, to get over the Snowy River; the crossing was named for the brothers who first drove their sheep across. The plains here are naturally treeless and windswept, with enormous granite boulders tumbled about like so much rubble on a giant's building site. The winters are cold: nights 15 degrees below zero are common. Moina Hedger from nearby Cave Creek station remembers a priest delivering a sermon during a bitter winter in her childhood and telling his flock they were all going to heaven, 'because we have all done hell here'. The summers are parched. Dalgety lies in a notorious rain shadow; residents joke blackly that when the good Lord made it rain for forty days and forty nights, Dalgety got 40 points (about 1 centimetre).

But the plains' very harshness makes them excellent sheep country; perhaps as a defence against the cold and lean pickings, the sheep grow extraordinarily fine wool. In due course, a surveyor, J. R. Campbell, laid out a town plan at Buckley's Crossing, at the request of the government, and renamed the village Dalgety, his wife's maiden name, at the request of no one. The Catholic Church, built in 1878, was named Our Lady Star of the Sea because the roar of the Snowy reminded its builders of the crashing waves of the ocean. The year 1888 saw the school open and a sturdy iron bridge constructed to carry stock over the Snowy.

At the turn of the last century, Dalgety looked set for big things when a NSW Royal Commission toplisted the town as the site for the new national capital. Dalgety had two main advantages: the Snowy River for water and power, and a good deepwater port nearby at Eden. The new federal government duly passed legislation in 1904 excising the area in a strip down to the coast, but Sydney's powerbrokers opposed the site. Dalgety was too

Delivering prize rams over the Snowy River in the nineteenth century. *Source: Rix Wright.*

close to Victoria and they feared Eden could develop as a rival port to Sydney. The federal government compromised and chose Canberra in 1909, 150 kilometres to the north and safely within the sphere of Sydney's commercial and political influence.

After all the excitement, Dalgety rolled over, slipped into slumber and the world started passing it by. It remained a mecca for trout fishermen, who booked out the rambling Buckley's Crossing Hotel a year in advance, but they stopped coming after 1967 when the Jindabyne dam turned off the Snowy River and the fish disappeared. By the early 1990s, Dalgety was in grave danger of dying in its sleep.

Below Dalgety, the Snowy River begins cutting a tortuous, 200-kilometre path up to 700 metres below the surrounding plateaux. This is the middle catchment, 'where the river runs those giant hills between', as A. B. 'Banjo' Paterson wrote. Explorer Angus McMillan described the high, broken ranges and dense scrub as 'a fearful country' when he rode through in 1839 scouting for new grazing land.[14] Sixty years later, Victorian Government geologist W. H. Ferguson described the scenery in the area below McKillops Bridge as 'wild and rough and grand in the extreme … in no place else in Victoria are there such dizzy precipices, such sheer bluffs, or gorges with such vertical sides'.[15]

Monaro people refer to the middle catchment as 'tiger country', reflecting its rugged mysteriousness rather than its abundant snakes. 'People die in there — the crows eat you,' Dalgety grazier Garry Suthern told me. He knows first-hand, after a three-day hike with a couple of mates turned into a six-day nightmare. 'It was much rougher than we expected,' Suthern said. 'We ran out of food after three days, and spent half a day going 300 or 400 metres, it was that steep and rocky — too rough even for a rabbit, and we know because we were looking for one to shoot. Our families were beside themselves with worry.'

Most of the tiger country is dry, with a bony, hungry-mongrel appearance; summer temperatures over 40 degrees are common. The rocky slopes are cloaked in native evergreens, called white cypress but identical botanically to the Murray River pine. The cypresses have black trunks showing through a mosaic of white patches and pale green lichen festooning the branches. The effect is striking. Donnie Wellsmore from Roslyn station south-east from Jindabyne, loves it down there, but not through rose-coloured glasses after mustering cattle on his father's lease as a young man.

'We camped under the pine trees and it was pretty rough. We would take a big hunk of cooked meat and bread — the bread was pretty stale after three or four days and no matter what we did, a blowfly always seemed to

Near Tulloch Ard Gorge in the middle catchment 'where the river runs those giant hills between'. *Photo: Craig Ingram.*

get into the saddle bag with the meat. It was hard work — there was nothing romantic about it. There wouldn't be much tucker and it would be hot and hard going, and you come back home glad to be out of it. But after a few weeks, you get the hunger again, to go back in. The Snowy River shines like a thread of cotton through the hills and it is beautiful. There is something special about the tiger country.'

The Snowy's notorious floods originate here, rather than up in the Snowy Mountains. Geologically and climatically, the middle catchment is rather impervious to rain and prone to thunderstorms. The water runs off rather than soaking in, causing devastating flash floods. Down on the flats around Orbost the weather can be sunny, warm and benign, when a high wave of angry brown water comes surging from the gorge at Jarrahmond, sweeping away houses, crops, livestock and people.

White people did their best to tame the tiger country before it was declared a national park in 1979. Dotted throughout the bush are crumbling cattle and brumby yards, tumbledown huts, charred stone fireplaces, broken crockery, rusting tools and the odd fruit tree from a homestead orchard. There are trees with distinctive triangular-shaped axe marks, or blazes, marking the packhorse mail routes and dating from the days when the forest was still open and it was easy to see from one blazed tree to the next.

Other trails were blazed with spade-shaped marks, pointing the way to copper, zinc, silver and gold mines. There are numerous mineshafts and tunnels; one of three tunnels boring into Campbells Knob near Gelantipy still has iron tram tracks and trolleys inside. 'The early settlers were looking for grass, and they went through the country that was arable,' said Paul Sykes, who grew up in Gelantipy. 'But the miners went everywhere because they wanted to find the exposed reefs. They opened the country more than the settlers, but the miners just disappeared and their family names were not known, so they get little credit.'

History is signposted everywhere in other ways. Graveyard Creek near Tubbut is where William Whittaker buried his two infant daughters in 1856 and 1858; Slaughterhouse Gully near Buchan is where a group of Aborigines were killed for taking sheep. Wheeler's Saddle on the steep road from Wulgulmerang to McKillops Bridge is where police magistrate Mr William Edward Wheeler fell off his horse and died from an apparent heart attack in 1884. Wheeler was a big man, and nearby settlers decided it was too difficult to get the body out in such hot weather. They dug a grave on the spot, but a doctor and policeman arriving from Bairnsdale refused to let them bury Wheeler. The body was put on a stretcher made from saplings, and it took a dozen men 'all their strength', working in relays, to drag the body out.[16] There is some hearsay that Mr Wheeler was gutted to reduce the weight; it seems unlikely but the embellishment makes a good story better. Incidentally, Wheeler's Saddle is also known locally as the 'Oooh, Aaah' lookout, on account of visitors' awed reaction when they turn the corner and the Snowy River valley opens before them.

McKillops Bridge is perhaps the most visible sign of another era, along with the marvellous bark slab schoolhouse at Suggan Buggan. Pioneer Edward O'Rourke built the schoolhouse in 1865, then hired a teacher to live on the remote property and educate his thirteen children. The schoolhouse was certainly built to last. Clive Richardson lives nearby, on a property his father selected in the 1950s. The first year or so, the family lived in the school house until a house was built. Richardson was only four, but has vivid memories of being bathed outside in winter, with frost thick like snow on the ground, and being taken inside to dry by the big wide fireplace. The schoolhouse was restored by the Gelantipy historical society in 1972, and is maintained by O'Rourke clan descendants.

When I first saw McKillops Bridge after the precipitous drive down into the gorges from Wulgulmerang, I wondered why on earth anyone would bother building such a grand structure in the middle of nowhere. Vehicles pass along the road maybe once every two or three hours on a busy day. But when the bridge was built in 1934, traffic of a different kind was heavy. About 40,000 cattle and sheep a year were driven through here, from the Monaro Plains down to the markets in Bairnsdale in Victoria. Land had also been opened for selection around Tubbut and Bonang, on the far side of the Snowy River. With more people coming to live in the region, an all-weather path across the Snowy seemed justified.

The bridge was built near McKellar's Crossing. Duncan McKellar was one of several men who operated government-funded punts across the Snowy. McKellar lived by the Snowy in his hut from about 1890 until his death in 1923. He would carry people and belongings over the river; livestock generally had to swim. His hut on the eastern bank offered rudimentary accommodation. Gippsland constable Alfred William Howitt observed that 'the men camped in the open where they were much troubled by fleas and the ladies and children were given one room in the hut where they were disturbed by bed bugs'.[17]

Travellers could be there awhile. David Ingram, a former parks ranger and fourth generation descendant of Bonang's Marriott and Ingram families, said his grandfather, Harry Ingram, was once stuck at McKellar's Crossing for three months waiting to get cattle over the Snowy. 'When it is wet and you get these east coast depressions, the tail end of cyclones, then you will get floods,' Ingram said. 'One of the men did not like the look of the crossing with some foam in the middle, so they had lunch and waited to see what happened. The river rose six feet in an hour while they had lunch. They could have got them over the day before.'

Heather Livingstone's father, Ted McDonnell, knew McKellar well from years of droving cattle and hauling with a bullock team between Wulgulmerang and Delegate. Heather retells the story her father told about the night in 1914 when McKellar helped protect two runaway children trying to reunite a tragedy-struck family. After losing his wife and two sons, a grief-stricken Dan Reidy had allowed a couple in Delegate to care for one of his daughters, Ida. Every year, her brother Laurie would ride across the Snowy River from Gelantipy to visit Ida, but her foster parents would not allow her to go home for a visit, not even for Christmas. Twelve-year-old Ida pined for her family, so Laurie, fourteen, took a spare horse on his next visit and the pair took off into the bush after dark. Whenever Ida tried to pull up, Laurie would say he could hear riders galloping behind them, and whack her horse on the rump.

The children arrived at McKellar's Crossing about midnight. Ida was too sore to keep going. McKellar assured Laurie he would shoot anyone who came in pursuit. Safe, the pair rested for a few hours, then continued their

Duncan McKellar standing in his boat, c1910, near present-day McKillops Bridge.
Source: Heather Livingstone.

flight early the next morning, back home to Gelantipy for a tearful and joyous reunion. Ida visited her foster family years later as a married woman, and was forgiven. 'They were heartbroken to lose her — but so were her father and brothers, and sisters,' said Livingstone, who lives at Wulgulmerang.

After McKellar died, the Victorian Government decided to build a bridge, so that stock traffic was not confined to summer months when the Snowy's flow was low and rather less hazardous: drownings and near-drownings were common. The bridge would have to be substantial to withstand the notorious floods. That meant steel truss on concrete pylons, with timber decking; the designers boasted the bridge would be indestructible. It also meant upgrading the 'Turnback' cattle track down from the Wulgulmerang plateau into something resembling a road.

It must have been a hell of a job. The road is still not for the faint-hearted: it is unpaved, perhaps one and a half cars wide, full of blind corners, and it hugs the mountain with a sheer drop on one side for much of the way. In the 1930s, the road was even rougher and narrower. Trucks carried two girders at a time, overhanging the front and back. Jessie Coates, eighty, from Buchan, remembers her father, Alex Ramsay, driving the heavily laden trucks with their awkward load down the tortuous track. The girders overhung the edges of the road and ' he would have to jack the truck around the corners,' she said.

The bridge was built during 1931–32, with up to 400 workers living in tents by the Snowy River. During construction, David Ingram's grandfather Harry met two young men camped on the road between Bonang and Orbost. Two elderly Snowy country stockmen, brothers Matt and Billy Coe, were also there. 'Matt and Billy asked these two young blokes what they were doing, and they were engineers who designed McKillops Bridge,' David Ingram said. 'Billy asked them how high the bridge would be.' It would be 15 metres high — 3 metres higher than the previous recorded flood — and 250 metres long. 'How high is that on the big currajong tree by the crossing?' Billy asked Harry Ingram. On hearing the answer, Billy said, 'I have seen floods bigger than that down there. I will not live to see it but Harry will: that bridge will wash away.' The engineers laughed. 'It is high enough,' they said.

They should have listened to the old-timers. The bridge was finished and named after explorer George McKillop, who travelled through this way in 1835. A grand opening was arranged for 19 January 1934. On 8 January, the construction crew watched a spectacular storm away up in the hills to the east. What they could not see was the cloudburst. Tom Warne had only just moved his wife Queenie and four-year-old daughter Ada to Deddick when

The wreckage of the first McKillops bridge, swept away in a flood a week before its scheduled opening in January 1934. *Source: Ada Healey.*

the storm struck. Ada Healey, now in Orbost, has vivid memories of a wall of water thundering past in the Deddick River while she cowered in a tent, terrified she would be swept away. 'I was standing at the door of the tent, and the river was at my toes — and then suddenly the water was gone as if someone had pulled a plug. It was 2am and my father and his workmate Wally Walsh said, "The bridge!"'

The ensuing flash flood, thick with uprooted trees and rocks, swept out of the tributary just above the new bridge, shot across the Snowy River and smashed against the far bank, then swung downstream. The water level was 4 metres higher than any flood recorded before. The force tore the bridge's steel trusses from the pylons. The tangled wreckage came to rest a few hundred metres downstream. The construction foreman, Edward 'Ted' Kay, contacted Orbost with his short-wave radio to advise the opening should be cancelled.[18]

The bridge was rebuilt 4.5 metres higher than the original, and opened on 6 December 1935. Its strength was tested in 1971, in a flood worse than 1934. Ian 'Blue' Minchin from Wulgulmerang went to the bridge opening in 1935, and went down to see the 1971 flood. He said the fast-flowing river looked like a rolling sea, ghostly with a dull and sullen roar. The water was so high it left debris behind in the trusses under the decking. Standing on

The rebuilt and much higher McKillops Bridge, which withstood (just) the record 1971 flood. *Photo: George Collis.*

McKillops Bridge today, high above the Snowy, it is difficult to envisage the narrow valley brimful with water like a lake, but it is only a matter of time before it happens again.

‿

> *My mother's people, the Prestons, settled 'Snodgrass' [deep in tiger country, northwest of Delegate]. The Prestons spent their time chasing brumbies and catching wild dogs, and they were robbed out there by bushrangers. There was a saying there was a bottle of rum in every hollow log at Willis. My grandad would say he was going down there chasing brumbies, and my mum wondered why he went in a new hat, moleskins and Driza-Bone. He would come home ragged 'cos it was just a big booze-up.*
>
> EMMA SELLERS, MANAGER, BLACK MOUNTAIN STATION, NEAR WULGULMERANG.

A. B. 'Banjo' Paterson accurately described the tiger country, where the hills are 'twice as steep and twice as rough/where a horse's hooves strike firelight from the flint stones every stride' — not to mention the 'pine-clad ridges', a reference surely to the native white cypress. This spare landscape is nothing like the dense, lush forests and luxuriant grazing country around Corryong, on the western side of the Divide. Yet Corryong promotes itself as the home of the Man, claiming a reclusive bushie named Jack Riley inspired Paterson with tales of his exploits when the poet and his friend Walter Mitchell stayed overnight in Riley's hut at Tom Groggin. The claim rankles with Monaro people, not least because Corryong is in the upper Murray River valley and has no links to the Snowy River.

A lot of energy has been wasted trying to identify Paterson's Man from Snowy River, despite the poet explaining his character was a prototype. Paterson encountered many stockmen on his many trips into the Snowy Mountains, and would have been familiar with their daredevil stories. In 1938, Paterson wrote in the *Sydney Mail* that he composed the poem to describe cleaning up wild horses in his district. It was 'rough enough for most people, but not nearly as rough as they had it on the Snowy. To make any sort of job of it, I had to create a character who would ride better than anybody else, and where would he come from except from the Snowy?'. When people persisted in claiming this or that local hero as the Man, the Banjo said, with some exasperation, 'the verses are intended as a ballad and not as a newspaper account of a sporting event'.[19]

If not for some inspired editorial judgment, there would not even be a Man from Snowy River. The poem was originally called *The Man from Araluen*, a now obscure gold mining town near Goulburn in New South Wales. *The Bulletin's* founder and editor, J. F. Archibald, persuaded Paterson to change the title before the poem was published in the magazine in 1890.[20] The last stanza however still read: 'And down by Araluen where the stony ridges raise/Their torn and rugged battlements on high'. The Man was also described as being astride a 'small and graceful beast'.

Paterson kept the title and made some minor but significant changes before the poem was published again in 1895, in his best-selling collection, *The Man from Snowy River and other verses*. The Man now rides 'a small and weedy beast', and his exploits are recounted, 'Down by Kosciuszko, where the pine-clad ridges raise/Their torn and rugged battlements on high'.

The Snowy River became a household name and the Man came to personify national characteristics. We like to think of ourselves as the plucky underdogs who thumb our noses at misplaced authority, whose abilities are not to be underestimated in a tight spot, and who can be relied on in situations where others might quail. We told the world as much when dozens of 'Men and Women from the Snowy River' galloped around Sydney's Homebush stadium in September 2000 to introduce the opening ceremony for the Olympic Games.

Setting aside the validity of Corryong's claims, the Snowy River country has, of course, produced many superlative stockmen. 'Owing to the nature of things — cattle, bush, remoteness — we had some extraordinary riders, blokes who fitted into a saddle as though they'd been moulded there,' said Jack Mustard, who grew up around Bendoc in the Depression, and lives now in Bonang.[21]

'With the hats, oilers and spurs, they looked something out of a Hollywood movie, and a lot of 'em acted better. There was always something fearsome about a bloke who'd clump into the [Bendoc] pub in high heels, carrying a whip, and covered in dust from head to toe and obviously ill at ease on the ground. They didn't walk in, they'd sway in, as though they were still astride something on the move — and you always knew they were going to try awful hard to drink the pub dry. And what's more, you didn't ever find one on his own, they was like the cattle they drove, forever in a bloody great mob.'

Brumby chasing was (and still is) a popular high country sport, and nearly every enthusiast has exciting tales of hair-raising rides. In researching this book, variations on Paterson's daredevil story abound. 'Some of the finest horsemen ever in Australia were from this country. There was Joker Johnson, Charlie West, the Richardson brothers and Ernie Bass. I don't think many men before or since could follow them downhill. They were magic, wizards,' said the late Clem Ingram in a 1992 recording.[22]

One of the first was Dick, an indigenous stockman who worked for settlers at Ingebyra, south of Jindabyne, in the mid-1800s. 'Dick had a reputation of being absolutely fearless and was a splendid horseman,' wrote Arthur Hunt, who had a reputation himself as a daredevil canoeist on the Snowy. 'One day some cattle broke away from him and ran out on a spur. Dick rode hard trying to wheel them. He was galloping fast when he saw that the timber ended abruptly, and he pulled his horse to a slithering stop at the very edge of a precipice. It was the only time Dick ever admitted being frightened.' The sheer drop towers over the Snowy River a few kilometres above its junction with the Jacobs River; it is still known locally as 'Where-Dick-Got-Frightened'.[23]

Joker Johnson was another brilliant Snowy stockman, but an even better opportunist. Alan Neven, from Tubbut, said Johnson borrowed money from the bank in his old age in the 1930s. When inspectors came to check his assets, Johnson paraded a mob of cattle. Then he got another mob, and another. The inspectors were impressed, but being city blokes, they did not realise Joker was bringing the same mob past every time. Nor did they realise the cattle were not Joker's at all, but a mob he found minding its business nearby in the bush.

Tommy Ventry from Deddick said everyone knew if Johnson went through because there would be a sheep fleece stuck in the fence. 'He would have slaughtered it for tucker, but he wouldn't hide it. He'd say, "Well, at least you got the fleece". Others would have stuck it in a log. I suppose you could say he was an honest rogue.'

David Ingram chuckles at the thought, and said Johnson was plain rogue in his family's folklore. 'Joker was always lifting things,' said Ingram. 'Dad caught Joker one day putting Dad's saddle on one of Joker's horses. They were at a show, and Joker said to Dad, "That saddle looks good on my horse!" "It looks good on my horse, too, Joker — take it off," Dad said. I guess Joker was a loveable rogue, you might say — but his old man was supposed to have ridden with one of the bushrangers and buried his gold coins somewhere in Deddick, from one of the hold-ups.'

Charlie West was among the last of the Snowy's legendary stockmen. He had several cattle runs on the lower Snowy River near Buchan, and lived rough and ready and all alone. His saddlebags were not much more than wallaby skins with the head cut off and the insides removed. He stashed food throughout the bush, tins of beans and sardines in hollow logs, so he was never caught short for tucker if far from home. He was illiterate, but usually had the last laugh. 'He was only a little bloke but he could fight like a thrashing machine,' said Chris Hodge, from Orbost. 'One time he was giving this bloke who deserved it an awful hiding after the Buchan sales. The other bloke could not get a hand on him, then Charlie said, "Stop, stop, you are too good for me!" Later, asked why he let the other bloke win, Charlie said, "He really thinks they can fight now and he will pick on someone else. They will give him a hell of a hiding and then he will get two instead of one."'

The hermit did not always live alone, though. He was married briefly to Alma, whom he met in Melbourne in 1916. Before long, she got a little too friendly with Charlie's neighbour and mate, Jim Charles. 'He was caught en flagrante with Charlie's wife,' said John Coates, sixty, who owns Mooresford, one of West's old properties. 'She would hang out a white sheet, and Jim would know Charlie had gone. Charlie cottoned on and one day he doubled back and gave Jim a hiding. He thought he had killed him, so he went into town to turn himself into the police. When the police got out to the hut, though, Jim had taken off.' Alma left, too, and they were formally divorced in 1922. Charlie died in 1958, aged eighty-two.

My Dad and his droving mates were camped at McKellar's Crossing one trip, bringing cattle through Tubbut. They were sitting around the campfire when they heard a dog whining. Dad coaxed it out of the shadows and found it was a little fox terrier. He fed it and made a fuss of it, and it attached itself to him. The men found it very strange that a little dog would be so far from civilisation. They came to the conclusion that it probably belonged to a swaggie and something must have happened to him. They searched but there was no sign of the dog's master, so Dad named him Scottie, and loaded him on a packhorse and brought him home.

We grew very fond of that dog, but we came to realise the drovers' theory was probably accurate. Scottie was the greatest thief. He would raid the neighbours' hen houses and carefully deposit the eggs on the back step. One time he raided the local café in Orbost and dragged off a leg of ham with Mr Drousou in hot pursuit. These were embarrassing incidents but his lost owner had trained him well. Some of the kids left their bikes in our yard for safety — he would let them put the bikes in but wouldn't let them take them out.

We always wondered what happened to Scottie's master. Many swaggies were humping their blueys in those days looking for work and we suspect that many would have died in some lonely camp, far from civilisation.

HEATHER LIVINGSTONE, WULGULMERANG

The pioneers lived off the land as best they could, but grinding poverty is a recurrent theme. Heather Livingstone, seventy-nine, said her family, the McDonnells at Gelantipy, ate everything they could catch — kangaroos, wombats, possums. Her Uncle Donald hated roast echidna. 'He said he could taste the ants,' Heather said. 'They ate everything but the "coola" bears, which they said were too cute.'

Jock Coates, eighty-four, from Buchan, said his maternal grandfather, Dr John Wallace Mackieson, and his wife Mary Roberts selected a few acres at Mountain Creek, across the Snowy River from Gelantipy in the 1860s, but, 'it did not go well'. Their cattle died from anthrax, and the property had to be left unstocked for two years. The birth of their first two children, Lelia and John, aroused the curiosity of the Aborigines who had never seen white babies before. They found Lelia's blond hair particularly fascinating, and began to camp nearby so they could watch her. The Mackiesons grew nervous — Aborigines had already been accused of taking a white baby at Black Mountain. 'It was a shocking life up there,' said Jock. 'They needed medals, because they had nothing.'

The supposedly kidnapped baby was Elizabeth O'Rourke. She was about eighteen months old in March 1866 when she went missing. Her family and thirteen men searched high and low, but could find no trace. It was widely and wrongly assumed Aborigines stole Elizabeth, until a year later when her remains were found on the banks of a creek about 1.5 kilometres east from the house. She had apparently fallen and broken her neck. Aborigines found the body and alerted the family. Elizabeth was buried in the O'Rourke family graveyard at Black Mountain. An O'Rourke descendant, Nigel Hodge from Gelantipy, thinks there may be up to seventeen people buried in the graveyard, but only one of the clan, Christopher O'Rourke, is marked with a gravestone; he died in 1854.

Hodge is among the last of the once-large O'Rourke clan who is still living in the Snowy's middle catchment; he is also the last of the Hodges. The Hodges were early settlers around Gelantipy and by 1960, there were seventy-two Hodges living in the area. Nigel said the Hodges and Rogers women kept the school open for years with their families of eighteen and more children, inspiring the local saying there was nothing but Hodges, Rogers and rabbits north of Buchan.

The O'Rourke family graveyard at Black Mountain. *Photo: Claire Miller.*

Making a go of it required ingenuity. Rix Wright's grandparents, Arthur and Ada Wright, settled at Tombong, north-west of Delegate, in 1880. They selected adjoining properties, one each, to maximise their holding. Under the laws to break up the vast tracts of land claimed by squatters, selectors had to sleep on their properties in order to prove they lived there. Ada and Arthur built their house, 'Mimosa', straddling the boundary between their properties. The line went straight through the bedroom and the double bed, so that each did indeed sleep on their own land. Wright said they had ten children, so there must have been a bit of trespassing.

Rix Wright's wife Jenny, whose ancestors took up land around Delegate Hill, said there was a lot of fighting among the pioneers. 'It is fairly dramatic country and wild stories come out of there,' she said. 'There was this tremendous amount of land but a lot of it was marginal and of very little use, so people fought over all the basic things they do when they are struggling to exist.' A small marble memorial marks the spot where the Scottish Earl of Ancram died in 1895 in mysterious circumstances down in the Quidong River gorge. Rix Wright says the Earl visited the area as the aide de camp to the New South Wales governor, and apparently flirted with the young governess on the property where Earl was staying. The property owner 'Old Edwards' also had his eye on the governess. 'Now, deer had been released into the Quidong and Snowy rivers, and it was a great thing for the young gentlemen to go deer hunting. The official story is that Earl of Ancram shot himself while getting on his horse. Now, you wouldn't accidentally shoot yourself getting on a horse, and the jackeroos that were there that day, their boss, Edwards, would not allow them to attend the inquest. He went on to marry the governess as his second wife. Ancram's parents put up the little memorial after their son's body was shipped back to England.'

The Wright household was a bastion of propriety in this sea of lawlessness. One time the patriarch Arthur Wright had to go into Cooma to serve jury duty in winter. Unlike the circuitous route by road today, the trail to Cooma by horseback was direct, over the Snowy River and up through Dalgety. Arthur dressed in his best and set off. He returned a few days later to find the Snowy River swollen by rain the previous night. Arthur stripped off to his boots, wrapped his good gear in an oilskin to stop it getting wet and strapped the bundle onto the saddle. He slapped the horse on the rump to swim over, and jumped in himself, with his bowler hat on his head. Arthur was swept a little downstream, but made it out okay.

'He wrung out his socks and removed his boots and took off his hat, and looked around for his horse,' said his grandson. 'He saw it grazing and went to catch it. The horse threw up its head, took one look at this pink creature coming at it, and galloped off. Grandpa swore he would have its hide. He caught up with the horse at the first slip gate, but then it jumped the gate and galloped away again. It did that several times, over several gates, until they got home. Grandpa was freezing and all the scrub had torn him to bits, but when he got to the top of the hill and could see the homestead below, he stopped.

'He knew the family would be nervous about his welfare when they saw the horse come into the yard riderless, but he was modest, and did not want his daughters to see the master of the house come home naked. So he stayed up in the bush until dark, then crept into the stableyard, caught the horse, got his dry clothes and got dressed. He had to keep his dignity, so he would not tell his family what happened.'

In such remote country, families had to make their own entertainment. Donnie Wellsmore and his brother John nearly burnt their parent's house down when they were boys in the 1940s. Bored, they took to teasing a turkey hen on a nest beside the house. Eventually they set fire to the nest to see if that would make her abandon her eggs. She sat and sat as the smoke curled up and her feathers began to singe. Just as she leapt squawking and took off across the yard, their father Ossie came leaping out from the house, yelling blue murder. He was in the bathroom when he smelt the smoke. 'There he was, leaping about in the nuddy, flapping at the fire with a towel and swearing at us' laughed Wellsmore. 'He wasn't a pretty sight!'

⌐

The storms, the wildness, the brumbies, the Joker Johnson people and the characters — it is very special country … It is beautiful country, and the people who live here love it and stick with it through fire and flood and famine and hell and high water. It gets into your blood and you can't get it out, and you don't want to. It is not like the softer tablelands. It is like typical western country, but hilly. It is tough country, but if you go with it, you will get on all right.

RIX AND JENNY WRIGHT, RUBIDA, NEAR TOMBONG

The settlers gradually abandoned their cattle runs and homesteads as the middle catchment degraded under the onslaught of cattle and sheep; the 1913 rabbit plague was the last straw. Nineteenth-century accounts describe the gorge country as open forest, well-grassed beneath the trees with reasonable topsoil, although not suitable for cropping. By 1890, Gippsland magistrate Alfred William Howitt reported that changed fire regimes and overstocking were taking their toll. Annual fires lit by the Aborigines prevented seedlings taking hold and kept insects in check, but white settlers put fires out. The result was whole tracts of country covered in forests of young saplings, while the grasshoppers and caterpillars ruined crops and ate grass into the ground. 'At present time, these [saplings] have so much increased and grown so much that it is difficult to ride over parts which one can see by the few scattered old giants, were at one time open grassy country,' Howitt wrote.[24]

By the 1930s, the livestock and rabbits had eaten out the Snowy River's tiger country, and the topsoil had washed away, exposing the stony ground beneath. Former Snowy River National Parks' ranger David Ingram said today's thick under-scrub was also a legacy of possum hunts. The possums, hunted almost into oblivion for their fur, kept the scrub down by eating all manner of seedlings. The rabbits promoted the scrub by eating out the grass and edible seedlings, leaving the tough, woody scrub like tea tree to take over.

Rabbits and livestock overgrazing on the Monaro plains are also to blame for the massive sediment load choking the Snowy River. William Crisp, whose father Amos Crisp established Matong station in 1831 and Jimenbuen in 1835, described the Matong Creek of his youth as a succession of deep waterholes without high banks, and grass to the edge. By the early 1840s, this little creek was a bed of sand, in which water came to the surface only in floods. In the following decades, the sand bed deepened into a badly eroded gully.[25] The same fate befell the other creeks on the Monaro feeding into the Snowy River.

The rate of erosion peaked in the 1890s, and has been declining ever since, but not before the Snowy River got a gutful of sand. The Snowy could cope with the added load while it still had the power of its headwaters to sweep the sand to the sides of the main channel and keep it moving downstream to the sea. Once the Snowy Mountains Hydro-Electric Scheme dammed 99 per cent of the Snowy's headwaters, the sand spread and accumulated, filling in the channel and choking the river like cholesterol in the arteries of a heart attack victim.

The scheme put an end to excitement in the class experienced by Gordon Ballard, when he and several friends canoed the length of the Snowy River in homemade canoes. Ballard filmed their adventures on several trips from 1947–49, giving us the only moving footage of the river before it was dammed. You can see how the Snowy got its wild reputation. The trip from Jindabyne to Dalgety was made in November, after a big snow season. There was still plenty of snow on the mountains, and the Snowy was at the peak of its annual surge. Its power is breathtaking, and the wonder is watching these blokes push off into the raging ice-blue water in two fragile wooden vessels without helmets or life jackets. At one point Ballard films his mates climbing over rocks, picking up the pieces of one canoe smashed to splinters. All four men then pile into the other canoe to complete the journey. The film is held at the Mitchell Library in Sydney, and is highly recommended viewing.

Yet while the Snowy River may be a shadow of its former self, it is still the backdrop for many a modern adventure. The names of the rapids in Tulloch Ard Gorge should be warning enough: George's Mistake, Triple Drop, the Washing Machine and Gentle Annie — who is anything but. In 2000, former journalist Graham Pike feared he had lost the newly elected independent member for Gippsland East, Craig Ingram, in Tulloch Ard Gorge. 'Craig is a superb canoeist, a bit of a daredevil, strong and built for it,' said Pike. 'It was late. We had done 30 kilometres and had another day to go and we came to the top of a rapid. Craig and [local newspaper owner] Bob Yeates were in the canoe in front of me. I could hear this roaring, but I could not see the bottom of the rapid from the top. I heard Craig say to Bob Yeates, "Will we go for it?". Bob looked around reluctantly and said, "Oh, yeah" and down they went and disappeared.

'All I saw next was a blue esky with a white lid going into orbit. I knew it was roped down in the centre of the canoe. It flew up and dropped back on the rocks near the top. Usually you then see bodies swimming behind the rapid coming out, but there was no sign of life — no sign of anything except this esky in the rocks.

'I thought, "oh great, we have drowned the local member and the local editor". I had this fear I would have to mount a major rescue, and went scrabbling over the rocks and still could not see them, and then I saw the canoe with its nose dented from hitting the rocks and Bob soaking wet and full of water. "Where is Craig?" I yelled. "Shit, I don't know," Bob said. He was a bit stunned. "Is he in the bottom of the pool or what?" I shouted. And then I finally saw Craig crawling up the rocks on the other side, after the esky, which had all our supplies. "Jeez, that was fun, wasn't it, Bob?" he was calling out. By this time, they were cold and wet and Craig was walking over these rocks in bare feet. He was in his element.'

Roddy Kleinitz, who runs the Wildernest retreat for jaded city slickers on the Snowy River near Buchan, used to get his thrills riding the flood waves in wet years in the 1980s. He would get out there in a canoe after the debris had gone past and have the ride of his life. 'I would have been doing 20 kilometres an hour!'

They were invincible days, when Kleinitz did not even bother wearing a life jacket. Then, one day, his canoe capsized in a whirlpool and he came close to drowning. 'It was so turbulent in the gorge, and muddy and murky, that I did not know if I was going up or down,' he said. 'By the time I worked out which way was up, I was nearly drowned. The water was 15 feet over the rocks. I grabbed hold of a little wattle and pulled myself out. I never saw the canoe or bits of it again. I took the river for granted until then. It is very unforgiving.'

Fires, as well as floods, defined life along the Snowy River. Donnie Wellsmore's earliest memories are of the 1939 bushfires that swept out of the Snowy River country. He was four years old on 13 January 1939, when he sat in his grandmother Celie's arms as she cowered in the chemical wash in a metre-deep concrete sheep dip along with seven other people. Embers blowing over the edge burned his grandmother's arms, and she cried when told the house she had struggled to put together was gone. When the clothes on a neighbour's baby caught alight, Wellsmore's father Ossie grabbed a bucket thinking it was full of water and threw it over the child. 'It was pure arsenic, but the baby survived although it was a bit yellow for a while.' His mother drove everyone into Dalgety after the front passed. 'They did not know us at the pub, we were such a mess with all the ash and arsenic and sheep piddle,' Wellsmore recalls.

The Snowy River country bared its teeth again in January 2003, when bushfires roared through Wulgulmerang and Suggan Buggan and down into the Snowy River National Park. The community was left facing the dragon alone when authorities in the fire command centre 100 kilometres away miscalculated. Fire trucks were pulled back from Wulgulmerang to Gelantipy for lunch on the basis that the front was still three days away. The firefighters had barely touched their first sandwich before the front swept out of the Alpine National Park to the west and cut Wulgulmerang off. The residents were told they were on their own, facing the worst of the catastrophic fires that ultimately burned more than two million hectares in Victoria and New South Wales over six weeks.

The fire crews could only listen helplessly as families called over their two-way radios to neighbours for help as the embers showered down. But there was no one who could help — every property was under attack and everyone frantically battling to save their own houses, livestock and themselves. The trembling voice of Jess Moon, fifteen, was almost too much to bear over the airwaves. 'Dad? Dad — are you there? Where are you? Come in Dad — please!'

Jess was sheltering under the house with her mother Sally Moon, brother Nich, and neighbour Mac during the height of the inferno. Sally tried not to think about her husband's fate as she desperately sought to stop the ember-laden gale blowing the door in. 'I can't hold it!' she cried out as some particularly strong gusts buffeted and rattled the door in its frame. Then, above the roar of the maelstrom outside, she heard her husband Gordon bellowing, 'Open the door! Open the bloody door!' as he battered his fists against it on the other side, trying to get in.

When it was over, nine of the district's eighteen houses were gone. So were the sports pavilion, the roadhouse, hay sheds, fencing, wildlife and most of the little grass the dry spell had left in the paddocks. Hundreds of cattle and sheep perished. The wonder is no one died. When David Woodburn gave up the fight to save the eccentric Seldom Seen roadhouse, he sprinted down his burning paddock to shelter in his dam, along with his dog, nine geese and a passing kangaroo. Bill Livingstone was inside in his house waiting for the front to go past — until he realised the house was on fire. He ran out, crashed down through the burning veranda, and headed for the other farmhouse across the yard, only to realise it was also on fire. He took cover behind his grader, crouched against a tyre with a blanket over his head.

'We can laugh about it now,' said Helen Bowman of the gallows humour rippling around her neighbours as they gathered by the roadhouse ruins to tell me the tale a few weeks later. 'But at the time it was desperate. It was the most horrific day I have ever had in my life.' One of her sons had to prise the hose from her hands, saying gently, 'It's gone, Mum. You can stop now.'[26]

The 2003 fires were the worst catastrophe since the 1939 Black Friday fires. The heat was so intense it baked the ground and killed the seeds of tomorrow's forest in the Snowy's gorge country. It also killed mature eucalypts, which are normally virtually indestructible and among the first plants to put out new green shoots after a fire. Whole hillsides of white cypress trees are also dead.

Two years after the fires, little other than grass has grown back in the Byadbo wilderness and wildlife has all but disappeared. It will take decades for the tiger country to recover, but what will never come back is the heritage. Old cattle yards, the remains of huts, scar trees, blaze trees — much was lost forever.

*We fished and swam in the river as children and when masks
became available, we dived. I have memories of walls of fish at
times, and the wonder of diving through murky fresh water into the
clear salt water. It was like going from a room in darkness into a
place of light.*

JIM NIXON (92), ORBOST, NOVEMBER 2002

The Orbost floodplains from the top of Newmerella hill present a bucolic picture. The alluvial plain is a patchwork of farms, mostly dairy interspersed with the occasional field of rudely healthy corn. Through the middle snakes the Snowy River, its course marked by a line of huge old mahogany gum trees. It is hard to believe this manicured agrarian landscape was once a near-impenetrable tangle of dank jungle and swamp, in stark contrast to the steep, dry, open forest a few kilometres upstream in the gorge country.

Baron Ferdinand von Mueller, the botanist who originally designed Melbourne's botanic gardens, visited the area in 1854, some ten years after white settlers began taking up land. He recorded dense vegetation tropical in character.[27] Norman Wakefield, the eminent East Gippsland naturalist, in 1954 described what von Mueller saw as a botanical wonderland, with its lilly-pilly trees, flowering clematis, vines as thick as a man's body, giant maidenhair ferns, tree trunks blanketed with epiphytic ferns, and cabbage tree palms. This riotous glory was testament to the fertility of the soil below, a rich, metres-deep loam built up over hundreds of thousands of years.

It only took twenty years for white people to render this primeval forest a sepia memory. By the 1870s, most of the giant mahoganies, lilly-pilly and kanookas had been felled and burned, with the ground ploughed, fenced and bearing boom crops of maize, beans and giant pumpkins.[28] Today, the merest shadow of the former glory remains at Lochend, a bluff on the Snowy River bank south-west of Orbost, along with a few giant mahoganies along the banks and just 2–3 square kilometres of wetlands representing less than 4 per cent of the area covered in 1865. The wholesale pillage took its toll on the river also. An 1865 map shows the Snowy was originally only about 50–100 metres wide across the floodplain; by 1934, desnagging and removing riverside vegetation had allowed the river to spread 150–375 metres wide.[29]

In the 130 years recorded since 1874, the Snowy River at Orbost has flooded 125 times. The floods can occur in any season, and, in some years, three or four times; certain decades, like the 1890s and the 1950s, were particularly wet. 'Why are the people of the Snowy River so passionate about it?' said Gil Richardson, a fourth-generation farmer on the Orbost floodplain. 'The answer is in its wildness, its extremity. It can flood like no other.'

Most floods are more nuisance value than anything else, with farmers rushing to get livestock onto higher ground and wives rushing to move household valuables up out of the way. The biggest problem in the early days was the lack of warning — it could be sunny and clear skies in Orbost when a flood wave came down from torrential thunderstorms upstream — coupled with the suspense of not knowing how bad it might get. The positive aspect was a renewal of fertile silt and recharge of ground water.

There was nothing positive about the monster floods for which the Snowy River is famous. There have been six of these: 1870, 1893, 1934, 1952, 1971 and 1978. Each time the river rose more than 9 metres. The two worst recorded were 1934, when the river rose 10.34 metres and swept away the newly built McKillops Bridge, and 1971, when it rose 10.79 metres. 'But the wild, wild Snowy River/He's a rough, tough mountain "bloke"/Nought can bind this fierce loose-liver/on his periodic "soak", wrote poet C. J Dennis after the 1934 flood.[30]

'It comes out of the hills at such a fast rate,' explained Gil Richardson's wife, Heather. 'One moonlit night in 1983, Gil and I were standing down on the river watching. We had a dry bed; the river had stopped running. It had not rained down here, but we saw the first wave come, and it was six inches. The second wave was 18 inches, and the third was 3 or 4 feet deep, with an incredible roar.'

That was just a routine flood. Heather Richardson will never forget the day the water started rising in January 1971. Being a city girl who grew up in Melbourne, she had no experience of the Snowy in a rage. She went out to look over the levee bank and was horrified. Big old mahogany gums were snapping like matchsticks, and the water was roiling from the sides into the middle with a terrific force so that the level was higher than where she stood. The Richardsons were lucky that time. When the flood receded after three days, it left behind debris on the top of the levee, but did not breach it. Elsewhere, the floodplain was a disaster zone. 'You think you have control, but the river brings you down to earth,' said Richardson. 'You are never in control. It looks very tame and mild most of the time, but you can never trust it. Yet it is the lifeblood of Orbost. It gets into you.'

ᔕ

The Snowy River winds its way through the story of Australia. It was a potent life force in Indigenous lore, and A. B. Paterson used it in his *The Man from Snowy River* poem to define a young nation's emerging character at the turn of the nineteenth century.

Sixty years later, the Snowy Mountains Hydro-Electric Scheme appropriated the Snowy and its mythology to help define the modern nation in terms of industrial development and greening the desert. 'The Man from Snowy River, he rides a tractor, now,' as the Snowy Mountains Authority's rollicking construction song went. The scheme all but killed the river that inspired its construction, and that might have been the end of the story if not for an unlikely group of people with almost nothing in common except a one-eyed commitment to a common cause: keeping the Snowy River and all it represents alive. Supported by hundreds of people from the Snowy River and beyond, they are the authors of the latest chapters in the Snowy River story.

Glossary

Above-target water The Snowy Mountains Hydro-Electric Scheme traps about 2410 gigalitres a year. Irrigators are entitled to 2100 gigalitres a year from the scheme, which usually holds another 1000 gigalitres in storage. This reserve is called 'above-target' water, and is the most valuable in the scheme. It can be used at the discretion of the operators to generate power at premium prices to meet demand spikes. It can also be sold to irrigators to top them up in droughts. The Snowy River Alliance argued that some of the reserve could be used to restore an environmental flow to the Snowy River.

Bridges Only three bridges cross the Snowy River: Dalgety; McKillops, halfway down in the remote wilderness region; and Orbost.

Council of Australian Governments Better known as COAG. State and federal government leaders and ministers regularly hold COAG meetings to discuss issues requiring national cooperation. COAG in February 1994 endorsed a strategic framework for reforming water management, aimed at more sustainable use. It led to the creation of a water market, but, significantly, the environment was recognised for the first time as a legitimate water user whose needs must be accommodated. The framework legitimised the community campaign for the Snowy River, which then became a test of the governments' sincerity in restoring environmental flows.

Corporatisation The process of turning statutory government bodies into commercial, government-owned companies operating under corporate laws, with their first and foremost purpose being to return profits.

Dalgety The smallest of two towns on the Snowy River, 30 kilometres downstream of the Jindabyne dam in New South Wales. Permanent population in 2004 was approximately seventy, with another 200 or so in the surrounding district.

Environmental flow Water allocated for environmental purposes, separate from agricultural, industry and urban consumption. Ideally, water is allocated on the basis of restoring and maintaining clearly identified ecological functions, such as native species habitat and sediment clearance. Usually, however, it is an arbitrary and inadequate amount determined after taking account first of human demands.

Flow rates in the Snowy Estimated average flow rates in the upper Snowy before it was dammed vary between 1121 gigalitres and 1168 gigalitres a year, including the Mowamba River.

The Snowy Mountains Authority says it released an annual average 33 gigalitres into the Snowy River (9 gigalitres from Jindabyne dam and 24 in spills over the Mowamba weir in wet years). This is about 3 per cent of the original flow. Other figures suggest the mean was 7–10 gigalitres, or less than 1 per cent.

These variations mean figures vary throughout the book, depending on the organisation doing the calculations, and the period. Victoria in 1999–2000, however, worked on the basis that a 28 per cent flow in the Snowy translated to an average annual 327 gigalitres. Assuming the Snowy got an average 33 gigalitres already from the scheme, Victoria and New South Wales had to come up with another 294-odd gigalitres.

The Dalgety and District Community Association worked out its figures based on flows under the bridge at Dalgety. Before 1949, the mean daily flow was 3200 megalitres. After 1967, when the Jindabyne dam was completed, the mean daily flow under Dalgety bridge was 25 megalitres, or 0.78 per cent of the original level. The Association says the Snowy Mountains Authority monitored water levels in Dalgety and adjusted releases from the scheme so daily levels did not exceed 25 megalitres.

Gigalitre 1000 megalitres.

LandCare Government-funded but community-based and directed program to address local degradation issues such as weeds, pest control, revegetation and erosion.

Mean daily flow The amount of water flowing in the river on most days.

Megalitre One million litres, or an Olympic swimming pool full of water.

Orbost The largest of two towns on the Snowy River. Situated on the flood plain near the river's mouth in Victoria. Population: approximately 2500 people.

Privatisation Selling government businesses and services to the private sector, usually after they have been corporatised. Alternatively, government services may be tendered to private providers.

Snowy Hydro Ltd The name of the company created when the Commonwealth, New South Wales and Victoria corporatised the Snowy Mountains Hydro-Electric Scheme, and abolished the Snowy Mountains Council and the Snowy Mountains Authority.

Snowy Mountains Council The joint-government body that administered the water and power-sharing agreements that governed the Snowy Mountains scheme. The council consisted of eight representatives, one from each of the energy and water departments in the Commonwealth, New South Wales and Victoria, plus two from the Snowy Mountains Authority.

Snowy Mountains Hydro-Electric Authority More commonly known as the Snowy Mountains Authority or just 'the Hydro'. The SMHEA was a federal body responsible for operating and maintaining the Snowy Mountains scheme. It took its instructions from the Snowy Mountains Council, but its Commonwealth-appointed commissioner was answerable to no one.

Snowy River Alliance coalition of local groups that joined forces in March 1996 to campaign for a minimum 28 per cent of the Snowy's original flow to be released from the Snowy Mountains scheme. At its height in 1999, the Alliance had several hundred members and more than seventy affiliate organisations.

Water savings The recovery of water lost through evaporation, seepage, waste or inefficient irrigation. The Murray Darling Basin Commission estimates that at least 3036 gigalitres are lost each year in the Murray and lower Darling River systems.

Bibliography

Andrews, G. and Andrews, N. (1990), *Snowy River Pioneers*, Gordon and Nina Andrews, Netherbyre, Orbost.

Armstrong, A. (1982), *A History of Buchan*, a personal account of J. S. Armstrong, a third-generation pioneer, 'as learned in his 78 years'.

ABARE (1997), 'The Snowy River: opportunity costs of introducing environmental flows', *Australian Commodities Forecasts and issues*, Australian Bureau of Agricultural and Resource Economics, Canberra, vol. 4, no. 1, March 1997.

Buchan Historical Society (1989), *Bukan-Mungie: 150 Years of Settlement in the Buchan District — 1839–1989*, Buchan Sesquicentenary Committee.

Byrne, G. (2000), 'Schemes of Nation: a Planning history of the Snowy Mountains Scheme', PhD thesis, Department of Art History and Theory, University of Sydney.

Collis, B. (1990), *Snowy: The Making of Modern Australia*, Tabletop Press, Canberra.

Commonwealth and States Snowy River Committee (1950), *Diversion and Utilisation of the Waters of the Snowy River*, final report of the committee, Commonwealth of Australia, May 1950.

Davidson, B. R. (1969), *Australia, Wet or Dry?*, Melbourne University Press, Melbourne, Victoria.

Dempster, M. G. (1934), 'Road Bridge over Snowy River, Woolgoolmerang, Vic.', *Commonwealth Engineer*, 1 September 1932.

Dempster, M. G. (1934), *Commonwealth Engineer*, 1 March 1934.

'Expert Panel Environmental Flow Assessment of the Snowy River below Jindabyne Dam', for the Snowy-Genoa Catchment Management Committee, February 1996.

Gilbert, M. (1972), *Personalities and Stories of the Early Orbost District*, Orbost Historical Society, Orbost.

Green, O. S. (1989), *The Snowy: its Cattlemen, Rivermen and Engineers*, Acacia Press, Blackburn.

Howitt, A. W. (1890), 'The Eucalypts of Gippsland', extract from *Forest Grower Canberra*, Section 26, 1993–94, vol. 16, no. 4.

Larkins, J. (1980), *Story of the Snowy Mountains*, A. H. & A. W. Reed, Sydney, NSW.

McHugh, S. (1995), *The Snowy: the People Behind the Power*, Angus and Robertson, Sydney, NSW.

McKay, R. T. (1939), 'Water Conservation and Irrigation From 1884 to 1917', paper delivered to the Institution of Surveyors, NSW on 24 October 1939, later reprinted in *The Australian Surveyor*, vol. 8, no. 1, pp. 32–42.

Meeking, C. (1968), *Snowy Mountains Conquest*, Hutchinson, Melbourne.

Murray Darling Basin Commission (1999), *The Salinity Audit of the Murray-Darling Basin. A 100-Year Perspective, 1999*, Murray Darling Basin Commission, Canberra.

National Archives of Australia, Snowy Mountains Hydro-Electric Authority, Folder 61, Documents 2275–2310.

Parkinson, T. (2000) *Jeff: The Rise and Fall of a Political Phenomenon*, Viking, Penguin Books Australia, Ringwood.

Seddon, G. (1994), *Searching for the Snowy*, Allen and Unwin, Sydney, NSW.

Smith, S. (2000), *The Future of the Snowy River*, Briefing Paper 2/2000, NSW Parliamentary Library, Sydney.

Snowy River Country, (1985), vol. Winter, Cooma, 'The Man From Snowy River', pp. 22–24.

'Snowy River Downsteam of Lake Jindabyne, Environmental Flow Scoping Study Summary', draft 1995 report prepared by NSW Department of Land and Water Conservation, Victorian Department of Conservation and Natural Resources, Snowy Mountains Hydro-Electric Authority.

SRICC (1993), 'Resource Management Issues in the Snowy River Catchment', report of the Technical Working Group of the Snowy River Interstate Catchment Coordinating Committee, October 1993.

SWI (1998) 'Snowy Water Inquiry, Final Report', 23 October 1998, published by the Snowy Water Inquiry, Governor Macquarie Tower, Sydney, jointly sponsored by the Victorian and NSW Governments.

Thain, S. (2004), '2020 vision or acute myopia — the unforeseen consequences of Australia's plantation policy', report prepared by Skye Thain, BA Environmetal Studies.

Wesson, S. (2000), *An Historical Atlas of the Aborigines of Eastern Victoria and Far South-eastern New South Wales*, Monash Publications in Geography and Environmental Science, No. 53, Monash University.

White, M. E. (2000), *Running Down: Water in a Changing Land*, Kangaroo Press, New South Wales.

Wigmore, L. (1968), *Struggle for the Snowy, Background for the Snowy Mountains Scheme*, Oxford University Press, Melbourne.

Young, M. (2000), *The Aboriginal People of the Monaro*, compiled by Michael Young with Ellen and Debbie Mundy, NSW National Parks and Wildlife Service, Jindabyne.

Endnotes

PROLOGUE

1 John Harrowell, submission to Snowy River Shire Council, on behalf of a community delegation, 17 December 1991.

CHAPTER 1

1 Quote from 1946 report included in final report of the Commonwealth and States Snowy River Committee (1950) 'Diversion and Utilisation of the Waters of the Snowy River'.
2 Neal, L. (1976) *Cooma Country*, The Cooma-Monaro Historical Society, p. 249.
3 Wigmore, L. (1968), *Struggle for the Snowy, Background for the Snowy Mountains Scheme*, Oxford University Press, Melbourne.
4 Wigmore, L. (1968) op. cit., p. 85.
5 Unnamed reporter cited in Larkins, J. (1980), *Story of the Snowy Mountains*, A. H. & A. W. Reed, Sydney, NSW.
6 Cubic feet of water per second.
7 NSW Water Conservation and Irrigation Commission, Document No. 61/17086, signed by the senior hydrographic engineer, 6 June 1961. Letter sent to Snowy Mountains Authority on 22 June 1961.
8 Grose, S. (1994), 'When the River runs dry', in *Canberra Times*, 9 January 1994, p. 17.
9 This figure can be misleading. It is the long-term average, including major floods. This distorts the real impacts. A more accurate measure is the mean flow, which is 39 per cent of the pre-scheme level. The Snowy River at Orbost also now experiences drought-level summer flows virtually every year, compared with one in twenty years before the hydro-electric scheme.
10 *Snowy River Mail*, 'Fear that entrance would silt up', 9 February 1949.
11 State Rivers and Water Supply Commission Archives, 14/2/49, PRO,VPRS 6008, Box 578, file 50/4912.
12 *Snowy River Mail*, 'Public Meeting Re Snowy River Diversion', 2 March 1949, p. 1.
13 *Snowy River Mail*, 'Snowy River Diversion', 9 March 1949.
14 National Archives of Australia, SR committee, notes of meeting 11/12/13 April 1949, p. 4 NAA MP831, 1955/714, part one, file 8/9.
15 *Snowy River Mail*, 'Effect of Snowy Scheme', 4 May 1949, p. 1.
16 National Archives of Australia, SR committee, Minutes, 23 May 1949, NAA MP831, 1955/714, part 1 (file3/9).
17 Commonwealth and States Snowy River Committee (1950), *Diversion and Utilisation of the Waters of the Snowy River*, final report of the committee, Commonwealth of Australia, May 1950.
18 National Archives of Australia, Snowy Mountains Hydro-Electric Authority Folder 61, Documents 2275–2310, Item 34.

19 *Snowy River Mail*, 'Snowy River Scheme', 22 June 1949, p 2.
20 *Snowy River Mail*, 'Snowy Water Loss All State's Problem', 5 August 1964, p. 1.
21 *Cooma-Monaro Express*, 'River reduced to 'water holes'', 22 March 1965, p. 1.
22 *Cooma-Monaro Express*, 'Diversion scheme upsets people of Dalgety', 12 April 1965, p. 1.

CHAPTER 2

1 SRICC (1993), 'Resource Management Issues in the Snowy River Catchment', report of the Technical Working Group of the Snowy River Interstate Catchment Coordinating Committee, October 1993.
2 West's quotes recorded in Harrowell's letters in response, letters dated 24 August and 12 October 1992.
3 Letter from John Harrowell to Jim Snow, federal MP for Eden-Monaro, 24 September 1992.
4 *Cooma-Monaro* Express (1992), 'This Association has no fight with the SMA', 27 August 1992.
5 Letter from John Harrowell to Jim Snow, federal MP for Eden-Monaro, 12 August 1992.
6 Quote from letter drafted by John Harrowell and sent to Senator Bob Collins, Minister for Primary Industries, signed by Jo Garland as president of Dalgety and District Community Association, 5 April 1994. Same point made less concisely in numerous letters and press releases starting from John Harrowell's first media release on 13 July 1992.
7 Quotes paraphrased from letters exchanged between John Harrowell, politicians and engineers throughout 1992 and 1993.
8 Memo from John Harrowell to committee members on the Dalgety and District Community Association, 3 September 1992.
9 Letter from Geoff Coleman, Victorian Minister for Natural Resources, to John Harrowell, president of Dalgety and District Community Association, 3 March 1994, ref. DG20421.
10 *Summit Sun*, 'John Harrowell heads for greener pastures, but the show will go on' 30 September 1993, p. 20.
11 Letter from R.A. Higgins, chairman of the Snowy River Council, to Brett Miners, coordinator of Snowy-Genoa Catchment Management Committee, 15 September 1995, ref. sr/smd/0044ms-94/9507.
12 'Expert Panel Environmental Flow Assessment of the Snowy River below Jindabyne Dam', for the Snowy-Genoa Catchment Management Committee, February 1996.
13 'Snowy River Downstream of Lake Jindabyne, Environmental Flow Scoping Study Summary', report prepared by NSW Department of Land and Water Conservation, Victorian Department of Conservation and Natural Resources, Snowy Mountains Hydro-Electric Authority, p. 22.

CHAPTER 3

1 Grose, S. (1996) 'Snowy trade-off draws local ire', *Canberra Times*, 1 July 1996, p. 4.
2. Explained at Dalgety community meeting, 16 March 1994. Meeting convened by Department of Water Resources as part of the ill-fated joint government scoping study.

3 Account of meeting drawn from interviews with people who were there, including Alison Gimbert and Brett Miners.
4 NSW Legislative Council Hansard, 'Snowy River Water Flow', 8 April 1997, pp. 7188–89.
5 NSW Legislative Council Hansard, 'Snowy Mountains Hydro-Electricity Authority Privatisation', 23 April 1997, pp. 7905–06.
6 This account rebuilt from interviews with Ian Cohen, Richard Jones, Jeff Angel, David Crossley and Peter Staveley, and *Hansard* reports.
7 NSW Legislative Council Hansard, 'Snowy Water Inquiry', 25 June 1997, pp. 11106–07.
8 *Sun-Herald*, 'The damn from Snowy River', 13 July 1997, p. 61.
9 Paul Leete interviewed on the *Today Show*, Channel Nine, 4 July 1997.
10 Account of inquiry hearing gleaned from Senate official committee Hansard, Finance and Public Administration Legislation Committee, Friday 26 September 1997, F&PA41–69.
11 Letter from Max White to Jeff Kennett, dated 20 August 1997; Glenice White's letter to Alan Stockdale, dated 5 September 1997.

CHAPTER 4

1 Discussions on plight of other rivers taken from TEC transcripts of phone hook-ups throughout 1998.
2 Report from Genevieve Fitzgerald to Fran Kelly at Total Environment Centre, 'Funding Issues — Where's the Money?', 18 March 1998.
3 From an unpublished transcript of my interview with Lady Southey on 24 August 1999. Transcript formed basis for article published in *The Age*, 4 September 1999, p. 20: 'One Lady's fight to let a river run free'.
4 Glasson quotes from a copy of his speech before the Snowy Water Inquiry hearing.
5 'Snowy water Inquiry begins at Orbost', *Snowy River Mail*, Wednesday 24 June 1998, pp. 1–2.
6 'Snowy River area rich in Aboriginal history', *Snowy River Mail*, Wednesday 24 June 1998, p. 13.
7 'Tourist potential linked to a healthy river', *Snowy River Mail*, Wednesday 24 June 1998, p. 4.
8 Gillespie, R. (1998), *Economic benefits of environmental flows for the Snowy River*. Unpublished report for the Total Environment Centre, Australian Conservation Foundation and Snowy River Alliance by Gillespie Economics. Lodged with the Total Environment Centre, Sydney
9 Bruton, J. (1998), 'Snowy Inquiry debate', in *Country News*, 6–12 July 1998, pp. 1 & 3. No one living along the Snowy River was ever compensated for losing their water. The Snowy Mountains Authority did pay for fencing when the river was no longer wide and deep enough to act as a natural stock boundary.
10 Agreement negotiated by the Murrumbidgee Water Management Committee, comprising representatives from the Department of Land and Water Conservation, the Agriculture and Fisheries Department, the Environment Protection Authority, Murrumbidgee Irrigation Ltd and community stakeholders.
11 MDBC (1998), Murray Darling Basin Commission draft issues paper on Snowy Corporatisation and Water Inquiry, commercial in confidence briefing for the Murray Darling Basin Ministerial Council, July 1998.
12 'Energy Update', advertising supplement in *The Australian*, 23 September 1998. Similar quotes and arguments in many other sources, including *Weekly Times*, 17 February 1999.

13 Snowy Hydro (1998), 'Managing the Dynamic Balance', Snowy Hydro Trading Ltd submission to the Snowy Water Inquiry, 22 May 1998, submission no. 160.
14 The Australian Greenhouse Office, National Greenhouse Gas Inventory 2002 executive summary, <www.greenhouse.gov.au/inventory/2002/>
15 As it stands, the coal-fired power industry enjoys the lion's share of Commonwealth funding and other support. 'Securing Australia's Energy Future', white paper released by Prime Minister John Howard, 15 June 2004, copies available at <www.pmc.au/energy_future>
16 Commonwealth Government (2000), 'Corporatisation of the Snowy Mountains Hydro-Electric Authority Draft Environmental Impact Statement', June.
17 Calculation based on information available on the Snowy Hydro website, <www.snowyhydro.com.au>
18 Snowy Hydro Ltd annual financial report 2003–2004, p. 11, <www.snowyhydro.com.au>
19 Max White, letter to Marie Tehan, 5 May 1998.
20 Details in letter from Fran Kelly to the Snowy River Alliance, dated 27 August 1998.
21 Account of schism reconstructed from interviews, letters and minutes of meetings.
22 'Snowy Water Inquiry Final Report', published by Snowy Water Inquiry, 23 October 1998, p. 12.
23 Quoted from minutes for Snowy River campaign phone hook-up, 28 October 1998.
24 Accounts drawn from TEC transcripts of phone hook-ups on 28 October and 18 November 1998.

CHAPTER 5

1   'Minister questioned on Snowy River flow', Snowy River Mail, Wednesday 26 May 1999, p. 1.
2   Letter from Victorian Premier Jeff Kennett to New South Wales Premier Bob Carr, 15 May 1999.
3   Snowy River Mail (1999), 'Ride for Future nears Melbourne', 15 September 1999, p. 22.
4   From TEC transcript of Snowy campaign phone hook-up on 3 June 1999.
5   Miller, C. (1999), 'Bid to help shrinking river falls on deaf ears', The Age, 21 July 1999, p. 7.
6   Miller, C. (1999), 'One Lady's fight to let a river run free', The Age, 4 September 1999, p. 20.
7   Snowy River Mail, 'Ride for Future nears Melbourne', 15 September 1999, p. 22.
8   Miller, C. (1999), 'Bid to help shrinking river falls on deaf ears', The Age, 21 July 1999, p. 7.

CHAPTER 6

1   Poem read out on Neil Mitchell's morning talkback show on 3AW on Thursday 23 September 1999.
2   Interviewed on ABC TV's 7.30 Report, 12 October 1999.
3   Hannan, E. (1999) 'Backflips: Staying Alive', The Age, 2 October 1999, p. 1.
4   Transcript of Bob Carr's doorstep media conference, Melbourne, 7 October 1999.
5   Letter from Jeff Kennett to Bob Carr, 8 October 1999.
6   Transcript of Jeff Kennett interview on CO-FM Rural Report [Albury-Wodonga] 13 October 1999.
7   Country News (1999), 'Drought conditions pushed farmer to brink of despair', 4–10 October 1999, p. 5. (Country News is an insert magazine in the Shepparton News.)

8   Mitchell, B. (1999), 'Growers threaten court action', *The Age*, 13 October 1999, p. 6.
9   Casey, M. (1999), 'Angry rice farmers in water rally', *Daily Telegraph*, Wednesday 13 October 1999, p. 17.
10 Press release issued 8 October 1999 by Richard Amery, New South Wales Minister for Agriculture, Land and Water Conservation.
11 Quotes taken from television news bulletins and the *Shepparton News*, 'Small but vocal band of protesters in Sydney', 13 October 1999, p. 1.
12 Letter from Jeff Kennett to Bob Car, 13 October 1999.
13 Michael Egan's statement faxed to Victorian Premier's Office on 14 October 1999.
14 Hannan, E. (1999), 'Sucker punch downs a Premier', *The Age*, 18 October 1999, p. 1.
15 'I gave my all to this state', Jeff Kennett's concession speech, published in *The Herald-Sun*, 20 October 1999.
16 Miller, C. (1999), 'Ingram: still slightly uneasy', *The Age*, 19 October 1999, p. 4.
17 Miller, C. (1999), op. cit., 19 October 1999, p. 4.
18 Costa, G. (1999), 'Voters back three independents', *The Age*, 1 November 1999, p. 2.

CHAPTER 7

1   This analysis drawn from conversations with sources in the New South Wales Environment Protection Authority, responsible for implementing the NSW Government's 10 per cent environmental flows policy.
2   Riverina wants to secure Snowy supplies', in *Weekly Times*, 22 December 2000.
3   Donovan quoted in Woodford, J. (1999), 'Men from Snowy River ride tide of political chance'. *Sydney Morning Herald*, 8 October 1999, p. 2; Bortoli quoted in Miller, C. (1999), 'Snowy users plan PR attack', *The Age*, 31 October 1999, p. 10.
4   'Food Bowl — the Other Side of the Snowy', undated statement accompanying *The other side of the Snowy*, brochure produced by Rice Growers Association of Australia, Murrumbidgee Irrigation, Murray Irrigation, MIA Council of Horticultural Associations and Coleambally Irrigation Corporation.
5   Murray Darling Basin Commission (2004) 'Murray Darling Basin Water Resources fact sheet', <www.mdbc.gov.au>
6   Calculations based on figures in the Murray Darling Ministerial Council's confidential issues paper for the Snowy Water Inquiry, draft, 6 July 1998, and a NSW Treasury briefing note, 1 October 1999.
7   ABARE (1997) 'The Snowy River: opportunity costs of introducing environmental flows', *Australian Commodities. Forecasts and Issues*, Australian Bureau of Agricultural and Resource Economics, Canberra, vol. 4, no. 1, March Quarter 1997, pp. 67–78.
8   Analysis by F. J. Bell and Associates, 1998, for the Australian Conservation Foundation, Total Environment Centre and Snowy River Alliance.
9   Smith, S. (2000), *The Future of the Snowy River*, NSW Government briefing paper.
10 Colebatch, T. (2004), 'Water study reveals massive river loss, suggests $824 m plug to remedy it', in *The Age*, 10 December 2004, p. 7.
11 Victoria in 1999–2000 worked on the basis that a 28 per cent flow in the Snowy translated to an average annual 327 gigalitres. Assuming the Snowy got an average 33 gigalitres already from the scheme (9 gigalitres from Jindabyne dam and 24 gigalitres in spills over Mowamba weir in very wet years), the states had to find another 290-odd gigalitres.
12 Smith, S. (2000), op. cit.
13 Australian Bureau of Statistics, Themes — Environment Land and Soil Agriculture <www.abs.gov.au>, accessed 8 June 2004.

14 ABS, op. cit.
15 Murray Darling Basin Commission (1999), *The Salinity Audit of the Murray Darling Basin. A 100-year perspective, 1999*, Murray Darling Basin Commission, Canberra. Also, Snowy Water Inquiry final report.
16 Seddon, G. (1998), 'Saving the Throwaway River', submission to Snowy Water Inquiry, May 1998. Professor Seddon is Professor Emeritus (environmental science) at Melbourne University and author of *Searching for the Snowy* (1994).
17 See Davidson (1969), *Australia, Wet or Dry?*, Melbourne University Press; and Francis Grey, 'Give the Horse a Drink! The Economic Framework of the Snowy River Trade-off', a submission to Snowy Water Inquiry on behalf of the Snowy-Genoa Catchment Management Committee, 21 May 1998, prepared by Economists at Large and Associates, Melbourne.
18 Chulov, M. and Marino, M. (1999), 'No-flow threat to Bracks', *The Sunday Age*, 14 November 1999, p. 9.
19 Victorian Government calculations were based on an average annual flow of 1168 gigalitres in the Snowy River pre-1949, and 33 gigalitres after the hydro scheme was completed. Figures include flows and spills from the Mowamba River. Other figures suggest the pre-1949 flow was 1121 gigalitres, and the mean annual release after the scheme was built was around 7–10 gigalitres.
20 Miller, C. (1999), 'Bracks rejects NSW Snowy offer', *The Age*, 9 December 1999, p. 4.
21 Miller, C. (1999), 'Hill signals hard battle for Snowy', *The Age*, 25 October 1999, p. 3.
22 *The Australian* (1999), 'Premier counters claim of cash for contact', p. 6.
23 Miller, C. (1999), 'Snowy flow to be investigated', *The Age*, 16 December 1999, p. 6.
24 Letter from South Australian Environment Minister Dorothy Kate to Victorian Premier Steve Bracks, 3 November 1999, DENR33/0214 Pt 4.
25 Interview with Matt Peacock and federal Environment Minister Senator Robert Hill, on AM on ABC radio, 20 December 1999, <www.abc.net.au/am/s74435.htm>
26 Transcript of doorstop press conference with SA Premier John Olsen, 20 December 1999, State Administration Building, Adelaide.
27 Comments from my notes of an interview with Steve Bracks' media spokesperson on 20 December 1999; article published incorporating some comments on 21 December 1999, 'Snowy tensions erupt', *The Age*, p. 1.
28 This analysis based on comment piece I wrote: 'River of Opportunity', published in *The Age*, 19 January 2000, p. 15.
29 'Environmental Impact Statement welcomed', press release issued by federal Resources Minister, Senator Nick Minchin, 20 January 2000, 00/13.
30 Miller, C. (2000), 'Snowy decision delayed six months', *The Age*, 21 January 2000, p. 4.
31 Letter from Tim Fisher to John Della Bosca, assistant Treasurer, NSW, 21 March 2000.
32 Commonwealth Government (2000), 'Corporatisation of the Snowy Mountains Hydro-Electric Authority Draft Environmental Impact Statement', June 2000.
33 Miller, C. (2000), 'Victoria rejects report on Snowy', *The Age*, 8 August 2000, p. 3.

CHAPTER 8

1   Quotes from Jindabyne speeches cited in Miller, C. (2000), 'Rebirth of a river may be first of many', *The Age*, 7 October 2000, p. 4.
2   'Snowy package welcomed by irrigators' council', NSW Irrigators Council press release, issued 6 October 2000.
3   Quoted in the *Express-Summit Sun*, 'Saving the Snowy River, Alliance campaign to continue', by Judy Young, 10 October 2000, p. 5.

4 Quoted in *Sydney Morning Herald*, 'Snowy to flow but they can't walk on water', by Paola Totaro, 28 August 2002.

5 For example, *Weekly Times*, 'Snowy savings best left for a rainy day', 21 August 2002, p. 14.

6 Net present value is an economic formula to calculate the total benefit or total loss into the foreseeable future, usually twenty years.

7 Quoted in *Herald Sun*, 'Mighty Snowy ready for a new least of life', by Mark Scala and Natalie Sikora, 19 August 2002.

CHAPTER 9

1 Figures from several sources, including Murray Darling Basin Commission and Collis, B. (1990), *Snowy. The Making of Modern Australia*, Tabletop Press, Canberra, p. 297.

2 Quotes from 'Succour for a broken spirit of the wild', by Claire Miller, *The Age*, 26 April 2003, 'Insight', p. 5.

3 Thain, S. (2004), '2020 vision or acute myopia — the unforeseen consequences of Australia's plantation policy'; report prepared by Skye Thain, BA Environmental Studies.

STORIES FROM THE MEN AND WOMEN OF THE SNOWY RIVER

1 Much of the bitter internecine fighting that mars contemporary Indigenous society can be traced back to people left holding frayed scraps of their heritage, with little idea what the fabric looked like as a whole and where they fitted into the weave. There will be Indigenous people who will challenge the authority of the storytellers cited in this chapter. That cannot be helped. I have trusted in recommendations from people working closely with the Indigenous communities of East Gippsland and on the Monaro.

2 Michael Young's *The Aboriginal People of the Monaro*, published by the NSW National Parks and Wildlife Service in 2000, is an excellent documentary history that seeks to fill in much of the missing history of the Ngarigo.

3 Wesson, S. (2000), *An Historical Atlas of the Aborigines of Eastern Victoria and Far South-eastern New South Wales*, Monash Publications in Geography and Environmental Science, No. 53, Monash University, p. 126.

4 Wesson, S. (2000), op. cit., pp, 19–20.

5 Gilbert, M. (1972), *Personalities and Stories of the Early Orbost District*, Orbost Historical Society, Orbost.

6 Neal, L. (1976), *Cooma Country*, Cooma-Monaro Historical Society, Halstead Press, Sydney, p. 35.

7 Young, M. (2000), op. cit.

8 Accounts of the massacres are drawn from several sources, but mainly the *Aboriginal Historical Places Project, East Gippsland*, Moogji Aboriginal Council, 1993. The project is a compilation of historical references to Indigenous people in East Gippsland.

9 Neal, L., op. cit., p. 27.

10 Neal, L., op. cit., p. 34.

11 Nyol and Dulagars described in Moogji Aboriginal Council's *Aboriginal Historical Places Project, East Gippsland*, 1993.

12 Meeking, C. (1968), *Snowy Mountains Conquest*, Hutchinson, Melbourne.

13 Green, O. S. (1989), *The Snowy: its Cattlemen, Rivermen and Engineers*, Acacia Press, Blackburn, p. 2.

14 Wakefield, N. A. (date unknown) 'Aspects of Exploration and Settlement of East Gippsland', paper by N. A. Wakefield, naturalist, Monash Teachers College, Clayton Victoria, p. 13.

15 Green, O. S., op. cit., p. 24.

16 Account drawn from *The Bairnsdale Advertiser*, 2 December 1884.

17 Green, O. S., op. cit., p. 63.

18 Account drawn from several sources, including a memoir by Edward Kay's son Ian, Ada Healy, and *Commonwealth Engineer* journal.

19 *Snowy River Country*, vol. Winter 1985, Cooma, 'The Man From Snowy River', pp. 22–24.

20 Green, O. S., op. cit., p. 1.

21 Thomas, M. (1991), *Mountains of Memories, A Life in Australia's Past*, Hutchinson Australia, Milsons Point, NSW, p. 110.

22 Recorded interviews for ABC Radio National series: 'Mapping of Memory — the telling of place', 1993, by Duncan King Smith, Melbourne.

23 Hunt, A. (1937), 'Down the Snowy by Canoe', *The Sydney Mail*, 21 July 1937.

24 Howitt, A. W. (1890), 'The Eucalypts of Gippsland', extract from *Forest Grower Canberra*, Section 26, 1993–94, vol. 16, no. 4.

25 Hancock, W. K. (1972), *Discovering Monaro, A Study of Man's Impact on his Environment*, Cambridge University Press, London.

26 Account of the Wulgulmerang fires from my notes for a newspaper article published 22 February 2003, 'After the inferno, hope, acts of kindness and red tape', in *The Age*.

27 Von Mueller, F. (1854), 'Second general report of the Government Botanist on the vegetation of the colony, in *Victorian Parliamentary Papers*, Government Printer, Melbourne.

28 Wakefield, N. (1954), 'Snowy River Saga', *The Victorian Naturalist*, August 1954, vol. 71, pp. 61–65.

29 White, M. E. (2000), *Running Down: Water in a Changing Land*, Kangaroo Press, East Rowville, NSW, p. 120.

30 Dennis, C. J. (1934), 'Snowy on a spree', in *The Herald*, 28 February 1934, p. 6. Written under pen name 'Den'.

Acknowledgements

This story could not have been told without the help and encouragement of many people who generously gave me their time, cups of tea and stories. There are too many for me to name every one, but I thank you all from the bottom of my heart for making this book possible.

In particular, I am indebted to the following members of the Snowy River Alliance: Glenice and Max White; Genevieve Fitzgerald; Chris Allen and Lynette Greenwood; George Collis; Craig Ingram; Jo Garland; and Paul Leete. I would also like to thank Graeme Enders for his encouragement and attention to details and Brett Miners for his insights.

I was shown great hospitality during my travels in the course of researching this book. I especially want to thank: Emma Sellers and Peter Telford, Black Mountain; Joanna and Kevin Parker, Deddick; Grant and Roslyn Shorland, Deddick; David and Jane Glasson, Jimenbuen; and Bronwyn Kaye and Guirec Danno, Sydney.

I would also like to thank the following people who helped me in myriad ways, including research, constructive criticism, 'fly-on-the-wall' observations, and their professional expertise: Rob Hudson, Robyn McLeod, Graham Byrne, Maureen Bridges, David Crossley, Peter Christoff, William Birnbauer, Susan Davies, Kate Houghton, Graeme Turner, Campbell Fitzpatrick and Kevin Love. To my friend Sue Sedelies — thank you for always being there.

And finally, I would like to thank my husband, Chris Agar, who has made many wonderful things possible.